WANDERER OF THE WORLDS

ASH FITZSIMMONS

WANDERER
OF THE
WORLDS

THE CROSSING
2

WANDERER OF THE WORLDS. Copyright © 2023 by Ash Fitzsimmons.

Print Edition ISBN: 978-1-949861-55-6

Cover design by MiblArt.

www.ashfitzsimmons.com

PROLOGUE

When I was a junior at Harris County High, back in the good old days when my biggest battles were haggling with my dad over curfew and trying to avoid extra chores at our family's general store, my guidance counselor called me in for a chat about my future. A gray-haired matron with a professionally pleasant smile, she sat across her cheap pine desk from me and reviewed my records on her monitor before asking whether I'd given any thought as to what I wanted to do post-graduation. In fact, I had, and I proudly informed her that my best friend, Mia, and I were applying to the same list of colleges in hopes that we could go together. The counselor murmured her approval, then asked, "After that? I know you kids get tired of the question, but what do you want to do with your life, Susan?"

I didn't have a ready answer that time. Mia, now, had her life planned out: four years of college, then a prestigious internship with a big-name publication that would inevitably lead to an editorial career. She'd get out of Cole's Crossing and never look back. As for me, I knew what I *didn't* want, and that was to stay in my hometown and take over the family business. Of all the places I could have been abandoned at birth, the Crossing wasn't the worst, and my adopted dad and uncle had been the best family a girl could have wanted...but I itched to see the wider world. Seeing as "professional traveler" wasn't a standard career path, however, I tried to offer a reasonable response: the Peace Corps, I proposed, or maybe Teach for America. Or graduate school, an answer that received another satisfied grunt from my counselor.

One career option that surely hadn't made it into the files was "sword-wielding monster slayer," yet there I was. Magic sword? Check. Fights against night-stalking creatures from beyond our world? Check, check, and *check*—and the souvenir scar cutting down my cheek served as a fresh reminder every time I caught a glimpse of myself in a mirror. Sure, Mia's career plans had gone off the rails, too, but nothing in our humanities degrees had prepared us to go, for lack of a better word, *questing*. It's not the sort of thing one puts on one's nametag at the tenth high school reunion.

When my Uncle Malachi died, I'd been confident in my basic knowledge of my place in the universe: good old Earth spinning around the Sun, one of eight or nine planets of our solar system, all slowly orbiting the center of our galaxy—in other words, a tiny blue dot of minimal significance to anyone who didn't live upon it, and a perfectly acceptable home to those of us who did.

Three weeks later, I wasn't so sure.

My universe, it seemed, was only one among others with inhabited worlds. At least four such worlds—Ildon, Honslia, Kopaat, and Ga'besh—had developed within the sphere of an etheric force known locally as the Aen, a force that could be channeled and wielded in ways that looked suspiciously like magic. From time immemorial, connections between those four worlds had spontaneously arisen, tunnels allowing the natives to mingle and colonize and establish trade routes and start religious wars with each other. Occasionally, one of those tunnels would open onto Earth, allowing humans to spread into the four worlds. Little traffic went the other way, however, as the very atmosphere outside the Aen felt unpleasantly different, almost prickly, to those accustomed to its embrace.

But while the tunnels allowed the peoples of the four worlds to flourish, they brought with them a massive danger. Tunnels were weak points between the worlds, and monstrous creatures from beyond the Aen—"Outsiders," they were called—began to slip in, following the scent of the Aen to their easy prey. Even those peoples naturally adept with magic—maladetas, elves, and dwarves—found the Outsiders difficult to kill. Faced with the choice of losing their tunnels or continuing to lose their soldiers, they joined with the human settlers in search of a third option. And about four and a half centuries before my birth, they found one.

All of the tunnels were closed but for one per world. These were anchored to a fifth world that no one cared about—Earth—meaning that whatever Outsiders came through would do so on that world. The four primary tunnels were long, and the scent of the Aen distant and faint, but the path to the surface on Earth was a short, easy climb. To draw Outsiders onto the surface and away from them, the peoples of the four worlds created a magically forged weapon, a sword set with crystalized Aen that would both power it and act as a lure. One spell that had been worked on the sword kept it close enough to the tunnels' intersection, the so-called Crossing, that it would always be the strongest source of Aen available to any Outsider that ventured in. Another bound a kidnapped air elemental to the sword and drew upon his life force, which gave the spells that made the weapon deadly to Outsiders the power necessary to function but kept the hapless elemental in continual pain.

And then there was the spell binding the sword to a single wielder for life—the Watcher. Chosen by the elemental in the sword and unable to free himself, the Watcher was condemned to remain within a short radius of the Crossing, fighting the Outsiders drawn to him until his last breath. The first Watchers were Native Americans forced into the job by maladetas who spoke of sacred duty, but then came Samuel Cole, a settler who happened to chance upon the then-current Watcher as he was dying. The sword needed a host, Samuel was stuck with the gig, and my hometown—Cole's Crossing—grew up around the hidden tunnels. Without fail, as soon as each Watcher died, the sword passed to another Cole man, nine in a row, until there were only two left: the Watcher, Malachi, and his older brother, Barnaby. Neither married or fathered children, and they assumed I was safe. After all, I was the *adopted* Cole, and surely I'd be spared the curse that had haunted their bloodline for three hundred years.

Ha.

I got the sword, all right. And with a little nudge from my neighbor—a maladeta, to my surprise—I set off for the four worlds beyond my own with Mia to return it to its rightful owners. Trouble was, no one wanted it back.

Oh, and as it turned out, Mia wasn't entirely human after all.

Neither was I, for that matter.

And my long-lost mother wanted me dead.

Sitting in my guidance counselor's office all those years ago, I'd never have envisioned myself on the run with an elf, a dwarf, a magic sword, and an elemental talent I could barely comprehend, but hey, life's funny like that.

Assuming you can stay alive long enough to laugh at the absurdity.

CHAPTER 1

It's said, in times of crisis, that one should be gentle to oneself, forgiving of one's own mistakes, understanding of one's limitations. That's all well and good until one ends up dunked in a cold, foul-smelling river because one is exhausted and can't steer for shit.

In fairness, I was doing the best I could to survive. Having barely spent two weeks exploring the four worlds tethered to mine, I'd discovered my nascent abilities with water, picked up a small posse, pulled together a freaking thunderstorm in the middle of a drought, and orchestrated an escape from the filicidal mother I'd only just met. Hell, I'd even made our getaway boat out of water. For a rogue elemental flying blind, I'd performed satisfactorily in light of my on-the-job training. But as my *control* of my power was still in desperate need of finessing, I was lucky to steer us down the river as long as I did before capsizing my strange little craft. That I'd failed to stick the landing, instead accidentally releasing my hold of the boat when we went over a ten-foot drop, was perhaps forgivable, though a cold dip was low on everyone's wish list that morning.

First to haul himself to the bank was Fanakel, whose slowly browning sunburn hadn't been helped at all by the previous day's river cruise. The elf dropped his borrowed duffel onto the rocks and wrung out his tunic, but any attempt he might have made to get dry would have been futile—roomy as the duffel was, it was anything but waterproof, and his extra clothes were undoubtedly drenched. His shoulder-length hair looked closer to brown than to its usual reddish hue, and his patchy four-day beard added unwanted color to his peeling face. Sure, he was still a beautiful specimen—I had yet to meet an ugly elf—but if one overlooked the ears sticking up through his wet hair, he might have passed for a particularly good-looking, if sun-fried, human.

Something told me that for the prince, that sentiment would constitute fighting words.

Close on his heels was Mia, who swam remarkably well for a woman burdened with a loaded camping backpack and a newly augmented body. That Mia wasn't a garden-variety human had come as a shock to all of us—her dormant tekorish genes seemed to have awakened after enough days in an Aen-bathed world—but she'd soldiered on, replaced her wardrobe, and made the best of it. True, it was awkward for her, but she could have suffered a worse transformation than going from "stick-thin and reasonably pretty" to "knockout with a pinup figure," and her newfound ability to incite men into doing whatever she wanted had certainly come in handy.

Mia swam with one arm wrapped around Anji, holding the dwarf's head above water where the river was too deep. I suspected that the exercise was humiliating for the princess—Anji was tough, scrappy, and someone I never wanted to cross in a dark alley—but she stood barely four feet tall, and Mia wasn't about to let her drown. The careful combing and beard-braiding on which Anji had spent hours the day before was almost for naught, and she stumbled up the bank as bedraggled as any of us.

And then there was me—tingling with my own sunburn, itching where my nasty facial scar was trying to heal, and smelling far funkier than the river. At least the others had been able to bathe before we made our escape from Deoni—I'd have given a hundred dollars for a couple bottles of cheap hotel shampoo and conditioner, and my hair was edging toward a matted disaster. As I slogged out of the river, disoriented and cold, fatigue called to mind an image of the mother I'd just evaded, the camera lingering on her unfairly perfect chestnut ringlets.

You know she has a staff, right? Erianthe can't possibly look like that by herself.

The voice in my head was still new enough to make me twitch, but I recognized Terj and calmed before I could start searching for the speaker. The elemental imprisoned in the sword at my side had only just recovered sufficiently from his Aen-less centuries on Earth to make himself heard, and as he'd promised, he was anything but quiet.

She's pretty, she's thin, and she has good hair, I mentally grumbled. *Why couldn't I have ended up like that?*

She seems unhealthy, he replied. *As for the hair, yours is different when it's cleaned and combed.*

She's still prettier than me.

His reaction felt like a shrug. *If you say so. I'm no judge of human beauty.*

"Is everyone all right?" Mia asked, clambering up the rocks. "Anyone hurt?"

"I'm sorry," I mumbled as I neared the bank. "Lost control—"

"You brought us safely from Deoni, lass," Anji interrupted, twisting her beard to wring out the water, "and we survived the fall. Let's walk from here, eh? Give you a rest."

The others eagerly agreed with the plan—I wouldn't have trusted myself as a boat pilot then, either—and we started on our squelchy way beside the river. I looked back at the drop over which we'd plunged, grateful that the rocks below hadn't been sharp enough to injure us, and noticed that the shoreline vegetation pattern we'd seen all along had continued: a gradual browning, then die-off within inches of the water. The river was dead, unable to sustain life without its elemental.

My father, apparently. Lost somewhere in the dry wastelands of Echoril, Kopaat's largest continent.

Anji and Fanakel had attempted to educate Mia and me

as to the world's geography as we'd floated downstream the previous day. The tunnel between Earth and Kopaat opened in the Great Desert, halfway between the Meali Republic and Daril—the kingdom of which I, to my continued disbelief, was somehow meant to be crown princess. Daril's main cities and towns snaked along the Falova River and its tributaries, but with the river's death, it relied more than ever on its northernmost port city, which opened onto the narrow stretch of ocean between Echoril and Genutil, a sparsely inhabited polar continent. The sea, at least, was still very much alive.

We'd been following one of the Falova's spurs toward the sea, eschewing Darili territory for the relative safety of the woodlands. Even with the river's death and the die-off at its edge, there remained enough moisture for a forest to grow near its banks, a buffer between the more inhabited regions of Daril and the desert to its west. We'd spied a few cultivated fields through breaks in the trees, but I'd kept us moving along, and no one had given chase.

Our destination was the settlement of the Taln'een clan of maladetas. What, exactly, a maladeta *was* remained a touch fuzzy to me, though perhaps that was my lack of sleep talking. They looked human enough—hell, one of them had lived beside me back in Cole's Crossing—but they could manipulate the Aen, and according to the relative experts in our group, they could live for a thousand years. Part of me flat-out refused to square the idea of Ardith Quince, my kindly neighbor known for her award-winning blueberry crumb cake, with an ageless, inhuman sorceress, but my world had fallen apart in the last three weeks, and perhaps I'd reached my mental capacity for weirdness. Putting aside the idea of what Ms. Quince might or might not be, I tried to focus on the lessons that my guides offered as we traveled north.

Allegedly, the Taln'een lived somewhere along the coast, just west of Darili territory. I'd wondered aloud if they ever clashed with Daril over resources, but the more experienced members of our party had chuckled at the notion. "Maladetas make good neighbors," Anji had explained. "They're peaceful, they seldom take more than they need, and they're surely not in competition with Daril."

"And if crossed, they're *incredibly* dangerous," Fanakel had added, "so no, I doubt that Daril is suicidal enough to attack whatever fishing boats the Taln'een put to sea."

I'm sure there was more to their lecture, but I probably only registered a fraction of it. Between trying to keep my water boat together and on course, I had little mental energy for geopolitics. Making matters worse, by the time I crashed us, I hadn't slept in two days, and the adrenaline surge of escape had petered out to a trickle. Oh, and I'd barely begun to process the fact that my own mother had tried to kill me *twice*, but stuck as I was in survival mode, I pushed my breakdown to the back burner, shook myself dry on the riverbank, and tried to keep trudging through my thickening mental fog. I shuffled along behind Anji, a soaked zombie with my eyes at half-mast, doing my best not to trip over roots and rocks.

You seem uncomfortable, Terj remarked.

Yeah.

Is it because you're wet?

I took stock of my physical complaints—exhaustion, hunger, stiff muscles unused to the punishment through which I'd put them over the last weeks of hiking, a dull headache from the strain of the river journey—then grunted. *Part of it.*

So why not will yourself dry?

That momentarily snapped me from my near-doze. *You think I can?*

Why not? You can repel water, can't you? Will it off. There's no need to add to your misery.

"Hold on," I told the others, then closed my eyes and concentrated until I could feel the water droplets within my clothing like pinpricks of light in the darkness. With a brief thought, they began to coalesce in front of me, and I opened my eyes to bone-dry clothes and a blob of water floating at waist height. I tossed it into the woods, where it splashed harmlessly against a tree, then repeated the process with my hair and my backpack—though I took care not to summon the contents of my water bottles as I dried myself. Within moments, the clamminess subsided, and my wavy hair sprung to its full dirty, frizzy glory. I didn't need a mirror to tell me I still looked like a disaster, but at least my socks were no longer squishy with river water.

"Better, Suze?" Mia asked.

I twisted my neck until it popped. "Yeah, that helps."

"Mind sharing the love?"

"Huh? *Oh*," I mumbled, seeing my three companions standing there dripping. "Uh...sorry. Just a minute..."

By the time I finished, the mood had moderately brightened, and even Fanakel patted my shoulder as he pressed on up the trail. *Thanks*, I thought to Terj.

I might as well try to be useful, he replied. *Having put you in this position in the first place...*

His guilt came through loud and clear, but I barely had the mental capacity to deal with my own emotions that morning, let alone his. Just walking was becoming a greater challenge with every passing minute, and when I strolled straight into a tree and fell like a flipped turtle, Anji took a long look at me and called a halt. "Rest, Susan," she urged, helping me sit up and remove my bag. "We should be safe enough hiding here for a time."

Really, I tried to protest. The longer we spent in the open, the greater the chance that someone—or worse, some*thing*—would find us. But there was soft grass where I'd fallen, and the dwarf's no-nonsense expression suggested that resistance would not be tolerated.

I think I mumbled something in the affirmative before curling up and passing out, but the specifics were lost to dreamless sleep.

When Mia nudged me back to consciousness, the sun was high, but the trees beneath which I'd collapsed had kept me cool. "Come on, sleepyhead," she said, pulling one of my water bottles from my bag, "drink up. Time to move."

Groaning, I took the bottle from her and drained half of it in two long gulps.

"Hungry?"

I wiped my mouth against the back of my hand. "Nah, I'm okay."

Liar, said Terj.

He must have broadcast his sentiment that time, as Mia glanced at the sword with a smirk. "Busted, babe. Here, I'll get you a granola bar."

"Save it," I said, screwing the cap back on my bottle. "You'll need it more than I will."

She started to argue, then rolled her eyes and gave up.

I didn't want to say it, but we both knew the danger of allowing her to grow too hungry. Mia had always been blessed with a lightning-fast metabolism, but now that her tekorish side had come to the fore, she had a new food source: the life energy of the one unfortunate corporeal male in our band. Terj had assured me that elementals were immune to the hypnotic powers of tekoraet, and Mia had sworn up and down that Fanakel was off the menu, but none of us had seen her truly famished yet, nor were we eager to put her willpower to the test.

As I packed my water bottle away, Anji marched over with a veritable spring in her step. "She's awake? Ah, good," she said as I groggily waved. "Join us—the view is lovely."

I climbed to my feet and staggered after her, passing through the tree belt until we reached a breeze-rippled meadow, where the three of them had pitched Mia's tent. Fanakel was standing a slight distance away from the impromptu camp, shading his eyes with one hand as he stared north. Curious, I started to join him, only to receive a sharp arm to my stomach before I could stumble down the steep hillside past his post. "Careful, now," he said, watching me secure my footing. "It's traversable—the road's just beyond," he added, pointing to a brown track cutting through the grass and down the hill—"but I'm sure you'd prefer to descend on your feet instead of head over heels, eh?"

"I'll have you know I'm the epitome of grace," I replied.

He chuckled. "You hide it well. And..." He scowled, then licked his thumb and jabbed it toward my face too swiftly for me to retreat. "Dried spittle. There, that's the best I can do," he said as I rubbed my sleeve over my cleaned chin. "We should aim for a better impression than we made in Deoni. Do you, um...want to brush your hair or something?"

I gave his sleek auburn locks a jealous glance. "My hair is *sad* right now, and I'd rather not be here all day. You think it's safe to go by road?"

"Safer than the river. I take it you've not seen what lies ahead, then?"

As I frowned, he beckoned for me to follow him, then led me across the meadow, back into the trees, perhaps thirty yards along the river...and straight to the edge of another drop, this one at least four times the height of the fall that had capsized us. The river plunged over the cliff into churning foam, and I stood at the top of the waterfall, sick to my stomach and wondering how the hell I'd *missed* it. If anything, the noise should have suggested imminent danger.

You were exhausted, said Terj. *Distracted. It's understandable.*

"Yeah, until I kill everyone," I muttered.

Fanakel arched an eyebrow. "What was that?"

"Nothing. Shit. I'm sorry I almost dragged us all into mortal peril again."

"Apology accepted," he replied. "But you see why we'll be proceeding on foot from here."

With the quick repacking accomplished, we set off

through the meadow toward the road. Looking north, I could just make out the shimmering line of the sea in the distance—though really, visual confirmation was unnecessary, as my awakening water-tuned senses were practically screaming with such abundance nearby. The road, I noted, followed the seeming cliff downward at its gentlest angle, opting for a slope instead of steps hewn into the rock. Below, the path remained narrow, a straight brown line heading toward the sea, cutting through vast, summer-green fields and terminating in what appeared to be a town. The hardships of the continent's dry season appeared nonexistent this far north—probably due to the moist sea air, I surmised—and if my rural childhood had taught me anything, the people living below wouldn't be going hungry that winter. Past the fields, the river curved to meet the road, and the two ran in tandem for a time before the river bent again and flowed into the ocean.

"Is *that* where we're headed?" I asked, pointing to the unassuming buildings on the coast.

Fanakel peered in that direction, then nodded. "I would think that's Taln'een, yes."

Something seemed off about his answer, and I rummaged through the detritus in my exhaustion-jumbled memory. "Wait...that's the clan name, right? They're the Taln'een?"

"Yes," said Anji, coming up beside me, "but it's also the name of their settlement. Maladetas are fairly flexible about where they live. If something should happen to this place, they'll rebuild elsewhere and call it Taln'een."

"If you ask a maladeta for directions, make her draw a map," Fanakel added.

Anji sniggered at that. "Sounds like someone speaks from experience."

"Someone does," he muttered. "And it was a *long* two-day ride back the other way."

From the rear of our pack, Mia asked, "Are you sure that's the place? It doesn't look like much."

"What do you mean?" said Anji.

"It's supposed to be a major town, right? So where are the fortifications? Heartfast is walled, the big tree fort in Nokan'ti—"

"Caritulo," Fanakel interjected.

"Sure, whatever you call it. It's got a fence and manned gates and, you know, *elevation*. And Deoni has a wall and the freaking river on one side. That place down there looks like a little fishing village by comparison."

Mia had a point—every prominent city we'd come across until then had been walled and defended. But Anji and Fanakel shook their heads. "The Taln'een is among the most powerful of the Kopaati maladetan clans, but maladetas aren't known for opulent construction," he explained. "Functional, not beautiful. You won't find palaces in their settlements."

"And they don't *need* walls," said Anji. "Attacking a maladetan clan is a shortcut to the afterlife." Sweeping one hand across the panorama before us, she continued, "This farmland must support the settlement, and I suspect they have a robust fishing fleet. If I'm remembering my Kopaati geography well, Genutil isn't far across the sea at this point—the continental gap is narrowest near Daril—and much of that land is uninhabited. There's probably decent hunting south of the tundra. Oh, see the stilts?" she asked, pointing toward the town. "If I had to guess, that's protection against flooding, not a siege."

"They could probably hold back the sea with their power, were they so inclined," Fanakel added. "They tend to be a self-sufficient lot until they interject themselves into our affairs—"

Anji snorted. "And how. My father hosts one or two every few months."

"As does mine—and Erianthe must as well, I'm sure," he said, glancing back at me. "I won't say it's bad luck to turn them away, but it's not *prudent*, either."

"And what are their thoughts on visitors?" I asked.

"Are we talking about something more on the dwarven or elven end of the spectrum?"

Fanakel huffed his indignation. "We are a *highly* hospitable people—"

"To other elves, maybe," Anji muttered.

"To guests who come invited," he countered. "You barged in without permission."

They were just as uninvited in Ildon, Terj offered, *and yet, Rokund didn't have them abused and imprisoned. He fed them and gave them beds, as I recall.*

"*Thank* you," said Anji, looking up at Fanakel with a smug little smile. "That's his impression, not mine. The elemental's unbiased."

I cast my mind back to our night under the dwarf king's roof, which felt like months before but was really a scant two weeks. "Wonder if the maladetas have indoor plumbing," I whispered to Mia, who groaned with our shared longing for hot showers and flush toilets. Camping had never been my forte, and experience hadn't made me any fonder of the great outdoors or of what passed for bathrooms in the four worlds.

Walking single-file, we navigated the sloping, rutted dirt road down to the fields, then pressed onward through them, where plants I couldn't name rose almost to eye level. I'd have thought we were traversing a corn field had it not been for the globular fruits hanging in pairs and trios from the stalks like pink softballs. Heading off Mia's and my questions, Anji murmured, "Kirta. The pods grow to head-sized when they're mature, and the flesh has a variety of uses."

"Raw, it's almost sweet," said Fanakel, keeping his voice low, "but most of them are dried and powdered. Excellent for bread."

"You've made it?" she asked.

"A time or twenty. What, are the princesses of Blackhorn Mountain too delicate to dirty their hands?" he teased.

"Wouldn't say that. I've had plenty of blood on them. Sometimes even my own."

Fortunately, before those two could come to blows, a man stepped out of the field to our right, dragging a long, dripping hose. Seeing us, he stiffened and stopped in his tracks, giving me a chance to take a good look at him: superficially human in appearance, with an olive complexion, brown hair, and a short-cropped beard. He wore a dark blue tunic with no sleeves, showing off powerfully muscled arms, and a hood, which he kept raised against the noon sun. A small bag, a sheathed knife, and a curved metal tool hung from his belt and bounced against his loose gray trousers.

"My translators are one-way," Anji reminded us, but when I floundered for an opening, Fanakel took the lead.

"Good day to you," he said, dipping his head toward the maladetan man, "and may the Divine bless your endeavors. We seek the great mother of the Taln'een. Does she await us ahead?"

The man considered that briefly, then tightened his grip on his hose and nodded.

"May we pass?"

He stepped back toward the field, having said not a word, and watched us as we trudged by.

"Think they get visitors often?" I whispered to Anji once he'd disappeared on his watering errand.

"Unlikely. It's also probably jarring that we allowed the man among us to speak."

"Huh?"

"They're matriarchal," said Fanakel, clustering closer to us. "I've never even seen a male. I mean, that one might have been human," he allowed, "but I can't imagine the Taln'een hiring field hands from Daril."

After another half hour's walk along the dirt track, we left the kirta fields behind. The next crops were a bushy green plant—even the knowledgeable half of our group couldn't name them, but they guessed that we were seeing something with tuberous roots. More of the maladetan men were bent over in the fields weeding, from the look of it. Another held up a hose and passed his own curved piece of metal over the opening, and suddenly, water spurted forth. To a man, they wore tunics cut in the same fashion—hoods and no sleeves, cinched with a utility belt—but their skin tones ran from ebony to light brown with angry red undertones, a tan in the works. As they noticed us, they stopped, raised up from their work, and stared like the maladetan version of startled meerkats, but no one tried to halt our progress.

"Is anyone else *slightly* weirded out right now?" I murmured, trying not to be overheard by our silent audience.

"A touch," said Mia. "Just checking, but maladetas don't lock each other inside, say, giant wicker statues and burn their victims alive, right?"

Anji's expression spoke of horror and not a little concern for Mia's sanity. "What could *possibly* give you such an idea, lass?"

"Too many movies at an impressionable age."

Though the dwarf seemed unsure, she shook her head briskly and carried on. "*No*. The only religions I've ever known to ask for blood sacrifices are practiced by a few fringe human groups in Honslia—"

"We've eradicated most of them," said Fanakel.

"Oh?"

"Self-preservation. They're not picky about the identities of their sacrifices."

"Glad *they* didn't have anything to do with the sword, then," she replied, cutting her eyes to the scabbard at my side.

I gave it a pat, partly to remind myself that it was still there—over time, my leg became almost desensitized to its presence—and partly in a futile attempt to reassure Terj. I couldn't tell whether the others were picking up on his trepidation or whether that was something I was tuned in to by virtue of our bond, but his anxiety was enough to set my own stomach knotting. *Okay in there?* I asked.

Fine.

Liar.

Relatively fine, then. The pain is no worse than it always is.

You say that, but I get the sense that if you had guts, you'd be puking them out on the side of the road right now.

Terj said nothing for a long moment, then seemed to sigh. *I don't like this place.*

Bad memories?

Fear, panic, agony...yeah, you could say so.

Maybe they'll help us, I thought, trying to comfort him. *Ms. Quince isn't a monster, right? She had to come from somewhere.*

Recall, if you will, the part about how she never told Malachi that the magic keeping him tied to the Crossing only worked in your world.

She told me.

Perhaps because you're female, he replied. *Notice anything odd in the fields?*

I cut my eyes from right to left, but I saw nothing of interest beyond the unnamed crops and a handful of curious workers. *What am I looking for?*

They're all male, aren't they?

So? Maybe the women stay home and cook.

Possible, but unlikely. I've felt male and female maladetas—they move through the Aen differently. The women are bright with the Aen—powerfully talented, he clarified. *I can sense that much. The men...well, honestly, they feel like humans. No power at all. It's like putting Ardith and Malachi in the same room, only Malachi had a flicker of talent by the end of his life.*

The mention of my uncle, only three weeks dead, sent a pang through my heart, but though I tried not to let on, Terj picked up on my sudden sadness. *I'm sorry, Susan*, he hastily said. *He was my frame of reference for years, and—*

It's not your fault, I told him, cutting his apology short.

But it is. You're grieving. I should have been more careful.

In truth, I didn't know how to answer that. So many of

my uncle's misfortunes—being magically leashed to his hometown, tasked to fight otherworldly monsters every night, and forced to accept life as a veritable hermit—were ultimately Terj's fault. He'd chosen Uncle Malachi, just as he'd chosen all of the Watchers in the long line before him...and now me. He could have glommed on to anyone in Cole's Crossing—hell, to anyone on Earth or on any of the four worlds of the Aen—but once the first Cole moved into the area, he'd stuck to the family like a generational curse for centuries. He'd ruined a long string of lives, consigning Watchers to loneliness and constant danger—and, I assumed, more than a few premature deaths in the woods. Sure, Uncle Malachi had died of a heart attack, but I couldn't help but wonder how things could have gone differently had he not been tethered so close to the tunnels between the worlds that he'd been forced to defend. Had he, say, been able to live in town without attracting monsters into the streets of our community, close enough to paved roads to make calling 911 more than an exercise in futility, or been able to visit a cardiologist outside of Cole's Crossing, he might still be alive. Instead, I'd lost the only family I'd ever known in less than eighteen months, with my dad and Uncle Malachi dying in quick succession, and all I had for it now was Terj, who'd reluctantly cursed me in turn.

But the hell in which Terj was trapped wasn't his fault. The Taln'een had done it to him. And I wasn't leaving without answers.

We'd been walking through the expansive fields for nearly an hour when one of the farmers finally did more than stop and stare.

"Your pardon, friends," said a white-haired man, who stepped down from what appeared to be a perfectly static hovering wagon, a wooden platform with upward-curving sides. As the wagon was floating only about a yard off the ground, I saw that the front third was loaded with gardening tools and a haphazard jumble of clay pots and jugs—the leavings of the workers' lunch, perhaps. Like the other men, he wore a hooded tunic, but his was gray and had long sleeves, protection from the afternoon sun. He moved quickly for his apparent age—the creases in his deeply tanned face spoke of decades outdoors—but as I glanced at Anji, I could see her sizing him up, just in case.

We stopped and waited as he neared our pack. "Your turn," Fanakel whispered, nudging me in the side, and I tried to formulate something appropriately diplomatic that wouldn't result in the men in the fields rushing up with their hoes and shovels.

The man paused a respectful distance away and folded his arms, tucking his hands into his sleeves—a little reassurance that he wasn't about to go for a weapon, I suspected, considering that between Fanakel's, Anji's, and my blades and Mia's pistol, we had the advantage. "Might I ask who you are and why you venture onto Taln'een lands?"

I cleared my throat and hoped that my nap had restored sufficient clarity to my thoughts so as to avoid another night incarcerated. "I'm Susan Cole," I told him, taking care to keep my hands empty and visible. "My companions and I are trying to get to the, uh…the great mother?"

His eyebrows rose. "For what purpose?"

Unsure of how much of our recent history was safe to reveal to the old man, I settled for punting. "Ardith sent us."

"Ardith?" he repeated, cocking his head as he frowned.

Ardielta, Terj reminded me.

"Uh…sorry, nickname," I said, and tried again. "Ardielta. Do you know her?"

The man's surprise seemed closer to shock, and he took a step back from us and slightly bowed. "Indeed, and if the first daughter has sent you hence, I am in no position to question her reasons or judgment." Giving us another quick study, he said, "You carry packs. Have you walked from Daril?"

"Deoni," Fanakel interjected, "and we came largely by river, may the Divine be praised for their mercy. This land is unforgiving to the south."

"In the dry season, most assuredly," said the man with a sharp nod. "Come, ride with me," he offered, giving the floating wagon a pat. "The day will only grow warmer."

My tired feet informed me that we would *not* be turning the offer down. Sparing a quick glance at Fanakel in case he was poised to object, I hoisted myself over the side of the wagon, lost my balance, and tumbled into its wooden bed with a grunt. The others followed me up, with Mia offering Anji a bent-knee hoist, and we settled in for the trip to town.

"The epitome of grace, you were saying?" Fanakel murmured as I made myself comfortable.

"Oh, go soak your head."

Overhearing us, the old man chuckled as he pulled one of the seemingly ubiquitous curved metal pieces from his belt. He held it aloft like a conductor poised for the downbeat, then executed a complex looping pattern. The wagon began to float along with barely a jolt—our driver, at least, didn't even waver in his footing—and picked up speed until we were skimming over the dirt road at a fair clip. Only once I noticed the plants waving with our passage did I realize that the cart came with an invisible windshield of sorts, as I wasn't buffeted by so much as a gust.

Any idea how this thing works? I asked Terj, as much for information as to distract him.

Not specifically... He paused, then said, *You understand the basic concept of mechanics, yes? Like, there's more to a car than the visible bits.*

I can change my own oil, you know.

I beg your pardon. Then think of those sort of mechanisms

working all around this vehicle, only invisible, and they're conduits for energized Aen. The metal things the men wield seem to start and stop the flow. I suppose they're necessary, seeing as the men have no ability with the Aen whatsoever.

His voice seemed oddly brittle, and I patted the scabbard at my side. *It's going to be okay, Terj. I'm not going to let them hurt you.*

Too late for that, he replied, but I felt a shading of gratitude beneath the neon blast of his fear.

CHAPTER 2

Growing up, I'd never been able to pin an age on Ms. Quince. She'd refused all attempts to coax it from her, instead teasing that once a lady reached a certain point, numbers were irrelevant. As I'd gotten older, I'd laughed at the absurdity of her reticence, deeming it nothing more than a silly throwback to a time when ladies wore gloves to church and made weekly trips to the salon. Unlabeled by something as base as a date of birth, she'd always seemed ageless to me, a woman permanently perched on the cusp of her middle years, with fine lines and a few gray hairs interspersed among the brown to give her character. Having since come to learn just how long a maladeta could live, I better understood her reluctance to give me the truth.

With that information in mind, I'd expected the Taln'een clan mother to be a wizened old woman, perhaps a crone with eight or nine centuries of experience behind her...but as had happened with far too much regularity of late, I was surprised.

Our driver stopped the wagon outside an unassuming building a few hundred yards off the beach, a long wooden house raised on ten-foot stilts. Wide windows opened to admit the sea breeze, though they were framed with thick shutters in case of storms. The only ornamentation beyond the purely functional was color: the window casings and shutters had been stained bright blue and violet, making them pop against the weathered walls. A pair of staircases spiraled up from the ground beneath the building, but the wagon rose to the level of the balcony and slid atop a docking platform. Cutting its magical engine with another flourish of his metal tool, the old man stepped out onto the platform, then opened a gate in the balcony's protective railing and beckoned for us to follow.

He led us not into a majestic throne room, but rather to an unguarded door, on which he rapped twice and waited. When it swung open, he stepped into the room beyond and bowed. "Good afternoon, Mother. I apologize for the interruption—"

"You're never an interruption, my darling," a woman's voice—a much *younger*-sounding woman's voice—replied. "What can I do for you?"

His spine seemed to straighten with the warmth of her greeting. "Mother, I found travelers approaching and brought them here. They said that the first daughter bade them come."

"She did," said the woman, "and thank you for escorting them. They're on the balcony?"

"Yes, Mother."

"Show them in, please. I can manage from here."

He bowed again and stepped out, then gestured for us to proceed. "Thanks for the ride," I murmured, and he smiled before taking his leave.

Following Anji through the doorway, I found myself in a pleasant space that I gathered was a sort of office. A low table had been positioned near the far wall, behind which sat a dark-haired woman on a thick blue cushion. Between us was a woven rug in cool tones, on which a selection of coordinating cushions had been arranged like the sophisticated answer to beanbag chairs. Around the room hung crystalline globes the size of grapefruits—lamps, I supposed—while a selection of potted flowers enjoyed the sun falling through the pair of windows.

Catching Anji's pointed stare, I attempted to take the lead and nodded to the seated woman. "Um...are you, uh..."

"Welcome, Watcher," she said, saving me from myself. "Ardielta misjudged your travel time—you came down the river, I trust?"

"Most of the way."

Her pale lips curled into a teasing smirk. "Found the falls, did you?"

"Unfortunately."

She laughed softly and beckoned us into the room. "Close the door and have a seat, if you like. Let me see if I have this straight in my mind...Anjikora of Blackhorn Mountain," she said, extending a hand to the princess, "and Mia..."

"Randolph," Mia offered. "From, uh...Cole's Crossing..."

Even as she spoke, I could see Mia remembering the problem: the pendant she wore, one of Anji's creations, could translate anything the wearer heard, but it wouldn't translate the wearer's speech in turn, unlike Fanakel's two-way translator ring. Having been branded by the magical sword I wore, I could understand and be understood—which, considering my ignorance of protocol, was more a liability than a boon.

But when the woman nodded at Mia, I realized we were in luck. "Ms. Randolph, be welcome," said the woman—to my astonishment, in perfect English. "Ardielta speaks well of you."

I wasn't the only one who'd picked up on the linguistic switch. "How—" Mia began.

Because she's Ganeel of the Taln'een, Terj cut in, and I knew he wasn't just offering me his commentary. *Once known as Nellie Jones. She babysat Zachary—Pericles's uncle*, he explained. *And since he was stuck as the Watcher for forty-seven years, she had ample opportunity to practice.*

If Ganeel was surprised to hear Terj, she showed no indication beyond a slow blink. "Ah. Ardielta warned me that the forging was...imperfect."

Imperfect? he cried, making me wince with the mental

shout. *I'm terribly sorry, would you be happier if I dropped dead?*

A muscle twitched in her otherwise still cheek, the only crack in her calm façade. "It was not intended for you to survive the process. None of our modeling suggested that you would live. That you *have* is testament to your strength, not to mention a sign that we should revise our thinking on the nature of elementals—"

Who gives a damn about that? Do you have any idea what you've done to me?

Maybe, I thought, sensing the warning tremors of a headache coming on, Terj was using fury to cover his fear—I could still feel it radiating off of him. More likely, his erupting anger had been building for a *long* time.

"Yes," said Ganeel, staring at the sword, "I know exactly what was done. And that's why you weren't meant to survive it." Sighing, she glanced at Fanakel. "A son of Nokan'ti, yes?"

"Uh…yes," he replied, rubbing his temples.

"And the elemental is correct—I'm called Ganeel. Now," she said, closing her eyes as she massaged her forehead, "Ardielta provided me with a rough sketch of why you're sitting in my office, but I need to hear it properly. If you'd be so kind, would someone like to tell me just what in all the hells is going on?"

The others looked my way. "You're the cursed one," said Mia. "Want to kick this off?"

Feeling the weight of Ganeel's eyes on me, and hoping to avoid yet another jail cell, I offered a brief, silent prayer for patience and calm before beginning. "So, uh…my uncle died about three weeks ago, back in Cole's Crossing. I went out to his place a few days later to go through his stuff and found this waiting for me," I said, pointing to the sword. "I picked it up, and it burned me—"

The translation mark, Terj offered.

"Yeah, that. Mia and I were attacked by Outsiders that night." *First night of many*, I wanted to say—even when I woke without having to fight otherworldly monsters, creatures twice my size with fangs and claws and an appetite for flesh, I couldn't escape them in my dreams— but I tried to stick to the facts. "The next morning, Ms. Quince—"

Ardielta.

Ganeel nodded and gestured for me to continue.

"She told me I was the new Watcher. First I'd ever heard of it. The sword had attached itself to my uncle, and now it was my turn to have my life ruined."

"Your uncle," she said, "was that…Pericles's nephew? Remind me."

Helpfully, Terj seemed to know the Cole family tree better than I did. *No. Pericles was Zachary's nephew. Susan's referring to Malachi, Pericles's grandnephew.*

She offered me a brief, wistful smile. "I remember Pericles when he was a boy. Rambunctious to a fault, but he grew into a fine young man. I don't suppose you ever met him."

"Died before my time," I replied, trying not to think of Uncle Malachi as my throat tightened. "Anyway, Ms. Quince told me I'd be stuck by the tunnels for the rest of my life, fighting whatever came through them. Doesn't seem quite *fair*," I said, hearing the edge creeping into my voice, "so Mia and I decided to go in search of someone who could take the sword back. They're your monsters, so it only seems right that you defend yourselves and leave Earth out of it."

Ganeel didn't respond, but she didn't disagree.

"We ended up in Ildon first," said Mia, picking up the narrative. "Luck of the draw. Made it all the way to Heartfast, but the king wouldn't help us."

The clan mother's glance slid toward Anji. "And so Rokund sent a daughter in his stead?"

"It was my choice," Anji replied. "He agreed that I could assist them as long as I was quiet about it. So I accompanied them back to the Watcher's cabin, and those *things* attacked again. I *saw* them," she said, staring Ganeel down. "Massive and deadly. The lass has almost no training, and beyond the inherent cruelty of the arrangement, she's unfit for the job. You don't ask babes to fight your wars, do you?"

"Of course not," said Ganeel, calm in the face of Anji's agitation.

"We packed up and tried Honslia next," I said before Anji could escalate her argument. "I thought maybe the Twins would help me, but, uh..."

"She said something that might have been construed as threatening to my father," said Fanakel, picking a bit of grime off a cuticle. "They were detained with the intent of being returned to the Crossing before any more Outsiders could find their way into Nokan'ti."

Ganeel gave him a long, searching look as he studiously avoided her gaze. "You helped them flee?"

"It wasn't his idea," I said, trying to leave it vague.

But Fanakel sighed and finally met her brown eyes. "Mia's tekorish. She didn't understand what she's capable of doing."

"Yes," said Ganeel, seemingly as unbothered as if she were discussing the odds of rain on a cloudless day. "Ardielta mentioned that."

To my relief, she didn't immediately call for Mia's head.

"I've got it under control," Mia hastened to interject. "Really. I mean, I used it to get us out of Deoni," she admitted, "but I think that's excusable, don't you?"

"Probably," replied Ganeel. "But child, if you have been aware of your abilities for only a few days, then you are most certainly not in control of them, and—"

"I vouch for her."

Ganeel turned to Anji, who stared at her with her jaw set. "In what regard?"

"Your men are safe. Mia won't touch them."

"Your confidence is surprising."

"I've seen something of her," said Anji with a shrug. "She's as yet given me no reason to question my trust."

The clan mother quirked an eyebrow, then pivoted back to me. "So, you were saying that you fled Nokan'ti?"

I nodded. "An elemental guided us back to the tunnel—"

"Kingkiller," Fanakel muttered.

"—and we got some more supplies and came to Kopaat."

Ganeel frowned and stroked her chin. "You crossed the wasteland on foot?"

"No. Kingkiller suggested that I create a rainstorm to attract the attention of an air elemental, and it worked."

"It *worked*," she repeated, her incredulity almost turning the statement into a question.

Susan is a rogue, Terj volunteered. *Their talents are unpredictable.*

"I'm well aware of that, but calling forth rain in the desert…"

No small feat. She's impressive.

Thanks, I silently told him.

His response came with a flash of amusement. *Putting a bit of fear in the old girl. Remember that insignificant body of water we saw just north of town?* His next thought was wordless, an imagining of a tidal wave slamming into Taln'een at horrific speed, which strained my ability to maintain a poker face.

Fortunately, Fanakel provided a distraction. "We stopped to assist a village under attack by Outsiders," he said. "Susan revealed herself, they took offense, and we were brought bound to Deoni. Erianthe proved less than sympathetic."

"She was going to kill Suze," Mia interrupted. "Let's not sugarcoat it."

Ganeel looked my away again. "Is this true?"

"Yeah," I murmured. "Once she saw me playing with water, she told me about this Darili princess who'd had a fling with a water elemental and abandoned her baby in Cole's Crossing. That baby would be *me*, the elemental is probably the one taken from the Falova River—"

"And the only Darili princess who fits the timeframe is Erianthe," Anji finished. "Unless we're gravely mistaken, Susan is, by right, the crown princess of Daril."

"Forget that," I said. "I'm not here for a throne—I just want to be free of the sword, and so does Terj."

Ganeel's head tilted in query. "Terj?"

Me.

Her bemusement only seemed to deepen at his response. "I didn't think your kind took names."

What kind? he retorted, his anger coloring the thought like a stage light in a smoky room. *I barely remember life before this torment. I couldn't have been much older than Susan when you people bound me. So if I'm not your expected elemental, please forgive me,* he said with all due sarcasm. *It's been centuries since I could speak, much less associate with another elemental.*

"Your frustration is understandable," replied Ganeel in perhaps the understatement of the day. "Truly, no one intended to cause you pain—"

No, just kill me.

"It...was unfortunate, yes, but for the sword to work—"

You tried to take my life. If Terj had teeth, I imagined he'd be gritting them. *What can you possibly say to mitigate that?*

She hesitated before speaking again. "Your sacrifice has kept these worlds safe for nearly five hundred years—"

It wasn't my sacrifice! You sacrificed me! You sacrificed all the Watchers! The volume of his mental shout made my head throb. *Undo this.*

"I—"

If there is any shred of decency in you, Ganeel, you will undo this. Softening ever so slightly, he added, *You saw what became of Zachary, did you not? Or would you rather forget?*

Before Ganeel could shut *that* down, Mia asked, "What happened to him?"

He was sixty-six when he died. Old before his time. Lame from an Outsider two years before. He lived on a homestead alone—

Ganeel certainly couldn't be bothered to leave town and share the dangers, he spat.

"Stop," Ganeel begged.

Terj ignored her. *And then, one night, he wasn't quick enough. He stabbed an Outsider, but not before it bit his other arm off. He bled out in the dirt. She found him the next afternoon on one of her biweekly visits, and then I damned Pericles in his place. Ganeel stayed only long enough to give the boy his sentence before she returned to Kopaat.*

"Enough."

She didn't even stay for the funeral.

"I said, *enough!*"

I screamed and covered my head as the pair of globular lamps nearest us shattered and the shutters rattled against the wall. When the last of the shards had tinkled to the floor, I dared to look up again and caught Ganeel's haunted, guilty stare, which began to retreat behind her professional mask as her breathing slowed.

"Forgive me," she said between deep breaths. "My, uh…my emotions can get the best of me from time to time…"

Though I suspected it was roughly the antithesis of wise to provoke a maladeta, Terj didn't seem to care that he'd touched a nerve. *He shouldn't have died like that. He should have married Sarah and had a litter of children, just like Matthew and Betsy. He should have had his brother's happiness. But all he had was loneliness and a miserable end. That blood is on your hands, Ganeel.*

"I had no part in Firebrand's forging," she muttered.

And what about Pericles, hmm? That rambunctious boy you remember died at seventy-eight. At least his nephew was visiting the cabin that night—one of Homer's boys, Ezekiel. An Outsider disemboweled the old man, and Zeke took up the sword to kill it. He thought he'd condemned himself, poor fellow. I chose Malachi instead—Zeke was in his fifties with four daughters and a heart condition. I couldn't do that to him.

Ganeel appeared to shrink into herself with every word.

Malachi was twenty-three. He'd so hoped to avoid the family curse. Zeke's family moved away three months later—guilt, I suspect—and it was just Malachi and his brother for years. Malachi desperately wanted a family, but he knew he couldn't have one. Not with Outsiders hunting him every night. He died alone, too. Shall I tell you about the ones before Zachary? I remember them all.

"You've made your point."

Have I? Because I don't think you feel the full weight of those lives you people ruined. The lives you made me ruin. Short little lives on another world you don't have to think about, perhaps, but I saw everything.

"Please," I said, "all we want is our freedom. Surely there's a way to destroy the sword, isn't there?"

Ganeel held her silence for a long moment, then sighed and rose from her cushion. "I will think about the best course of action. For now, you are my guests, and you'll be treated as such." The fingers of her left hand began to twitch as if she were playing an invisible instrument, and I heard a chime ring deep within the building.

Not even a minute later, a blonde woman who seemed no older than Mia and me knocked at the office's inner door and poked her head into the room. "Yes, Great Mother?"

"Daughter, my guests are weary," she said as the rest of us found our feet. "Take them to my dining room and see that they're well provisioned, if you will."

She nodded and stepped aside, opening the door more widely.

"Go with Satamun," Ganeel told us. "Rest. I'll join you later this evening."

As frustrating as the dismissal was—whatever I felt, Terj only amplified it—I knew there was no point in refusing her hospitality. Mumbling thanks, I followed the woman out.

The maladetas appeared to dine communally, as Satamun

led us into another building filled with long tables—a banquet hall, perhaps. The men laying plates and goblets paused at our arrival and offered shallow bows to our escort, who returned the gesture as a nod and swept onward past the trolleys loaded with dishware. Passing through a door and down a short corridor, she opened another door into a much more intimate space, a room with a rectangular table set for fourteen. "Leave your belongings against the wall, if you like," she suggested. "I'll speak with the kitchen."

We discarded our packs, but experience had made me wary, and the sword stayed belted on. My companions must have shared my paranoia, judging by the amount of steel we wore to the table, but we sat ourselves along one side and waited—though whether for a meal or an ambush, I couldn't say.

As we settled in on the creaking wooden chairs, Mia murmured, "Thanks, y'all."

"For what?" asked Anji.

"Not making me out to be a complete monster. Appreciated."

The princess chuckled. "Maladetas are unaffected by attacks from tekoraet. Anyway, seeing as you and Ganeel are both female, she was never in any danger."

"Do we know about the males, though?" asked Fanakel.

Mia shrugged. "Doesn't really matter, since I'm not going to feed on anyone." Leaning past Anji to look down the table at him—I couldn't help but notice that he'd taken the opposite end of our line—she said, "Were you planning to introduce yourself to Ganeel at some point? I didn't want to assume."

"She recognized who I am," he replied, frowning. "What more would you have me do?"

"Considering that we've come as escapees from Daril and are seeking her assistance," said Anji, "it might be helpful if you offered your name."

The elf stiffened. "You want me to abase myself?"

If you can't show a drop of humility in front of a maladetan clan mother, then where can you? Boast all you like of elven skill with the Aen—you know she's your better on that count.

"I don't see *you* coming before her on hands and knees," he retorted, glowering at my hip.

Considering my present condition, such would be impossible, Terj snapped. *And I have a right to my anger. You're asking a favor. I'm demanding justice.*

"Boys," I interrupted, massaging my head, "could we please not do this now?"

I registered Terj's surprise, then a surge of guilt. *You're in pain.*

"I'm fine."

No, you aren't… He hesitated, then asked, *Did I—*

"It kind of hurts when you shout," I said, and the rest of the table grumbled their agreement. "I get it, you have every right to be angry, but, uh…could we keep it down for just a little bit? Maybe until my brain stops throbbing?"

I'm sorry. Of course. Just…don't be an ass, Fanakel, he concluded, and fell silent.

Fanakel regarded the three of us, none of whom were jumping in to contradict Terj, and cleared his throat. "You really think it would be helpful if I offered?"

"It couldn't hurt," said Anji. "Particularly coming from a son of Nokan'ti."

He sighed but mumbled, "I'll think about it."

Before long, Satamun returned with a trio of men bearing platters and jugs, which they spread before us on the table before taking their leave. As the door clicked shut, she pulled out the chair across from Mia's and gestured toward the spread. "Help yourselves, please. If nothing here suits, I'll ask the kitchen to make accommodations."

"This is most generous, thank you," Anji hastened to reply before anyone could make requests, and filled her goblet with a golden liquid before pouring for Mia and me.

"Juice," she murmured as Fanakel took his turn. "It shouldn't make us drunk." Lifting her goblet, she turned to Satamun and smiled. "To the great mother's health."

Satamun joined Anji's toast and drank with us. "You are Ildoni?" she asked as Anji picked up the fish fork.

"Of Blackhorn Mountain." She squinted at the woman, then asked, "Are you using a translator?"

"No, no," she replied with a soft laugh. "I spent time among your people in this world, to the south."

"You have an ear for accents, then."

She bobbed her head at the compliment. "My grasp of Common Elvish is somewhat weak," she said, glancing at Fanakel, "but I trust that ring is a translator."

He spooned a pale green mush, somewhere between the consistency of pudding and mashed potatoes, onto his plate. "Correct."

"You must excuse Mia," said Anji, passing the fish. "The only translator she has is a one-way piece of my making, a poor thing. She can understand you"—Mia nodded at that—"but the other direction might be difficult."

"I take no offense," said Satamun. "The great mother informed me of who and what Ardielta was sending this way. And besides, you've had a long journey. I don't expect you to entertain me at the table."

"Thank you," I said between bites of the green mush. Texture-wise, it was nothing great, but the taste was faintly sweet and reminded me that I was starving. "Are you, uh...you're Ganeel's daughter?"

"We are all her daughters," Satamun began, then caught herself and grinned. "*Ah*—you mean by blood? No. I'm the fifth daughter. My sisters and I serve our clan mother and the Taln'een, but to answer your question, no, she did not give birth to me. In fact," she mused, "aside from her daughter in Silverhold, I believe her only blood child now living is Hakesh...I saw him ferry you here."

Thinking of the old man and his floating wagon, I

frowned and shook my head. "No, that was an elderly fellow…"

"Not so old. He's perhaps seventy," said Satamun. "He and one of my sons were playmates. My poor boy was lost in a hunting accident across the strait years ago, but he'd have been about Hakesh's age."

I knew I wasn't the only one of our party regarding her with confusion.

Satamun cocked her head. "You haven't had many dealings with my people, have you?"

"Personally?" said Anji. "No. My father has hosted several…"

"Mine as well," Fanakel added.

Mia and I looked at each other and shrugged. "Just, uh…Ardielta," I told her.

"I thought as much." After taking a sip of juice, Satamun pushed her goblet aside and lightly steepled her fingers. "The humans' confusion I expected. When your people first crossed into our worlds, we believed you to be like us, but the truth soon made itself known."

"No talent for magic," I replied.

"That was only part of it. Tell me, how long do your men live?"

The question struck me as odd, but I played along. "Very few live past one hundred."

"Mm-hmm. And your women?"

"About the same…maybe a little longer on average, but centenarians are rare. And since you live *quite* a bit longer than that—"

"Our *women* do," said Satamun. "Our men are like yours, short-lived and unable to speak to the Aen. And so they serve our clan in different capacities than we do—in the fields, in the forests, at sea, in construction, in the kitchens. Our women, by contrast, may live ten times longer. We have the years necessary for a proper education—it makes us more suited to clan leadership, you see. Mastering one's connection to the Aen is not accomplished overnight," she said with a slight chuckle. "But it works out. Male children are born so much more frequently than female that we never want for labor, and when they grow too feeble to work, they're provided for, just as they provided for the rest of the clan. But that is why Ganeel's son seems more aged than his mother," she explained. "As for those first humans we encountered, our history recounts that they were perplexed—they sent their men to negotiate, we sent our women, and neither side could understand why."

I couldn't help but notice that Satamun kept her attention focused on Mia's end of the table instead of Fanakel's, and judging by the looks I sneaked between bites, it hadn't been lost on him, either.

As I grabbed a second helping of fish, Satamun said, "A few of our men do leave us, especially with all the human settlements these days. It's a pity, but we wish them well."

"Can't imagine why," Fanakel muttered under his breath.

But Satamun, apparently, had excellent hearing. "You think we mistreat them?" she asked, leaning closer for a better look at him. "They are weaker and die quickly, yes, but we care for them. And they are as vital to the survival of the species as we are, which is a fact to be respected."

"You condemn them to servitude."

"We task them with the responsibilities to which they are best suited," she countered. "Some leave us for the human settlements in hopes of a different life—I won't say *better*. Even a few mothers have taken their sons beyond the Crossing. The women can never stay long—our aging is far slower than yours," she said, glancing at Mia and me—"but their sons make lives for themselves."

"Wait, *wait*," Mia interjected, "you're saying there are maladetas on our side of the Crossing?"

Satamun looked to me for a translation, then nodded. "A few have gone, all male. I cannot say where they are now. The last that I know of who left us was taken...oh, a hundred years ago, easily. He must be dead by now."

"But if your people have intermarried with ours..." I began.

She interrupted me with laughter. "Nothing to worry about. Any man who leaves us is treated first."

Fanakel dropped his fork, but she reassured him before he could object. "Merely to prevent them from siring daughters. We can't risk allowing women to be born with our power and no restrictions."

I thought of the rogue that the air elemental who'd carried us across the desert had described: a daughter born to a male maladeta and a fire elemental, killed as soon as her father's people learned of her existence. Perhaps her father had sneaked off without the full treatment. But though I understood Satamun's concern, the cavalier way in which she offered these tidbits rubbed me wrong. "You've never lived with a Watcher, have you?" I asked.

"No," she said with obvious relief. "I was slated to be posted after Ardielta, actually, but seeing as you're here—"

"Never lived with humans?"

"Uh...no, nothing more than a day or two in transit. I've spent most of my postings outside Taln'een with dwarves."

I paused long enough to take a sip of juice and tamp down the worst of my indignation. "What are your thoughts on the Watcher arrangement, then?"

"What about it?"

"You know, how the Watcher's stuck with the sword for life, fighting things that would never have appeared in our world if you weren't sending them our way...any of that sound familiar?"

Satamun considered me, her expression suddenly guarded. "The service you render is an honor—"

"Oh, bullshit," I snapped, pushing back my plate. "This is fine by you? Terj in constant pain, me and all the Watchers before me stuck by *your* damn Crossing, doing the work that *you* won't do? Our lives are ruined, and that's not a problem?"

Perhaps sensing the hostility from the rest of the table, Satamun chose her words carefully. "Think of all the good you do—"

"For my betters, right? People like you? I mean, I'm not going to live any longer than one of your men, so this is the best thing for me, isn't it? Just follow the plan you've set up—"

You might live quite a bit longer, actually, Terj whispered to me. *Rogues are unpredictable.*

I pushed that to the side, the better to concentrate on Satamun, who looked less comfortable by the second. "Tell me, if it's such an honor, then why do you ask strangers a *literal* world away to do it?"

She floundered briefly, then managed, "You're angry, I sense that—"

"Furious," I said, fighting to maintain control.

With a little nod, she rose from the table and smoothed her dress. "I, uh...I'll see about a next course," she mumbled, then slipped out of the room.

"There is a reason that I had decided to send Satamun after Ardielta's return," said Ganeel, closing the dining room door behind her and latching it.

None of us had risen from the table since our escort's flight. The kitchen hadn't sent anything further to eat, but then we'd hardly expected more. Satamun's excuse had been as flimsy as wet toilet paper. Instead, we'd remained in our row, picking at the dishes on offer—well, all but Mia, a longtime member of the clean plate club whose appetite had returned with a vengeance.

Ganeel didn't take Satamun's vacated seat, instead choosing another chair across the table from us. The silver threads in her dark hair twinkled in the sunlight through the window, but the only other sign of her age was the weariness in her expression as she considered our silent pack. "The girl is intelligent and has performed well in her prior postings, but her empathy could be improved."

"So you were going to foist her onto me?" I replied. "Let me be her learning experience?"

The clan mother winced at the edge in my voice. "My time with Zachary was…eye-opening. I had hoped for a similar result with Satamun, but…" She shrugged. "All a matter of supposition now, isn't it?"

Cut to the chase, Terj interrupted. *Will you free us, yes or no?*

Ganeel hesitated, her fingers whitening as she laced them together and squeezed. "I can't. Please understand," she said, raising her voice above our protestations, "I appreciate your position, and I wish the situation were otherwise. But I cannot destroy the sword."

You made it!

"We did, yes, with help from Nokan'ti and Blackhorn Mountain and Daril, and in tandem with the finest forgers of the age. The work that went into its creation was unlike anything seen before or since. Creating the *Crossing* was a novice's exercise by comparison."

"Assume for a moment that we don't know anything about magic or the Aen or whatever you want to call it," said Mia, mopping up the last of the fish's buttery sauce with a roll. "In layman's terms, what would it take to unmake the sword?"

Briefly, she scowled in thought. "Twelve of our clan mothers came together to make it. Ours led the effort. She saw the solution to the problem of powering the weapon, but she knew that working that sort of bind would be fatal. Using the Aen for destruction is possible, you see, but the consequences are steep. Trapping an elemental, killing him, and turning his life force into a source of energy for the sword is the sort of magic that one wouldn't attempt without either dire need or a death wish."

And she still failed, Terj muttered.

Ganeel's lips pursed. "Yes. But cast your memory back

to that time—Outsiders slipping into our worlds, soldiers being slaughtered at every tunnel mouth, all of us at each other's throats. She thought her sacrifice would be worthwhile in furtherance of the greater good, and the other clan mothers agreed. Undoing their work would take at least as many us as made it, and convincing enough clan mothers that we should render our foremothers' sacrifice meaningless would be next to impossible."

"Not to put too fine a point on it," said Mia, "but fuck your foremothers."

I held my breath, but Ganeel proved to be less touchy than the Twins of Nokan'ti. "Even if I had the necessary talent here," she continued, "there's a second problem. We entered a pact with the sword's other makers."

Mia huffed. "So break it—"

"It's not that simple, child. Understand that we were all at risk and anxious to protect our own people. The pact ensured that no one would build in loopholes to protect themselves at the others' expense. No one would harm the others…and no one would harm the sword," she explained. "And while I was not personally a signatory to that pact, my clan was, and it remains binding upon us. Which, I would venture, is another reason why your fathers are so reluctant to render aid," she said, looking at Anji and Fanakel. "Blackhorn Mountain and Nokan'ti signed—indeed, the Twins are personal signatories. Attempting to destroy the sword or release the Watcher could be considered a violation of that pact. And the protections we built into the pact are *powerful*."

"Meaning?" I asked.

She flashed a grim smile. "Let's just say that if the effort of unmaking the sword didn't kill me, the penalty for breaking the pact would."

"What if you could bring the signatories or their representatives together and unmake the pact?" Fanakel ventured. "If everyone agreed—"

"Son of Nokan'ti, do you honestly believe that your

father and your aunt would support such a plan? Free the Watcher, leave their people vulnerable?"

"Fanakel," he murmured. "And can't you *try*?"

Ganeel straightened in her chair and studied him for a long moment before slowly nodding, an acknowledgement of the gesture. Elves didn't give their names lightly—it was an admission that the recipient was the giver's equal, and for a race with a firmly established superiority complex, offering one's name to a foreigner had to be a humbling experience. I knew Fanakel's name only because Mia had asked while he was under her power, and seeing how uncomfortable it made him, I tried not to use it. That he had given Ganeel his name told me one of two things: either he believed in the rightness of our cause, or else he *really* didn't want to be sent home to face his father.

"Please know that I don't say this lightly," Ganeel finally told us. "I would help if I could, but even bringing us past the danger of the pact would take impossible political maneuvering. If the gods themselves appeared and started giving orders, then *maybe* we could bring the necessary parties to the table. But short of a miracle?"

That's it, then? Susan and I are damned, and you won't lift a finger?

"You didn't allow me to finish. There...*may* be a workaround."

I leaned forward, staring at her across the table. "Anything. What do we do?"

Ganeel took her time in answering. "Firebrand was forged for a purpose, and that purpose directs much of the magic worked upon it. If that purpose were to be removed, the sword *should* fall apart, and the elemental would be free."

"How do we do that?"

She exhaled slowly. "Well, the purpose of the sword is to kill Outsiders. If the threat of Outsiders were to be eradicated..."

"Like...destroy the Crossing?"

"No. You would need to go Outside and see where they come from and how they can be stopped."

That's madness! Terj protested. *You would have us go beyond the Aen—*

"Incredibly dangerous," Ganeel agreed. "I can open a path Outside for you—we would use the same weakness in the Crossing that the Outsiders exploit—but my people would not make the journey. It's never been done in living memory, and those explorers spoken of in our histories failed to return. But I fear it's the only way," she said, holding my gaze. "You want your freedom, Susan, and I understand that. How far are you willing to go?"

What do you think? I privately asked Terj. *Do we have a chance?*

I don't know, but if our options are take the risk or live like this...

I'm willing if you are.

Then I'm with you.

"We're in," I told Ganeel. "Point the way."

CHAPTER 3

While I was eager to hit the road, Ganeel put the brakes on my plan for immediate departure. "Your party needs rest, and *you* in particular need training," she said. "How would you describe your skill with a blade, minimal or nonexistent?"

"Uh…minimal," I mumbled.

Anji snorted. "If that."

"Which is why you'll be remaining with us for the immediate future," said Ganeel. "I'm not sending you Outside until I'm confident that you have at least a small chance of returning."

"The longer I'm here, the more Outsiders you'll have in Kopaat," I reminded her. "We fought them in Daril."

"I've put watchmen on our borders, and we can be ready to fight in short order—you're as safe here as anywhere on this continent, and if we're overrun, we'll flee across the strait. But you're not ready for the Outside," Ganeel insisted. "Rest and train. I'll equip you as well as I can."

I couldn't help but notice that she didn't volunteer to come along on our expedition beyond the world.

Moreover, there remained the minor matter of our recent flight from Daril. While Taln'een received few visitors, a search party from Daril couldn't be ruled out, either by land or by sea, and the clan mother decided to take precautions.

Before nightfall, Fanakel was dismissed to one of the men's communal lodges, where his red hair and scraggly beard were dyed dark brown. Desperate though he was to shave—facial hair was a giveaway that he wasn't of purely elven extraction—Ganeel ordered him to let it grow, the better to make him blend with the other men. They outfitted him with a hooded tunic from the stockpile, and one of the older men thought to finish the look with a simple knit cap, which disguised Fanakel's pointed ears. "I'm not sending you to the fields or the boats," Ganeel assured him when we reconvened for a late dinner. "You'll be training as well. But should a Darili scout approach, I'd prefer to hide you."

Mia's appearance was next on the agenda. While there was no way to diminish her natural beauty, Ganeel did what she could to disguise it, cutting her blonde waves into a simple bob and dying it brown. Rendered nearly shapeless in a baggy dress and cloak, Mia could hide herself well by pulling up her hood, which satisfied the clan mother. "Acceptable," Ganeel decreed, inspecting Mia from several angles. "Though I do have one final request: stay away from our men. I don't want you nibbling on them."

"I *wouldn't,*" Mia protested. "I swear, I'm not going to hurt anyone—"

"See that you don't." Softening a degree, she added, "We'll keep you fed, dear. You're not the first tekori I've entertained."

Anji presented a slightly trickier problem. In light of her short stature, Ganeel thought it best to dress her more like an older child than a grown woman, which meant a knee-length dress over leggings and boots instead of the adults' floor-skimming style. Anji had no problem with that—given what I'd seen of her tunic-and-trouser wardrobe to that point, I doubted that the princess owned more dresses than the absolute minimum dictated by necessity—but then came the delicate conversation about her hair. "It's a lovely color," said Ganeel, smoothing Anji's blonde tangles over her back. "But, uh...the beard."

Her shoulders tensed. "What about my beard?"

"I think you know where this conversation is going, dear. As long as you're sporting one, there's no disguising what you are." When Anji didn't waver, Ganeel took a knee in front of her and waited until Anji met her eyes. "I wouldn't ask it of a dwarf if I knew of another way. But if the Darili were to learn that we'd sheltered you…"

She didn't have to complete the thought. When Ganeel presented her with a bone-handled razor, Anji grunted and headed for the bathroom—which, to my great relief, was inside the guesthouse in which the three of us were staying. Any facility better than an outhouse, a bucket, or a hole in the ground constituted an improvement over our recent options. But before Anji could take two steps, Mia stopped her. "Wait," she said, and rummaged in her pack for a sample bottle of body wash. "It's not great, but it'll help. And does anyone have scissors?"

Mia insisted on doing the barbering for Anji, explaining that at least she knew how to use a razor in relative safety. When they emerged from the bathroom twenty minutes later, my jaw dropped. Anji had remarkably delicate features hidden beneath the beard, and Mia had given her mane a bit of a shaping trim and braided it after tackling her face. But it was clear to anyone with eyes that Anji felt uncomfortably denuded, and she clutched a thong-tied bundle of long hair in one hand—the remains of her beard, which Mia had carefully snipped and set aside for her.

As for me, I was the simplest of the bunch, and Ganeel decided that I'd pass muster after a shower, particularly if I kept my hood up. She did, however, send for the second daughter, who served as a sort of healer and midwife for the clan. The woman considered my scarred cheek, applied a sweet-smelling lotion, then covered the wound with a flesh-colored bandage. "Not as noticeable from a distance," said Ganeel, "and the moisture will help with the healing. But I'll still ask the four of you to stay away from the road and the sea, just in case."

That night, once we were fed again and left to our own devices, Mia, Anji, and I made ourselves comfortable in our communal bedroom, leaving the windows open to catch the cool breeze coming off the sea. I wasn't complaining—finding myself atop a real mattress, a pad stuffed thickly enough to render back support, was a relief after four nights on the ground, in a wagon, in a cell, or without sleep at all. But despite our general exhaustion, we tossed and shifted beneath the blankets, listening to the distant hiss of the waves.

Finally, Anji huffed an impatient sigh and flopped one arm against her pillow. "This is wrong."

I rolled over and raised myself onto my elbow to see her by the moonlight. "What in particular? I can think of a few things."

"Ganeel wants us to go *Outside*. You heard her—no one they've sent has ever made it back. What would give us any greater hope of success? She's feeding us, offering the rudiments of preparation, and ushering us to our deaths."

"I'm not asking you to go," I murmured. "Or you, Mia. You've done enough for me—"

"You can stop that, lass," Anji interrupted. "I'll see this through at your side."

"You just said it was suicidal—"

"But all I've been hearing is that my people helped orchestrate this injustice. *My* grandfather oversaw it, and he can answer to the High King for it. As for me, whether I'm destined to explain myself to the High Queen sooner or later, I'll damn well have a proper accounting for her."

"And you know *I'm* not leaving you, Suze," Mia chimed in from the next bed over. "If you're going exploring, I'm coming along for the ride. We've already hit three worlds in the last three weeks—what's one more stamp in the passport, eh?"

I laughed weakly and stretched out again. "We survive

this, and you can pick the destination. Maybe somewhere with fruity cocktails and infinity pools. I'll sell the house if I have to."

"Somewhere with bikinis," said Mia. "Scenery to admire. We'll find you a pretty cabana boy or something."

"Generous of you. Does that mean we're going somewhere with real cabanas?"

Anji snorted at our scheming. "You know, wisdom dictates that those who make plans for after the battle without first making plans for the battle itself seldom live to enjoy their plans."

"Killjoy," I muttered.

"I'm merely trying to keep us alive," she retorted, and sighed as she searched for the sweet spot on her mattress. "In all honesty, you'd probably be safer returning to the Crossing and living as the Watcher. With a bit of training and experience, you'd have a decent chance of survival…"

Maybe," I replied, "but I don't want to live that way, and I'm not doing that to Terj. This is about more than just me now."

I waited for his input, but he'd been quiet all evening. Not knowing if elementals slept, I didn't try to draw him into the discussion in case he was out cold. Terj had said that his bindings kept him in pain, and if he was getting a reprieve, I wasn't about to take that from him.

"This might just be me spitballing," said Mia, breaking the momentary silence, "but we could have better odds than the maladetas of surviving this trip."

Anji sat up in bed and stared at her. "Than *maladetas*? They have the strongest gifts of all of us—"

"With the Aen, right? Do they rely on defensive magic?"

She considered the translated term, then said, "I suppose…yes. Destructive magic can kill them, but they're deadly if provoked."

When Mia replied, I heard the smug smile in her voice. "What happens to them when there's no Aen to play with?

If that's their best defensive weapon, and they find themselves in a world beyond the Aen, what's their backup?"

The question gave Anji pause. "Blades, I suppose. Bows. Conventional weapons."

"But are their women taught to fight like that? Or do they leave the swords to their men and focus on magic instead?"

"Let's say a bunch of well-trained maladetan women went Outside," I said, picking up Mia's thread. "Once they left these worlds, all that skill in magic would be useless. Us, now, we're not relying on the Aen—"

"Except Fanakel," said Anji. "He's decently skilled if given time—quite helpful in our escape."

"But he can use conventional weapons, too," said Mia. "And *you*—I mean, I'm pathetic with swords next to you, but I don't see any reason why my guns wouldn't work Outside."

The princess sat in contemplative silence for a long moment, then stretched out again and rolled over toward Mia. "It's a nice thought. Perhaps not accurate, but a pleasant thought to sleep on."

The ropes supporting Mia's mattress creaked as she shifted positions to face Anji in the near-darkness. "I'm not giving up hope yet."

"Neither am I. Goodnight."

Mia hesitated, then murmured, "Hey, Anji?"

"Mm?"

"I know you hate your new look, but would you kill me in my sleep if I told you that you're pretty?"

I lay still, waiting for an explosion, but Anji just groaned. "Haven't been this hairless since I was eight. I look like a *babe*."

"Not from where I'm sitting."

"How you find this attractive, I'll never know."

"What can I say? I like blondes."

"You know what I mean."

Mia laughed to herself and adjusted her blankets. "If it'll make you feel any better, I'll shave my legs in solidarity."

"Why would anyone do *that*?" asked Anji.

"Ooh, smooth legs, clean sheets...you don't know what you're missing."

"*Humans*," she said with a sigh, and pulled her covers over her head.

Soon enough, I heard their breathing slow, leaving me alone with the sound of the sea and my restless mind. Closing my eyes against the moonlight, I tried ineffectively to will myself unconscious, and I'd just reached the point of envisioning sheep to count when I heard Terj's faint voice in my mind: *Susan?*

You're awake? I replied.

I don't sleep. Not in any form you'd recognize as such, he amended. *Drifting, you might call it. But yes, I'm awake.*

I peered across the room to the corner where I'd left the sword propped in its scabbard. *Anything I can do to make you more comfortable?*

No. He fell silent for the space of a long breath, then said, *I'm sorry. I'm so sorry for getting you into this mess. If I'd known the only solution was to go Outside, I'd never have done this to you.*

Terj—

If you want to go back to the Crossing, I'll understand. I've ruined your life—I can't ask you to sacrifice it, too.

Well, I don't plan to live like Uncle Malachi did, and I'm not going to let you suffer, so Outside it is. Can't promise miracles, but I'll do my best.

I thought he'd started to drift again when he said, *Malachi was always proud of you.*

Thanks.

He so wanted to keep you. Would have given anything to have a wife and children. But he knew he couldn't protect you at the cabin or provide the sort of life he wished for you, and he and Barnaby agreed that it would be best for Barnaby to raise you.

My throat tightened as Terj's low voice echoed in my thoughts.

It broke Malachi's heart. He loved you from the moment he laid eyes on you, he continued. *Barnaby adored you, too, but Malachi saw you more like a daughter than a niece. Either of them would have died to protect you. You should know that.*

Though I offered no reply, Terj picked up on my query. *I'm telling you this now because of Erianthe. She cut you to the core.*

His words only served to confirm what I'd begun to suspect the longer I lay still: the generalized disquietude keeping me awake could be partitioned, and one of those chunks had my mother's name all over it. Sure, a much larger chunk outfitted with a flashing sign concerned the Outside and my odds of surviving the trip, while another reminded me that if I came back without finding the cause of the monsters, Terj and I would still be trapped. A piece that kept bumping its way to the fore insisted that if anything happened to my companions, their blood would be on my hands. And of course, there was the bit that had lurked at the back of my mind for weeks pertaining to the mourning I'd barely started to process. But that night, lying in a real bed for the first time in days, I finally had a chance to reflect on the truth that the loving mother about whom I'd fantasized for much of my life had in fact left me in the woods to die, then prepared to kill me two days ago as an inconvenience. I hadn't been stolen from her and dropped for Uncle Malachi to find—I'd been discarded as the evidence of her indiscretion and an impediment to a marriage treaty. My existence wasn't cause for joy and relief, but rather a new problem for her to fix.

I didn't *want* to think about her. God knew I had bigger problems to address than my disappointment with my mother, but still, as I'd been given a break from immediate peril, she wormed her way toward the front of my thoughts.

Erianthe was cruel, said Terj. *I suppose it's only natural to be wounded when the person who's supposed to love you does not. But you had a family, and they loved you very much.*

Had. I curled up and tightened my grip on the blankets.

I'm sorry. Malachi's death is still fresh, and you've yet to fully cope with Barnaby's.

At that, my anger rose like prickling spines. *Don't suppose you ever had parents, huh?*

No, he admitted. *But I've witnessed this cycle play out for centuries. Malachi mourned his mother for the better part of two years. Barnaby was closer to three. Add to that their father's death two years after hers, compounding the loss. But there was healing after a time. Scars, perhaps, but healing. You're not there yet. I'm sorry,* he said again. *You should have had time to grieve without this being thrust upon you. And I'm making it worse now, aren't I?*

Thanks for trying.

His frustration translated as a mental sigh. *I'm finally heard again, and all I do is cause pain. I've spent most of my life ruining others'—why should this be any different now?*

As he berated himself, understanding dawned, and the last of my sudden anger faded. *Terj—*

I'm so sorry.

You miss him, too, don't you?

I don't have that right. After everything I did to Malachi—

You're allowed to mourn him, I said as gently as I could. *Hell, you lived with him for, what—forty years?*

I trapped him. He wanted so much more than that life, but he was the stronger of them, Barnaby couldn't have done it as well, and they knew it—

Terj—

The elemental continued as if he hadn't heard me. *And he's dead with nothing to show for it, just one more soul I've damned, and...*

The mental transmission I was receiving ceased to translate into words, then, instead morphing into an overwhelming wave of sorrow and guilt. Wading through it, I saw flashes of faces: Uncle Malachi's, prominently, but others whose names came to me from Terj's memory.

There was Dad and Uncle Malachi's granduncle, Pericles, the previous Watcher. Before him, a colorized version of Pericles's uncle, Zachary, whose photos I'd only seen in black and white. Two men in overalls—Richard, Zachary's uncle, and his own uncle, Joseph, both Watchers who'd died within four years of each other. The faces and names and more continued to swirl around me—stories of children dying young and survivors being encouraged to flee the family land, of sons and nephews in mourning suddenly finding a familiar sword wrapped in leather and knowing the curse had fallen upon them, of men who'd passed their nights keeping lonely vigil over the woods, of grief for shattered dreams, of death in the jaws of creatures from beyond our world.

And in the midst of Terj's outpouring, I caught a glimpse of myself at the kitchen sink with Mia doctoring the bleeding gash down my face.

I forgive you, I told him. *You're a victim in this, too. If you hadn't chosen me, it'd be someone else.*

I should have tried harder to fight it. The pain worsens if I wait to choose a Watcher, if I try to thwart the spells, but I could have done it, I could have said no...

He sounded so miserable that I was momentarily tempted to get out bed and hug the sword, for all the good that would have done. *I forgive you,* I repeated. *And if Uncle Malachi had known the truth, I think he'd have forgiven you, too.*

I ruined everything for him—

You didn't want to. The damn sword forced you to choose. And if I know my uncle at all, if he'd had the first inkling of what was really going on, I bet he'd have ripped Ms. Quince a new one.

He was in love with her, Terj said.

He still would have been furious. Am I wrong?

After a long pause, I heard a soft, *No.*

I know you're sorry, I continued. *None of this was your idea. So if you miss Uncle Malachi as much as I do, you don't have to hide it from me. I'm not somehow offended that you wish he weren't dead.*

Thank you, Susan.

When all of this is said and done, you and I can give him a proper send-off, eh? Do all the mourning then that we can't afford to do now.

I'd like that.

Curling up in my borrowed bed, I could still feel Terj's guilt-tinged sadness, which, if a strange sensation in my mind, at least served to distract me from my own spiral of rumination. *He's free now, you know,* I thought at the alien consciousness. *Wherever Uncle Malachi is, he's free, and I bet Dad's with him.*

Nice thought.

We'll get there, I promised, then whispered, "Goodnight," and listened to the moon-kissed waves until I fell asleep.

Morning dawned foggy and cool, a relief after our recent days in the sun. As the three of us puttered around our suite, taking turns with the blessedly hot shower, a knock at the door heralded Fanakel's surprise arrival with a basket of food. "I went back to the dining hall in search of breakfast, and Ganeel sent me here with this," he explained. "She also said to tell you that training begins after we eat. So…hungry?"

We admitted him, pushed the table closer to the window, and tucked in. While we found no maladetan version of coffee hiding in the basket, there *was* a flask of reddish-orange juice that tasted like liquid sugar, which was good enough for me. "She said to wear what you like today," Fanakel told us, having glimpsed bits of our new garb strewn over the beds. "Something comfortable. We'll be working in a training field well away from the road and the sea, so our chances of detection should be minimal. The weapons master has been informed of the situation." He took a bite of bread, then squinted at Anji and tapped a spot on his beard corresponding to the spreading blood along her jaw. "Nicked it, did we?"

She swiped her thumb along the wound, saw the blood, and groaned. "Sorry, I thought it had stopped—"

"Cold water and pressure. Pull the skin taut—less chance of snags that way. Make sure your blade is sharp. And I find that it's easier *after* bathing, not before," he added—fair chastisement, as Anji was the only one of us in the room with dry hair. "Did it yourself?"

"Mia demonstrated the basics yesterday," she replied stiffly, holding a napkin to her face.

In truth, Mia had offered to help when Anji slid out of bed that morning and grumped her way to the bathroom, but the princess had declined, insisting that she could attend to her own toilette. Even through the closed door, we'd heard her muttered curses for a solid ten minutes while she made her awkward first attempt.

"And how often does Mia shave her face?" Fanakel asked, glancing her way.

"Techniques used elsewhere are transferrable," Mia replied.

He paused at that, looking increasingly uncomfortable as he pondered her statement, then returned his attention to Anji. "Let me work with you tomorrow. It's one thing I can do reliably well." When she seemed poised to object, he said, "No throat cutting, I swear it."

She held out a moment longer, then gave a curt nod and returned to her meal with a mumbled, "Thank you."

Maybe it wasn't a sweeping improvement in dwarf–elf relations, I thought, peeling a hard-boiled egg, but that morning, I'd count progress on any count as a win.

The weapons master of Taln'een was a tall, brawny man with a thick shock of silver hair, a neatly trimmed beard, a translator around his wide neck, and hands like catcher's mitts. Though his hair made him seem older, his face suggested early middle age—maybe forty or so, I thought, sizing him up. Like the men we'd seen in the fields, he wore a sleeveless tunic, though his was black and lacked a hood—and that was the first critique he offered upon seeing Fanakel in his maladetan best. "Hoods are liabilities," he said. "They catch, they twist, and they give your opponent something else to grip. Take it off."

To my relief, Fanakel didn't argue with him, and his shirt joined our pile of water bottles at the edge of the dirt training field, a space roughly the size of a baseball diamond and surrounded by thick trees. A single path led from the village to the field, and aside from the occasional calls of the men working with the crops beyond the tree buffer, we might have been alone in the woods.

The weapons master introduced himself as Rinnik, and he wasted no time with pleasantries. Pointing to a jumble of wooden practice swords, he instructed us to arm ourselves, then gestured toward the far more substantial weapon hanging at my hip and scowled. "Why would you bring that? You think you're ready to fight with steel?"

"If I don't carry it, it follows me anyway," I replied, unhooking my bungee belt. "And if you don't like that, take it up with Ganeel. *I* didn't put the spells on the damn sword."

He grunted as I dropped it with the rest of our gear. "You're the Watcher, then?"

"I am."

"Don't suppose the sword could have chosen someone with a bit of muscle, hmm?" He marched up to me, then clamped one hand around my upper arm and squeezed. "Barely anything but *fat*," he announced with disgust. "Have you never attempted physical conditioning, girl?"

"Hey, Suze didn't ask for this," Mia snapped, "and it's been a rough year—"

He spun on her and shrugged. "I don't care. Your excuses are meaningless now. The great mother wants you prepared for whatever awaits Outside, and we have a *very* long way to go." To me, he said, "Ready yourself and step closer. Let's see how well you defend."

To no one's surprise, the answer to that was *poorly*, and I ended up on my back in the dirt thirty seconds into our practice bout. Rinnik grunted again as I picked myself up, then summoned Mia to take my place with a crooked finger. She performed moderately better—it took him perhaps forty-five seconds to lay her out flat—but he looked no more pleased with his students when Fanakel approached for his turn. At least the elf put up a fight— Fanakel *had* spent seventy-odd years as a palace guard, after all, and though he wasn't a great swordsman, he knew more than the rudiments of combat. Still, Rinnik soon had him pinned at wooden sword-point, but his grunt was accompanied by a brief nod as Fanakel returned to our line.

Last to test her skill was Anji—who, I had to admit, looked like a child beside Rinnik. But though she was at least two feet shorter than the weapons master, the cut-off sleeves of her undershirt revealed ropy muscles, and she passed the practice sword from hand to hand, gauging its weight. Unlike the rest of us, she never took a firm stance, instead slowly circling Rinnik, sizing him up, as he smirked at her.

"You'll need to be quicker than that, little girl," he taunted.

Anji didn't waste time with a reply. Like a lunging snake, she struck hard before he could put her on the defensive, then parried and ducked as Rinnik tried to catch her. Her wooden sword sliced and beat against the back of his legs, and when he let down his guard in surprise, she leaped onto his back and put him into a sort of headlock with the fake blade at his throat. "Congratulations, lad," she said, pulling the sword against his neck so hard that he staggered back. "You've been hamstrung, and now I've cut your throat."

She released him and jumped down, her point made, and eyed the weapons master as he rubbed his neck and kept a wary distance. "Never fought a dwarf, have you?"

"No," he admitted. "You're a master, then? The great mother never mentioned—"

"I'm but a student," she interrupted. "Barely forty years of training. Would you like another chance?"

The Anji who'd worked with Mia and me in the clearing by Uncle Malachi's cabin had been demanding but fair, doing her best to encourage us while beating us black and blue. *This* Anji was a different sort of creature, highly focused and lightning fast. She didn't goad Rinnik, but then again, he was already so discombobulated by the unexpected defeat that she had no need to mess with his mind. They circled each other, Rinnik tense and staring, Anji moving as easily as if she were strolling in the park.

And then she smiled.

That time, she didn't stop with her sword around Rinnik's throat. When he hit the dirt, she compounded the insult with a boot atop his head and the sword at the back of his neck. "You're a master, are you?" she said as she released him. "Of *what?*"

He pushed himself off the ground, his tunic streaked with sweat and mud, and cringed as she took two steps closer.

"You're a big lad, I'll give you that," she murmured. "Could be faster. I suppose you're a marvel next to all the farmers in town. But you have much yet to learn. *I* have much yet to learn. And *they*," she continued, jabbing her sword toward the rest of us, "are trying their best. The lasses are virtually untrained, and I doubt he's seen much of true combat," she added, jerking her head at Fanakel, who affirmed with an emphatic nod. "But we're here because we're willing to go Outside. Can you say as much?"

Rinnik seemed to shrink in his silence.

"I didn't think so. The skill is lacking in your students, but the will is there. Respect that, lad, or I'll dismiss you now and let you explain yourself to Ganeel."

The clan mother apparently being the scarier of the two options, Rinnik brushed himself off and cleared his throat. "You and you," he said pointing to Mia and me. "With me. We will, uh…practice blocks?"

Anji nodded as he looked her way for approval. "They'll be doing basics," she said to Fanakel as Mia and I walked off with the embarrassed weapons master. "If you'd like, I could show you how he put you on the ground. It's simple to defend against if you know how it works."

"That…might be useful," he replied, and then, far more softly, I heard him mumble, "Thank you."

CHAPTER 4

And thus began my descent into the fresh hell of basic training.

I've never been described as "svelte." At first, my dad thought I might turn out tall, given how quickly I grew in comparison to my classmates, but by middle school, my vertical growth had slowed to a crawl, while my baby fat blossomed into its more permanent form. My transition from juniors' to women's clothing was nothing more than an ignominious switch from size eleven to size twelve. Top the whole thing off with a mild case of teenage acne and an uncontrollable mass of brown hair, and…well, suffice it to say that even in my small high school class, I knew damn well that I'd never be homecoming queen.

Life might have been easier if I'd been blessed with even modest skill at any sport. But no—I had butterfingers on the softball field, two left feet in soccer, and bad aim in basketball. My one summer of tennis lessons had ended with me collapsing on the clay from heat exhaustion. I could swim—adipose tissue is *great* for floating—but I much preferred lounging to the backstroke. Dad had never seen the need to force me into dance lessons, which was for the best, as my flailing at school dances revealed that I had little sense of rhythm on the floor. And while I could ride a bike, I preferred to do so at moderate speed, and only when I had a destination in mind. Going for long rides out in the country—or worse, long jogs around the neighborhood—sounded more like torture than a good time.

My talents lay in other areas. I was a good student, a decent singer in the school choir, and handy with a pen or paintbrush. Mural needed sprucing up? I was all over that. Yearbook needed a layout editor? Give me the photos and the software. Mascot costume had devolved into a moth-eaten mess? My work with fake fur wasn't going to win awards, but at least our jaguar looked less like a mange victim once I was finished. Still, none of those activities involved strenuous physical exertion, which suited me nicely.

Thus, I came to Rinnik more or less a blank, squishy canvas, resigned to the work ahead but not at all thrilled with the itinerary. Running laps around the training field as a warmup did nothing but wind me and start the sweat flowing. Fanakel and Mia could carry on a conversation during our morning runs, but I gasped along behind them, at first cursing the blisters my boots gave me, then cursing the uneven ground when I tossed the boots aside and ran barefoot. Strength training followed, a battery of exercises involving rocks and metal weights that left me with gelatin limbs, then a too-brief lunch. Only in the afternoon, once I was exhausted and ready for a nap in the grass, did Rinnik turn to the business of combat instruction. Releasing Fanakel to Anji's custody, he made Mia and me drill with wooden swords until our hands ached. As the sun set, he'd free us to stagger away to the dining hall, and I'd drag myself behind Mia to join Anji and Fanakel at the end of the table we'd staked out as our own. While I could dry our sweat—useful once the temperature began to fall and the sea breeze kicked up—I couldn't do anything about our stench, but perhaps it served to keep curious maladetas at arm's length.

Although she'd been dismissed from our sessions with the weapons master, Anji had embarked upon training of a different sort. She worked with Fanakel in the afternoons, freeing Rinnik to concentrate on basics and giving herself a bit of exercise, but she spent her mornings at our guesthouse table with a stack of books taken from the clan's extensive library, which Ganeel had delivered after our first training day as Mia and I moaned on our beds. "Your forging is satisfactory for a novice," she'd said, dropping the leather-wrapped tomes onto the table in a puff of dust. "The translators you made show a modicum of promise. I fear that our weapons master's lessons may be too elementary for you, so perhaps you would prefer to occupy yourself with the improvement of your skill."

Anji had inspected Ganeel's books with a bemused frown. "I appreciate the offer, but these are far too advanced for one such as I—"

"A challenge, then," the clan mother had replied with a smile.

"But...but forging without guild oversight is outlawed..."

At that, Ganeel's smile had sharpened. "Not in Taln'een, my dear."

How much Ganeel's assessment of Anji's work had been downplayed, I couldn't say. Though my knowledge of dwarven culture was sketchy by the most generous assessment, I'd learned early on the faux pas of gushing over a dwarf's handiwork. Genuine praise from a foreigner came across as almost sacrilegious to the dwarf, and so the polite alternative was to keep one's compliments to a minimum. Given her age and experience, I assumed that Ganeel was aware of these norms—and considering what Anji had accomplished with the translators, Ganeel *had* to think more highly of Anji's skill than she let on. Forging magical items was a practice unique to dwarves, usually accomplished in teams of two: one to work with the physical objects, the other to channel the Aen. That Anji could forge solo was notable; that she could already do so as a young woman in her fifties was, I assumed, remarkable. The pair of translator pendants that she and Mia wore were beautiful pieces even without their magical effect. But there was room for improvement, as the translators only worked for the wearer's ears and not for her mouth. I certainly had no idea how much more difficult a two-way translator would be to forge, but the thick books seemed daunting, and Fanakel muttered more than once that she was taking out her frustration on him in their practice sessions.

If we had to be miserable in our own ways, at least we could gripe about it together. While Fanakel had been relegated to a bed in one of the men's lodges, he took to visiting our guesthouse for evening commiseration sessions. With Anji's books hidden out of sight in a chest, we lounged around the room, eating whatever snacks we'd convinced the kitchen staff to relinquish and cataloguing our injuries. Ganeel had been merciful enough to send us a tub of pain-numbing salve, which, combined with Mia's amateur masseuse skills, worked wonders on sore muscles.

Finally, after four days of work, Rinnik informed us that we'd have the following day off. "The great mother's orders," he said. "She thinks you're due regular recuperation." He looked like he was poised to disagree, but whatever self-preservation instinct he possessed made him bite his tongue. "Use it wisely. If you were to start the morning with weights, you'd do yourself no harm."

But weights were the furthest thing from my mind the next day. Having learned not even two weeks before that I possessed unusual abilities with water, I'd pulled off a few large-scale tricks flying by the seat of my pants, but I'd hardly *practiced*—and quite honestly, playing with the next-best thing to magic trumped physical conditioning any day. While Mia and Anji went for a long walk along the shore in their maladetan disguises, I borrowed a large clay bowl from the kitchen, filled it with water, and set it atop the table in our room. Closing the shutters for privacy, I lit the lamp on the wall—Ganeel had left one of the metal pieces for us, a sort of key given to their men to allow them to manipulate the spells the women crafted—then settled cross-legged on my bed and contemplated the bowl.

In recent days, I'd grown sensitive to the presence of water, a highly specialized sixth sense that made me a somewhat human dowsing rod. Most of the time, I was able to ignore the feeling—I really didn't need a precise mental map of what everyone in the dining hall was drinking, for instance. Had I not been able to tune it out, the proximity of the sea would have overwhelmed me like an air-raid siren splitting a silent night. But when I closed my eyes, quieted my mind, and allowed myself to listen to that weird new sense, I opened myself to a wealth of information. To the north was the sea, present as a thumping bass line in a nightclub, rolling onto the land and retreating. I could have drawn the contours of the coast, which registered as a void beside that great well of power. To the southeast, snaking its way toward the ocean, was the spur of the Falova on which we'd fled. I could map its bends and trace it over each plunge as the river followed the land to its edge. All around me, buoyed up by the constant wind, was a shining cloud of moisture, a billion stars against the expanse. The humidity of the seaside town was as an abundance of wealth after my experiments in the wasteland. But if I concentrated and narrowed my focus, I could easily sense the water in the bowl, just waiting for me to command it.

It rose.

I opened my eyes and watched the water swirl upward like a tornado in reverse, a funnel narrowing and stretching to the ceiling. With a touch of my will, it spun itself down and around my arm, a bracelet of moving water that didn't leave so much as a drop on my bare skin. I split it and wove the strands together as a braid, then undid my work, split it into three times as many pieces, and maintained the stability of one braid while I worked on the other two.

Having fun?

I turned and smiled down at the sword, which I'd left sheathed on the bed beside me. The more I got to know Terj, the worse I felt about constantly propping him up in the corner until I needed to stab something. *Better than running laps*, I replied.

You're sweating less.

This is easy.

His response was colored with amusement. *It should be. Ask one of us how he learned to manipulate an element, and you'll get nothing but confusion from him.*

You didn't have to practice, then?

No. It's instinctive. Under other conditions, I would demonstrate, but...

Don't want to blow the roof off? I asked, chuckling.

I can't. Not bound as I am.

I dropped the water back into its bowl and shifted on the bed to give the sword my full attention, as if I might find Terj looking back at me through the leather sheath. *I thought that since you're back in an Aen-rich environment—*

It's not enough. The spells draw on my essence—they pull less here, with the Aen to power them, but that only leaves me strength enough to be heard. I can no more control the air now than you can.

Terj didn't sound angry, but rather merely resigned to his damnation. "I'm sorry," I murmured.

I'm used to it.

Curious but hoping not to upset him, I hesitated before asking, *Do you remember what it felt like?*

One never forgets what it is to ride the wind, Susan. Never. After a moment of melancholy silence, he said, *You have yet to feel the pull, correct?*

What pull?

The only elementals to remain free-roaming are those of us of the air, he explained. *We all roam at first, but after a few years, the others are driven to settle down. You haven't sensed any unexplainable urge to jump into the sea and never surface, have you?*

Pretty sure I'd drown if I tried.

Perhaps before, but your talent has awakened now. It's possible that you'll feel the pull someday.

I tried to imagine myself plopped in the middle of a river, floating with my eyes and nose above the surface, but the thought didn't spark any deep longing in me.

Terj's laughter reminded me that he was better at seeing my thoughts than I was at picking through his. *Perhaps not*, he allowed. *Rogues are unpredictable. Anyway, you should worry more about that water bowl than running in circles for Rinnik.*

Levitating the water to me again in the form of a glistening sphere, I replied, *Feel free to tell him that yourself. I'm trying not to make him angry while Anji's not around as backup.*

Think about it: the sword is deadly against Outsiders, yes? You're no great warrior—

Gee, thanks.

I'm only speaking the truth, he said. *But look how many you've killed without any particular skill at arms. All you need to do is make contact—you need not fight with Anji's skill, nor even Fanakel's. And he's better than you think he is*, Terj continued. *He's not the dwarf's equal, but then she's among the best I've seen. The woman's a natural.*

Fine, but if I actually learn how to fight with a sword, maybe I won't get sliced open again, I countered.

That's fair. But if you drown your opponent, then stab him while he's trying to gasp for air, you won't need any particular skill.

Drown him how? We're going outside the Aen again, remember?

You don't need Aen to manipulate water, Terj replied. Before I could argue with him, he said, *Forging and the sort of magic that maladetas and elves use is entirely Aen-based. What we do isn't magic at all—it's who we are. Maybe your talent didn't reveal itself until you crossed into one of these worlds—hell, maybe the spells on the sword sparked something in you—but what you can do with water doesn't require magic.*

Surprised at the news, I lost focus, and the floating sphere fell onto my bed like a burst water balloon. I swore and summoned it back into the air, leaving my bedding dry once more, and looked at the sword. *So, assuming we don't land in another desert…*

You have a skill that Rinnik can't touch, he finished. *Don't be afraid to employ it.*

I considered that as I turned the water over in my hands, watching the lamplight glint off its surface. *Is it limited to water?*

Terj sounded bemused when he answered me. *Unless your mother was an elemental as well—*

No, I mean…well, look. Dropping the water into its bowl, I flopped onto my back and stared at the ceiling. *Air elementals have power over air, right?*

It's in the name, yes.

What does that even mean? Define "air."

I…don't follow you.

Think about it. If you were free right now, you could manipulate the atmosphere around us, correct?

Yes…

But what part of it? Oxygen? Nitrogen? Carbon dioxide? What about water vapor? There's lots of that in the air here.

By then, Terj seemed unsettled by my line of questioning. *All of it, I suppose.*

What about other gasses? Like, say I had a tank of helium and released it into the air—could you play with it?

I don't see why not.

Okay…so "air" for an elemental is basically "any accessible gas."

He mulled that over for a moment before rendering a verdict. *That sounds reasonable. I never tried to separate gasses, but it might be possible.*

What about "water," then? I continued. *Are we talking purely water, or does it extend to liquids in general? And I know I can tease moisture out of air, but can I play with ice?*

I can't be entirely certain, but I think I rendered him speechless for a few seconds.

Water elementals' power is limited to the body of water in which they reside, he finally replied, *but beyond that, I have no idea. These aren't the sort of questions that anyone has ever posed me…*

Then I guess we experiment. Sliding off the bed, I belted the sword on and headed for the door. *Let's see what the kitchen has on offer.*

I suspect that the kitchen staff hated the sight of me by the end of the day, as I kept returning in search of new items to test in the privacy of my guesthouse. Water was easy—liquid, gaseous, or frozen, I could make it do almost anything I desired. Wine was simple, though the thick, almost yellow chiquiw milk was harder to coax from its bowl, and the sweet sap that tasted like almond-flavored maple syrup moved only with heavy concentration. When I tried to manipulate a broth-based vegetable soup, the broth rose at my command, but the solid bits wouldn't budge. A chunky green sauce similarly separated into water and the firmer components left behind.

Next came trials concerning proximity. Water that I touched was easiest to move, but it wasn't markedly more difficult to draw it forth from across the room. I then switched from bowls to closed containers, which *were*, surprisingly, harder to deal with. But as soon as I could make the water in the container sufficiently slosh around so as to knock off the lid, victory was mine. By dinnertime, I'd concluded that anything water-like and in a breakable container was fair game for me, which led me toward a troubling query.

"Can you manipulate air inside a living body?" I murmured, pouring the last of my practice water over the railing and onto the scraggly grass growing below.

I've never tried, said Terj. *Why do you ask?*

Think about it. A body's not even a closed container—you've got orifices to consider. So if you could reach into someone's lungs, say, and pull the air out...

That's only mildly horrifying.

And we haven't even gotten to liquids yet. Blood, sure, but imagine what you could do with stomach acid in the wrong location.

Do I want to know? Hey, where are we going? he asked as I grabbed the sword again.

Beach. I need more practice.

Staying clear of the fishermen hauling up the last of the day's catch, I marched barefoot across the dark sand, looking for a secluded spot and a target. After a ten-minute walk, I found both: a little patch of seashore on the far side of a stone breakwater and a freshly dead fish—a victim of the tides and not the seabirds, I thought, as the corpse was nearly intact. I closed my eyes and concentrated, tuning out the waves lapping over my feet to focus on the moisture within the fish. There wasn't much—barely a drop beside the literal ocean of potential—but with a moment's work, I could pick out the coagulating blood in its veins, all stilled by death. Slowly, I coaxed the blood into movement once again until it was running through a loop, faster, ever faster, forcing its way toward an exit…

Um…Susan?

Startled out of my trance by Terj's voice, I opened my eyes to see blood pouring from the fish's open mouth and fumbled backward up the beach. As I stared at the draining fish, the weight of the knowledge I'd just acquired slammed into me.

"Oh, my God," I whispered.

No wonder rogues were feared. I'd already been told that I was stronger than my presumptive father, but to make matters worse, I was unbound. He could make a river rise and fall, but if I could squeeze blood from a body…

Ganeel was taking a risk by sheltering me. Could she continue to do so in good conscience if she knew that I could remotely exsanguinate?

Or, more worryingly, could she afford to let me live?

While I considered the ramifications of my newfound talent, Terj said, *We're not going to tell the others about this yet, are we?*

No, I replied, feeling a little queasy, *we are not.*

Calling upon a few convenient waves to do my bidding, I returned the fish to the sea and washed away what evidence I could, then buried the leavings with my foot. As I smoothed the sand flat, I heard a pointed throat-clearing behind me and whipped around, afraid I'd been discovered. My fear, however, was for naught; Fanakel had spotted me, and it seemed that the fading light had disguised the worst of my expression.

"Good evening," he said, smiling as I straightened and batted the hair out of my face. "Did I disturb you? I thought you'd be at dinner—the others passed me some time ago, heading in that direction."

Unlike me, Fanakel had thought to tie his hair back against the sea wind, and it hung almost neatly beneath his hat, though his hood had fallen to his shoulders. I couldn't say that his new look didn't suit him, but then again, I was hard-pressed to imagine a scenario in which the elf would seem less than beautiful. Even filthy, the man radiated sex appeal, and a week-old beard and a handknit cap did nothing to diminish the effect.

"Not hungry just yet," I replied, which wasn't entirely false. "I wanted some air. Did you go exploring?"

"Up and down the coast," he said, joining me at the water's edge, and I took care to keep the waves away from his boots. "Nice to have a day of rest, though I thought the walk would keep my muscles from stiffening tomorrow. Anji is merciless."

"Terj said she's a wonder."

"I'd believe it. Should you ever attribute that to me, now, I'll deny it before any gods you like."

I glanced up in time to catch his teasing smile. "There's nothing wrong with being nice to her."

Snorting at my suggestion, he cracked his back and stared out at the sea. "You're new here, aren't you?"

Baby steps, Terj whispered to my mind, and I bit back my sarcasm.

"So," I said instead, "you didn't want to go hiking with Anji and Mia, I take it."

"I've missed solitude," he replied, and looked my way again with a curious expression. "Though I'm surprised you didn't accompany them."

I shrugged. "Work to do here. Why? You thought we were joined at the hip or something?"

"No, but I…" He paused, and even in the twilight, I detected the sudden uncertainty on his face. "That is, I, uh…you and Mia…"

After a moment, I understood the thrust of his awkward babbling and laughed. "Oh, no, *no*, she and I aren't a couple," I assured him. "We've been friends for most of our lives—she's like a sister to me—but we're not in a relationship like that."

He seemed to deflate with relief. "Glad to hear it. I didn't want to be the herald of bad tidings, but Mia and Anji…"

"I'm not the only one seeing things, you mean?"

A grunt was the only confirmation required.

We stood together by the sea for a time in almost comfortable silence and watched the stars pop out as the light faded. Eventually, however, Fanakel murmured, "Do you suppose it's infatuation?"

"Couldn't say," I replied. "Mia had a bad end to her last relationship about a year ago, and I haven't seen her interested in anyone since. And Anji's just a closed book."

"A dwarf and a tekori."

"*Half* tekori."

"Still won't work. Even if Mia were a dwarf as well, Anji's royal—we do tend to have standards. Most of the time," he amended. "I still don't know what my father was thinking in siring me, but that's unimportant tonight."

I thought over what Anji had described of elven cultural norms and tried to pick the truth from the dwarven propaganda. "You, uh…I heard that monogamy's not really a thing for your people."

"It is to an extent," he said, unfazed. "Father and his sister married their consorts in a joint ceremony shortly after their elevation, and most of their children were born within their marriages. It's expected." He paused to raise his hood against the deepening chill of the evening and hug himself. "But the four of them have all produced children with other partners. It's said that taking a new partner for a brief time every so often brings one closer to one's spouse. The Divine sanction it, in any case. I suppose they realized that bedding only one person over eight or nine hundred years would be terribly dull."

I watched the waves roll in, trying to think of a way to ask the question on my mind without coming across as desperate, as settled for a less than suave, "So, uh…is there anyone special in your life?"

If Fanakel drew any conclusions from the tenor of my query, he kept them to himself. "No. Nor will there ever be."

That took me aback. "You're not interested in a relationship?"

"I wouldn't say that, no. But relationships require a partner, and…well, I'm not ideal for anyone I'd choose to pursue."

"But your father and mother—"

"The True have bedded humans on occasion, yes," he said, avoiding my gaze. "But those are brief affairs, and they seldom end in half-breeds. We're best avoided, you understand. And as I'm tainted, I'm not fit marriage material."

His voice was nearly monotonic, but I caught the slight tightening of his shoulders as he stared at the horizon.

"You wouldn't consider a human, then?" I asked. "Elves might be stupid about it, but, I mean, it's not like you're *hideous*…"

That garnered only a fleeting grin. "Recall that practical reason why our flings with humans are necessarily brief. I'm ninety-nine years old, girl. *Young*. And you are…"

"Almost twenty-three."

"Right. So, assume that we threw caution off a cliff, said to hell with all the gods, and embarked upon a torrid affair."

Honestly, it didn't sound like such a horrible idea.

"Maybe we'd run off to some quaint little settlement on Ga'besh," Fanakel continued. "In another thirty years, I'd look like your son. In sixty, your grandson. In ninety, you'd be dead. What's the point?" Giving me a quick glance, he mused, "Perhaps not *you*. I suppose you'll know better in a decade or two—"

"Know what?"

"How quickly you'll age. I've never known a rogue, but what I was taught of elementals suggests that they don't die of natural causes."

We're difficult to kill, Terj chimed in. *That's what makes us great indefinite power sources for cursed weaponry.*

I stepped back on the wet sand, frowning as I processed that. "So...you're suggesting..."

"Mia may live five hundred years if her tekorish side is strong enough," said Fanakel. "Anji might see eight hundred, and I could go a bit longer...I mean, one of True could, so who knows about me?" he muttered. "But you show elemental abilities in a physical form, and that's..."

Largely uncharted.

Fanakel shrugged. "Somewhere between a human lifetime and an indefinite span, then, and who's to say for certain? Assuming, that is, we don't all die a quick and painful death once we step Outside."

Still trying to come to terms with what the two of them had so casually let slip, I forced myself not to ask the first question that popped into my head—*Would you be interested in someone like me?*—and tried instead to pivot. "Okay, so elves are out, humans are out, you don't seem too keen on dwarves..."

He dignified that with a brief, incredulous chortle.

"And not big on tekoraet, for obvious reasons."

"Affirmative," he muttered.

"Maladetas?"

Shaking his head, he said, "No. Too risky. I mean, I suppose there wouldn't be a problem if I preferred men in my bed, but I'm partial to women—"

Hope fluttered within my chest like a stupid, manic bird before I reminded it that my handsome companion was in no way infatuated with me and pushed it deep down again.

"—and if I were to sire a child on one, even odds we'd have to kill it at birth. Can't afford to leave a female maladetan cross alive. Understandable in theory," he said, lowering his voice as the waves continued to roll in around the dry patch I'd left him, "but if that were your child, you know...you've waited, you hold it, only to realize that you have no choice but to destroy it..."

"Slightly horrifying," I concurred.

"So you see why entanglements with maladetas are to be avoided—that, and the fact that their women think they're so much more *advanced* than their men. The air of superiority they affect...it's infuriating how they look at you almost with pity—"

Now, where have I heard that before?

Fanakel glared at the sword hanging from my waist. "I suppose you're referring to the True, yes? Consider yourself clever?"

Did I say that?

"I think I liked you better when you were silent."

I think I prefer you with a modicum of humility, Fanakel, but maybe that's just me.

The elf twitched at hearing his name, and I could almost feel the smirk in Terj's thoughts.

"In any case," said Fanakel, "they barely take partners. The women come to the men's lodges at night, their chosen men depart with them, and half the time, when they partner off again, it's with different people. Obscene. There's nothing like marriage among them, you know," he told me. "Probably half the men I've asked can't name their father. The clan raises the children together."

Methinks someone's peeved that he hasn't been invited for a night out.

"*Ha.* These women are barely plain beside the ugliest

girls of Nokan'ti." Glancing at me, he asked, "What about you, then? Some village boy back beyond the cabin in the woods?"

"Nope."

"Hm. Village girl?" he guessed.

"That's Mia, not me. I just haven't found anyone yet."

"And what would you be looking for?"

If Fanakel knew how uncomfortable his prying made me, he played it perfectly cool. "The usual, I guess," I managed to spit out. "Love, faithfulness...if he were good looking, I wouldn't mind. Might be nice if he thought I was smart or funny or something."

He considered my list, nodding to himself. "Nice to dream, I suppose. Realistically speaking, you'll never get that."

"I'm not saying he has to be *beautiful*—"

"It's not the looks you need to worry about. You're the heir to Daril, remember?"

"Technically," I mumbled.

"Let's pretend that you went back, reconciled with Erianthe, and took your place in the succession. Politically speaking, you'd make a highly desirable match, but that wouldn't mean you'd have any choice in your pairing. Royal weddings among near heirs are like breeders swapping chiquiws, only with lands and lives mixed up in the arrangement."

I stood silently and listened as a pair of seabirds called to each other while swooping in tandem to the shore. "Real romantic, aren't you?"

"Pragmatist," Fanakel corrected. "I'm virtually worthless as a political match, so my father has made no move to marry me off. Some of his other children have married because of the mutual benefit to the parties. They don't necessarily *love* their spouses, but even where the soil is too thin to cultivate love, fondness can flower."

"Centuries stuck married to someone you don't love? That sounds ideal to you?"

"It's the way of life, girl—I never said it was ideal. So should you find acceptance with your mother, prepare yourself for marriage. Erianthe and Narod were betrothed as children—you're already behind. I'm sure there's a match in planning for Edes," he said with undisguised distaste.

The mention of my mother's son left me with a grab bag of emotions: curiosity, though tempered by Fanakel and Anji's disdain for him, jealousy that our mother had kept him after dumping me to die, but also a twinge of guilt. According to my better-informed companions, if I was truly Erianthe's firstborn, then I was by right the crown princess, no matter who or what my father had been. Seeing as she'd tried to kill me, I doubted that Erianthe had told her other children about their older half sister, meaning that Edes had surely grown up secure in the knowledge that he would inherit Daril. What would he do once I entered the picture?

If I entered the picture, I mentally amended. First, I had unknown horrors to slay and four whole days of proper arms training behind me. If I made it back alive, then theoretically, I'd be free of the spell tying me to Cole's Crossing. I'd be able to go anywhere, to restart the life I'd put on hold when Dad died. Why would I return to *Daril*, a place I'd fled to avoid execution?

You had strength enough to cry when Malachi found you, but you were lethargic, Terj murmured. *Ant bites on your face—he brushed the rest of the bugs off your arms and legs. You were filthy and still tethered to the afterbirth. Cold. Hungry, I'm sure. He wrapped you in his jacket, held you until you quieted, then put you beside him on the seat of his truck and drove to Barnaby's house as quickly as he could. Almost hit a tree or two. He couldn't accompany you to the hospital, so he poured himself a stiff drink and sat on the porch when Barnaby left. Only once Ardith came over to investigate did he realize that he still had blood on his hands.*

Shocked though I was by Terj's unexpected trip down memory lane, what surprised me most was the undercurrent of anger beneath his words. *What are you getting at?*

You deserve justice, too, Susan. I'd settle for freedom—there's nothing that Ganeel or anyone else can offer me in recompense, and I'm not strong enough to force the great powers of these words to a reckoning. But you could take on Erianthe. Remind her and the scions of all the lesser houses that consequences attach to the actions of the small and great alike. He paused, then added, *The humans of much of Kopaat have a saying: the gods demand truth. I believe they use it in lieu of making the other person swear an oath—it's a reminder that lies tend to come out in spectacular fashion. Erianthe lied to Narod about her infidelity, she lied to her people about the cause of the Falova's apparent death, and she tried to cover up her lies by disposing of you. Bring that to light.*

Still, I wavered. Couldn't freedom be enough? If Terj and I could break the sword, if I could find my father and restore him, if I could win back my life—couldn't I write Erianthe off? So I had a terrible mother. I could still make something of myself.

Sell the store, if you like. Sell the house and the cabin. Take the money and see your world, said Terj. *And while you do so, remember that your mother's on a throne, your brother will sit it at her death, and they will either pretend that you don't exist or never know the truth.*

I sighed and hugged myself against the wind. "It's a nice evening, isn't it?" I said to Fanakel.

"Pleasant," he agreed.

"Too bad this is temporary, eh?"

I jerked when I felt his hand unexpectedly land on my shoulder, and he turned the gesture into an awkward pat. "Dinner?"

"Sure," I said, and followed him up the beach as the roosting birds in the nearby woods trilled their last for the night.

CHAPTER 5

My first two weeks in Taln'een passed in a grueling cycle of exercising, training, and collapsing, punctuated by the occasional day of playing with anything conceivably liquid in my vicinity. Under Rinnik's tutelage, I ran until my skin flushed scarlet and beads of sweat dripped into the dirt. I slammed my wooden sword into Mia's until my palms calloused over and her attacks became as familiar to me as long-practiced choreography. I fell into the grass time and again as Rinnik demonstrated variations on techniques and scowled at my uncoordinated attempts to defend myself. I limped into the dining hall with Mia to gorge myself on anything even vaguely palatable—and as luck had it, the maladetas were better than decent cooks. I washed the salt and grime and streaks of dark soil away in a cloudy swirl, letting the beating shower tenderize my aching body before Mia took her turn with salve and pressure. And then I stretched out in my bed, muscles taut, flesh bruised, blisters stinging, and waited for sleep to come.

I wanted so badly to quit. I wanted another option, a solution involving more talking and fewer attempts at effective shielding, a visit from a group of responsible people who would take pity on me and make the problem go away. I wanted to wake up in my childhood bed and discover that the last month had been nothing more than a vivid nightmare. But no one came to save me. No one shook me awake and reassured me that all I'd faced was my own overactive imagination. And there was *never* enough moleskin to pad my injuries when I woke to find myself curled into a sleep-stiffened ball, burrowed beneath the covers against the sea breeze.

After the initial days of communal commiserating, as we settled into our training routines, I knew better than to gripe about my aches and fatigue. Though the others never brought it up, I knew too well that they were only stuck in Taln'een because of me, and I had no room to complain. Of course, it didn't help my mood to always be the worst in our practice sessions—the slowest runner, the weakest with weights, the loser in bouts. Every time I lagged behind or hit the dirt, part of me wondered why my companions should risk themselves on my behalf when I couldn't even keep up.

But then there was Terj, who often spoke to me out of the others' hearing. Where Rinnik offered frequent beratement, Terj countered with a more balanced commentary: *That was better. You're still exposing too much of your flank. You've doubled your weights this week, and strength doesn't build overnight. Pick yourself up. That was good.*

Terj had never been trained at arms, and being incorporeal, he couldn't have pulled a muscle if he'd wanted to. But he'd been a silent witness to five centuries of Watchers fighting for their lives, and he'd picked up a thing or two about the mechanics and nuances of combat. If Rinnik intended to shame me into shape, Terj offered encouragement instead—and more.

He knew my family better than I did. Embarrassing stories about Dad and Uncle Malachi? He had them in *spades*. Tidbits about the grandparents I'd never known outside of photos? Having lived with Pericles Cole, Terj had known his nephews and watched to see which of them might be damned in their uncle's stead. That they'd escaped due to Pericles's longevity didn't mean that Terj had forgotten their names and faces. He told me about my great-grandparents, Homer and Betsy, and about Homer's uncle, Zachary, who'd done his time under Ganeel's supervision. They'd been farmers, mostly, those Coles, a family that had gone west, stumbled onto the Watcher at the hour of his death, and inherited the burden. For generations, parents had encouraged their children to move away, hoping to spare them, but a son or two always remained—someone to care for the farmland and the store and their aging parents. Usually, Terj's choice had come down to two of the younger Cole men, almost always nephews of the previous Watcher, as the Watchers seldom married or left families. He told me of the Coles who'd gone off to war, of the ones who'd set tongues wagging before they were properly married, of the feuds and petty sniping and reconciliation that pock any extended family's history. He'd watched it all play out like a soap opera in real time, a distraction from his torment, and I heard the cast of melancholy in his voice when he spoke of the Watchers who'd come before me.

I think, in his way, he'd loved them. Though they'd never known of his existence, though they'd cursed the sword and railed against the injustice of their selection, he'd known them and missed them.

They would be proud of you, Susan, he often concluded. *Especially Malachi. He was always proud of you.*

But as pleased as I was to hear stories of Coles past, my connection to them seemed more tenuous than ever. These were Dad and Uncle Malachi's ancestors, not mine—I was the foundling brought into the fold, the outsider to whom the curse had fallen when there was no true Cole left in the Crossing to bear it. The family that was mine by blood—the Fulquirs of Daril—had cast me out. And as I lay in my guesthouse bed night after night, exhausted and scabbed and sore, I thought of what Erianthe had said to me in my prison cell: I could die as punishment for abandoning my post at the Crossing, or I could return, do my duty, and erase my shame.

My shame.

My mother was ashamed of me. Her other children had been raised as princes and princesses, but she'd have been thrilled for me to spend my life alone in a sad little cabin, fighting monsters until one of them slashed me somewhere more important than my face. I was a problem to be fixed, nothing more.

Anger always filtered into those circling thoughts. Surely precious little Edes had never found himself in a maladetan guesthouse, stuck between certain death in Daril and likely death Outside. If he'd had combat training, it must have been with a kinder, gentler teacher than Rinnik. No one had stuck *him* at the edge of the Crossing and told him to have a nice life.

But when my mind had spiraled far enough, I'd hear Terj interrupt: *It's not fair. None of this is fair. And if we survive the Outside, I'll help you make it right.*

How?

I don't know yet, he'd say, *but this I swear to you.*

After three weeks of basic training, I noticed something peculiar: an unfamiliar hardness in my arms and legs, either fast-growing tumors or the beginning of actual muscle tone. Banking on the latter, I flexed in front of the mirror and took stock of what I was seeing. My face was looking better—the scar, at least, had faded slightly—and if I weren't mistaken, my arms had begun to tighten.

I paid attention during my workout that day, trying to track any change over the last weeks, and realized that I'd made *progress*. Sure, I wasn't toned yet, and my clothes weren't falling off from the pounds I hadn't miraculously shed, but I was lifting more weight, putting greater strength behind my sword, and feeling ever so slightly less like I wanted to die when I ran laps.

And then it happened, the great miracle of the afternoon: when Rinnik tested me, I held my ground for almost a full minute. I ended up sprawled in the dirt like always, of course, but his grunt sounded pleased as I picked myself up.

That night, when Fanakel skipped dinner for an early bedtime, Mia and I teased each other at the table about our lucrative future careers as bodybuilders, striking exaggerated poses and making jokes in terrible Austrian accents and just *laughing* for what felt like the first time in a month, and for a brief hour, life felt normal again. I hadn't realized how much I craved the comfortable familiarity of sitting down with food and my best friend, talking about everything and nothing, not worrying if what we said would translate. Neither of us mentioned home or the jobs we'd abandoned—the store was in good hands, but I had to imagine that Mia had lost her waitressing gig by then. Instead, the conversation turned back to college, when things were simpler and we thought we had all the answers, when the maps of our futures were contoured if not fully shaded in. We talked of the better days when I had a family and Mia's mother was speaking to her, when the world lay spread out before us and the biggest challenge in our lives was exam period. For that hour, my heart was light, and the dining hall of Taln'een almost seemed like our favorite college cafeteria with its unofficial pajamas-all-weekend dress code and endless frozen yogurt. But then we noticed the tables around us clearing off as the clan dispersed for the evening, and I reminded myself that if I stayed up all night, I'd be in for a world of pain in the morning. Mia smiled sadly as we bussed our dishes, but she held my hand while we walked back to the guesthouse, and in the darkness, I could almost pretend that nothing had changed.

Anji hadn't made an appearance at dinner, nor was she in bed when we returned to our room, but that didn't surprise me. Having plowed through Ganeel's books, Anji had taken her independent study to the clan's modest forge, a workshop on the edge of town. I didn't know what she did there—Rinnik hadn't suggested a field trip, and any question posed to Anji regarding the mechanics of magical forging resulted in a barely comprehensible lecture about Aen flow—but whatever she was up to had become a minor obsession.

Two nights later, Fanakel let slip that he'd been enjoying his afternoons alone, as Anji had begged off combat practice so as to continue her work in the forge. "I don't know what she's making in there, but if it means I get a nap, I won't complain," he told Mia and me over dessert.

"I thought she was working on translators," Mia replied through a mouthful of cake.

Fanakel shrugged. "Whatever it is, I hope someone's been leaving food for her. Fainting in a forge seems unwise."

Troubled, Mia and I brought a covered plate back to the room, but Anji didn't return before we went to bed, and when I woke to the sound of footsteps pounding up the staircase, I saw that her dinner remained untouched. I'd had no plans to be up at dawn that day, it being our abbreviated weekend, but before I could roll over, Anji threw open the door and bellowed, "Finished!"

As Mia groaned, I sat up and took Anji in. The princess almost vibrated with energy—whether from adrenaline or the maladetas' *highly* stimulating tea, I couldn't say—and her face and clothes were so streaked with grime that she looked like a chimney sweep. But she was grinning, and she held a cloth-wrapped bundle in her arms.

"Big translator," I said through a yawn.

Her excitement dimmed only for a second. "I'm still working on those. This is another project. Hurry and dress—I want to show Fanakel."

Mia and I slid out of bed and threw on our off-day garb, then shuffled down to the seaside lodge where Fanakel slept as Anji exhorted us to pick up the pace. She ran up the staircase and knocked, only to be greeted by a confused older man. "Are you lost, uh…girl?" he asked, perhaps thrown by the combination of her juvenile dress and copious blonde stubble.

"Looking for the elf," she explained.

"Ah." Turning over his shoulder, he called, "Hey, elf boy! You've got visitors!"

A moment later, Fanakel stumbled across the room, half dressed and rubbing sleep from his eyes. "Anji? I'm not late…"

"Come *see*." Grabbing him by the wrist, she tugged him past us, and Mia and I followed them beneath the lodge to the shaded gallery of stilts and sand. Fanakel leaned against a post, cutting his eyes to me for an explanation, but before I could do more than shrug, Anji had unwrapped her surprise and presented him with a quiver of arrows. "Finished last night," she said, cradling it in both arms. "The interior is worked steel, but the leather around it should prevent chafing."

He took it from her, inspecting the plain brown exterior, the handmade chest strap, and the six feathered arrows sticking out of the top. "Uh…thank you?"

"Get the bow, give it a try."

Humor her, Mia mouthed when Fanakel hesitated.

We waited on the beach while he retrieved Uncle Malachi's compound bow from the lodge, and then he slipped the quiver over his bare chest, sighted a tree in the distance, and shot. Nodding, he said to Anji, "Good weight to that one. I think it flew straight."

"Again."

He did as she bid, shooting six times to empty the quiver. But when she urged him to loose a seventh arrow, he said, "You only gave me six," then reached over his shoulder, felt the shaft of one of the arrows that had been repopulating the quiver all along, and stared at her as a wide smile spread across his face. "How did that…"

"Set with a decently large Aen crystal in the base, hidden in the leather," said Anji. "It recreates arrows taken from the quiver. Since you won't have any Aen to work with Outside, I thought it might be useful to secure sufficient ammunition instead."

Fanakel dropped the bow and swung the quiver off his shoulder, giving it a closer study as he beamed. "Anji, this is—" he began, then paused, cleared his throat, and affected a more sober attitude. "This is adequate. Thank you."

She dug the toe of one boot in the sand. "It's a poor thing, I know, but—"

"*Most* adequate. I appreciate the labor."

"The High Queen guides my hand," she replied, and then, as if the anticipation of seeing the quiver in action had been the only thing keeping her on her feet, Anji yawned and pointed vaguely in the direction of our guesthouse. "I...should sleep."

"I'll make sure she doesn't collapse in a dune," said Mia, wrapping an arm around Anji's shoulders. "Come on, you, bedtime."

Fanakel and I watched them wander away, and then he picked up the bow and whistled softly as he swung the quiver back into position. "Did I do that properly? Thank her?"

"I think so, yeah."

"Good. She has a surprisingly firm fist." He waited until Anji and Mia had disappeared around a shed, then said, "This thing is *incredible*. I've never seen its like."

"Ganeel loaned her a bunch of books on forging," I said as we started up the stairs to the lodge. "I thought she was working on translators, but I guess that's the next project in line."

He paused at the door and stared out at the retreating fishing fleet. "You know, growing up, I heard that forging produced little of value. Trinkets, but nothing worthwhile. Dwarves can't channel the Aen without their toys, yet another reason for their inferiority."

I smirked. "But?"

"*But*. And she made it for *me*," he said bemusedly. "Why would she go to the trouble?"

I rolled my eyes and sighed. "I don't know, maybe she

figured you were more useful alive and armed."

"It's better than I deserve."

"*Anji* is better than we deserve." I patted his arm and started back down. "I'd better not go in there with you. People will get the wrong idea."

His soft laughter followed me as I descended, and he waved from the landing. "Thank her for me again, won't you?" he called. "She's less likely to punch you in the face."

Anji hit the bed that morning and didn't stir until sundown. She rose in high spirits, showered and shaved— only nicking herself twice, a new record—and joined the rest of us for dinner, where Fanakel peppered her with questions about the forging process.

"I thought it requires two dwarves," he said between bites of baked fish. "That's what I was taught, anyway."

She nodded as she picked a bone from her fillet with the point of her knife. "That's not wrong. Forging is best accomplished with a partner. One makes the physical item and holds it steady in preparation, and the other works the Aen through it. People tend to favor one job or the other when they begin forging, and it's best not to fight the direction of your talent."

"But you made that quiver alone."

"It's a poor thing."

He sighed and put down his fork. "*Anji.*"

Continuing to work on her fish, she said, "Some of us can forge alone. I favor metalwork, but I've learned to weave with the Aen. The books have helped."

"A rare skill?" he pressed.

Her shoulders tightened. "Not so common, no."

"And her work is perfectly adequate," Mia interjected, breaking a roll in two, "so let's move on to more important matters: how long do you think it's going to be before Rinnik breaks one of our arms?"

Snorting into his goblet, Fanakel replied, "Not for lack of trying. Are we working together tomorrow, then?" he asked Anji.

She shook her head. "Sorry, but I need to return to the forge. Perhaps you could assist Rinnik with the lasses."

"But I don't particularly *want* to break an arm."

"Then keep your shield up," she said, grinning as he pouted.

That meal was the last we saw of Anji for nearly a week. She stopped coming back to the guesthouse, and Mia took to leaving food outside the forge twice a day. The unnerved maladetan blacksmith had ceded the place to her—he spoke of incomprehensible chanting, strange lights, and metal that moved in *decidedly* unnatural ways— and so Anji worked in solitude.

I'd joined Mia and Fanakel for dinner on our off day when the door to the dining hall slammed open, revealing Anji on the threshold. I knew her only by her stature, as her face, her hair, and most of her clothing were black with soot. But her dark eyes held a look of triumph, and she marched between the tables toward us with no regard for the concerned diners on either side of her path. "*There,*" she said, dropping a grimy pair of crystal-set pendants onto the yellow tablecloth in front of Mia. "Try it."

"Let's, uh…let's get you something to drink first, okay?" said Mia, going to her feet for the leverage necessary to shove Anji into a chair. "Maybe a few napkins—"

Anji grabbed her wrist and squeezed. "Try it," she insisted. "I need to be certain."

Perhaps unwilling to risk further agitating Anji, who was giving off the same vibe as a computer science major I once knew who drank coffee and coded for four days straight before we dragged him to health services, Mia took off her pendant, wiped one of the new ones clean, and threaded it onto the chain in the old one's place. Anji removed her own pendant, leaving her without a translator, and gestured for Mia to begin. "Am I coming through?" Mia asked, absently rubbing the black streak on her wrist where Anji had clamped down. "Does it work?"

The dwarf beamed, a flash of white teeth in middle of her bristly, blackened face, and nodded. "Perfectly. Do you understand me?"

"As usual. Well *done*, lady," she said, holding up her hand for a high-five.

Anji cocked her head at the gesture, then shrugged and punched Mia in the palm. "High Queen be praised," she said, then folded her arms on the table and nestled her head into the depression, and was snoring almost as soon as her eyes closed.

The three of us considered our unconscious companion, then the staring diners around us, and silently decided that dinner was over. As I bussed the plates, Fanakel pulled Anji out of her chair and slung her over his shoulder with a grunt, then staggered toward the exit. Mia and I followed, offering assistance, but he refused. "More awkward with two carrying," he explained, though he strained under his burden—Anji might have been short, but she was dense.

Instead of carrying her to the guesthouse, however, Fanakel dropped her onto the beach near the lapping waves. "If you track that much soot into the room, you'll never see it clean again," he explained, his smudged clothing standing as proof. "Do your thing, Susan."

Though I hated to dunk Anji in the cold ocean, my talent didn't extend to *heating* water, and so I stayed well back from her in case of angry flailing. Calling forth a blob of seawater, I floated it over to Anji and unceremoniously dropped it from above her. She sputtered as it exploded, soaking her, and woke enough to screech with the chill.

"Sorry," I said, and hit her again.

By the time the third blob had crashed into her, Anji was awake and struggling to her feet. "Stay down and keep your eyes closed," I snapped. "The sooner the worst is off, the sooner you get a hot shower."

Maybe she was too exhausted to fight that night, but Anji surrendered and let me drench her. A bit of concentration pulled the water from the ocean along an invisible pipeline and showered it over her, but even when I increased the pressure to massage levels, she still looked like she'd spent a month in a coal mine.

"It's going to take soap and elbow grease," said Mia, appraising my handiwork. "I've got it from here."

"You sure?" I asked, dropping the water I'd siphoned back into the ocean.

"Positive. Not the first incapacitated girl I've walked home by a *long* shot. Come on, Anji," she said, tugging the dripping princess to her feet. "I've got the translators nice and safe. Let's get you cleaned up."

Anji's teeth chattered, but she managed to nod and let Mia help her to the guesthouse. As they climbed up the dunes, I heard Terj say, *You know, there's probably a good reason why dwarves forge in teams.*

"Yeah. Good luck with that," Fanakel muttered, and headed off into the night.

With her success in the forge, Anji turned her focus back to Fanakel, who seemed to limp almost as badly as Mia and I did when he joined us at dinner. We'd just settled down to our meal one night about two weeks after Anji's return, three of us sporting fresh bruises and decent tans from our six weeks outside, when a sound like a church bell began to ring in the distance. A closer neighbor picked up the chiming, echoing the first a fifth higher, then another bell with the minor third. The four of us watched with concern as the maladetas abandoned their dinners and ran for the door, men and women alike, and I said, "Terj?"

Sounds like an alarm to me.

"That's what I was afraid of." I rose, checked the

tightness of the bungee cord at my waist, and started off after the crowd, and my companions fell in behind me.

The tolling of the bells was far louder beyond the insulated walls of the dining hall, and I had no idea where to go in the chaos outside. People ran in all directions, some unarmed, some carrying swords and bows. Carts floated by, driven by both women and men, and after a moment's observation, I realized that all were heading south, following the road toward the fields. As I debated whether to follow them, a cart stopped in front of me, and I recognized the elderly driver as Hakesh, Ganeel's son. "What's going on?" I called, running closer. "Are we under attack or something?"

The greenish light of the crystal lantern affixed to the vehicle cast a sick pallor on his craggy face. "Outsiders," he said. "Will you come?"

I swung myself into the cart, and the others followed suit. "I'm unarmed but for a dagger," Anji told him as he sped toward the road.

"Take what you need," he replied, gesturing behind him at the pile of weapons tossed haphazardly into the cart. "Swords, short swords, bows, axes…whatever you can wield."

She, Fanakel, and Mia scrambled to outfit themselves as we flew along, while I headed for the front of the cart. "How many, do you know?" I asked Hakesh. "If it's only three or four, and with a whole clan of maladetas here—"

"I cannot say, Watcher," he murmured, "but I wouldn't expect so many bells for three or four of the creatures."

Too soon, we'd reached one of the distant fields of kirta, where the bulk of the maladetan defenders was gathering. From my perch atop the floating cart, I had an excellent view over the head-high stalks, though I wished I didn't.

By the light of the defenders' lanterns and torches, I counted at least a dozen Outsiders—some seemingly lupine, some ursine, some insectile, and one that looked like an upside-down squid attached to four legs. Two of the creatures were flapping along on bat-like wings. There was no accounting for the variety of monsters that slipped between the worlds from the Outside, and no one with whom I'd yet spoken had mentioned any sort of attempt at taxonomic classification. But whether the beasts appeared with fur or flesh, talons or tentacles, sharp beaks or bared teeth, a few constants remained: they were no shorter than eight feet tall, strong, heavily armored, and on the hunt. They had no natural predators within the four worlds—or on Earth, for that matter—and something instinctive drove them toward the scent of the Aen, where prey was abundant and unlikely to do much damage.

But the maladetas could put up a fight. To my astonishment, I saw perhaps thirty women standing on carts like mine around the field, chanting with their arms outstretched. Light streaming from their fingertips wrapped around the pack of Outsiders, each woman's strands weaving with those of others to form a magical net. Another group of women whispered fireballs into being, white-hot orbs the size of dinner rolls that they flung toward the creatures. Their shots struck true—frankly, with the number of Outsiders trapped within the netting, it would have been difficult to miss—but they seemed to do little but burn and anger the creatures, and the women who threw them cried out with pain. I was puzzled for only an instant, then recalled the great check on maladetan power: using destructive magic was harmful to them, even fatal. As for their men, magic wasn't a concern, but the arrows they shot through the net were brushed aside like beestings.

I felt queasy just looking at the monsters, but seeing as I was the only person for miles around equipped with a magical sword, it would have been rude not to employ it. *Ready?* I asked Terj.

Please don't get yourself killed.

That's always the goal, I replied, and looked back at the

others. "How do we want to do this?"

Anji, armed with her dagger and borrowed sword, joined me at the front of the cart. "If Fanakel stays back and shoots for the eyes," she murmured, "we can take them as he blinds them, but—"

"They need to split the herd," Mia interrupted from behind us. "Run that netting or whatever through the pack and make it more manageable. I'd rather try for two at a time than twelve."

Anji's mouth tightened as she considered the sword in Mia's hand. "You're a distance fighter, too. Go back and get your guns—"

"No time, and I like to think I've learned *something* after six weeks with Rinnik. You, me, and Suze go in, Fanakel stays back and harries them."

The elf pointedly cleared his throat until we turned. "You know, if you're going to talk about me, be so kind as to do it to my face."

"How many arrows have you found in here?" Anji asked.

He hefted a quiver jammed full of them. "Not as pretty as yours, but under the circumstances…"

"You know what to do. Terj, can you get Ganeel's attention?"

From here? Yes.

I spotted the clan mother in the front line and saw her twitch with the message, but Terj soon had a response: *They'll do it. Be patient, but be prepared.*

Mia, Anji, and I watched from the safety of the cart as the maladetas' nets shifted and rewove themselves, splitting the pack into clusters of three. "Guess that's doable," said Mia as the last of the nets solidified. "Left to right?"

"Agreed. High Queen have mercy on us all," Anji muttered, and leapt to the ground.

The women working the nets at the point where we wanted to enter created a hole large enough to admit us, and as we passed through, the men ceased firing on that clump of Outsiders—all but Fanakel, who shot for their eyes with surprising accuracy. Wounded, the creatures bellowed and thrashed at the unyielding nets, giving us little room to work. But Anji, quick as ever, jumped onto the nearest beast's scaly back, distracting it as I plunged my sword into its gut and yanked upward. Ichor poured onto the trampled crops, but I withdrew before the Outsider could catch fire and turned to the next one, which Mia was harassing from behind. Half blinded, he turned in a circle, trying to catch her with his claws or swipe her with his barbed tail, but she managed to keep her feet until I could slice the thing in half.

You've grown stronger, Terj remarked as I gutted the third.

I'm going to pay for this in the morning. That time, I held the blade in place until the body began to smoke, then slipped through a fresh hole in the nets as the dead smoldered behind us. Emerging, we found ourselves facing a line of wide-eyed women and bowmen…and one shocked face gave me particular joy. "We'll be by for practice after lunch tomorrow," I said, flashing Rinnik a tight smile, and followed Anji into the next magical makeshift pen.

With the three of us, Fanakel, and the men shooting from the ground, it took nearly half an hour to reduce the Outsiders to corpses. As I set the last of them on fire, the nets collapsed, and Ganeel strode forward to meet us. "That was incredible," she said, waving her thanks to Fanakel on his perch. "I've never seen so many of them in one place, even before the sword was made…"

"*Great.* They're multiplying," I muttered, looking down to see that I was soaked with ichor. "Mind if I shower?"

"You've done more than your share," she told us. "Return to the village and take your rest. We'll see to the disposal."

I was the last to swing myself aboard Hakesh's cart for the journey back, and though I kept my silence, Terj knew too well what I was feeling. *It's over,* he soothed as I squeezed the sword's scabbard to reassure myself that it was still there. *Relax, Susan.*

It's never over.

It will be.

One way or another, I replied, sick to my soul with the reminder of my fate. The weeks we'd spent among the Taln'een were nothing but a respite. My choice now was to either go home and continue killing those creatures or venture into the uncharted Outside and tackle them at their source.

True, there was no choice at all, but that didn't mean I had to like my options.

As hopeful as I was to receive some small commendation on my performance from Rinnik, we never made it to practice the next day. While the four of us were finishing a leisurely breakfast—the kitchen staff made no move to kick us out—Satamun burst into the dining hall, cloak askew and panting. "You're wanted," she called down the length of the room. "Ardielta has returned."

After hastily returning our dishes to the kitchen, we ran after Satamun to Ganeel's office, where we found the clan mother sitting on her cushion across the table from my old neighbor, both drinking tea from delicate mugs. They rose as we piled in, and Ganeel dismissed Satamun with a wave.

When the door closed behind her, I folded my arms and looked the newcomer up and down—at once familiar and foreign in her long maladetan dress. "Ms. Quince."

"Hello, my dear," she said, absently smoothing her dark hair and straightening her skirt. "Are you hurt? And Mia, how are you?"

"Nothing new," I said. "A little sore, but that's to be expected after last night."

"What took you so long?" Mia asked.

She sighed and cut her eyes to Ganeel, who nodded. "I've been trying to monitor Erianthe's movements. She wants you dead, Susan."

"No surprise," I muttered.

"She was flustered and paranoid when I arrived, but once more reports came in of Outsiders in the hinterlands, she went public with your escape. You're Daril's great scapegoat now, and as far as the queen is concerned, the sooner you're dead, the sooner the sword will choose a worthy host."

If anything happens to Susan, Terj interrupted, *I'm going to Erianthe. Tell her that, if you like. It might slow her search.*

Ms. Quince stiffened in surprise before recalling the elemental in the sword. "You...can't do that, can you? She's a sitting queen, she has no tie to Cole's Crossing—"

Would you rather I choose you?

"No," she said quickly.

Then don't question me. I've done your damn bidding long enough.

She coughed, perhaps stalling, then looked at me again. "The Outsiders who attacked last night are probably the ones who've been harrying every desert settlement from Meoni to Daril. The fighting forces sent to the borders have kept them largely in the waste, and I suppose they moved north in search of food. But the kingdom and the republic alike have suffered casualties and fatalities, and everything I hear suggests that the situation is much the same at the end of the other tunnels."

Anji looked a little green at that, but Fanakel remained stoic.

"Erianthe tried to send word to your fathers of your whereabouts and your actions," Ms. Quince told them, "but neither messenger returned. This is no time to be sending lone riders. She asked me to pass the message through our channels. Needless to say, I did no such thing," she muttered, glancing at Ganeel, "but word from our sisters in Blackhorn Mountain and Nokan'ti hasn't been encouraging."

"I know," said Ganeel. "My sisters have called a

meeting for this evening. I would have you join us, daughter."

Ms. Quince's head bobbed in acknowledgement. "And them?"

The clan mother gave us a long, searching look. "Perhaps. I'll ask you to keep yourselves available," she told us. "This concerns you, after all. I'll send word to Rinnik that your lesson has been canceled for the day. Why don't you rest?" she added. "Sleep. I'm certain you could use it."

She wasn't wrong on that count, and we took our leave. But before I could get far, I heard Ms. Quince call my name and waited as she ran down the staircase after us. Cupping my face in her hands, she studied my features for a moment before her expression shifted toward pity. "I see it," she murmured, releasing me. "See *her*. Susan, honey, had I suspected, I'd have said something, but I left this world when Erianthe was just a little girl. I never knew her. Seeing her now, though…"

I shrugged, trying to play it off. "Skinnier, better hair…"

"Okay, first, your hair could be styled like hers if you had servants to manage it, and second, she barely eats. You look good, by the way," she said, giving me another once-over. "Healthy. Sea air agrees with you?"

"I think it's mostly Rinnik's doing."

"Well, then, I'll be sure to make his acquaintance."

She smiled wanly and turned to go, but I called after her, "Ms. Quince? Why didn't you tell Uncle Malachi that he could come through the tunnels?"

I held her gaze while a flush ran up her face, and when she spoke again, her voice was low and strained. "When I arrived in Cole's Crossing, I intended to follow the orders I was given. Once I met Malachi, I thought he would die in a matter of months, that he was too weak to be the Watcher for long. After a few years, once I understood how wrong I was…well, by then, I was too selfish to tell him the truth."

"Selfish?"

"I couldn't bear to lose him," she replied, her smile brief and far too tight. "See you this evening, Susan," she said, and walked off through the scrub grasses before I could demand anything further of her.

CHAPTER 6

Fanakel remained close to our pack that day, eschewing the men's lodge for our guesthouse and joining us for picked-at meals. No one had much to say. Anji, I knew, was worried about the threat to her people from Outsiders, and even if Fanakel was frustrated with his father, he surely felt *something* knowing that Nokan'ti was in the line of fire. Reminded once more of the threats outside Taln'een's borders, I sat on my bed and played with a bowl of water to distract myself, occasionally making idle chitchat with Terj. But Mia stepped into the breach, organizing an afternoon walk, making tea, and cajoling us to eat when we pushed our food around. "Whatever happens tonight, we might as well face it on a full stomach," she said. "Hunger never solved any problem."

Shortly after we returned to the guesthouse following dinner, Satamun knocked. "The great mother requests that you come," was all she told us, though she pursed her lips when she noticed Fanakel sprawled across Anji's bed.

We trooped after her, me with the sword strapped on as per usual, but instead of Ganeel's office, we were escorted to a smaller building next door. There, we found the clan mother seated on a green cushion, one of perhaps two dozen arranged in a circle. Small metal discs had been placed atop the other cushions, while another hung suspended in midair several feet away from Ganeel. At the squealing of the door's hinges, she turned and beckoned us in, then motioned to Ms. Quince, who was sitting on a cushion against the wall. "Join Ardielta, if you would," she said, gesturing to the empty cushions around her. "We'll begin shortly."

As we settled in, I caught Ms. Quince's eye and whispered, "What's going on? Where is everyone else?"

"The clan mothers across the four worlds need to meet every so often, but doing it in person is impractical," she whispered back. "This is how they discuss matters as a group."

I considered the setup, then recalled the compact-like device Ms. Quince had used to speak to Ganeel when she found us outside Deoni. "So...maladetan video conferencing?"

Her mouth twitched into a brief smile. "More or less, dear."

Just as I found a comfortable spot on my cushion, the discs began to light up, one by one. A few seconds after each illuminated, a hologram—or the Aen-powered equivalent—appeared, revealing a ring of woman in varying styles of dress and disarray. A dark-skinned woman with a complicated updo of braids sat on a simple wooden chair, glaring around the circle. A paler woman, her eyes sunken with sleeplessness, appeared to be seated on a stone bench, and her hands worried the hem of her gray cloak. Then there was the brown-complexioned woman two seats down from Ganeel, who dripped with sweat. Her face and the bodice of her red dress were stained black with ichor.

"What—" I began, but Ms. Quince hastily shushed me with a finger to her lips and a vehement shake of her head.

Studying the setup, I assumed that the disc floating in front of Ganeel acted like a camera, projecting her image to the other clan mothers in turn. From where she'd positioned us, we were invisible to the rest of the maladetas...which, I mused, considering their expressions, probably wasn't a terrible thing.

Ganeel clasped her hands in her lap. "Good evening, sisters. Or morning, as the case may be." A few nodded in acknowledgement, and one stifled a yawn. "How fare you?"

The one with the ichor facial barked an incredulous laugh. "How *fare* we? There are Outsiders in the four worlds, Taln'een! The tunnels are impassable. Every night, we've been attacked. I've had perhaps five hours of sleep in the last five days."

"Likewise," said the yawner. "The casualties are mounting. It's the far-flung villages I fear for the most, but even within fortified walls—"

"This is untenable," the woman with the braids interrupted, staring at Ganeel. "I understand you know of the Watcher's whereabouts?"

Ganeel hesitated before answering her. "I do."

"And you've yet to return the Watcher to the Crossing because…"

"Because," said Ganeel, "the Watcher is a twenty-three-year-old novice who is in desperate need of training. I've put her to work with our weapons master to learn the rudiments of combat, but she has a long path yet to tread."

"Let her learn as she goes," the pale woman suggested. "Firebrand burns Outsiders, does it not? Let her swing it like a cudgel until she develops the necessary skill—the fire should keep her alive for a time."

Unfortunately, it was impossible to punch a hologram, though my hand had preemptively begun clenching into a fist.

The other clan mothers muttered their thoughts as to their sister's idea, but Ganeel raised a finger to draw their attention. "The Watcher is…*highly* reluctant to return to her post. She refuses."

"Then *force* her," Ichor Woman said. "People are dying—"

"She is aware of this fact and distressed. But sisters, hear me: she is so young, and—"

"I carried children to the pyres today," she snapped. "Girls and boys of four and five, disemboweled and beheaded. I carried tiny limbs to join the blaze, not knowing whose they might be. Our worlds are in peril because of that selfish brat, so stop coddling her, stop trying to negotiate, and drag her back to the Crossing where she belongs!"

Ganeel waited until the rumblings quieted, then said, "It's not only the Watcher at issue. Firebrand is...well, *peeved* would be putting it mildly."

Braid Woman cocked her head. "Firebrand has developed sentience?"

"No. Firebrand is largely powered by an elemental. One whom our sisters bound to the blade. They thought the forging would kill him. It did not."

The yawner shrugged. "Then he is doing the rest of us a noble service as well."

"He says he is in constant pain," Ganeel murmured, "and has been since the forging. My sisters, this is unjust."

Pale Woman frowned into her disc. "And what would you have us do? Taln'een helped *create* Firebrand. You're not suggesting that Taln'een will now break faith, are you?"

"All I'm suggesting is that we should explore alternatives. There are two beings before us, bound by no fault of their own and condemned—"

But Ichor Woman wasn't having it. "Two lives for how many? I guarantee that far more than *two* have died in the last weeks. Probably more than that in the last night. Innocents, sister, all of them! What makes the lives of the girl and the elemental worth any more than theirs?"

Ganeel's hands tightened in her lap. "They are worth no more or less. But the price for the safety we have bought ourselves has been the lives of the Watchers and the elemental. It is *Taln'een* who monitor the Watcher beyond the Aen," she continued, looking around the ring of faces. "I have lived with their people. What we ask— nay, what we *demand* of them is nothing less than their freedom and safety."

At that, Ms. Quince rose, crossed the room, and knelt behind Ganeel's cushion. "I just came from the Crossing, great mothers," she said, her head bowed but her voice firm. "Forty years among them. The last watcher lived in a hovel in the woods, all alone, far from civilization. He refused to risk drawing Outsiders into town, you see. He never married. No children. Even a child he found abandoned, a child he desperately wanted to keep, had to be given to another. His was a lonely, *awful* life."

I knew I wasn't imagining the hitch in her voice.

"It is the custom of many of their people to bury their dead on blessed ground," she said. "The Watcher's ancestors were buried in the usual way, and he—Malachi—had a place saved for him. But he insisted that he be cremated instead, and his ashes spread onto moving water. He refused to be bound to that land in death, too..." As her head rose, I saw the sheen in her eyes. "Malachi was a good man. He deserved a chance at happiness."

"His sacrifice saved countless lives," said Braid Woman.

"But that was not *his* sacrifice," said Ms. Quince. "*We* sacrificed him. The humans of the Crossing are not ours to sacrifice," she continued, her voice rising. "We are no better than the tekoraet with their herds."

A few of the woman hissed or recoiled at her words, and Ganeel murmured, "Ardielta—"

"I meant what I said," she insisted. "We call the tekoraet parasites for using the life force of others to sustain themselves. How is the Watcher system we've created any different?"

Several of the women began to talk at once, and by the tenor of their comments, it was clear that Ms. Quince's sentiment was shared by none of the clan mothers. Finally, Ichor Woman gained control from the ruckus. "Taln'een is entitled to its opinion," she said, glaring at Ganeel. "And since you allowed one of your daughters to insult the rest of us, I can only believe that you share her sentiments. But Taln'een's qualms are not Gerian's."

"Nor Erefuri's," said Braid Woman.

"Yrton sees the daughter's logic but disagrees," Yawning Woman added.

"I propose a vote," Ichor Woman said. "Who would have Taln'een return the Watcher to her post?"

Even as hands began to rise, Ganeel said, "I have given the girl sanctuary here. You have no right to order me in such a fashion."

"Perhaps not," said Pale Woman, "but Gerian gives voice to what we know must happen. Whether Taln'een does so voluntarily or by force, the Watcher must return."

"And how," said Ganeel with remarkable calm, "does D'pell propose to *force* us? If the tunnels are impassable, I dare say you'll have difficulty reaching us from Honslia."

Her bloodless lips moved into a tight line. "Do not think yourself invincible, Taln'een. All it will take will be a quiet word to Daril and Meali and Ti'cal, and you will see what desperation can achieve. Remember that yours is not the only clan in Kopaat."

Ganeel looked to her left to a redheaded woman in a black dress. "You've said nothing, sister. Would you risk the desert to inform Daril?"

The woman glanced at her, then at the rest of the circle. "While Furnig respects Taln'een's supremacy among the clans of Kopaat, we will do what is necessary for the greater good."

"I see," Ganeel murmured. "But I ask my sisters this: if we force the Watcher back to her post, how do you propose we force her to *remain* there? She knows the four worlds are open to her."

"We could post a guard at the end of each tunnel," Braid Woman suggested. "Someone to repulse her, should she attempt another stunt like this."

"Or we kill her now and let Firebrand choose a better Watcher."

The eyes of the circle turned to Ichor Woman—the clan mother of Gerian, I thought, trying to keep them straight so I could deal with them personally at a later date.

"You would kill a child?" Ganeel asked.

She shrugged. "Humans mature quickly. The girl is young, but she is surely no child among her people. Certainly old enough to bear responsibility for her actions. Kill her now and end this madness," she continued, staring at the others in turn. "Let a more deserving Watcher take up the blade."

Ganeel nodded as if considering this course of action, then said, "There is, I fear, a problem with your plan."

Ichor Woman's eyes narrowed. "Oh?"

"The elemental fears for the Watcher's safety, and it is he who selects the next to carry the burden. He has informed me that should harm come to the Watcher, he will choose one of us to guard the Crossing in her stead."

No, I didn't, Terj whispered to my mind. *I said I would conscript Erianthe if something happened to you.*

I think Ganeel is improvising, I replied, hoping the maladetas' discs couldn't pick up on our conversation.

We spoke undetected, apparently, as silence fell over the circle following Ganeel's fib. Finally, Pale Woman said, "He can't do that, can he? Firebrand must be wielded by a human."

Ganeel shook her head. "Nothing in its forging requires that. Firebrand was *forced* upon a human, and it has passed to humans ever since, but nothing would stop it from attaching itself to one of another race."

"Perhaps the elemental is bluffing," Pale Woman tried again. "Surely he understands what harm it would do to rip one of us from our clan and our daughters… indefinitely…"

I didn't think it was possibly for her to blanche, but she managed the trick.

"It is…*unpleasant* outside the Aen," Ms. Quince offered. "Having just come from my posting there, I can speak to it better than anyone. An almost negligible amount of the Aen trickles through from the tunnels. The crystals in the sword, now, *those* are pure Aen, and proximity to them helps, but I never did grow comfortable with the air."

The others sat quietly for a moment, digesting this.

"You're certain that the elemental could do this?" Braid Woman asked. "That he *would* do this?"

"I'm confident that this would be within his power," said Ganeel, "and if the Watcher were to die at our hands, I cannot imagine that he would show mercy." When no one rushed to dispute that, she said, "There is another option, one that the Watcher seems to favor. She's willing to go Outside."

The circle erupted at that, but Ganeel waited patiently for the outcry to subside before explaining. "The Watcher does not only wish to be free of Firebrand—she wishes to free the elemental as well. I cannot do this for her without breaking the pact to which Taln'een swore, but if she were to destroy the Outsiders or find a way to prevent them from attacking our worlds, then the sword should recognize that its purpose had been fulfilled, and both the Watcher and the elemental should be freed."

"But if she takes the sword Outside and breaks it," Ichor Woman protested, "or if it's lost beyond the Aen, we will be defenseless."

"No more so than we were prior to Firebrand's forging," said Ganeel. "If the worst comes to pass, then I will do what is necessary to create a second sword. I will accept this responsibility."

"You decree your own death," Ichor Woman countered.

Ganeel inclined her head. "I have done what I can to see that the Watcher is trained and prepared to survive the journey. If you could give us more time—"

"*No one* has survived that journey! Return her to the Crossing and let her die there if she isn't strong enough to do her duty. Then the sword will choose another human, as is proper." Ichor Woman looked at the others, then said, "Again, I call a vote. Who would have Taln'een return the Watcher to the Crossing?"

That time, Ganeel sat and waited as every hand slowly rose. When the clan mothers' votes had been cast, she bowed her head and sighed. "My sisters, I understand your position, and I do see the wisdom in it. Perhaps...perhaps my time in the Crossing has unduly softened me toward those who wield Firebrand."

"Yours is a good soul," the redhead from Furnig reassured her. "It is no true failing to show compassion, my sister, but when so many are being wounded or killed as a result..."

"Outsiders have attacked Taln'een. I am well aware of the danger in which I've placed my people," Ganeel replied, and glanced up again. "The clans have spoken. I will see the Watcher back to the Crossing, whether she wishes to go or not. This, I swear to you."

One by one, the women said their farewells, and the discs winked out. Once the last had vanished, Ganeel disengaged her own and pushed herself to her feet, only to find me on mine, clutching the hilt at my side. "You needn't draw that, child," she said, her voice low and weary.

"I'm not going back."

"Damn straight she's not," Mia chimed in, joining me, and Fanakel and Anji likewise took their places with us.

Ganeel considered our quartet—well, quintet, technically—for a long moment, then folded her arms. "Do you truly believe I meant what I told them?"

"You swore an oath..." said Anji.

"Not all oaths are sacred," the clan mother replied, "nor are they intended to be binding. The gods know what is said in truth and falsehood."

Fanakel crossed his arms in mirror of Ganeel's. "So...you lied."

"A useful skill, I assure you, and one with which your

esteemed father is intimately familiar. *And* yours," she said to Anji. "The kings may be reasonably honorable in their daily dealings, but I've seen another side of them both."

I cut my eyes to Fanakel, then looked back at Ganeel. "Why should *we* trust you, then?"

"Because," she said softly, "I was Nellie Jones once, long before your time. And I remember far too well how Zachary's body looked when I found him. Gray-haired and wrinkled, he was, sinewy and strong but too old for his years. His left arm was gone but for a ragged stump, and the dirt in which he lay had only partially soaked up the blood. He died with Firebrand in his hand, and in his open eyes, I saw nothing but horror. *That*," she said, holding my stare, "is a face I will never forget, though not for trying, to my shame." She looked away and cleared her throat. "If you wish to go Outside, Susan, I will help you make the journey beyond the Aen. But you must decide tonight. I don't trust my sisters to keep their silence for long."

"I'll go," I said without hesitation. "The Watcher, the sword—this ends with me." Turning to my companions, I said, "Something tells me we're not ready, but it looks like we're out of time. If you'd rather sit this one out—"

"Don't be stupid, lass," said Anji, and Mia and Fanakel nodded. To Ganeel, she asked, "How do we get there?"

"Unfortunately, we'll need to return to the tunnels," she replied. "They're weakest at their intersection, and Ardielta and I should be able to open a way for you at that point."

I grimaced. "If the tunnels are being guarded, though…"

"And we'll need to pass through Darili territory, will we not?" asked Fanakel. "Surely Erianthe has told her men to look for two human women, an elf, and a dwarf. We can only disguise ourselves to a point."

"True. And that's a journey of days, I fear," said Anji. "Even with swift chiquiws—"

"How did you make the trip so quickly?" Mia

interrupted, looking at Ms. Quince. "Suze and I left Cole's Crossing the day after you explained the sword, and I guess you had a head start on us to Kopaat while we went to Ildon. By the time we found you in the woods, you'd obviously been home and were headed to Deoni. How'd you do it?"

"Good fortune," said Ms. Quince with a sigh. "As I was heading down the Kopaat tunnel, a dwarven merchant caravan overtook me. Their carriages brought me across the desert and as far as Deoni—I'm estimating, but they can probably reach forty miles an hour, which is remarkably rapid around here."

"I've got an idea," I said. "Worked once before."

Elemental? asked Terj.

"Exactly."

I would help you, but I'm not strong enough—not bound in this fashion.

"Don't worry," I told him. "Let me see if I can hitch us a ride."

Ganeel frowned. "Is that wise to attempt? Elementals can be unpredictable."

Terj didn't have a throat to clear, but the mental sensation of his indignation was unmistakable.

"Unless you've got another caravan handy, I guess we'll find out, won't we?" I said with forced cheer, and started for the door. "I'm going to the beach. Don't wait up."

A month and a half prior, I'd managed to produce a rainstorm at the edge of the Kopaati tunnel, which opened onto a desolate waste. The desert was still well within its dry season, but in Taln'een, at the edge of the sea, I had plenty of water to work with and weeks of practice.

That still didn't make my task *easy*.

I settled in, making a depression within the cool sand, and looked up at the cloudless sky. The unfamiliar stars of Kopaat twinkled brightly—whatever could be said for the place, their light pollution was far less than what we had at home—but when I closed my eyes and opened my other senses, I could feel the potential around me like a cloud. The air was heavy with moisture, and mere yards ahead of where I sat, the cold sea rolled in and retreated, a churning power source at my fingertips that almost seemed to glow.

I felt more than heard Terj's presence just outside the core of my mind, watching and metaphorically holding his breath.

"I've got this," I murmured.

I know. But I worry about you. This is more than should be asked of one so new to herself.

"What," I joked, "you've never made your own weather?"

We ride storms, Susan—we don't produce them. Maybe the odd gust of wind, but nothing of the scale you're attempting. This is far beyond typical elemental behavior, you realize.

"And when, exactly, have I been typical?"

Amusement mingled with his concern. *Seldom. Is there anything I can do to help?*

"Not unless you've got a way to text someone instead."

The number of elementals with cell phones being approximately nil, and cellular service in Kopaat being nonexistent...

"Wishful thinking."

And since I've been gone all this time, I wouldn't have anyone's number. He paused, then told me, *I don't even know the water elementals closest to the shore.*

"Kingkiller knew you," I pointed out.

Kingkiller knew of me. I've been dead to my brothers and sisters for almost five hundred years. But you don't need to hear me gripe tonight, he continued. *Do what you can, and I'll try to keep the others from distracting you.*

"Thanks, Terj," I said, and directed my focus to the water within my grasp. That I could manipulate it, I had no doubt, but convincing it to form the necessary beacon was going to take some doing.

It's much easier to produce thunderheads with midday heat fueling their growth. The cooling air at Taln'een's shore as the night wore on sapped energy from my creation, making me work all the harder to force the storm into coalescing. But unlike my last attempt, I had a literal ocean at my fingertips from which to steal moisture, and I toiled steadily through the night, drawing water that glittered in the place behind my eyes into a swirling vortex above me. Every so often, I made myself pause to take stock of my body—cramping, cold, a little salty, but still breathing—and thus reassured, I returned to my labor.

Terj moved like a shadow on the edge of my consciousness, and at times, I thought I heard him speak—to Mia, perhaps, or to Ganeel. I *know* I overheard him when he spoke to an unfamiliar elemental, and part of me distantly suspected that one of the ocean's guardians had finally approached to investigate. No one broke my concentration, however, and so it came as a shock when I felt the first raindrops fall upon my bare head.

I opened my eyes to a sky that would send storm chasers running for their vehicles. Clouds stretched to the horizon in all directions, and as the drizzle headed for a downpour, lightning cracked over the sea.

"Whoa," I croaked. "Didn't know I could do that."

There's a massive amount of energy in that storm, said Terj, who sounded almost awed. *How do you feel?*

"Like I don't really want to think about standing up just yet." I tentatively stretched my stiff legs and groaned. "Time?"

Perhaps an hour after midday. Difficult to tell without the sun, but Mia came down to check on you before lunch, and that wasn't so long ago. Are you hungry? Thirsty? He hesitated, then said, *Look, I realize I'm no expert on corporeality, but even I know you need to feed and water yourself.*

I tilted my face to the heavens and let my mouth fill with rain, which went a ways toward easing the ache in my parched throat. *Do you think that did the trick?* I asked him mentally, as my mouth was otherwise occupied.

I think it should generate some interest…ah. There.

Swallowing quickly, I straightened up and looked around until I spotted a figure approaching through the blowing rain—or rather, I spotted a distortion in the storm in a vaguely humanish shape. Weary, I raised a hand and thought, *Hi.*

The voice I heard in return seemed to laugh. *I thought that might be you, little sister. You have quite a way about you.*

"Oh!" I said, recognizing the elemental who'd carried me across the desert, and pushed myself to my feet. With a few pulses of will, I managed to put up an invisible umbrella and dry myself, though I could do nothing about the sand. "Hello, again. We've got to stop meeting like this."

He cocked his head. *This displeases you?*

A joke, Terj offered. *She means that she wishes you two were meeting under better circumstances.*

The other elemental quickly drew closer. *Who are you? Where are you?*

I am called Terj now, he replied, *and I am within the blade Susan carries.*

I could feel the elemental's shock, which quickly gave way to horror. *I had heard you were dead! That the maladetas murdered you!*

They thought they had, he replied bitterly. *But no, I'm trapped here now.*

The newcomer turned to me, suddenly angered. *Free him at once! How could you—*

She's trying, Terj interrupted. *No one who built my prison is willing to break it, so the plan now is to venture Outside and see what can be done to fix this. Susan has done more for me in a few weeks than anyone has done in the last few centuries.*

His mood softened as quickly as it had flared. *I see. My apologies, little sister,* he told me. *Do you require assistance?*

"Well, actually," I said, rubbing my elbow, "I was hoping someone might be willing to help my crew get back to the tunnel. It's a long way on foot, the queen of Daril wants to kill me, and lest we forget, this place is now crawling with Outsiders."

I had noticed the creatures, he replied. *But what came of you in Deoni? Does the queen hold you responsible for the attack on that village? If she does not believe your account of the events, I suppose I could add mine...*

"That's only part of it. She's my mother," I muttered, "and she abandoned me to die. *Whoops.*"

The elemental made no attempt to mask his surprise. *Erianthe Fulquir joined with...* He paused, then asked, *Was I correct about your father? A water elemental?*

"Yeah. She wouldn't tell me his name, but I think it was Falova."

I could feel his excitement spike. *He lives still—I told you this, did I not? Deep in the desert. I could take you to him.*

As much I wanted that, I had to consider my priorities. "Thank you, and I do mean to seek him out," I told the elemental, "but none of us are safe as long as there are Outsiders in this world, and besides, the bonds on Terj keep him in pain. I've got to free him first."

He considered this briefly, then nodded. *You need swift passage back to the trunnels?*

"At this point, I would love anything speedier than walking."

Ooh...no. I have witnessed humans attempt to cross the desert on foot during the dry season. Most fail. Even venturing as far as the tunnels would be inadvisable. You could try to find a merchant caravan bound for the Meali settlements, he mused, *but even with desert-bred chiquiws, they move slowly.*

A chiquiw-drawn wagon would be a plodding trip, and I'd spent long enough astride a chiquiw on Honslia to know that a long journey in the saddle would be hell. "Just how far is it to the tunnels, anyway?"

The elemental mulled over the question. *By foot? Or riding?*

Reminding myself that he probably wasn't familiar with

any of the units of measurement I knew, I said, "Either. How long would it take to get from here to there?"

Well...assuming you could travel straight through Deoni, which is probably inadvisable for you at this point...if you were walking at a constant pace for half the day...twenty days, perhaps. Practically, I believe it would be longer, considering the season, but you could take the Falova upstream to the south, then cut west across the desert. Mind you, there is plenty of traffic on the river, so if you seek to avoid detection, that might not be wise.

Three weeks. Three weeks of traveling by night, dodging anyone who might look askance at a brunette with a weird accent and a fancy sword, and trying to trek across a freaking desert without turning into the local equivalent of vulture chow.

Before I could ask, the elemental said, *Or I could carry you. You'd be safer in the air, anyway, especially if we traveled by night.*

"Would you? It would be several of us..."

I would not have offered were I unwilling. And if this venture of yours could free my brother, then I will assist as needed. His head turned, or so I thought—honestly, picking his shape out of the rainstorm took a bit of practice. *This close to Deoni, I might counsel waiting for full dark. Meet me here at sunset.*

"I owe you," I told him. "I don't know how to repay you for this, and for getting us across the desert in the first place—"

Do not trouble yourself, little sister. And brother?

Yes? said Terj.

It is good to hear you. I will return, he promised, and leapt into the storm.

I stood on the beach for a moment in my bubble, watching the rain pound against the barrier and drip to the sand like water running down a window. "Guess we should probably tell the others," I said.

Guess you should eat before you collapse.

"I'm not—" I began, only for my growling stomach to prove the lie.

Eat, Susan.

"Fine, *fine*," I said with a sigh, and started walking toward the dining building. "Someone's bossy today."

I'd just like to keep you alive and functional, if it's all the same to you.

"Seeing as I'm no good to you if I'm comatose, right?" I joked.

Terj said nothing for a moment, and I'd thought he'd let the matter drop when he quietly said, *I know it must not seem like it, considering how you came to be here, but I do care about you.*

"Uh…thanks. I, um…I care about you, too," I replied awkwardly. "Might have let myself get electrocuted back there in Deoni otherwise."

Please don't remind me. He paused again, then said, *I know this will sound weird, but I've been conscious of you, to one extent or another, for most of your life. I recognized the elemental in you, at least, and Malachi was always happy when you visited. But being with you over these last weeks, connected like this…*

I could feel his distress and stopped walking, giving him a chance to put his thoughts in order.

I'm so sorry, Susan. Of all people, I wouldn't want to hurt you, and yet—

"It's okay."

No, it isn't. I…I want you to find happiness, he said. *Safety. Love. You should be exploring California or Paris or the Outback right now, not stuck hiding on a beach on Kopaat.*

"To be fair, had I known Kopaat was an option, and were I not being hunted, this might be nice. The beach ain't half bad, and say what you will about the maladetas, but they can cook."

A minor positive in a pile of negatives.

"Hey, not every vacation can be a winner."

Susan, I'm serious. I'm sorry, and I don't know how I can ever make this up to you—

"It's okay," I repeated, trying to make that sound believable. "And for what it's worth, if I had to get stuck with someone for the rest of my life...you know, I could probably do a lot worse than you."

That's better than what I deserve.

"We're going to figure this out," I said, gripping the hilt of the sword at my side as if I could somehow take his hand. "And once we're free, where do you want to go?"

He seemed to chuckle in my mind. *What do you mean?*

"Well, is there a special someone here you'd like to meet up with again, or do you want to see more of Earth beyond Cole's Crossing? I swear, there are more exciting corners of the world. Or could you even come back? Without the Aen—"

I believe I could.

"All right, so we go back," I said, leaning against a stone retaining wall, "you and me, maybe Mia if she's not sick of us yet, and we pile in my *sweet* Accord—"

Not Malachi's truck?

"That thing's fifteen years old. Hell, no. We take the car and drive west...wait, do you think you can ride in a car?"

Why couldn't I?

"You're incorporeal," I pointed out. "What happens if I hit seventy and you go flying through the rear window?"

Unless the interior of the car is a vacuum, don't worry. If you have air in there, I have my ways.

"Good to know. So, that's you, me, possibly Mia, an old-fashioned road trip...where to?"

Malachi always wanted to see the Grand Canyon.

"Done. We'll drive all the way to California, stick our toes in the Pacific. Eat greasy burgers in shitty roadside diners. We'll have so many car singalongs, you'll be begging me to drive you back to the Crossing," I teased.

Death by karaoke is probably not the worst way to go.

I laughed softly and folded my arms as the rain continued to pour around us. "But we could throw together an awesome trip—*after* I find Falova, of course."

Naturally.

"Free ourselves, find him, put thousands of miles on

my car, and then you can get back to your life." I could feel his mood shift and frowned at the sea. "What?"

I barely remember what it was like before, said Terj. *I was very young when they grabbed me—I don't know the precise date on which I came into existence*, he admitted, *but I was probably about your age.*

"Shit," I muttered.

Yeah. It's been so long since I've been around my own kind that I'm afraid I wouldn't know what to do with myself. I'd probably use the wrong fork...if we had a need for utensils. You know what I mean.

"I wouldn't mind if you stuck around. Eased into it."

Like a baby bird at a rehab center? "Oh, look, it's finally flying away!" Cue the happy crying from the volunteers.

"How much TV *did* Uncle Malachi watch?"

I'll be honest with you: there's not much to do when you're alone in that cabin. Nothing I'm going to discuss with you, anyway.

"Oh, *God*," I muttered. "Did you have to go there?"

I said we're not discussing that, he protested.

"But you brought it up, so now I'm thinking about it, and ew."

Come, now. I've never known a Watcher who didn't engage in such activity.

"Yeah, but he was my uncle," I protested. "That's like imagining Dad with the house to himself, and *shit*, now I'm thinking of that—"

Eat, Susan.

"Ugh. Yes. Fine," I groused, and started on my way again. "I'll make you a deal."

Oh?

"You never mention Uncle Malachi's happy fun solo times ever again, and once we get free, I'll let you hang out at the house."

Terj's amusement wrapped around me like a warm blanket against the damp chill. *Deal.*

CHAPTER 7

As night fell, Mia, Anji, Fanakel, Ms. Quince, Ganeel, and I trooped back to the beach with our gear packed. The maladetas traveled light—each carried a waterproofed satchel slung over her chest and tucked beneath her cloak—but the rest of us had crammed everything we could carry into our backpacks, since we had no idea what awaited Outside besides a never-ending stream of hungry creatures out of my nightmares…who would be drawn to the crystals in my sword as the closest source of Aen. I tried *really* hard not to think about that sobering fact as I rolled up my shirts and double-checked for my tent.

Anji and Mia had helped me prepare that afternoon, insisting that I rest after my night on the beach while they hauled back the food supplies the kitchen had thrown together and wrapped for transport. After an early dinner, we dressed in maladetan garb and borrowed cloaks, and Mia, Fanakel, and Anji strapped on loaner swords from the maladetas' stash. Fanakel accepted a more comfortable canvas bag of local make instead of using Uncle Malachi's old duffel, but Mia and I insisted on keeping our clearly foreign backpacks. While my bag might attract attention, I'd finally begun to memorize where the pockets were, and I appreciated the sheer volume of gear it could accommodate. Thus rested, fed, and equipped with clean clothes, I was feeling, if not close to human, at least less likely to collapse by the time we reached the rendezvous point.

The elemental appeared right on time, heralded by a

distinct stirring contrary to the sea breeze as he shaped the air into an almost transparent body around him. *Six to transport, little sister?* he asked.

"Seven, technically," I replied, patting the sword at my side. "Is that too many?"

Should you become overly burdensome, I will drop the maladetas first.

While I picked up on the teasing color of his reply, Ganeel and Ms. Quince didn't look entirely reassured by this plan. Still, they refrained from screaming as the wind swept us off our feet and deposited us atop a cushion of air, and a protective wall seemed to form ahead of us like a windshield—a good thing, as I'd yet to find a method of transportation in the four worlds faster than elemental flight.

Our chauffeur took a seat behind us as he steered our course southward. *The tunnel lies to the southwest of Daril,* he explained. *While we should be able to safely traverse Darili territory, I think it would be prudent to avoid Deoni.*

He wasn't wrong. I glanced over my shoulder, catching a last glimpse of Taln'een and the play of the reddish glow of sunset on the northern sea, then turned around in an effort to avoid air sickness.

The elemental must have sensed my unease, as he quietly laughed in my mind. *You realize you are being carried on air, little sister, yes? Should you become ill, it would be no trouble to simply drop the evidence.*

Good to know, I replied, *but there's a certain stigma attached to tossing your cookies like that.*

Tossing your—

Violently expelling the contents of one's stomach, Terj offered. *Some perceive it as weakness.*

Ah. He paused, considering this information, then asked, *This is a human issue?*

Perhaps not one solely attributable to humans, but yes.

Interesting. But I have seen such expulsions, and they seem to be quite outside the afflicted's control. Why the shame? Does it discomfort those who witness it?

It can trigger a feeling of nausea in others—

Y'all, I begged, *speaking as the one of us with a stomach, could we please not talk about puking right now?*

Oh...sorry, Susan, said Terj with a flash of contrition.

The other elemental gave my mind a moment of more considered study. *You are afraid.*

I have a healthy respect for gravity, I countered.

You are safe with me, he insisted. *Truly, I was jesting about dropping the maladetas.*

I appreciate that, and I do trust you, but I'm also squishy and breakable, and some primal parts of my brain are freaking out right now. It's nothing personal.

This is not uncommon with humans, Terj told him. *Adding altitude to speed sits poorly with their self-preservation instincts.*

But this is far better than walking across the desert, so thank you again. Really, I said, smiling at the elemental. *I mean it, I owe you.*

There is no debt, little sister. And as night is falling, perhaps the scenery will not be quite so troubling before long. His hand, barely substantial enough to see, gave the floor of our conveyance a pat. *Or you could sleep. You need not worry about entertaining me.*

"I might just do that," I mumbled, and stretched out.

"Do what?" asked Anji.

"Sleep for a bit. Rest up for tomorrow."

"That's wise," she replied, and slipped off her backpack. But almost as soon as she lay down, she sat up again and looked toward our pilot. "Uh...sorry, I don't know what to call you..."

I am myself, the elemental replied.

"Yes, I see that, but how do you refer to yourself when among others?"

To my mind, at least, he seemed bemused by the question. *I am myself. Others are themselves. Why do you insist upon assigning sounds to beings?*

"You've never lived in a city, have you?"

His first response was a ripple of distaste. *I would never choose a single place for habitation. Others of my brothers and sisters do, but not we of the air. To be trapped like that—*

The thought ended abruptly.

It's not ideal, said Terj.

I did not intend to grieve you—

You speak the truth, he replied. *And you didn't do this to me.*

I glanced at the maladetas in time to catch Ganeel's wince.

"Anyway," continued Anji before the tension could worsen, "what I was going to say is that should we pass over any burning villages or attacking Outsiders tonight—"

"For the mercy of the Divine, *do not stop*," Fanakel interjected.

"Right. What the elf said."

"Aw, look," said Mia, "you two are bonding! We've found some common ground, eh?"

Anji and Fanakel locked eyes only for an instant. "I wouldn't call this a great step forward in our peoples' relations," she replied as Fanakel flopped down behind her, "but...I suppose..."

"The bar is low," Mia finished.

"What bar?"

"Idiomatic." She stretched out in turn, a buffer between Fanakel and Anji. "I'm guessing that pole vaulting isn't a popular sport with dwarves."

"I've never heard of such..."

As Mia explained the concept, I rolled over and closed my eyes. The sword rested on the impossibly solid nothingness beneath me, and I patted the scabbard. *Good night.*

See you at daybreak, Terj whispered to me, and I surrendered to the white noise of the wind.

Honestly, there are worse ways to spend your night than

resting on air. I slept deeply and woke shortly before dawn when we began to descend. "Are we there already?" I mumbled.

No, said Terj. *Mia requested a pit stop, and since there's nothing around, it's safe to land for a while.*

I sat up and watched as the dunes below us swelled. The elemental gently sat us down between two massive mounds, and I stepped out onto the night-cooled sand. Above us stretched a cloudless sky, its stars already beginning to fade with the coming sunrise. My feet sank as I took a few test steps, and I shuddered at the thought of making the long desert trek.

"Okay, people, here's how this is going to work," said Mia as the others disembarked. "Fanakel, go that way," she ordered, pointing toward the left dune. "Ladies, follow me."

The bathroom situation was, in a word, grim, but after that many hours without a break, no one seemed too picky. With our shovel, travel toilet paper, and solemn promises to turn our backs while we handled matters one at a time, the five of us made the best of it and returned to find Fanakel lounging on our makeshift conveyance, eating granola. "What took you?" he asked.

"*Men*," Ms. Quince muttered, and climbed aboard.

After generous squirts of hand sanitizer—Anji wasn't sure about it, but Ms. Quince insisted the goop was a healthful thing—the rest of us joined Fanakel in scrounging together breakfast while the sun rose behind us. The elemental had kept to a fairly southerly course during the night, avoiding the larger settlements along the banks of the Falova, and now veered in a more westerly direction above the open waste. Looking down, I saw little but sand and the occasional glimpse of what might have been small animals. The heat of day would be miserable, I thought—back home, it was mid-July, and Kopaat's northern hemisphere seemed to be on a similar schedule— but for now, the morning was pleasant, and I relaxed with my water bottle.

Until, that is, an all-too-familiar screech sounded below us.

Rising to my knees, I peered down and spotted a winged monstrosity gaining altitude. The creature looked like the love child of an eagle and a pterodactyl, covered with glossy black feathers but about three times too large. Its claws had to be bigger than my head, and when it opened its hooked beak, I caught a flash of serrated teeth within.

"Ms. Quince?" I called as my hand went to my sword. "I thought these things were nocturnal!"

"They are!" she called back. "Mostly…"

"Maybe it's hungry," said Mia, digging her handgun from her pack.

The thing let out another screech as it drew near, and I unsheathed my blade. "You *think*?"

"Yeah, that was dumb," she conceded. "Anji—"

An arrow whizzed past us through the supporting air and into the Outsider's right eye. It reeled with the hit, flapping and screaming, and I nodded to Fanakel, who knelt behind us with another arrow nocked and ready. "Nice shooting."

"Thanks," he grunted, lining up the next shot. "Now, if it would just…level…"

A blast from beside me made my head whip back around, and I saw that Mia's .454 had put a hole through the creature's skull just before it fell from the sky. By the time the Outsider's corpse hit the sand like a meteorite, the elemental had slowed us to a halt, and he waited while we checked for signs of movement.

"Do you think we should go down and burn it, just to be certain?" asked Anji.

"It's half blind and missing a chunk of its brain," I replied. "Burning would probably be overkill at this point."

Would you like to land? It would be no trouble.

"Thanks," I told the elemental, "but just in case any of

its friends are hunting around here, I think we should push on for the tunnels."

"You do remember the part about how they *come* from the tunnels, right?" Fanakel muttered.

"All the more reason to get there while we still have daylight."

The elemental sped us onward, but I kept an uneasy eye toward the east until the sun had cleared the horizon, imagining hunting cries in the distance.

Our pilot estimated that we would reach the tunnel opening by midday, and so, as we ate an early lunch in preparation, we tried to cobble together a plan.

"Keep your hoods up and your heads down," Ganeel instructed us as she tore off a fresh piece of bread from her small loaf. "You are maladetas, and we are traveling to see a clan in Ildon. I'll speak for us all. If anyone of consequence is guarding the tunnels, they should know my name."

"What if they question us?" asked Fanakel. "I'm conversational in Common, but I don't speak more than a few phrases of New Kopaati. Even if these guards have translators, they'll recognize that I'm not local."

"I don't suppose you can speak passable Old Kopaati, can you?" Ms. Quince queried. "That's what we speak among ourselves."

He grimaced. "I've not been taught."

"Nor have I," said Anji. "*New* Kopaati, yes, but I'm sure I have an accent."

"The solution is to say nothing," Ganeel explained. "Even if questioned. It's customary for the clan mother to provide answers for all, *especially* for men traveling with her," she added, glancing at Fanakel.

"But do we work as a group from a compositional standpoint?" I asked. "The clan mother, the first daughter, two more women, a man, and a child? What's our cover story?"

Ms. Quince quirked a brow. "Our story, dear girl, is that most inhabitants of the four worlds consider it best practice not to provoke maladetas. If there are guards at the tunnel, and if they have two brain cells among them, then they should step aside and send us on our way."

"And if they don't?" asked Mia.

A fireball bloomed in my former neighbor's hand. "They will."

Though I didn't fully share Ms. Quince's confidence, I tried to keep calm. As I'd seen with the dwarven guards back in Heartfast, attitude can get you a long way, and a pointy metal stick helps.

Of course, that didn't exactly work out for me in Caritulo with the Twins or in Deoni with my freaking mother, but hey, one in three wasn't *horrible*.

All too soon, the elemental said, *Do you see that rocky prominence ahead? That's the tunnel mouth.*

I found it easily, a darker brown splotch pocking the outcropping. We'd left the dunes about two hours before, but the shift in terrain was no more welcoming than the sand had been: a dry, undulating, treeless waste dotted with the occasional patch of bare rock, which poked upward like the ground-down stubs of ancient teeth. I wondered if this part of the continent was the last vestige of a mountain range, worn almost smooth with the passage of time. Dust rose on the warm air below us and swirled, making me all the more grateful for our conveyance's pseudo-windshield.

Squinting toward the tunnel, I spotted movement at the base of the hill and tried to count the bodies. "We've got at least four guards."

Ganeel grunted. "Four is manageable. But perhaps we should land and approach on foot—I would rather not alarm them more than necessary."

The elemental accommodated her wishes, depositing us behind a hillock about a fifteen-minute walk from the tunnel. "Thank you again," I told him, trying to pick out the detail in his barely visible face. "If I make it back, and if there's ever anything I can do for you…"

Free my brother, he said, and I felt a pressure like a hand squeezing my shoulder. *If you can accomplish it, free him. We are not meant to be confined.*

"That's my goal," I said, and he released me. To the others, I muttered, "Well, it's not getting any cooler, and the only shade around is the tunnel. Let's do it."

Hoods up and weapons hidden, we trudged onward behind Ganeel.

Maybe, I told myself, this would be simple. I'd heard how others here spoke of maladetas—if not with fear, then at least with a healthy dose of respect. Perhaps this would be as simple as a quick explanation from Ganeel and a "Have a nice day" from the guards.

As we neared, the four figures at the bottom of the rough path leading to the tunnel came into focus: all men, as expected, two with close-cropped hair and two with ponytails. They wore what I recognized as armor, shirts of silvery maille beneath vests of rugged leather protecting their chests, and carried swords belted over their hips. They had to be miserable in the summer heat, and their lack of anything approximating helmets seemed unwise, but what made my stomach sink was the decoration painted on the front of their vests: a square containing alternating wavy bands of blue and green, the flag I'd seen flying over Deoni.

They had pitched tents a little ways from the hill, near a sextet of bored-looking chiquiws, and I wondered if the night shift was resting. The last thing we needed was backup. Looking past the tents, I saw a pile of dark, half-burned flesh, proof that the guards were doing their job.

They noticed us quickly enough, and by the time we'd come within hailing distance, they'd taken up a rough formation in our way—none with weapons drawn just yet, but all at the ready. My fingers itched for the reassurance of the hilt beneath my long cloak, but I forced myself to keep my hands visible and my head lowered, hiding slightly behind Fanakel as we approached.

Finally, one of the guards, a blond with a messy ponytail, raised a hand to stop our progress. "Turn back," he said. "The tunnels are closed."

"*Closed?*" echoed Ganeel, putting an edge into her voice. "By whose authority, pray tell?"

"By order of the queen," he replied. "No passage without a pass and an escort."

Ganeel folded her arms and cocked her head. "If Erianthe Fulquir thinks she has the power to open and close the tunnels, then she should reacquaint herself with a map. This is not Darili territory."

The guards stiffened. "You may petition the queen with your complaint—"

"Oh, I *will* have a word with that little girl," Ganeel snapped, "but not today. I am Ganeel of Taln'een, and I have business in Ildon. You will stand aside, and I will deal with Erianthe later."

Judging by the looks on their faces, the guards weren't accustomed to their sovereign being spoken of in tones generally reserved for a misbehaving child. "Great Mother," said another guard, a stocky fellow with a brown crewcut, "we have no quarrel with you, nor does our queen seek to interfere in maladetan matters. But walking into the tunnels right now, especially with a party as small as yours, would be suicide."

She turned, gave us a brief look of appraisal, and faced him again. "You don't think that my first daughter, two of my other daughters, and I can fend for ourselves? I realize that humans labor under the misapprehension that the female is the weaker of the sexes, but trust me, young man, I am more than capable of seeing my people safely to their destination."

"I do not call your strength into question, Great Mother," he said placatingly, "but is Taln'een aware that

Outsiders are in the tunnels?"

"Outsiders are frequently in the tunnels. That is how they have always entered our worlds, is it not?" The guards regarded her bemusedly, and she sighed. "You boys don't know how the tunnels work, do you?"

"The Watcher is meant to kill the Outsiders before they reach the tunnels," the blond guard chimed in, "but she's abandoned her duty."

Easy, Terj whispered to me as my muscles began to clench.

"There is an offshoot tunnel that runs to the place where the Watcher has been," Ganeel told him. "Your ancestral world, in fact, beyond the Aen. But the tunnels remain the entrance point for Outsiders, and the Watcher has never *stopped* them from entering. They're merely lured away from the main branches." She shrugged. "Your education is not my concern today—and yes, Taln'een is aware of the Outsider situation. We have fought them within our own territory, and I go now to assist my sisters in Ildon. Stand aside."

The guards quickly conferred among themselves, perhaps debating which fate was riskier, disobeying Erianthe in distant Deoni or Ganeel standing twenty feet away. After a moment, they seemed to reach consensus, and the blond took the lead once more. "If Taln'een wishes to assume the risk of traveling the tunnels, we won't stop you."

"Thank you," said Ganeel, and started forward.

But he held up a hand. "We will need to ensure that your party is entirely of Taln'een. Darili are prohibited from accessing the tunnels. You understand, yes?"

"I assure you," she said dryly, "that we have no Darili among us."

Technically? I thought to Terj.

Not the time for technicalities, Susan.

"Your assurance is appreciated," said the guard with a bit more sarcasm than was perhaps wise, "but if your companions could lower their hoods—"

We'll never pass inspection, said Terj as Ms. Quince slowly complied. *Mia could be convincing until she opens her mouth. Fanakel's too pretty, and that's before you take his cap off and the ears pop free. And Anji didn't shave this morning, did she?*

I glanced at the dwarf and noticed her blonde morning fuzz. *Nope.*

She's only convincing as a child from a distance. These guys may have been sent here as cannon fodder, but they're not idiots. How do we play this?

Honesty?

Before Terj could weigh in on that, the guard came to me, and I pushed back my hood. When he saw my face, his eyes widened, and he retreated a step. "You!"

"Me?" I replied.

But he'd already drawn his sword. "The queen has ordered your arrest."

"Are you certain?" asked his apparent second.

He nodded. "Brown hair, scarred cheek, fat. That's in the warrant."

"And who are you calling fat?" I protested.

The other guard gestured toward me. "Maybe slightly overweight—"

"The warrant was *very* clear about the scar," said the first guard, "and look at her face! You are to be brought to Her Majesty at once," he told me.

"I don't think so." Sloughing off my backpack, I pulled the cord at my neck and let my cloak fall away, revealing the sheathed blade at my side. "She wants to execute me. I've got more important things to do."

The second guard, who was definitely the better informed of the spokesmen, noticed the hilt of my sword and gasped. "Is that…"

"I am the *fucking* Watcher," I said slowly, "and I'm coming through. Move."

He stepped aside, but his boss, who seemed to prioritize his orders over common sense, drew his sword.

"If you don't surrender, the queen will accept your head."

"Your queen," I replied, sliding my weapon free, "can kiss my ass. And you can tell her that Susan said as much. Now, here's how this is going to go: you're going to hang out in your tents for a few minutes, and you won't see anything. If anyone asks, we slipped right past you. Oops."

But he didn't stand down. "I don't want to kill you here, girl, but if you force me—"

If you kill her, said Terj—and by the guards' shocked expressions, I knew they heard him loud and clear—*then one of you will become the Watcher in her place, and you can fight Outsiders for the rest of your brief, miserable life. Is that what you want?*

"Who said that?" the guard demanded, looking wildly around for the speaker.

"Shadowbane's rather opinionated," I told him, turning the sword over in my hand so that the blade winked in the sunlight. "And his choice of Watcher can't be challenged. So unless you really like this posting and never want to see your home again…"

Blanching, he put his sword away and stepped back, and I nodded. "Smart man. Have a *nice* day," I muttered, then quickly dressed and led the way up the slope.

We'd almost reached the top when the second guard called, "Watcher?"

I whipped around, anticipating a sneak attack, but he remained emptyhanded. "Yes?"

"Why did you abandon your post? Don't you know how many have died since you disappeared?"

"I'm sorry for their deaths," I replied, staring him down, "but that blood isn't on my conscience. The responsibility lies with those who made this sword, then forced it into a stranger's hand and walked away. Your dead," I said, glaring at the quartet below, "are not my fault. But if you should see your queen, you can tell her I'm off to face the monsters that all of you in the four worlds are too afraid to fight. Look at you," I said with a smirk. "All the big, strong men of Daril, and you'd rather send one woman to fight your battles for you. Would anyone like to accompany us?"

None of them raced up the hill to accept the challenge, and I glanced back before stepping into the tunnel. "Didn't think so," I said, and proceeded into the darkness.

"The weakest point of the tunnels is at their intersection," said Ganeel, her voice echoing off the stone as we traveled along the passageway between worlds. "We designed it like that—"

"Yeah, Ms. Quince told us," Mia interrupted. "Thanks again for that. Real neighborly of you."

To her credit, Ganeel didn't try to defend the decision. "Dare I ask what *else* you told them, Ardielta?" she said, glancing to her right.

Ms. Quince didn't flinch. "I told them enough."

She was quiet for a moment, then murmured, "I suppose you did. Anyway," she continued, looked back at us, "I'm sorry for the long walk, but it can't be helped. Not unless we want to waste an enormous amount of energy breaking through to the Outside at a more reinforced location."

At a moderate pace, the Crossing was a four-hour hike—not a terrible stretch unless you were freaked out by the surrounding rock and the weird streaks of colorful lightning that flickered along the walls, always heading toward the tunnel exits. The passage had been shaped large enough for us to comfortably walk four abreast, wide enough for, say, a dwarven carriage...and, unfortunately, for a hunting Outsider. "What's your plan once we get there?" I asked.

"First, Ardielta and I will force an opening," Ganeel replied. "With any luck, we'll accomplish this with minimal work."

"Not to rain on your parade, but I think we should put

that off until morning."

She peered over her shoulder at me again, her brow furrowed. "You want to delay?"

I can tell you from long experience that the Outsiders come out at night, said Terj. *Susan, what time is it now at the Crossing?*

I glanced at the watch I'd borrowed from Uncle Malachi's dresser, a cheap, scuffed digital piece. "Little after three p.m."

If it's not dark by the time we arrive, then it will be once you force an opening. Seems safer to me to overnight aboveground and wait for daylight.

"A fair point," said Anji. "And I wouldn't mind a night in the reclining chair…"

"You say that, but the cabin's not designed to sleep six people," I replied. "Not comfortably, anyway. What if we split up? I'll stay at the cabin with the sword, and the rest of you could sleep in town. My house should still be standing, and since I automated my bills, the power should be on."

"That would work except for the part where we've been gone for a month and a half," said Mia. "If you or I, or Ms. Quince, are spotted in town, there'll be questions. 'What's with the getup, where've you been—'"

"'What happened to your face?'" I muttered.

"Oh, try, 'Jesus, how much plastic surgery did you *get*?'" she added with a weak chuckle. "Can you imagine what my mom would say if I ran into her looking like this?"

"Unfortunately," said Ms. Quince, "and if I know Janine Randolph…"

"She'd probably run for the pastor," Mia grumbled.

Glancing back to catch Anji's and Fanakel's blank looks, Ms. Quince explained, "The Randolphs are a fairly conservative, religious family. Mia and her mother don't really speak now as it stands—"

"No 'really' about it," said Mia under her breath.

"—and if her mother believed she'd had heavy surgery to give herself, um…"

"Sex appeal?" I suggested.

She seemed relieved to be spared a detailed recitation of Mia's late development. "Yes, that. It would only worsen matters between them."

Anji nodded, but Fanakel frowned at Mia. "What did you look like before?"

"You don't remember?" she asked.

"No. I recall being on duty outside your cell, but I didn't take a particularly good look at you before you started with the damn hypnosis—"

"Sorry."

"You didn't know," he said gruffly. "But everything between that point and the next morning is hazy."

"Ah." She kicked a pebble out of the way, and it ricocheted off the wall of the tunnel. "I was skinner. Pretty flat all over, even my hair. Wasn't quite so blonde."

"Your face changed a bit, too," I added.

"Yeah. In sum, factoring in the time I've been away, I look like I left town, had major surgery, and holed up somewhere to heal for weeks. Of course, how I would *pay* for plastic surgery like that is a mystery..."

I arched an eyebrow in the light of my glowing sword. "Bet I can guess what your mom would say."

"You're not wrong. Honestly," she griped, "just because *she* ran off on a bachelorette and got knocked up doesn't mean that *I* jump into bed with anyone who crosses my path. Unlike some people," she said, scowling into the darkness ahead.

I patted her shoulder. Four months after Mia's breakup, it was evident that she had yet to forgive Raquel the Whore.

"In any case," said Ms. Quince, "Mia's right. Overnighting in town would be too risky. I suppose we can make the best of the cabin, can we not?"

"Sure," I replied with a shrug. "And that way, you can all help me when the monsters come calling in the middle of the night."

Ganeel cleared her throat. "You do understand that it's very painful when we use our power for destructive ends, yes?"

I know damn well that you can shoot a rifle, Nellie Jones.

"Does the cabin *have* a rifle?" she countered.

In reply, Mia quickly loosened two straps and thrust her shotgun toward Ganeel. "Malachi had several long guns, and if you don't like what's on offer at the cabin, then you can borrow this baby. Personally, I think the .454's more useful, but take your pick of the rest." When Ganeel didn't exactly jump up and down at the offer, Mia snorted. "You're not afraid, are you?"

"I...prefer not to use violence unless the situation absolutely demands it," she admitted. "Aggression increases the risk of accidentally using our abilities to cause harm, and once you know that sort of pain—"

I don't want to hear one word about __pain__ from you, Terj snapped.

"My sisters have died from it!"

And you can't see it, but I'm playing the universe's tiniest violin for you poor maladetas.

I snickered before I could stop myself, and though Mia managed to control her laughter, she looked like she was struggling to bite it back. Ganeel's shoulders tightened, and though Ms. Quince turned and gave me a look I knew *quite* well from childhood, she said, "There should be a pair of rifles in the gun safe, and I believe Malachi had them inspected and repaired in March. We'll make do."

CHAPTER 8

After spending weeks on Kopaat, I better understood what Ms. Quince had meant about the air of home feeling prickly. My senses had tuned to the Aen bathing the four worlds, an easily tapped source of energy and potential, but hardly a trickle passed out of the opening to the Crossing and out into the community. We'd hurried to race the sun, and we emerged into the dimming glow of late afternoon, squinting even with the trees overhead after spending hours in the tunnels. The old "asbestos mine" appeared to be as abandoned as ever—at least we didn't see anyone trying to use the avoided site as a make-out spot—and once we ducked through the hole in the barbed wire fence, a twenty-minute hike brought us back to the cabin.

"All I'm going to say is thank God for automatic debit," I muttered, flipping the switch inside the door. Uncle Malachi's deer antler chandelier illuminated, revealing the fine layer of dust that covered the sparse furniture and much of the floor. "It's not great, but it'll do for the night," I told the others, dropping my gear by the battered leather recliner, and set about turning on the air conditioners in the main room and bedroom windows. Considering its age and construction, the cabin was decently insulated, but the July heat was moist and unforgiving, even in the woods.

Once I had the air flowing, I returned to find Ms. Quince rummaging through the remains of the pantry with Mia. "Looking for something?" I asked.

"Found it," Mia replied, holding up a box of spaghetti. "Just searching for sauce. Do me a favor and pull the venison out of the freezer, okay? We're going to have to defrost that in the microwave."

I did as she asked, though not without a pang of grief. Uncle Malachi had been a hunter, quick to share with Dad and me, and this was among the last of his frozen stock. Still, I popped the steaks into a bowl and started the microwave, then considered the rest of our group. The others had abandoned their gear in haphazard piles around the room, and while Anji had made herself at home in the recliner and Fanakel had pulled up a wobbly wooden kitchen chair, Ganeel stood awkwardly by the old TV, taking it all in.

"You left before the cabin was built, right?" I asked her.

She nodded. "Zachary had another home near the tunnels. Did Pericles construct this?"

"Yeah. He lived here, and then Uncle Malachi inherited it. As did I," I added with a shrug. "My place in town is nicer, but since I'd rather my neighbors not get eaten in their beds…"

She crossed the room and held her hand in the air conditioner's outflow, frowning. "An expensive purchase."

"Not really. When were you last here?"

"1944."

"They've gotten a lot cheaper since then. Dad wanted to install central A/C out here for Uncle Malachi, but *that* wasn't feasible."

"For several reasons," Ms. Quince added from the kitchen. "Imagine the cost of repairs if the unit became collateral damage in an Outsider attack." She pulled open the spice drawer and scowled. "Honestly, Malachi. How old is this oregano?"

"You're probably better off not asking," I said. "Okay, I'm going to run the vacuum and collect the dust kittens. If you're not cooking, why don't you hit the shower? With six of us, we'll have to stagger unless you like cold water."

Fanakel and Anji didn't need convincing—Fanakel especially, once I showed him Uncle Malachi's stash of razors—but Ganeel loitered by the door, regarding the old vacuum cleaner with suspicion as I halfheartedly cleaned. When I turned it off to dump the cannister, Ms. Quince called from the stove, "It's not going to bite you, Ganeel."

"It's rather *loud*," she said.

"Because it, like almost every other appliance in this shack, is a piece of shit," she muttered—in English, I noted, as if the familiar rhythms of the life she'd just left were returning to her.

"The chest freezer's good," I offered.

"Yes, as that's the only thing Barnaby didn't have to beg to replace. Your father kept trying to update the cabin, but Malachi wouldn't let him. Said it would be a waste." She turned to me, leaning against the counter with her arms folded as the pasta water heated. "That's what the curse did to him. He was so weary and beaten by the end of his life that he couldn't see the point in letting his brother buy him nice things. Couldn't have a family, couldn't leave…"

Well, at least he had you, said Terj, the thought dripping with sarcasm.

Her gaze dipped to the sword, which I'd propped in the corner while I worked. "I didn't think you'd be able to communicate here."

Sword recharged, so it's not drawing on me to that point yet. I mean, the pain's worse, but that's to be expected. As my guts twisted with guilt, he added, *It's fine, Susan. Nothing I haven't endured before.*

"I'm sorry—" I began.

I'd rather you not die in the tunnels before we get Outside. And since there's no Aen there, this is just easing myself into it.

But Ms. Quince wasn't ready to let the conversation drop. "I did the best I could for Malachi."

You never told him how to leave Cole's Crossing. You could have brought him to Kopaat and tried to make the case for him.

"Someone would have killed him," she protested. "You've seen what's happened to Susan!"

But you could have tried, or even given him the option. You let him suffer here instead.

"I didn't want to lose him like that!"

Oh? What were you afraid of? Best-case scenario, he's freed, and he finds someone who can love him?

"That's not—"

He loved you, Ardielta. That man loved you, and he trusted you, and you left him here to rot. When Ms. Quince didn't immediately deny it, Terj pressed on. *You say you loved Malachi? Look, I get it—humans don't live long. I'm well aware. But what was your plan? Enjoy his company while you held him captive here?*

"I didn't hold—"

You didn't try to free him, did you? You could have decided that his life was worth more than this damned arrangement you god-foresworn monsters made and tried to free him. If I knew Malachi, and I'm fairly confident on that count, then he'd have done anything in his power to help you, had your positions been reversed. Tell me I'm wrong.

Ms. Quince said nothing.

So you didn't love him enough to show him a possible path to freedom, but you loved him too much to risk a future in which Malachi was free to be with a true partner? You just couldn't bear the thought of Malachi not needing your companionship and maybe seeking out someone with whom he could build a life? Raise a family?

"That's enough from you," Ganeel tried, but Terj ignored her.

Well, he's dead now. Sixty-three, and his heart gave out. He collapsed in the woods and died alone—no spouse by his side, no children, just dirt and weeds and me and that poor kid who found the body.

"Please stop," Ms. Quince whispered.

It was Malachi who always wanted to be a father, you know. And even when Susan practically landed on his doorstep, he had to give her away.

"Please—"

Everything Malachi wanted in the short time allotted to him was snatched away because your curse made me choose. That was a maladetan addition to the sword project, was it not? A guarantee that there would always be an expendable human with the sword stuck in his hand? If you loved Malachi—if you truly loved him— then you could have fought for him. But you were too damn selfish.

"Ardielta followed her orders," said Ganeel, "and there is nothing—"

Spare me. She knows this is wrong—whatever else can be said for her, and believe me, I have a few choice thoughts, she does have a conscience. She disregarded her orders when she told Susan how to flee, didn't she? So why not do the same for Malachi?

"Because—"

"I *was* selfish," Ms. Quince interrupted, her arms tight across her chest. "All right? Is that what you want to hear? I knew that no one would agree to free him from his duty, and I didn't want to risk him being killed in the attempt. I *did* love him," she said softly. "And I thought he was safest here."

With no hope. In a shitty little cabin in the woods.

Her face started to crumple, but she fought for her composure.

You told Susan quickly enough. If you were so worried about safety—

"I watched her grow up!" she cried, her voice finally cracking. "That little motherless girl lost Barnaby and Malachi, and she deserved *something* good in her life, and you took everything from her!"

"Do *not* try to pin this on Terj," I said, and she jerked and turned to me as if I'd shouted in her ear. "No. The Taln'een own this. So do Daril and Nokan'ti and Blackhorn Mountain and everyone else who built your goddamn tunnels and your goddamned sword. You can justify your silence to Uncle Malachi however you like. Whatever lets you sleep at night. But you don't get to blame the victims of this little arrangement, understood?"

For a moment, I thought she might shoot me one of her familiar looks, the kind I'd received for picking flowers from the neighbors' beds or making too much noise when playing in the yard. Instead, she silently nodded, then turned back to her work.

I packed the vacuum into the closet and glanced toward the kitchen, catching Mia's eye. She made a face but said nothing, and the maladetas and Terj kept their thoughts to themselves until dinner was ready.

I took the first watch that night and stepped outside, partly to give the others a chance to clean up and rest but really to get Terj out of the house.

I'm sorry, he told me as I settled in on the porch steps after a perfunctory stroll around the quiet cabin. *Everything hurts worse, and I'm cranky, but pushing Ardielta wasn't helpful. She's grieving, too, in her way.*

I think she really loved him, I replied, keeping our conversation private.

Oh, she did. And that's what makes it so much worse. You know, the maladetan justification for a long time has been, "We watch over the Watcher, we make such a sacrifice, but it's all for the greater good." The thought flickered with disgust. *If she were so keen on sacrifice, she could have sacrificed her clan standing, brought Malachi back with her, and fought for his freedom. She could have sacrificed Taln'een's standing by breaking faith with the others who made the sword and seeking a way to destroy it. She could have been the one to go Outside in search of answers. Notice who's not coming along tomorrow?*

I chuckled. *No surprise there. But more importantly, is there anything I can do to lessen the pain for you?*

No, and I'm trying to prepare myself for what it will be like without even the little Aen that flows here.

You said the sword was charged up…

That won't last. The ambient Aen of the four worlds is sufficient to power the forging that holds the sword together. Outside of that, the forging is designed to draw upon its backup source. Lucky me.

What about these? I asked, tapping the Aen crystals set in the hilt.

Those are just the beacons for Outsiders, Terj explained. *If the forging tapped them, the sword wouldn't be so effective in luring the monsters here, you see? And since the energy necessary to sustain this delightful little torture chamber is considerable, the crystals would have been drained long ago. I'm a much better battery.*

Shit.

Yeah. These last few weeks were a nice reprieve, though, so thank you.

As I listened to him, a horrifying thought occurred to me. *How much longer will you be able to talk?*

Maybe a few days. The sword's not drawing on me completely yet. But don't worry, he joked, *you'll be getting a break from my complaining soon.*

"Terj," I muttered.

It's all right, Susan. Really. Nothing I haven't lived through before. And if this plan works, it'll be worth it in the end, yes?

What plan? Poke our heads out there and ask nicely if the locals could keep their monsters more securely penned? God, I said, *if this turns out to be, like, alien sheep that just need a better shepherd...*

He laughed in my mind. *You know the house three doors down from yours with the invisible dog fence?*

The absurd notion of Outsiders yipping like old Mrs. Sheridan's aggressive Jack Russell with his shock collar made me giggle, and from what I could sense, Terj seemed pleased with himself.

After a moment, he said, *There's something on your mind.*

I snorted. *You think?*

Not the obvious. Back of your thoughts.

Honestly, I was embarrassed to bring it up, but with the night momentarily calm and Terj prying, I relented. *I keep thinking about what that stupid guard said today. Ridiculous to worry about that tonight, I know, but—*

What did he say?

Heat bloomed in my face. *You know, the fat girl with the scarred cheek…*

You're not fat, Terj protested. *Average, I would think. More toned than you were two months ago, but not fat.*

I'm not thin, either, I countered, *and Mia—*

Comes from a species that has weaponized sex appeal. Why compare yourself to her?

I sighed. *Look, you don't have to convince me. I know this is dumb. It's just that…* I hesitated, trying to compress my twisted knot of feelings into words, then said, *I've never been a great beauty, right? Fine, I can deal with that. But add in the scar, and at the end of the day…who's going to want this package?* When Terj didn't immediately jump in to argue with me, I said, *Again, I know how ridiculous it is to worry about something as inconsequential as my looks right now, but he kind of hit a nerve. That's all. I'm not going to be a mopey mess tomorrow.*

I will never understand why humans put so much importance on their bodies' appearance, said Terj. *They inevitably change, they break down. As long as your body can accomplish the necessary tasks and keep your squishy bits contained, why fault it?*

I'm pretty sure it's not just humans who focus on aesthetics.

Fine, corporeal species. I still think it's silly to put so much stock in physical beauty.

So what do you look for in mates, then?

The question gave him pause. *Well…I can't speak for all elementals, and I haven't looked for one, but if I did…personality, ability to carry on a conversation, and so forth. "Who is this person?" instead of "Does this person's body meet a particular set of criteria?"*

You never wanted a partner?

I was too young to really consider one, and from what I understand, air elementals don't typically pair for long. Water and earth, now, they can bond, and I know of a fire elemental and a water elemental who've been together for ages—

That seems unlikely, I replied.

Ever seen a geyser? It works for them. And I could be mistaken about my kind, he admitted. *It's been centuries since I was around my brothers. But I believe that we, more than any others, prefer our freedom.*

And instead, you're stuck with me.

Hey, I'm the one who dragged you into this mess, he said.

Fine. New plan.

Oh?

Yep. We get Outside. We stop the monsters from coming in. We figure out how to get you out of the sword. And then we take you back to the four worlds, where you can finally look for a nice girl. Fire and earth, right? Those are the female elementals?

Correct, he said with what felt like soft laughter, *but believe me, I wouldn't be seeking a partner.*

Why not?

Because I'm what you'd call damaged goods. As I frowned, he explained, *The one who carried us across the desert, he and I spoke extensively while you slept. It's clear to me that I am...not right.*

You've been through hell, I protested. *That doesn't mean you're doomed to be alone...does it?*

Honestly? said Terj. *I don't know. But my mind and his are rather different, to the point that he frequently remarked that had he not known better, he wouldn't have thought me one of his brothers. I...I suppose it's to be expected that after so long away, I would seem strange, but not to* that *extent.*

I picked up on the faint cast of despair in his voice.

So even if your plan works, he said, *I don't think I'm going to be, say, Kopaat's most eligible bachelor. At best, I'm an anomaly.*

He fell silent, and I sat on the porch steps for a moment long, listening to the crickets and the hooting of a distant owl.

"Well, *shit*," I muttered.

Terj laughed then in earnest, though it sounded strained.

We make a great pair, I joked. *You're weird, and I'm not pretty.*

That doesn't seem accurate. Not as to you, I mean—I am *weird. But surely there's something about your body that would attract a reasonably decent human male.*

Let's be realistic: next to Mia, I'm unfuckable.

But you and Mia aren't searching through the same pool of partners, correct? What does it matter how she looks if she's not in competition with you? And since she seems to have attached herself to Anji...

You noticed that, too, huh? I replied.

I think there's reciprocity there.

Good for them. I pushed myself off the steps with a groan and adjusted my sword belt. *Want to walk the perimeter again?*

I wouldn't mind a stroll.

Says the one who's not actually walking.

We'd almost passed Uncle Malachi's truck when Terj said, *Susan—*

Yes? I asked, surprised by how abruptly his thought had cut off. *What's up?*

Never mind, he insisted, his mind as unreadable to me as blank stone.

I'd just collapsed into bed beside Mia and begun to drift when Anji shook me awake. "We've got company, lass," she said as I groaned. "Come on, we need all hands."

I rolled out of bed—quite literally, as I misjudged where the edge of the mattress was—then picked myself off the rug, unsheathed the sword, and hurried into the main room with Mia on my heels.

The place was pitch-black—there was no sense in helping the Outsiders find us, after all—but as my eyes adjusted, I made out Fanakel with his back almost pressed against the wall between the pair of front windows, turning ever so slightly to peer out at the night. Ms. Quince had taken up a position by the chimney, shotgun in hand, while Ganeel had retreated to the kitchen with another long gun, perhaps a rifle. As Mia traded places with Fanakel and he quickly unpacked Uncle Malachi's bow and his forged quiver, I murmured, "What's out there?"

"At least six of them," Ms. Quince replied. "Two

keep—" She paused as a pair of thumps sounded on the roof and claws began to scrabble above us. "Keep landing up there. The other four have been circling."

"Damn it." I joined Mia and glanced out the window in time to catch a hulking shape darker than the trees as it loped past. As much as I itched to turn on the porch light for a better view of our assailants, that would have been a terrible idea. "Any idea as to type?"

"Well, at least two are winged," said Ms. Quince, "but I don't know about the others…"

The noise above us headed toward the chimney, and Ms. Quince had just leveled her weapon when the first of the Outsiders plummeted down. She fired before the creature could rise, and a headshot from Mia's pistol ended its pained screeching. Apparently, the racket below scared off the Outsider's buddy, as the sounds from the roof suddenly ceased, followed by a thud as something heavy landed in the bed of the old pickup truck.

"That's my inheritance, you bastard," I grumbled. "You'd better not bend the axle."

Going out there? Terj asked.

"Don't have a better idea. Y'all?"

"With you," said Anji, who'd belted on her short sword and loaded her loaner .38. "Mia?"

"Ready."

"As am I," said Fanakel, rising from a crouch with an arrow already nocked. "How do we play this?"

"Distance weapons first," Anji replied. "Shoot from the porch and see what damage we can do. Then we'll use blades to finish them off. Susan, light it up."

A flicker of will was all it took to make my sword glow green, and I stood at the top of the steps while the others lined up down the porch, watching the woods.

We'd barely gotten into position before the first of the wingless Outsiders attacked. The thing that ran toward me did so on four hooved legs, and as it neared, I mused that it looked a bit like a deer…well, at least below the neck.

The thing's head was topped not with antlers, but rather with four sharp horns, and it opened its mouth to reveal serrated fangs just before Fanakel put an arrow in its eye. A shot from Mia's gun sent it to the ground, where it quivered its last in a spreading pool of ichor.

A second, more ursine, creature neared as the other winged Outsider decided to try its luck. Mia shot the bear-like creature in the head, while Anji and Fanakel blinded the winged one before it could launch itself at the porch. Instead, it staggered, threw itself toward us, and ricocheted off a porch column before I opened its guts and let the blade set it afire.

"That's four down," said Mia, the fire in the gravel throwing her face into odd, flickering planes of light and shadow. "Where are the—"

Two monsters like scale-plated gorillas came charging out of the trees before she could finish her thought, and the shotgun blast from behind me left my ears ringing. "Sorry!" Ms. Quince yelled as her target fell to its knees and bellowed. Mia finished him, and while Anji and Fanakel harried his friend, I stabbed him to be sure. By the time I had him on fire, Anji had disemboweled the other, and I beheaded him to put him out of his misery.

We stood there for a moment in the light of the burning Outsiders, listening, but the only sounds around us were the usual nighttime chirrups and the crackling of fat.

I don't sense any more, said Terj.

"Works for me. Y'all watch the corpses for a minute, okay?" I said to the rest of our party. "I'm going to get the fire extinguisher before the cabin goes up. We can haul them to the burn pit and finish this safely, yeah?"

When I stepped back into the house, I found Ganeel still in the kitchen, clutching her gun and staring at the front door with wide eyes. "It's over," I muttered, and brushed past her to pull one of Uncle Malachi's emergency extinguishers from beneath the sink. "You can relax now."

As I straightened, glowing sword still in hand, I saw the terror in her dark eyes. "Ganeel? You all right?"

"I hate it here," she whispered, gripping the gun to her chest. "There's no Aen, and it feels awful, and I…I'm almost powerless, and I hate it *so much*."

If she wanted sympathy, she was out of luck, as I was too damn tired and smelled of burned Outsider. "We're going to haul the bodies around to the back to dispose of them. Put that down and give us a hand."

"I…I don't…"

"*Ganeel*," I said, locking eyes with her, "put down the goddamned gun and come help us drag. Least you can do."

And though she whimpered intermittently until the last of the corpses had been reduced to ash, she did as she was told.

Morning dawned all too soon for my interrupted sleep cycle, partly cloudy and humid with the promise of afternoon storms. While Mia munched on a sleeve of saltines, I checked on the food in our packs and refilled all the water bottles. I barely paid Ms. Quince any mind when she stepped inside—she'd taken the final watch from the porch—but then she grabbed the truck keys and asked, "Does anyone have cash? I left my cards at my house in town."

I dug in the back of the pantry and pulled out Uncle Malachi's emergency fund, then handed her three twenties. "Is this enough? And do you need to borrow something to wear?" I asked, giving her wrinkled attire a once-over. Sure, Cole's Crossing wasn't the epicenter of the fashion world, but even still, the simple gray maladetan dress looked out of place.

"The drive-thru has seen worse," she replied as she took the money. "Back soon."

"What drive-thru?" asked Mia.

She glanced over her shoulder, already halfway to the door. "McDonald's. Nearest option that'll let me stay in the vehicle."

My town being as tiny as it was, even the closest chain restaurants were twelve miles away. About thirty minutes later, by the time the others were up and clothed, Ms. Quince returned with fragrant bags and six cups of coffee. Ganeel, Fanakel, and Anji regarded the paper sacks with curiosity, but Ms. Quince methodically unpacked and passed around sandwiches and hashbrowns, then slid a double portion in front of Mia with a knowing look. "Thanks," she mumbled, and wolfed down her meal.

"Right," said Ms. Quince as the rest of us tucked in, "here's the plan. Once we've eaten, we'll return to the Crossing and open a way for you. We will *keep* it open."

Anji frowned. "Won't that make matters simpler for the Outsiders coming in?"

"Perhaps, but they may get distracted by having Firebrand in their midst. That's a much closer source of Aen."

"Joy," I muttered into my biscuit.

"Anyway," Ms. Quince continued, "I'm more concerned about inadvertently trapping you over there, so Ganeel and I will remain in the cabin and monitor the Crossing."

It seemed that the clan mother hadn't been fully briefed on this part of the plan, as her eyes widened. "Wait, now, that wasn't what we discussed—"

"I will *remain*," Ms. Quince replied, staring her down, "because we owe them that support. If you wish to return to Kopaat, Great Mother, then that is your prerogative, but recall that the desert is wide, and there will be no chiquiw waiting for you at the tunnel mouth. Only Darili soldiers."

"We cannot stay here indefinitely," Ganeel protested.

"No. Ten days, I should think. If you need a longer time to scout," she told us, "simply return and let me know. But if we see no sign of you within ten days—"

"Then we probably won't be alive to send one," Fanakel finished, and sipped his coffee with a grimace. "Understood."

"I'm not sure there's enough food here for ten days unless you get into the questionable flour," said Mia, frowning at the pantry door.

Ms. Quince nodded. "Agreed. I'll slip back into my house tonight, exchange my wardrobe, and go shopping. If anyone asks whether I've seen you two…"

"My cousin in Louisiana had her baby prematurely back in May," Mia replied. "Suze and I went out to help, since it's just my cousin, her wife, and their two-year-old, and they're still dealing with the NICU."

My neighbor arched a brow. "Since when do you have a cousin in Louisiana?"

"Since May."

She grunted. "Fair. I can improvise around that if necessary." She paused, watching us eat, then asked, "Is there anything else you need before setting off? More food? Ammunition?"

"We've packed all the ammunition we can carry," said Anji as Mia nodded, "and the quiver takes care of itself. Perhaps extra bowstrings…"

"Already packed," Fanakel told her between bites. "There's no sense in stalling, is there?"

"None that I can see." With that, the dwarf wadded up her trash and rose. "Excuse me for a few minutes."

She closed the bedroom door behind her, and the mumbled bits I caught sounded very much like a prayer.

Soon enough, the last of the breakfast had vanished, our bags were double-checked, and all the necessary gods had been importuned. I handed Ms. Quince the keys to the cabin and my vehicles, and with her promise to keep the place intact, we set off for the Crossing.

My watch said it was barely eight by the time we made it through the fence and down the stairs into the darkness of the tunnels, but I kept an eye on the four branching arms, looking for Outsiders who'd decided to wait for sunset up top. "This will take a few minutes," Ganeel cautioned as she and Ms. Quince took up their positions in front of the stretch of wall between the Ildon and Kopaat tunnels, and then they began chanting in low voices and gesticulating in tandem.

At first, I wondered if there might not be enough Aen to power whatever the maladetas were trying to accomplish, but then the wall began to glow—a spot the size of a basketball, then a hula hoop, and then a semicircle half as wide as my garage door. Once the glow had stabilized, the stone within its borders seemed to slowly liquify, dripping down the wall and pooling on the floor.

"Laser hands?" Mia whispered to me.

"Hell if I know," I whispered back. "This is why you don't piss off maladetas, right?"

If they heard us, they paid us no attention. The wall continued to melt until finally, the stone began to fall away in chunks, revealing what appeared to be another tunnel of dark orange bricks on the far side. The air from the new tunnel swirled into the Crossing, and I felt the distinct prickliness of an atmosphere devoid of any trace of the Aen.

"*That* is the Outside," Anji murmured.

Fanakel nodded. "Shall we?"

She looked up at him, her face strained in the green light of my drawn sword. "You're not afraid?"

"Oh, no, I'm absolutely terrified," he confessed, "but standing here and contemplating the many ways in which this could go wrong will not make me feel any better." He sighed and shifted the straps of his pack. "May the Divine have compassion for us all."

When the maladetas moved aside, he stepped over the melted stone and into the brick tunnel, and Anji quickly followed suit. Mia paused at the edge to give Ms. Quince a hug, but before I could do likewise, I heard Terj's frantic voice in my head. *Susan?*

Are you okay?

I need to tell you something. In case the worst happens out there...I want you to know that you're beautiful. Not your body—I can't fairly judge that—but the parts that actually matter.

Terj, I said, surprised. *You don't have to—*

I mean it. Whatever happens, if this is the last time we speak, take that with you, for what it's worth.

This won't be the last time, I insisted, then hugged Ms. Quince, nodded to Ganeel, and stepped Outside.

We hadn't emerged at the end of a tunnel, as I'd imagined, but rather in the middle of one, and all I could see by the light of the sword was darkness on either end. I walked a few feet in either direction, looking for guidance, and rested one hand on the brick wall on the Aen side...which, to my shock, seemed to *give* beneath my hand. "The hell? Come here, feel this!" I told the others.

Anji arrived first, and when she likewise pressed on the wall, her hand sank through to the wrist like a fork slicing into gelatin. "High Queen have mercy," she said, yanking her hand back, "what *is* that?"

"We told you the Crossing was the weakest point," said Ms. Quince. "The walls are thin here. I suppose they're *permeable* from that side...fascinating..."

Left without a signpost, I asked, "Any idea which way we go?"

"I wish I could tell you, but from what I can see, one looks as good as the other."

"Well," said Fanakel, "we can't stay here all day. How about this way?" he suggested, pointing to the left.

With no better idea, we started off, but I hadn't walked ten feet from the hole when Terj's agony lanced across my mind. *It hurts,* he said, his words like a sob. *Oh, it hurts—*

Terj? I said, stopping in my tracks. *Talk to me. Are you all right?*

But though I could perceive him on the edges of my thoughts, he remained silent.

Noticing that I was falling behind, Mia called a halt and hurried back to me. "Suze? What's wrong?"

"I can't hear Terj," I said. "The sword must be drawing from him, he's in so much pain..."

"Do we retreat?" asked Anji, glancing toward the hole, which Ms. Quince and Ganeel were shrinking.

I gripped the hilt more tightly, feeling the Aen crystals press against my fingers and palm, and shook my head. "No. We stop wasting time," I said, and brushed past Fanakel to lead the way.

CHAPTER 9

At least the air was breathable. That, I mused as we trudged along the endless brick tunnel, hadn't actually been a given. The previous fools who'd ventured Outside might have died from, say, an atmosphere filled with cyanide. It was difficult to determine whether anyone's skin was turning blue, given that our only sources of illumination were Mia's flashlight and the sword, but no one complained about the quality of air.

No, it was the fucking Outsiders in the tunnel that got on our nerves.

They came through about once every half hour or so, crawling, skittering, scrabbling monstrosities that blocked the way forward and honed in on the Aen crystals I was carrying like piranhas to blood. Under other circumstances, I might have feared that the gunfire in the tunnel would have let the others know where to find us, but since the tunnel was as branchless as those between the four worlds, and since I was basically an ambulatory beacon, there was really no point in subtlety. We refrained from incinerating the corpses, trying to avoid smoking ourselves out, and left them behind as snacks for anything coming from the opposite direction.

That the Outsiders had consistently come from ahead of us suggested we were walking in the right direction, which offered me a modicum of comfort as the self-appointed line leader. Part of me feared that the tunnels went on forever, or that we might actually be trapped in some sort of monster-filled circuit. I'd wondered aloud if this might be all there was Outside, but Anji had vehemently rejected the notion. "Look at this," she said, and patted her hand against the brick wall—which, as we'd walked farther from the Crossing, had returned to familiar solidarity. "This isn't natural. *Someone* had to make these bricks, which suggests that there's an intelligent people out here. And if this is an artificial construction, it must end at some point."

Three hours into our trek, I hoped she was right.

Suddenly, Fanakel said behind me, "What's that ahead?"

I raised my sword, trying to illuminate more than the next few feet of darkness. "Outsider?"

"No, sorry, *sorry*," he hastily amended. "I thought I saw light."

Curious, I willed the sword to go dark, and Mia cut her flashlight. A few seconds later, once my vision had cleared, I noticed what he'd seen: a pinprick in our path, small but significant against the shadows.

"Think it's the end?" Mia asked.

Gauging distance wasn't easy in the dark tunnel, but I shook my head. "Too small, I imagine."

"Maybe it's a crack," Anji suggested. "If we could break out of here…"

That idea met with no resistance, and we hurried on toward the light.

Sure enough, the tiny glow was coming from a fissure in the brick wall, barely wide enough for an exploratory finger. Fanakel pressed against the wall around it, but the hole seemed to have come from a bit of weak mortar, not a widespread structural failure, and the wall held fast. As he stepped back to ponder the problem, Anji knelt and rummaged through her bag, then pulled out a metal disc roughly the size of a silver dollar. "You should stand aside," she told the rest of us.

Bemused, we retreated a few feet, and Anji placed the disc on the wall. It flashed gold as it adhered, then began to emit a beeping noise—steady at first, but quickly accelerating. Grabbing her gear, Anji ran down the tunnel to join us, then dropped to her knees again, tucked her head, and yelled, "Blast!"

I barely had time to get on the floor before the wall behind the disc blew up in a shower of brick shards. Fortunately, most of the shrapnel flew out of the tunnel, but we coughed for a moment as the dust cloud settled, then picked ourselves up and considered the roughly four-foot hole Anji had made.

"How…how long have you been carrying *explosives*?" Mia asked.

Anji alone seemed unfazed. "Standard kit when you live around mines, lass. Useful in case of cave-in." She brushed the grit off her sleeves and ran a hand over her chin stubble, then nodded toward the opening. "Want to see what truly awaits in the Outside?"

We started on, but I overheard Fanakel murmur, "Nice work."

"Poor things, really," Anji replied.

"Better than my kit."

"I don't recall there being much danger of tunnel collapse in Caritulo," she joked. "Your father would probably protest if you started blowing up trees."

But Fanakel didn't let it go. "Should we survive this, the next time I hear someone say that forging is a worthless art, I'm afraid I'll be forced to start an argument."

"Ooh, saying something nice about *dwarves*? Isn't that practically blasphemy?"

"You jest," he muttered, "but…"

Anji reached up and patted him on the back. "You're decent, son of Nokan'ti."

Before he could answer that, Mia reached the hole in the wall and said, "*Whoa*. Come see!"

We jogged up to join her, then stared out at the alien world beyond the tunnel.

A pale lilac sky stretched to the distant mountains on the horizon, from the peaks of which plumes of smoke seemed to rise at irregular intervals. Between us and the mountains stretched a field of tall yellow grass. I tore off part of a long blade and found it pliable in my fingers— alive, then, but strangely colored. There was no road running alongside the tunnel, but looking out across the prairie, I saw a collection of low buildings a mile or so away, perhaps a village. I was about to suggest we head in that direction when a six-legged creature with tawny stripes and large black eyes wandered up. As we froze in place, it regarded us with vague curiosity, then bent its head and resumed grazing.

I let out a sigh of relief. "Herbivore. Fantastic. Want to get out of here?"

We stepped over the jagged bottom of the hole and into the field of waist-high grass—well, closer to chest-high grass for Anji—then set off for the closest sign of habitation. Glancing up, I found the sun to be high overhead, suggesting that the local time was close to that of home.

"Hey, y'all?" said Mia. "Turn around."

I did as she said, then whistled low.

The tunnel stretched on for *miles*, cutting across the land like a dark orange oil pipeline. The direction in which we'd been going seemed to aim for the mountains, while a glance in the direction from which we'd come revealed nothing more than grass and grazing animals heading into the distance.

"So," said Mia, adjusting her pack, "do you suppose the folks around here are going to be upset that we blew a hole in their nice tunnel?"

"Once the first Outsider pokes its head through," Anji muttered. "Come. I'd prefer to put distance between that opening and Heart's Blood."

The rest of us shared her sentiment, and we pressed onward, trampling the grass while we made a path toward the village. "A thought," I said as the warm sun sent sweat trickling down my spine.

"What's that?" asked Mia.

"Assuming that settlement up ahead isn't populated by the things tracking me, what do we call the locals? I mean, technically, I guess they're Outsiders as well, but surely this place has a name."

"If it does," said Fanakel, "we've no knowledge of it."

"Nor do we," Anji added. "It's just…Outside. The gods set this land beyond the Aen, a barren place of monsters…" Her voice petered out as she scanned our pastoral surroundings. "Or so our priests say. What about yours?" she asked Fanakel.

He made a face. "Much the same, actually. The Outside is a realm cut off from the light of the Divine. It's a land of bloodthirsty, misshapen creatures who dwell in total darkness."

"Total darkness, eh?" I grumbled, wiping my brow. "I could go for a bit of that."

The elf and the dwarf walked along in contemplative silence for a few minutes, which Anji finally broke with a pointed clearing of her throat. "I would never suggest that our priests have been untruthful, but the High Queen, in her mercy, did give me eyes. Perhaps our priests are…mistaken."

"Perhaps ours are as well," Fanakel allowed.

Anji glanced up at him sharply. "But only as to the condition of the place beyond the Aen. I've seen no evidence to suggest a mistake as to the tenets of the faith."

"Nor have I."

"Very well. So we keep our mutual heterodoxy to a minimum, then?"

He nodded. "I believe the Divine would approve, as they've brought us here, after all."

They fell silent again, but only briefly that time.

"Do you *honestly* think the gods are siblings?" Anji asked.

Fanakel shrugged. "Why wouldn't they be? They had to come from somewhere, did they not? It makes sense that they would be sister and brother."

She grimaced at the thought. "That feels so *wrong*. And don't say it," she snapped as Fanakel smirked.

"I wasn't going to."

"Yes, you were. What, the Broken can't possibly understand the Divine? Isn't that what the True Children believe?"

He chose his words carefully before answering her. "That…is a common thought, yes."

"You agree?"

"Did I say that?"

She snorted.

"You do recall that I'm not True, correct?" Fanakel murmured.

Anji looked at him again, then grunted. "You're True enough."

"I'm not sure whether that was meant as compliment or insult."

"Well," she said, "since the True are so wise, you can figure it out."

"Play nice," Mia cut in, giving Anji a pat on the head.

The dwarf batted her hand away, but she didn't seem to be angered by the gesture.

"All right, then, explain it to me like I'm a fool," said Fanakel. "You have two gods. If they didn't come from the same place, then where did each arise, and how were they brought together?"

Anji huffed in exasperation. "They simply *are*. They always have been, and they always will be. They came from nowhere because they have no beginning or end."

"All things have beginnings," he countered.

"You know, I'm no expert in heathen theology, but I doubt your priests would approve of this line of enquiry."

"They're not here to criticize, are they? And since we're walking through absolute proof that they're not infallible—"

"Hey, y'all?" I cut in. "Crisis of faith later. We've got company."

We'd reached the end of the meadow, which gave way to a mown patch of vegetation...and a *very* surprised trio of apparent laborers, who'd been resting and eating their meal. They jumped to their feet as we emerged from the grass, then reached for the nearest makeshift weapons, which looked like old-fashioned scythes.

I felt a bit better with my sword in my hand, and cutting my eyes to my left and right, I saw the others arm themselves with anything convenient. We didn't move, but neither did the people upon whom we'd stumbled. As we stared each other down, I took their measure: humanoid, dwarf-sized but thinner, with skin in slightly varying shades of orange and hairless heads. They wore only loose gray pants and sandals, revealing the musculature of their arms and chests...and, I absently noted, they seemed to lack both navels and nipples. What truly drew my attention were their purple eyes—all four of them—which were multifaceted like those of a housefly. A primary pair sat in the expected location, while a smaller pair grew an inch or so behind them, in front of their small, rounded ears. Peripheral vision like that would be useful for a species small enough to make a decent snack, I thought, wondering what their world must look like through so many lenses.

"Hey, Anji?" Mia murmured. "Just how good *are* your translators?"

"Let's start with mine," I whispered, then lowered my sword and took a small step toward the three. They backed off as if we were dancing, and I held up my free hand in an effort to stay them. "Uh...hello," I said, trying to sound nonthreatening. "Sorry to bother you. We're new here."

The leftmost of the three cleared his throat—or maybe hers, I couldn't tell. "Where...where did you come from?"

"Back there," I replied, turning to point to the brick

tube snaking across the land. "We didn't know...um..."

I abandoned the rest of my thought as the three fell to their knees and prostrated themselves before us. "Oh, uh...that's really not necessary," I said. "We're just travelers..."

This elicited nothing but mumbled prayers from them—or at least I assumed they were prayers, though the actual wording was lost to the ground. The four of us stood there awkwardly while the laborers paid homage, until finally, they rose but maintained a respectful distance.

"Honored children of the Great One," said their spokesperson with a deep bow, "how may your humble people serve you?"

I looked at the rest of my posse, who offered no help. "Uh...could you take us to your leader, please?"

The spokesperson beamed. "Yes, yes, of course! Please come with us."

Walking backward and with much bowing, the three waited until they were sure we were behind them, then turned and set off for the village with a spring in their step.

"Did y'all follow that?" I whispered to my group.

"Every word," Mia replied in kind. "Nice first encounter, there. All we need is a flying saucer, eh?" she said, then nudged Anji. "And as for you, I don't care about blasphemy. Your translators are *damn* good, woman, and you should be proud of yourself."

Anji's face flushed, and she began to stammer. "I...that is, I...they're poor things..."

"You know," said Fanakel, gripping her shoulder, "sometimes, it's best to accept a compliment in the spirit in which it's given."

She started to speak, then snapped her mouth shut, looked at the road, and mumbled, "Thank you."

"And, uh...I think your gods did a pretty good thing when they made you," Mia offered. "So we could give them the credit, right?"

The princess glanced up and stifled her laughter.

"You're trying, aren't you, lass?"

"So hard."

She grinned, then reached over and squeezed Mia's free hand. Mia twisted her wrist until their fingers were interlaced, and the two of them walked on in tandem, like kindergarteners on a field trip using the buddy system.

I don't know if you can see this, I thought to Terj, *but they're cute when they think they're being subtle.*

He didn't answer me, and my heart sank as we followed our obsequious escorts into town.

The settlement was larger than I'd assumed from a distance; much of what I'd seen at first was situated on top of a rise, and the rest of the buildings extended down the slope and into the grassy yellow valley. Most of the structures were a story or two high—and even then, the ceilings were better proportioned for Anji—but the trio led us down the stone-paved main street and into the lower part of town, where a four-story building sat in a place of prominence at the heart of a manicured garden. Gnarled trees with spreading golden canopies grew around it, offering shade from the midday sun, while beds of fragrant blossoms lined the pathway to the wide double doors. While the walls were built of unornamented stone, someone had trained yellow-green vines to climb them in complex patterns as living decoration.

We'd had an...*interesting* walk to get there. As we'd reached the first dwellings, half of those who'd spotted us had run in terror, but those who'd remained had been treated to the cries of our guides, who sang our praises as children of the Great One. Some had seemed unconvinced by the message, but enough had fallen in behind us that when we arrived at our destination, we did so in a jubilant parade.

It was, I thought, entirely possible that these people believed we were some sort of gods. Part of me feared what would happen when they learned the truth, while the wiser part of me told the other to shut up and *roll with it.*

Just as we reached the first of the lovely flowerbeds, the front doors flew open, and another of the hairless orange creatures appeared on the threshold. This one wore a dark purple robe, which hung unclasped to reveal a bare chest and gray trousers. The drooping around its eyes and mouth suggested age, and a silver pendant in the shape of a swirling sigil hung from its wrinkled neck.

"Rejoice, Your Holiness!" our spokesperson called from the head of the parade. "These children of the Great One have blessed us with their presence!"

The older person—a priest of some sort, presumably—cocked its head and considered our pack. "Have they, now? Be welcome," the priest said, and beckoned the four of us inside. "I will hear their message and report."

The crowd outside was still babbling excitedly as the priest closed the doors and lowered a heavy metal bar across the inside to lock them. He—or so I guessed, based on the low timbre of his voice—sighed softly, then turned to us and folded his arms. "Who are you, really?"

"You don't believe we come from the Great One?" I asked.

"I know what Her children look like. Unfortunately," he muttered. "You're rather different. Also, I've never seen Her children clothed, armed, and carrying packs, which suggests to me that there has been a...misinterpretation."

I glanced at the others, who nodded encouragement. "You're right. I told those folks out there that we'd come from the tunnel, and they assumed. We're not from around here—"

"That's evident. Well, come in," he said, heading past us deeper into the building. "I told them I'd hear your message, did I not?"

Mia, Fanakel, and I stooped slightly to avoid low-hanging lanterns as we followed the priest up to the third floor, where he led us into a comfortable sitting room. A quartet of low couches had been grouped around a fireplace—cold at the moment, given the season—and he gestured toward them in invitation. "Sit, if you like. This is a place of sanctuary, and as long as you rest within these walls, it is my duty to ensure that no harm comes to you."

After a brief hesitation, Anji removed her bag and took a seat, and we followed suit.

Our host sank onto an empty couch and regarded us— or I thought he did, at least. With his peculiar eyes, it was difficult to tell. "Will you tell me where you come from?" he asked.

I waited, but when no one jumped in with an answer, I took the initiative. "We come from a place—er, *places*— outside your world. The tunnel that runs across your land reaches a...a thin spot, I guess you might say, and if you know what you're doing—"

"Or just hit the wall in the right way," Anji offered.

"Yeah, that. You break through between your tunnel and ours." Looking to Anji and Fanakel, I asked, "Would someone like to give me a hand, here?"

Anji jumped into the breach. "I come from Ildon. The elf is of Honslia," she said, nodding to Fanakel. "Two other worlds are connected with ours within the Aen."

The priest sat up a little straighter. "*Ah*. You come from Beyond."

I could almost hear the capitalization. "Beyond what, exactly?"

"Beyond our world," he replied. "Unara."

"Unara," Anji repeated, trying it out. "We call this place Outside."

"I suppose that's fitting," the priest said. "Are you lost? Did you intend to come here?"

"Well, we don't exactly know where we are," I chimed in, "but yeah, we meant to go beyond the tunnels...the known tunnels, I mean. You see, these monsters keep pouring in from your world—"

He nodded vigorously. "You speak of the children of

the Great One, may She show us mercy."

"Uh…all right," I mumbled. "You know about them?"

"Oh, certainly. The tunnel through which you came runs from the mountain where She lives to the thin point, then travels back again."

"Like this?" Mia asked, tracing a bulbous U in the air.

"Precisely. It allows Her children to reach the rift between our worlds and go Beyond, to spread." Cocking his head, he asked, "How *did* you leave the tunnel? Has a hole developed?"

"We found one," Fanakel lied with a straight face.

The priest grimaced and stood. "Excuse me. I must arrange a repair crew immediately. Most of the children never leave the tunnel, but I do not wish to risk a visit from them tonight."

When he hurried down the staircase, I looked at the others and spoke softly. "Think this is a trap?"

"That's not the feeling I have," said Mia. "And if things do get squirrelly, I can try to hypnotize him into letting us go."

"Are we sure the priest is male?" asked Fanakel.

She shrugged. "We might find out if I turn on the charm."

"Or you might kill him. We have no idea how your power affects these…uh…"

"Unarans?" Anji suggested.

"Sure. And since we're sitting in the nicest building in town, I think the locals might *strongly* take offense if we accidentally killed their priest." Fanakel glanced at our bags, then said, "Manners be damned, I'm starving. Do we have any of that crumbly mixed stuff?"

"You mean granola?" Mia asked.

"Chunky, grainy, has dried fruits and these little brown sweet bits…"

"Yup." She fished a sealed plastic bag from her gear and handed it over. "Stole this from the back of the pantry. It may be past the expiration date, but it shouldn't kill you."

I smiled sadly as Fanakel popped the seal and dug in. Uncle Malachi had had few true pleasures, but he'd been a sucker for the homemade granola from Cole's Cuts as long as I'd known him, and Dad had usually slipped a bag or two into my bike basket when I made delivery runs to the cabin. Somehow, I didn't think my uncle would mind sharing.

The granola bag had made it up and down the couches several times before the priest finally returned. "My apologies," he said, resuming his seat. "The village is in a festive mood with your coming, and it took a few...*creative* statements to convince them of the pressing need to patch the tunnel hole. Which I've now seen, incidentally," he continued, "and something tells me it was not a natural occurrence."

We deployed our best poker faces as we finished our handfuls of granola.

"In any case," he said, "we should be safe as long as the hole is filled by sundown. The children seldom venture abroad into the light."

"Might be a slight problem, there," I replied, patting the hilt at my side. "See the blue-green crystals in the sword?"

"I would have to be blind to miss them. Are they not glass?"

"Solid Aen," Anji explained. "Your *children* are drawn to it. Since that sword is now the nearest source..."

"Let's just hope your patch holds," I murmured.

The priest swallowed hard but maintained his composure. "What do you want with us?"

I shrugged. "Answers would be a good starting point. For instance, why the hell do you shunt your children into the Beyond?"

"Because the Great One commands it," he answered without hesitation. "When She came to us in the long ago, She ordered that Her children be sent beyond this world, where they could grow and thrive. Who are we to question the will of the gods?"

Anji began to bristle. "The gods would never—"

"Hold it," I told her, then turned back to the priest. "Putting aside issues of theology for the moment, the problem is that these 'children' are ravenous monsters. They kill indiscriminately in the Beyond, and so they're slaughtered wherever they're found."

His jaw began to droop.

"Why are you surprised?" I pressed. "You ran out of here to get the tunnel fixed—obviously, you *know* the little darlings are deadly."

"Well...yes," he admitted, "I know they are born hungry, but are you seriously telling me that when we help the Great One's children leave this place..."

"You're sending them to their deaths," Fanakel finished.

While it was difficult for me to fully read the priest's expression, there was no mistaking his distress. "But...but it's been ordained..."

"Maybe there's a better solution," I said gently. "One in which hordes of, uh...divine children don't get sent away from here to die. Maybe they should remain closer to their mother, you know?"

"But they can't," he protested. "We don't have the resources to sustain them all! The Great One has said—"

"Has She? Or has someone perhaps misinterpreted Her command? Because frankly, it seems odd to me that a mother would send her kids away to be killed," I said, deciding to leave my own mother out of the equation.

He mulled that over, rubbing his chin as he thought. After a time, he raised his head and faced me. "I am not one to ponder such notions—I'm but a village priest. You need to speak with my superiors in the capital, or possibly the queen herself. They would be able to better explain to you the will of the Great One."

I glanced at the others and saw their frustration. "And

how far is this capital of yours?"

"Two days' ride. I could take you," he offered. "I was planning to set off in the morning, so your timing is excellent."

The rest of our party began to nod, and I said, "Thank you, that would be wonderful. But, uh…there's no chance that we could leave today, is there?"

His head tilted. "You are in a great hurry?"

Again, I patted my sword. "There's someone trapped in here. Until this matter is resolved, he's stuck, and he's in severe pain. We need to get to someone who can help us as quickly as possible."

The priest frowned. "What manner of being could be trapped within a *sword*?"

"An elemental. Don't ask me the process—this is all new to me, too—but they're creatures of energy, and he's hurting. So please, is there any way we can leave now?"

Though he shook his head, his expression softened. "I am sorry, but no. Not until daylight. It's unsafe to be abroad at night."

"Robbers on the road?" asked Anji. "If so, we'll gladly provide security."

"No, not that. It's, uh…it's a precaution."

Her brow knit. "Against…"

The priest hesitated, then sighed. "You saw how the people here reacted when they believed you were the Great One's children? The tunnel is firm and was built well, and few outside the priesthood have any true conception of what the children look like. *I* know the children are hungry and prone to hunt, but that is not common knowledge." Shifting on his couch, he murmured, "Travel at night is reserved only for the direst of emergencies. We preach that the Great One commands this. In truth, it's a protective measure the high priests have long enforced, just in case of holes in the tunnel."

I started to argue with him, but that time, Anji cut me off. "If that's the case, then you should post a guard on the tunnel tonight. That sword will draw them here, and you may learn just how strong your masonry actually is." Giving the priest a hard look, she added, "Best be sure you don't put someone on watch who might hear scrabbling within the tunnel and try to help the creatures join us. I think we can all imagine how that might end."

The priest's orange complexion paled slightly at that, and bidding us make ourselves comfortable, he quickly took his leave.

I didn't want to spend the night in that little village, but things could have been worse. At least no one had locked us up yet, which had happened with unfortunate frequency in the last months.

The priest, who'd returned in time for dinner and finally introduced himself as Dagerah oo'Fin sha'Acanna—Dagerah, son of Fin, born in Acanna, he'd explained in the face of our befuddlement—had given us the run of a guest dormitory in the temple, a room with simple single beds for ten. Unfortunately, as the beds were scaled for the locals, the three of us above five feet tall had done a bit of creative rearranging to accommodate our oversized frames, though Anji, who seemed able to sleep anywhere, had settled in with a sigh and quickly passed out. Mia and Fanakel had soon followed suit, but I lay awake in the darkness, filtering through the information Dagerah had given us over the evening meal.

We'd popped through the tunnel near the village of Acanna, a little farming town of no great repute. Most of the settlements close to the tunnel were similar in size and stature, clusters of homes and perhaps a few businesses surrounded by open pastures and fields. Dagerah, who was rather frank with us after a couple glasses of a deep green liquid that smelled to me like pumpkin spice rubbing alcohol, said that the design was intentional: the high priests had ordained that the area near the tunnel be left underpopulated, ostensibly because the traveling children should not be subjected to the noise and sounds of city life, but in truth because they feared the consequences of a tunnel break in a high-density environment. "I don't know why the Great One's children can be so vicious," he'd confessed, refilling his cup. "If my superiors know, they don't see fit to inform those of us of lesser orders. But since showing the children in a negative light could cause the laity to doubt the benevolence of the Great One, we take pains to disguise the...unpleasant side."

"So why tell us?" Mia had asked.

He'd lifted his glass to her in salute. "Because you've already seen them. What's the point in subterfuge? You wouldn't believe me if I insisted they were gentle and harmless."

The tunnel was contained entirely within Banilgh, one of the kingdoms of Unara. "While it is our great honor and blessing to dwell in the shadow of the Great One," Dagerah had noted, "proximity does have its price. Banilgh built most of the tunnel to send the children on their way, though our neighbors send supplies and crews to assist in the general maintenance."

Dagerah—and now the rest of us—were bound for the Banilghish capital, Volng, at first light. There were, said the priest, a series of waystations along the route so that travelers would not be caught in the darkness. They were nothing fancy, he cautioned, but they were clean and decently maintained, and he volunteered to pay our lodging fee.

Fearing a long two days in a wagon, I burrowed down under my borrowed blankets, holding the cursed sword to my chest. I didn't think Dagerah would try to steal it— even if he did, it would inevitably return to me—but I hated to leave Terj propped in the corner.

He was in pain. My friend was hurting, and I couldn't help him—all I was doing was lengthening his torment by lingering in- Acanna. Our host refused to be swayed, however, and since I certainly had no clue about how to get to the capital on my own, we were stuck for the night. So there I lay, listening to my companions' slow breathing and running my fingers over the stitching on the sword's leather sheath. Though part of me knew it was stupid to cuddle up with the blade as though it were a particularly spiky teddy bear, I couldn't bring myself to leave Terj to suffer alone.

Hey, you, I thought, aiming for him alone. *I don't know if you can hear me, but if you can, I'm so sorry. This priest here is going to take us to someone who might be able to help, but he won't leave until morning. I tried, I told him what's going on with you, but he wouldn't budge, and I don't know the way…*

I didn't know what else to say. Hell, I had no idea if Terj could even sense me, or if too much of him was being used to keep the sword together in that Aen-less place for him to have any concept of what was happening around him.

But then, ever so faintly, I heard him whisper my name.

I'm here, I said, clutching the sword, and stared wide-eyed at the shadows as my heart raced. *Terj, I'm here. Can you speak to me? Are you okay?*

The silent seconds stretched between us, and I'd almost given up hope of a response when his voice floated into my mind like a sigh in the wind: *Sleep.*

Terj?

Sleep, Susan.

I tried for the next ten minutes to get a response from him, but once again, Terj had fallen quiet, and my efforts were for naught. Still, I held the sword close and reassured him that I was there until fatigue claimed me.

CHAPTER 10

A firm hand shook me awake, and I cracked open my eyes to see Fanakel standing by my makeshift bed, shirtless and holding a candle. Even unwashed and stubbly, the elf wasn't the worst view I could have had first thing in the morning…which, I realized, considering the candles sitting around the room, had yet to arrive. "Wazzt?" I mumbled, tasting something sour and unidentifiable.

"The priest says we'll leave at first light," he told me. "I thought you might want to bathe before then."

I groaned in the affirmative, left my sword atop the rumpled covers, and shuffled with Fanakel to the guest bathroom, an unadorned but functional space with a stone floor and windows set high in the wall for privacy. The sound of running water drew my attention to a plain wooden screen, behind which a deep gray tub sunk into the floor was rapidly filling with warm water. Whatever else could be said for the good people of the kingdom of Banilgh, at least they'd embraced indoor plumbing.

"Did you see this?" asked Anji, who'd already washed and dressed, and was combing her short, scruffy beard in front of the mirror. She pointed to the sink below it, then flipped a handle to turn on the water. "Looks familiar, does it not?"

I nodded. "Got to love pipes."

"If one lacks the Aen, I suppose one must do what one must." She cut the flow, then studied her reflection and snarled her nose. "I look like a *child*."

"You look fine," I said, slipping behind the screen,

then tossed my clothes over the top and sank into the steaming bath. My sore muscles relaxed in the warm water, and I spent a moment just luxuriating there before wading to the side to examine the soaps on offer. The bathtub was about three feet deep, and I imagined that the locals could practically swim in it.

The sky was just lightening toward purple—I was never going to adjust to *that*—when Dagerah knocked and checked in. Despite his drinking the night before, he seemed none the worse for wear—if anything, he appeared to have mellowed somewhat toward us. "I've packed breakfast for the road," he said, and glanced toward the window. "We should leave soon. Are you ready?"

Following him downstairs with our gear, we found an open wooden wagon standing outside the temple, hitched to a pair of the six-legged creatures we'd seen grazing the day before—lakils, he called them. "Peachy," I muttered to Mia as I stowed my gear and climbed up. She followed me, grimacing as she made herself as comfortable as she could on the low plank bench. Naturally, it was scaled for its makers, and so Mia, Fanakel, and I sat scrunched like parents trying out their kindergarteners' classroom chairs.

As Dagerah coaxed the beasts into motion and we rolled through the pale dawn, I asked, "So…this road goes to all the way to Volng?"

His head turned slightly toward me, and while I still couldn't read the expression in his eyes, he sounded surprised by the question. "Uh…I suppose so, yes."

"You don't know the way?" Anji queried.

"Oh, no, I know the way," he replied, chuckling. "Sorry, I didn't mean to frighten you. I haven't tried to travel to the capital by road in many a year. We'll take it as far as the waystation."

I glanced at the others, but they seemed similarly perplexed. "Waystation?"

The priest nodded. "I spoke of them to you yesterday, did I not? The attendants will tend to my wagon and my girls here while I'm away, and we'll be off with the morning departure."

"Departure in *what*?" Mia whispered to me, but I shrugged and let the matter drop.

We hadn't been on the road more than half an hour before a long stone building came into view. "The waystation," said Dagerah, pointing to the structure up ahead. "As I mentioned, it's nothing fancy, but we should be comfortable at night. Well, uh…" Turning back to examine us again, he winced. "*Anji* should be comfortable. I'm afraid we're unaccustomed to travelers of the rest of your, um…stature."

"If worst comes to worst, we did pack tents," Mia offered.

Dagerah looked horrified at the notion. "Surely we can do better than that. I'll have a word with the priest in charge of the waystation where we'll stop tonight—she's an old friend."

"Your priests cater to travelers?" Fanakel asked, frowning.

"Of course. The gods prize hospitality to stranger and friend alike. We ensure that all who travel this way do so in peace." He paused, then asked, "Yours have a different function, I suppose?"

"Uh…the rites, the ceremonies, discerning the will of the Divine…"

"But no direct service as such?"

"Nothing like that," said Fanakel, gesturing toward the nearing waystation.

Dagerah grunted. "Curious. There's nothing quite like encountering a traveler from a distant land to make one realize just how much of one's 'normal' is anything but."

"Well, *I* think this is lovely, so thank you," said Mia, doing her best to smooth over any friction while the day was young.

The priest smiled and coaxed his lakils onward.

Soon, we pulled up to the waystation and proceeded to

the wide barn doors, where an attendant in purple stood on duty. "Gods' blessings be on you," Dagerah called, pulling the lakils to a halt. "I have a reservation for ten days' maintenance."

The attendant stared up at us, mouth slightly agape.

"Pay no mind to my companions," the priest told him, and quickly dismounted. "Come, now, my son, let us make the arrangements before we miss our carriage."

Something in his tone drew the attendant back to his job, and he allowed Dagerah to direct his attention to his file of papers. A few coins changed hands, and then Dagerah returned to us and nodded. "Collect your things. We should be away."

Once I'd willed my sword invisible—I didn't want to worsen the perceived threat—he led us from the barn to an arched passenger entrance barely six feet high, and we traversed a short tunnel through the waystation to a wide platform beyond, upon which a few people loitered with their luggage. A pair in red robes sat together on a bench to my left, while another bench to my right was occupied by a person in a hooded black cloak. The hood was down, exposing the person's hairless orange scalp. Beside them sat a woven basket about the size of a basketball, which they kept touching as if for reassurance that it hadn't wandered away.

But it was the long, dark shape on the far side of the platform that made me laugh in surprise.

"What's so amusing?" Anji murmured.

"That." I pointed to the "carriage," which had to be a sort of train. Six metal-clad passenger cars were lined up behind a lightly smoking engine, and when I craned my neck to see past the end, I caught a glimpse of silvery rails shining in the morning light. "We have something similar."

"Do you?" She regarded the conveyance with evident mistrust. "Is that…smoke?"

"Probably a steam engine," said Mia. "You stoke the fire, water boils, and the steam pushes pistons. We've mostly moved on from steam locomotives, but they do the trick."

"So…there's a *fire* in that front box?"

Mia shrugged. "Yeah?"

"Is that not dangerous?"

I looked at Anji, then to Mia, and murmured, "Maybe we should talk about combustion engines at some point."

"I'm sorry, *what*?" the princess demanded, but Dagerah shepherded us toward a ticket window before Anji had long to fret about the implications of that phrase.

"Hello," he told the ticket attendant, who had pushed their chair away from the window in fright at our approach. "Dagerah oo'Fin sha'Acanna, checking in for Volng, and four more seats for my friends here."

The attendant's mouth opened and closed a few times before they managed to speak. "What…what manner of—"

"Travelers," Dagerah smoothly interrupted in the patient voice of one comforting a scared child, "bound to see the queen and the high priest. I'm escorting them. Now, if you would be so kind…"

It was, I mused, disconcerting to be unable to tell where a Unaran was looking, but my sixth sense suggested that at least one or two of the attendant's eyes remained on us until Dagerah completed the purchase and led us away.

A few minutes later, another group of purple-clad attendants opened the doors to the train cars, and we followed Dagerah aboard. While different from the photos of old-timey trains I knew, the car was recognizable: pairs of padded seats flanking a wide central aisle, an open area around the doors for mingling and movement, and metal racks overhead for luggage. Globular oil lanterns hung from the ceiling every few rows, glowing softly in the shaded car. The gray carpet muffled our footsteps as we found seats near the back—Anji and Mia shared a row, I sat across from them, and Fanakel and Dagerah selected the open aisle seats in front of us. With the car barely a quarter full, we had plenty of room to sprawl, or at least to stretch our oversized legs, and the rest of the passengers gave us a *wide* berth.

When the doors closed, an attendant on the platform hit a large gong, and the train jerked into motion. Anji and Fanakel bore the experience stoically enough, but I grinned—I'd never been on an antique train, and no matter how long the ride, it beat the hell out of two days spent plodding behind Dagerah's lakils.

As the train left the waystation and began to pick up speed, the priest leaned toward us and quietly asked, "Do you see the boy and girl in red near the front of the carriage?"

I peered up the aisle and spotted the pair from the platform. "Yeah."

"They've been selected to join the Great One."

Mia frowned. "Meaning?"

"Well," he explained with a little smile, "every so often, the high priest consults with the Great One, and She chooses new acolytes, who are brought to the mountain where She dwells to attend to Her. It's a high honor," he continued, "and a sign of great blessing upon the acolytes' families and villages. They will never leave Her presence, nor will they ever want for comfort." Chuckling softly, he said, "I used to pray that She would choose me, but alas, She still has better options. So I serve Her in a lesser capacity."

"If, uh...the Great One selects you," said Fanakel, "can you refuse?"

Dagerah cocked his head. "Are you in the habit of refusing your gods?"

"Hypothetically?"

"I've never heard of anyone trying to reject an honor like *that*."

"But...to leave your home, to never return..."

The priest smiled again. "While I have not been so fortunate as to be called into Her presence, the high priests teach that it is a joyous place, and the pain felt upon leaving Her is greater than the greatest sadness we know. What parent or child or spouse or friend would deny such bliss to a loved one? Trust me," he said, "those two with us know what happiness awaits them."

I sneaked occasional glances toward the two at the front over the next hour or so. With the few other passengers in the car clustering near them, I overheard snippets of conversation, mostly congratulations at their selection. The chosen seemed like older teenagers, excited and a little awkward, and they explained that they were newly contracted to be married. This was the greatest wedding present they could have received—to be united with each other in the presence of the Great One.

As I eavesdropped, Mia tapped my shoulder. "There's a bathroom behind us. Want to join me?"

That wasn't a true request. I stepped into the aisle, and Mia and Anji followed me into the cubicle at the back of the car. The little room only had two stalls, and as it was scaled for people half my size, cramming the three of us in there didn't leave much space for breathing, but Anji stepped atop a closed toilet to make room and bring herself to the neighborhood of our height.

"Is anyone else getting creepy cult vibes from the kids in red?" Mia asked, leaning in close to keep her voice down. "Because this feels like 'throw the virgin in the volcano' time to me."

Anji's face twisted in confusion. "*What?*"

"It's nothing we actually do, it's just a story," Mia explained. "Weird, remote cult demands a virgin sacrifice to appease their supposed volcano god, hero sweeps in and rescues her, the end." Looking back and forth between us, she said, "I get the feeling that the lucky ones selected don't have to worry about anything for the rest of their lives because they don't live long after meeting their god. Know what I'm saying?"

"That had crossed my mind," Anji replied. "Think

about it: the people believe this Great One of theirs is a wonderful, benevolent being who sends her children beyond this world to spread, yes? But most of them have no idea what those children are actually like. If we assume, as we must, that the child favors the parent in some respect..."

"The Great One ain't so great," I finished. "Maybe we need to kill her."

"You...want to kill a *god*?" Anji asked.

"What if she's not a god?" Mia countered.

"These people worship her as one. We can't just march into their capital and announce that we've come to slay their deity."

Mia arched a brow. "So we keep that bit on the down-low."

"On the...*oh*," she replied, catching Mia's meaning. "But how? And suppose we manage it—how would you like to escape this place if its devout citizens find out we killed the creature they worship?" When Mia and I weren't immediately forthcoming with an answer, she said, "Speaking for myself, if a group of bizarre-looking strangers announced that the High King and High Queen were really...I don't know, child-devouring monsters, and that they'd come to kill my gods, I certainly wouldn't believe them, first, and second, I'd do everything in my power to stop them."

"Anji's got a point," I murmured. "And forget the Great One—we don't know what we're dealing with when it comes to Unarans. All we really know is that they're short—"

"Careful, lass," the princess grumbled.

"Relatively speaking, and some of them are farmers. They've obviously got some degree of tech, considering this train."

"But no electricity that I've seen," said Mia. "Did you notice the lights in here? And the candles this morning?"

"That doesn't mean they haven't developed guns."

Anji winced. "I've not spotted any…"

"Yet. Again, we just don't know."

"So how do we want to play this?" Mia asked us.

When Anji didn't jump in with a plan, I ventured, "Diplomatically. Let's see if their high priest or the queen are willing to hear us out. The high priest, at least, has to know that the 'children' are a problem. If we can convince them to send their monsters elsewhere, maybe that will be sufficient to break the sword and free Terj."

Mia's forehead creased. "You really think that'll be enough? And how would one convey that development to a freaking weapon?"

"Ganeel said it should fall apart once the threat is eliminated."

"Would a treaty count as elimination? Could there be a workaround?"

We turned to Anji, who shrugged. "I'm no master, and I don't know how Heart's Blood was forged. Perhaps, once the threat is removed, a better forger could be convinced to help us."

"Unless your dad wants to keep the Watcher on standby in case this queen or whomever change their minds," Mia pointed out. "Or the freaking elves protest. Or Suze's mother throws a fit."

"One step at a time," I said. "We get to Volng, we find the folks in charge, we work something out about the monster problem, and if that doesn't do the trick, we get the hell back into the Aen so Terj isn't suffering as badly while we figure out plan B."

Anji and Mia nodded. "That's a start," said the dwarf. "How do we tell Fanakel?"

I tapped my temple. "Quietly. Leave it to me."

She seemed taken aback. "You can…"

"Elemental, remember? You've certainly heard Terj in your mind."

"But…*here*? Beyond the Aen?"

"It's not dependent on the Aen. I'll fill him in

eventually," I said, then flushed a toilet to help cover our tracks.

Back at our seats, I tried to play it cool while I fished for information. "Hey, Dagerah?" I asked, tapping him on the shoulder.

He turned. "Is everything all right?"

"Oh, just great," I fibbed. "May I ask you something about this, uh, carriage?"

"Ask whatever you like. I'm no expert, but I will do my best."

"Thanks," I replied, feeling a touch more confident about my scheme. "So...I noticed the vapor rising from the front car. What powers the carriage? Do you burn wood? Grass? Coal?"

The priest's head tilted. "Burn?"

"Yeah. This is a steam engine, isn't it? What makes the steam?"

At that, he laughed aloud. "Magic, of course. All carriages are driven by mages."

"Magic," I echoed, my confidence evaporating as quickly as it had appeared.

"Yes, magic. I'm afraid I've never had the knack, but the gods have seen fit to bless some of us with their gifts." He paused, then asked, "Do your gods not show their favor in such fashion?"

"It's, uh...it's a little different for us," I managed.

"Indeed? I suppose that explains your confusion, though I confess that the idea of a *fire* driving the carriage..." He chuckled and shook his head. "That seems unsafe, does it not?"

"I guess so," I said, deciding not to mention the book of old rail disasters I'd found in the library in the fourth grade, which had given me a healthy fear of burning trains until Dad had explained that the modern versions mostly ran on diesel...which, upon further consideration, wasn't all that much better.

Glancing across the aisle as Dagerah turned around

again, I noticed Mia watching me with a questioning frown. *The freaking train runs on magic,* I told her. *They've got magic. Shit.*

While she couldn't answer me in kind, her quick grimace said enough.

So if we do need to kill ourselves a Great One and the villagers get pissed, they're not going to come after us with pitchforks. There's no telling what they'll have.

She cut her eyes toward the bathrooms again in invitation.

No, too soon. Just…ugh, I griped, *why couldn't we have wandered into a world going through an industrial revolution, huh? I could deal with steam engines, oil lamps, maybe the odd rifle. But no, these folks have* <u>*magic*</u> *steam engines! What the hell, Mia?*

She shrugged.

What's next? Magic guns? Magic lasers? Magic flamethrowers? I've got a fucking magic sword, and I'm feeling a little outclassed right now.

At that, Mia leaned across the aisle and patted my knee. "Take a nap, Suze, okay?"

"It's too early for a nap."

"Then pretend you're going back to bed."

Though I glared at her, I slid further into the seat and rested my head against the window, telling myself I'd just close my eyes for a few minutes. But moving vehicles have hypnotic abilities, and soon, I drifted off to the rhythm of the wheels.

The wheels driven by a magical steam engine that was taking us toward a distant city, where we might try to kill a beloved god.

Shit.

The first day passed without serious incident, a long, surprisingly speedy ride by villages and fields. Occasionally, we passed a train going in the other direction, and once, we stopped for a herd of stubborn lakils on the tracks, but no calamity befell us as we rode onward. While I ate a late lunch from the stash in my bag, I looked out the window and considered the mountains rising in the distance, the seat of the Great One. Our train wasn't heading straight toward them, Dagerah told me—Volng sat to the southeast of the range, within sight of the peaks but far enough from them that the city's noise and smells wouldn't offend the god dwelling therein.

And far from the tunnel, I noticed. I glimpsed it on occasion out the windows on the other side of the car, but we finally made a bend away from the brick tube and headed toward more inhabited districts.

As twilight began to descend, the train pulled up at a waystation about twice the size of the one we'd left in Acanna, a three-story structure of pale gray stone with graceful arched doors. While most of the disembarking crowd hung near the pair in red, as if hoping their good fortune might rub off, Dagerah led us onto the platform and straight to a startled attendant. "Gods' blessings be on you, my son," he said before the attendant could ask any questions. "Please inform Vashir that Dagerah has come and needs to speak with her outside."

The attendant's training must have kicked in, as he hurried into the building without demanding to know what sort of creatures we might be. We stepped out of the way and waited, and a few minutes later, a person in a gray robe emerged from the door through which the attendant had run. The newcomer was dressed much as Dagerah was—gray trousers, no shirt, silver sigil pendant—and the open robe flapped as they drew near.

Dagerah smiled. "Vashir."

"Dagerah," the other priest replied in a voice of a decidedly feminine register. Other than that, I could find virtually nothing to distinguish her as female, either a testament to my ignorance of the species or evidence of minimal dimorphism. She paused a few feet from him and folded her arms as she looked up at the four of us standing behind him. "I...I have questions, old friend, but honestly, I'm not certain where to begin."

"At the beginning, then," he said, and gestured toward her as he turned to us. "This is Vashir oo'Sanival sha'Joh, the priest of this waystation. Vashir, my companions have come to us from Beyond.

"*Beyond?*" she whispered. Her eyes didn't widen—given what I'd seen of Unarans, I didn't that was possible—but her voice betrayed her shock. "How?"

"Through the tunnel. An opening formed near Acanna."

"One that I trust you have closed—"

"Of course, of course," he soothed. "But these travelers have questions that can only be answered in Volng. Questions pertaining to the Great One, may She show us mercy," he added quietly.

Vashir's head tilted. "Do they come with tidings of Her children?"

"Well...yes," he allowed, and pointed toward the warm lights of the building behind her. "Perhaps we should discuss this in private, hmm?"

With a grunt, Vashir turned on her heel and swept back into the building, and Dagerah shooed us in after her. Dodging light fixtures, we ducked through the narrow, low-ceilinged corridors, up a twisting flight of stairs, and into the priest's apartment. As she bolted the door behind us, she said, "My apologies for not suggesting the elevator, but I thought it best to draw minimal attention from other travelers. Now, *what* has happened?"

"Do any of you want to take a crack at this?" I muttered to my companions, who awkwardly shrugged. Mia motioned me on, and so I cleared my throat and said, "Basically, the children of your Great One are bloodthirsty monsters. When you kick them off your world, they end up in ours, and our only option is to kill or be killed."

One hand went to her breast. "You...you *kill* Her children?" she whispered, aghast.

"It's her children or our children," said Anji, "and no one in the Beyond recognizes the Great One as a god. Under those conditions, what would you choose?"

Vashir paused to consider that, her brow furrowing. "I suppose...if one knew nothing of the power and blessing of the Great One..."

"Blessing?" Fanakel echoed. "You consider her children such a *blessing* that you foist them onto us! If you're so fond of them, why not keep them here?"

"I know not why She ordained that Her children be sent elsewhere, but She did," Vashir insisted. "And we obey."

"I understand," I soothed, catching Anji's reluctant nod. "You're trying to do what your god wants you to do. Our concern, however, is that we're constantly under siege by her children, and they've *very* effective killers. Surely your god doesn't intend for her children to kill people who've done her no harm, right?"

Neither priest had an answer for that.

"Anyway, that's why Dagerah is taking us to the capital," I explained. "We're looking for answers, and maybe your high priest knows how we could work something out so that we're not constantly having to defend ourselves against your, uh...émigrés."

"I'm no theologian," Mia interjected, "but I have to assume that the Great One would prefer that *some* of her children live. Maybe there's been a miscommunication along the way. I mean, you two don't seem like the sort of people who'd want to see little kids eaten in their beds."

Vashir vehemently shook her head. "No, of course not. This is...troubling," she said, in what might have been the understatement of the night. To Dagerah, she asked, "Have you alerted the high priest to your coming?"

"I sent a message last night," he replied. "We're expected. But for this evening—"

"A private room, I should think. No need to frighten the others." She looked us up and down, then planted her hands on her slim hips. "Tall, aren't you?"

"If we could squish some beds together, we could make this work," I told her.

"I suppose that's the best we can do in these circumstances. But for now, sit," she offered, gesturing to the cushions scattered around the main room of her apartment. "I believe it would be best if you dined with me tonight."

The morning arrived with the sound of an insistent bell, which echoed throughout the waystation. "The wakeup alarm," Dagerah told us over our quick breakfast. "It would be inhospitable to allow travelers to miss the morning carriage, after all."

After saying our goodbyes to Vashir, we boarded the car we'd selected the day before and resumed our seats in the back. The pair in red once again sat near the front, as happy as ever, as did the person with the black cloak and the large basket. When the other passengers sneaked glances at us, I smiled and tried to seem non-threatening, but given how bizarre I had to look to Unaran eyes, I suspected that the effort was futile.

We'd only traveled for an hour or two when a loud crack sounded from the other side of the car. The person with the basket jumped and quickly opened the lid, then gasped and turned toward us. "You, sir," they said, pointing to Dagerah, "you're a priest?"

He beamed as he slid from his seat. "Is it time?"

The person nodded.

"First one?"

Again, they nodded, and Dagerah chuckled gently. "It's nothing to worry about. This, like all things, is in the gods' hands, my daughter. What's your name?"

"Hibil," she said softly. "Hibil oo'Dafin sha'Ton."

"Dagerah. May I see?"

I stood to watch as he approached her and peered

down into the basket. "A good size," he said, then reached within and nodded. "And active. I can speed this along, if you like, or you can let it happen in its own time. By the end of this journey, I should think." His smile widened as he raised his face toward hers again. "But there's no harm in helping the process. Are you ready?"

"I...yes. Yes, please."

Carefully, he pulled a mottled white and tan item from the basket—an egg, I realized, albeit one big enough for an ostrich. A dark fissure had formed near the wider end, and he flipped the egg around in his arms to orient the crack toward the ceiling. His knuckles gently rapped on the shell around the crack, and then he maneuvered a finger into the opening, widening it and pulling away pieces of the shell. After a moment's work, the hole was large enough for his hand, and he reached in to break off larger chunks.

"What the heck..." Mia whispered, standing in the aisle for a better view.

Suddenly, I realized why the Unaran torso was unmarred. "That's a baby," I whispered back.

"You think?"

Before I could answer, the broken shell fell into the basket, leaving Dagerah holding a tiny, wet, orange bundle. He eased the baby's neck straight and unbent its curled limbs, and as the cool air of the carriage hit it, the newborn began to wail.

"A son," he told Hibil, who eagerly reached for her crying child. "A strong one, judging by those lungs."

The rest of the passengers laughed with relief as she held the baby to her chest, warming him against her skin. "*Thank* you," she told Dagerah.

"Do you have supplies for him? He won't need to eat for a few days, but if you soak a cloth with water, he'll suckle at it."

"Yes, I came prepared," she replied, jutting her chin toward the bag above her, "just in case. We're meeting his father tonight—we were meant to be together for the birth, but I fell ill and was waylaid for a few days…"

"Then why don't we share the happy news with him now, hmm? Is your speaker—"

"Here." She shifted the baby and reached into a pocket of her cloak, then pulled out an item about the size and shape of the maladetans' folding communication devices. Dagerah depressed a button to open it and held it toward her, and Hibil slid a finger up and down the inner surface until she tapped it twice. A few seconds later, a light flashed on her face, and she grinned into the apparent camera. "My love?"

"Is everything all right?" asked a slightly tinny male voice. "Did you make your carriage?"

"I did. And with an extra passenger," she said as Dagerah tilted the device toward the baby. "Meet your son."

His wordless exclamation spoke volumes, and when I glanced at Mia, she pressed a hand to her breast and smiled.

"May I trade with you?" Dagerah asked Hibil, and passed her the device as he took the much calmer baby. "Where are we?" he asked, looking around the car.

"We just passed Fogash," another passenger replied.

"Very good." Cradling his burden, he placed his hand on the newborn's forehead and said, "Grow in peace and with the gods' blessing, Tarak oo'Hibil sha'Fogash, and may the Great One always favor you. As you are born a traveler, may the gods lead you along the right paths and bring you safely to your destination."

He handed the baby back to his mother, and she and the new father chatted for a moment before the rest of the passengers crowded around to congratulate her. Dagerah returned to us and sat with a contented sigh. "One of my favorite duties," he murmured, smiling. "I've named all six of my nephews and nieces. It's such a privilege to be there at hatching, you know?" He looked around at us and asked, "Do your priests do likewise? Attend at hatching?"

"Uh...not exactly," said Mia. "Priests tend to get involved later. Most of us have doctors around at birth, at least where Suze and I come from."

"Midwives for us," offered Anji, and Fanakel nodded.

The priest's head tilted. "Are your young generally unhealthy?"

We four traded glances, and when no one rushed to answer Dagerah, I leaned closer to him and mumbled, "We don't hatch. Females carry our young to birth."

He pulled away from me, shocked. "You...you *what*?"

"Yeah, it's a whole thing. Kind of messy. Pretty painful, apparently, but that's the way it goes."

"Got to say, that looks a whole lot neater," Mia added, cutting her eyes to Hibil. "Though I'd be nervous about breaking my kid's egg open prematurely..." Her voice faded, and she coughed. "Uh, Dagerah? What's she doing?"

We looked up the aisle to find Hibil on the edge of her seat, holding little Tarak under the armpits. The naked baby was bouncing on his spread feet and squealing as he looked up at his mother, and she cooed down at him.

"How the hell is he holding his *head* up?" I marveled.

"Forget his head, he's almost got his balance!" said Fanakel.

Dagerah's expression suggested deep bemusement. "The moving carriage isn't ideal, but the little one will compensate quickly enough. By lunchtime, he'll be walking just fine."

"Oh, um...that's good," I replied, and waited until Dagerah turned around again to contact the others: *Just thinking here, but maybe, as a safety measure, we shouldn't mention that our newborns are squishy and helpless.*

Anji grunted her agreement, and Fanakel, once he calmed from the surprise communication, locked eyes with me and grimaced.

By the time we disembarked that evening, Tarak was able to run from the carriage and into his father's arms, and we stood well out of the way as Dagerah negotiated our accommodations with the priest of the waystation. While he was occupied, the duo in red approached us, heads cocking inquisitively. "What manner of beings are you?" the female of the pair asked without preamble. "There has been much discussion at the other end of our compartment. Are you gods? Have you blessed that priest with your company?"

While common wisdom might suggest that the prudent answer to "Are you a god?" is a hearty "Yes," I didn't think we could maintain the charade. "Travelers from Beyond," I murmured, keeping my voice low. "We seek an audience with your high priest."

That answer seemed to sit well with the two. "From *Beyond*?" the male asked. "Then you have been blessed by the Great One and Her children."

"We absolutely have," Fanakel cut in, lying through his perfect teeth. "But our priests have some questions for your priests, so Dagerah is being kind enough to escort us."

They nodded. "Safe journey to you, then," said the girl. "We may not see you in the morning."

Fanakel frowned. "No?"

She pointed to a two-car train parked in front of ours. "We leave you here. By this time tomorrow, we will be in Her presence."

The chosen two looked like they were on their way to an all-expenses-paid eternal Disney vacation instead of a remote mountain.

"If I may ask one question?" I ventured. They gestured for me to continue, and I said, "What, uh...what will you *do* with the Great One?"

"Serve Her," said the boy with a beatific smile. "In whatever capacity She desires."

"We will be in Her presence," the girl repeated.

"Whatever She asks of us will be a trifle in comparison to the privilege of seeing Her glory firsthand."

"I see," I fibbed. "Well…best of luck to you both. Have a good trip. And, uh…congratulations?"

They thanked us and wandered off toward the waystation entrance, and Anji whistled low once they were out of earshot. "You know, I have a healthy reverence for the High King and the High Queen, but…"

"Virgins in the volcano?" offered Mia.

The dwarf made a face. "I don't know, and I don't like to rush to judgment, but…maybe?"

"Seems like a freaking cult to me," I muttered.

"I concur," said Fanakel. "Which leaves us with a conundrum."

Mia's eyebrows rose. "Oh?"

"Yeah. Do we rescue them by force, or do we let them meet their god?"

The question made my stomach twist, but common sense shouted a warning. "Remember that part about how we're outside the Aen?" I said. "You can't access your power. We're limited to the tools and weapons we have, and though these folks may be short—"

"Tarak did laps up and down the carriage all afternoon," Anji interrupted, "and beyond physical issues, we don't know the extent of their magic. We can't rescue them. It would be suicidal."

"I know," Fanakel mumbled, folding his arms as he watched the two in red disappear into the building. "But that doesn't mean I *like* it."

He jumped when Anji patted his back. "Decent of you, elf," she said.

Fanakel smirked. "And you'll deny ever saying that, should I repeat it?"

She squinted up at him, then gave her head a quick shake. "No. No, I don't think I would."

His smirk faded as he puzzled through that, then shifted toward a half-smile. "You're satisfactory as well, dwarf."

Anji grunted and rolled her eyes, but when she bade Fanakel good night later that evening, I heard something almost friendly in her voice.

CHAPTER 11

By the time we reached the platform the next morning, the two bound for the Great One were boarding for departure. Those waiting for our carriage stood around and waved as the short train pulled away with a double blast of its horn, and I hoped that wherever those two ended up, they'd be okay.

Our car held a different assortment of people that day—none of them willing to sit near us, naturally, but a new crew from the ones who'd journeyed with us from Acanna. The place where we'd overnighted, Dalienn, was a hub for traffic flowing near the capital, and I noticed several waiting carriages as we boarded, lined up on adjacent tracks. Many were outbound, and Dagerah pointed out a carriage destined for another hub on the far side of the capital, but ours was the first of three headed into Volng. "It's only half a day's ride to the main station," he told us as we settled in. "And the high priest is sending an envoy to escort you from that point."

I frowned, bracing myself against the back of his seat at the carriage began to move. "You're not coming with us?"

"I was not invited," he replied, "and it would be presumptuous of one such as myself to appear on the high priest's threshold without a summons. But you will not be mistreated," he insisted, looking around at our faces. "I assure you that the upper echelons of the priesthood are filled with good, honorable people, devoted to the gods and properly hospitable to strangers. You'll be welcomed guests."

"If you wanted to come, we'd vouch for you," Anji suggested. "Explain that we didn't feel comfortable trying to navigate the city alone."

Dagerah smiled at the offer. "I appreciate your kindness. However, I do have business in the city—my youngest sister is expecting her third child at any day, and I intend to be there for the blessed event, gods willing."

While I wasn't thrilled at the thought of losing our unexpected guide, I couldn't very well complain when Dagerah had done so much for us already. So I sat back as well as I could in the too-small seat and stared out the window as the fields turned to neighborhoods, which finally gave way to the glittering pink city walls of Volng.

"A sandstone unique to the area," said the priest when I asked about them. "Pocked with bits of quartz. Beautiful, is it not?"

While the city walls couldn't hold a candle to the jewel-studded black stone wall around Heartfast, Anji's hometown, they stood about thirty feet high and were at least ten feet thick, and the train had to pass through a tunnel with heavy doors on either end to gain access. As we crawled toward the waystation, I took stock of the city: impeccably clean, filled with three- and four-story stone and brick buildings decorated with colorful awnings and climbing flowers. We passed what seemed to be trolleys, but I saw no other vehicular traffic. Pedestrians bustled in the narrow roads, visiting shops and eating lunch at outdoor tables. From what I could tell, the city's designers didn't believe in a grid system of roads, and I sincerely hoped that we wouldn't be left to find our way to the high priest on our own.

"There," said Dagerah, pointing to a magnificent pink stone building visible in the distance as we rode past a park covered in neatly cropped yellow grass. "The temple. What do you think, eh?"

The place was obviously built to impress, a columned structure about twice as tall as the buildings on our side of town and surrounded by landscaped grounds. "Lovely," I said, resisting the urge to compare its hue to cotton candy. "And, uh, that's a temple for *which* gods?"

He chuckled. "All of them. The Great One receives particular worship, naturally, but those walls hear prayers to many gods. If you should feel the need to commune with your own," he added, glancing around our group, "I'm sure it would cause no offense if you stopped before an altar."

All too soon, the carriage pulled up to the waystation, a five-story structure similar in design to the ones in the hinterlands but proportionally grander. We collected our packs and followed Dagerah off, and he escorted us to a person wearing all white—loose white trousers, white sandals, and even a hooded robe that appeared to have been freshly bleached. In what I'd come to think of as typical Banilghish fashion, there was no shirt to complete the ensemble, but the person did sport a sort of draped metal headdress, a delicate silver and gold piece whose prongs fell between the center eyes and curved back around the outer pair.

Dagerah neared and bowed low. "Am I in the presence of the high priest's envoy?"

"You are," the person—female, I thought—replied in a bored tone. "Dagerah oo'Fin sha'Acanna?"

Having straightened, he bowed again. "Your servant."

She didn't bother introducing herself. "My master has received your message and will see your...guests," she said, turning slightly toward our uneasy pack. "I will escort them from here. Go on your way with his blessing."

He bowed a third time, then rose and turned to us. "Safe travels to you," he murmured, clasping his hands. "And I hope you find the answers you seek."

"Take care, and thank you," I replied, and the others followed suit.

With a final nod, Dagerah strolled off through the crowd, unburdened of his charges and en route to the hatching. I watched him go for a moment before looking at the envoy, whose voice suggested nonchalance but whose body language suggested she thought we might bite. "Thanks for picking us up," I told her. "Where do we go?"

"This way," she said, and strode through the press, which parted for her. We followed in her wake, which widened *considerably* once the other travelers saw what was coming, and passed through the arched tunnel out of the waystation to find a wheeled vehicle the size of a minivan waiting at the curb. The envoy made a flicking gesture, and the nearest door retracted into the roof of the vehicle, revealing several sets of padded benches within. "Climb aboard," she offered. "I will steer."

We tucked ourselves inside—Anji, ever the team player, headed for the back to give the rest of us more legroom—and our driver started the engine with the touch of a button. The vehicle hummed, but I had no idea how it was propelled...nor, considering the envoy's mood, did I think pressing her for a lesson in Unaran transport would be a fruitful endeavor. Assuming there was magic involved, I kept my mouth shut and my sword invisible, and stared out the window at the passing city as we wove through the winding streets and toward the temple at the center of town.

If you can hear me, I told Terj, *we're on our way to someone who might know how to stop the Outsiders. Or at least someone we can work with. Hang in there.*

He didn't answer me, but then I hadn't expected it. Terj had been silent since our night in Acanna, and though I worried for his safety, there was nothing I could do to check on him. At least we were finally getting close to someone in a position of authority, I told myself—surely we'd get some answers now.

About fifteen minutes later, our escort pulled up in front of the temple and said, "You may disembark."

We climbed out, adjusted our gear, and followed her up the grand staircase toward the pink edifice at the summit, saying nothing but sticking close together.

At the top, an attendant in gray opened one of the tall—well, by Unaran standards—wooden doors, bowed their head, and stepped back to admit us. Our escort paid the attendant about as much attention as one might pay a potted plant in the dentist's waiting room, but I nodded to them as I passed, trying not to be rude.

"So," I began, stepping into the temple, "are we going to meet the high priest…"

The sight within took my words and my breath. The silver-plated vestibule walls rose at least twenty feet to a gilded ceiling stamped with a pattern of swirling stars. Colorful windows that I had taken for stained glass from a distance resolved into mosaics of faceted gems. The pink floor remained uncovered, the primary paths of centuries of worshippers worn as grooves into the stone, but I could hardly keep my eyes downcast when the air was full of shimmering balls of light in every hue, which hung and bobbed like giant alien fireflies.

"Oh, my God," Mia murmured beside me.

I'd only seen the Great Temple in Heartfast from a distance, but something told me the temple in Volng would give even the dwarves' religious masterwork a run for its money. Glancing at Anji, who stared open-mouthed at the splendor around us, I decided that my bet was on the Unarans. Even Fanakel, hard-pressed as he was to find virtue in anything not made by elves, gawked at the extravagant design. I couldn't blame him—the place made the Vatican seem austere.

Our escort looked up at us as we soaked it all in. "You are impressed?" she asked, her voice warming fractionally.

"This is gorgeous," I replied with all sincerity. "A true monument to your gods."

She grunted softly but smiled. "One cannot help but strive for architectural perfection when one is blessed to live in the shadow of the Great One, as we are. She guides our steps, inspires our work…" Her hand swept around the room as if showing off the altars built into the walls. The largest, straight ahead, was twice the size of its nearest competitor and encrusted with jewels. "If you wish to worship, the high priest will not object to the delay."

"Uh...thank you," I told her, "but perhaps later. We'd hate to keep him waiting."

Her head dipped. "As you like. This way."

She led us into an elevator, which continued the silver-wall theme, and we rode to the top of the temple. While still ostentatious by any metric, the corridor in which we emerged was more modest than the ground level: eight-foot ceilings, tapestries instead of metal plating, and only a few gem windows. Our escort paused outside a set of wooden doors, then rapped three times and waited. When the doors opened from within, she took two steps inside, then knelt and bowed her forehead to the rug. "Your Grace," she murmured. "Your Majesty."

"Arise, daughter," said a male voice, velvety with a hint of rasp—the sort of voice designed for audiobooks. "Show them in."

Quickly, she pushed herself to her feet in a fluid motion, then stepped aside and beckoned for us to join her.

I was first into the room and found myself in a parlor of sorts, a place of fine furnishings and perfumed incense that felt almost cozy in comparison to the rest of the temple. Sitting on a padded black bench were two figures, one in a long white skirt with a purple cape clasped around its shoulders, the other sporting a green dress with much of the torso cut away but for the sleeves, a slight panel up each side, and decorative silver braiding linking the two sections. They wore a coordinating pale green veil, through which they watched us...or so I assumed, still unable to reliably discern the direction of the Unaran gaze.

The one in the white skirt motioned us closer, toward the cream-colored cushions arranged around the foot of the bench, and said, "Enter. Please be seated."

That one was male, then, and presumably the high priest. The one in green said nothing, but based upon our escort's reaction, I guessed she was the queen.

We shed our bags and sat on the cushions, and with much bowing, our escort took her leave. Once the doors had closed behind her, the high priest clasped his hands and seemed to stare at us each in turn. "The village priest who brought you here claimed you come from Beyond," he said, not bothering with pleasantries. "Did he speak truthfully?"

To my relief, Anji stepped to the fore. "He did, Your Grace. I'm afraid we imposed upon him, but he was an excellent host and most accommodating," she said smoothly. "I dare say he is a credit to your gods."

There were, I thought, definite perks to a royal education.

The high priest smiled briefly at her praise but quickly sobered. "He also said that you bear ill tidings of the Great One's children."

"Again, he spoke the truth," she said, and cleared her throat. "Permit me to introduce myself. I am Anjikora, daughter of Rokund III, under-king of Blackhorn Mountain. This," she continued, gesturing to Fanakel, "is a son of the king of Nokan'ti."

I was mentally praising her for not delving into the details of the elves' governing arrangement when she pointed to me. "Susan is the crown princess of Daril, and this is her companion, Mia."

I opened my mouth to protest, but a sharp look from Anji shut me down.

The high priest cocked his head. "We know nothing of these places."

"All in the worlds you call the Beyond," said Anji. "We understand from Dagerah that you have long sent the children of your Great One through a tunnel to a thin place between us. They come through daily—well, nightly, perhaps. We know they favor the dark hours. But while they may seem as children to you, they come to us as ravenous beasts. We have no choice but to kill them."

Neither the high priest nor the queen seemed shocked by this news.

"We mean no insult to your gods," Anji insisted, "and perhaps the children behave differently here. But within the Aen—"

"That what?"

"The ether of our worlds, you might say. They are drawn to it—we've long known this. But once they reach us, they kill indiscriminately. We slay them to defend ourselves."

That *we*, I thought bitterly, was doing a lot of work, but I held my tongue. Instead, I cut my eyes to the queen, who sat silently behind her veil.

"Dagerah said that your Great One has ordained that the children be sent elsewhere," Anji told them, "but perhaps there's been a miscommunication along the way. Surely a benevolent god would not send her children to slaughter us or be slaughtered."

To my surprise, the high priest nodded. "You're right. A benevolent god would not do such."

Her brow furrowed as she considered his response. "Then…are you saying that the Great One is not benevolent?"

"I'm saying she's not a god."

Anji looked at us for guidance, then turned back to the high priest. "If that's the case, then your priests appear to be misinformed…"

"Oh, they are," he replied with a chuckle. "Intentionally, I assure you." He turned toward the door, but finding it still firmly closed, he continued. "The children are no better behaved in our world than they are Beyond. This is why we send them away."

"You make them our problem," I muttered.

"We do what we must to protect our people," he countered, and sighed. "What you're witnessing is the result of a terrible mistake. Generations ago, the high priest was also a powerful mage, perhaps the finest in thousands of years. He thought he could open a pathway to the gods and perhaps convince one to dwell among us. He was horribly wrong."

Anji cocked an eyebrow. "The gods weren't amused?"

"He never reached them. He opened a way, but a monstrous creature came through. It took every priest in the temple to drive it into the mountains, and the high priest crafted a sort of energetic fence holding the creature there." His mouth moved into a thin line. "But he was proud and foolish, and he'd promised the people a god. So he lied—he announced that an unknown god had come to bless us, and he called it the Great One."

My guts clenched. "And no one ever spilled the secret?"

"He was a mage, remember," said the high priest, "and he worked his magic on the priests who knew what he had done. Most lost all memory of the true nature of the Great One, and those who resisted with their own power lost the ability to speak or write the truth. The only people who know the secret are the current high priest and the king or queen…and now you."

"Why us?" asked Fanakel.

"Because you already know the true nature of the children, and I'm no great mage. Certainly not strong enough to make you forget them, though that would be convenient."

"But what *are* they?" I pressed him.

His smile was weak and mirthless. "Her children. That's no lie—the creatures we send into the Beyond are the offspring of the Great One. It was only a few days after she was contained that the high priest returned and saw that she had spawned. Moreover, the energetic field was tuned to *her* energies alone—her children could pass through. Fearing a massacre, he put some temporary protections in place, then ordered that the tunnel be built, claiming it was a great revelation from the god. The children have been shunted away ever since, and our people live in peace. We know there is something in the Beyond that attracts them. It's been speculated that the Great One might have come from a place with similar conditions."

But as he spoke, a thought that had been darkening the back of my mind burst into the light. "The chosen ones— those who are selected to serve the Great One..."

The queen's hands balled into fists, but if the high priest noticed, he gave no indication. "It is unfortunate but perhaps should be expected that the Great One, whatever she is, must feed."

Never had I been so upset to be proven correct. "You *sacrifice* them?"

"If the Great One's hunger grows too strong, she will fight through her bonds and go in search of food. It's happened four times. Those who are sent to her preserve the lives of their families, their friends, their villages, this kingdom—"

"You sacrifice them," I repeated.

"We do what we must."

I thought of the pair in red in the carriage and how happy they'd been, how fucking *joyful* to be chosen to join their god, and tried not to throw up.

"She is incredibly fertile," the high priest continued. "If she were driven to roam free and her children were allowed to spread, they could wipe out our civilization. Our neighbors as well. So we do what must be done, and as a result, we live in peace."

"You murder your own people," I spat, and turned to the silent queen. "You sanction this?"

"*I* do," said the high priest. "And the Crown is wise to listen."

Anji caught my eye and made a subtle *simmer down* motion, then took the floor again. "We may have a solution to your problem," she told them. "Obviously, our people have no desire to keep fighting the children, and your people have been plagued by this creature long enough. Perhaps we can kill her. If we work together—"

The high priest's incredulous laughter interrupted her offer. "Our people *love* the Great One. They worship her, and they wholeheartedly believe that she blesses them. If we were to expose the truth, to show them that they have been worshipping a lie...can you imagine what damage that would do? It would be catastrophic enough if they believed us, but if they did not and learned that we had slain their god..."

"But you said yourself that she is no god," Anji countered. "Surely your true gods, whoever they may be, would prefer that you not waste your worship on a false deity."

He smirked. "You assume that gods exist, little princess."

Her eyes widened. "You're their *high priest*—"

"Which means I have seen and know far more than most, but I have yet to receive a missive from anything approaching divine. But no, I don't fear retribution from other gods who may be paying us any attention. We need the Great One to exist as she does in the minds and souls of our people, so no, I'm afraid I cannot allow you to threaten her."

"Then we must insist that you close the tunnels and prevent her children from infesting our worlds," said Anji with her best no-nonsense-royal voice.

"I'm afraid that you're in no position to make demands," he replied. "You were offered hospitality, though you came uninvited. Now you've threatened our god. Seeing as you may pose a threat to her safety and to the common good, you will remain in custody for the rest of your days."

Fanakel jumped to his feet, reddening. "You can't—"

"There are mages in this temple who will do what they must to protect the Great One. Because your lies may lead

the people astray, you will be silenced, and your hands will
be stilled. You see," he said with a faint smile, "it doesn't
matter what I tell you, as you will never share it with
another soul. Not in life, anyway. Perhaps you will find a
god who can loosen your tongues once you make your
final journey."

I froze where I sat. Staying in Volng forever might not
have been such a terrible punishment had it just been me,
but to condemn Terj to remain in agony at my side for
decades...

Or maybe centuries. Who knew how long a rogue
could live?

As the high priest started to rise from his bench, Mia
said, "Fanakel, plug 'em."

"Huh?" he asked. "Plug what?"

"Ears," she murmured.

He breathed sharply as he understood her meaning,
then jabbed his fingers deep into his ear canals and braced
himself.

The high priest frowned at him. "What are you—"

"Don't you think this can wait?" Mia interrupted in a
voice that would make a porn star jealous. "It's been such
a long day, and you're *so* tired."

He turned to her, but almost as quickly as his mouth
opened, his jaw went slack.

"It's all right," she purred, standing. "Why don't you sit
down, cutie?"

Wordlessly, he plopped back onto his bench as the
queen scooted to the far end.

"Now," said Mia, raising his chin with two fingers,
"you never told me your name." Putting on a sexy little
pout, she added, "I thought we could be friends."

The high priest struggled to produce sound for a few
seconds, then croaked, "Kirvva."

"Mm. Kirvva. That's *nice*. What's the rest?"

"K-Kirvva...oo'Salg...sha'Volng."

"Such a *pretty* name," she said, stroking his cheeks.

"And I want to learn *all* about you, Kirvva. But you need to sleep first. Gather your strength," she whispered in his ear, "so I can take you places beyond your wildest fantasies."

He swayed briefly on the bench, then slid forward onto the rug and lay still. Mia waited for a few seconds before nudging him with her toe, but he was out cold. "Cretin," she muttered, and gestured for Fanakel to remove his protection.

"*That*," said the elf, staring down at the sleeping high priest, "is still terrifying to watch, and you'll never hear a negative word about tekoraet cross my lips again."

"Aw, shucks." She flashed him a quick grin, then glared down at the queen. "Right, then, sunshine. Got any *thoughts* you'd like to share?"

"Why don't you let *me* go first?" I said, pushing myself from the floor, and yanked my sword from its scabbard. The blade, which had until then been invisible, gleamed in the light of the high priest's office, and the startled queen scooted too far and fell off her bench. Before she could pick herself up, I stepped on the hem of her long dress and held the point of the sword to her neck. "Here's how this is going to work, *Majesty*," I murmured. "You're not going to scream for help. You're going to take us to the Great One, and you're going to be a good girl while we clean up your damn mess. Understood?"

She shifted beneath my sword, then asked in a surprisingly high-pitched voice, "Do you truly believe you can kill it?"

"It's not a god, is it?"

"My understanding is that it's heavily armored. I've never seen the Great One, but that's what I was told." She paused, but when I didn't move, she said, "If you think you can kill it, I'll take you there."

I cut my eyes to Anji, who shrugged.

"You're not worried about the faithful rioting in the streets?" I asked the queen.

"That thing killed my parents," she said quietly. "I want its head."

I considered her response for a moment, then stepped back and allowed her to sit up. She stood and straightened her dress, then pushed back her veil.

While I was no expert on Unarans, even I could tell she was barely more than a child. "How old are you?" I demanded.

"Sixteen."

Anji swore under her breath.

"Awfully young to be queen," I said.

Her lips pressed into a thin line. "That's what happens when one is the heir and one's parents are murdered." Turning to the high priest, who'd begun to snore, she asked, "How long will he sleep? What did you do to him?"

"My little party trick," Mia replied, "and I have no idea how long it'll last, but I'm hopeful that he'll be down for a few hours."

"Can you kill him?"

She frowned, taken aback. "I mean…I'm *armed*…"

"You want us to kill him?" I asked the queen.

"I'm thinking," she replied, and folded her arms. "Kirvva is my mother's younger brother. She became queen, he joined the priesthood, and then he started trying to rule in her stead. When she and Father finally refused to follow his suggestions, he announced that the Great One had selected them. They really couldn't say no." Staring down at her uncle, she said, "That was only a few months ago. He told me the truth of the Great One, and he's been threatening to send me to her if I disobey him. If you could loan me a blade…"

"Best not to do it now, lass," said Anji. "Messy, and if he's discovered, someone will point to you. These matters need to be accomplished with *discretion*."

"Plus, we should really get out of here," Fanakel interjected. "Just in case Mia's not as effective outside the Aen."

I turned back to the queen and, as far as I could tell with her multifaceted purple eyes, held her stare. "You'll take us to the Great One?"

"I swear it by any gods you like," she replied, and extended her hand, palm up. "Sanniah oo'Kral sha'Volng."

Unsure what to do, I covered her hand with mine and said, "Susan Cole. And Anji exaggerated a bit—I'm technically a princess, but only the queen knows I exist, and she's not telling anyone."

"Good enough," said Sanniah, and flashed what appeared to be a genuine smile as she withdrew her hand. "Shall we? My conductor awaits below."

Though young, the queen appeared to have shared Anji's education in manners of carriage and bearing, as she dropped her veil and strode purposefully through the temple like she owned the place. We followed, a line of oversized ducklings, and tried to look like nothing was amiss—and it worked. People stepped aside and bowed to their sovereign, and if they peeked up to gawk at the weird strangers in their midst, they didn't stop Sanniah to demand an explanation.

She led us into the basement of the temple, then out a guarded but unornamented door at the rear, where a wheeled vehicle much like our temple escort's awaited. The windows were tinted black, however, and the driver emerged to assist the queen into the front seat as we piled in the rear. When the door descended and latched, we pulled out into the city, and Sanniah looked back over her shoulder at us and our gear. "It's a short distance," she said. "If you'll excuse me, I'll make arrangements for arrival." With that, she pulled what I recognized as a communication device from a pocket of her dress, opened it, and began tapping at the smooth surfaces therein.

The palace was only about a mile from the temple, a longer trip than it should have been due to the twisting roads of the capital and the frequent pauses for pedestrian traffic. The designers had eschewed the local pink stone, instead opting to build slender towers and connecting walls of blue-gray granite. It seemed short to me, more proportional to the locals' stature than the temple had been, but the floor of the expansive subterranean garage was polished to a shine, the doors were constructed of thick, beautifully carved wood, and the rugs within the palace proper looked nice enough that I almost offered to remove my shoes.

But Sanniah didn't waste time with a tour. A pair of gray-clad attendants greeted her upon arrival and followed us up a stone staircase and then an elevator to a generous tower suite, then stood watch outside the locked door as we dumped our bags in the vestibule.

"There," the queen said with a sigh, and pulled back her veil once more. "Speak freely—the walls are thick, this room is regularly searched for signs of magical espionage, and I trust those two on the door with my life."

"Great," I replied, rolling my unburdened shoulders. "How soon can we leave?"

"And how long is the trip?" asked Fanakel. "We saw a carriage leave for the mountains back in Dalienn this morning..."

Her face fell. "You did?"

"With two aboard."

The queen muttered under her breath. "Their blood will be on my uncle's head, and I hope the gods they meet after death will be kinder than the one who takes their lives. But there will be time for mourning later." Straightening, she said, "The lair of the Great One is a day's journey by carriage from Dalienn, but I have a private conveyance that can take a more direct route—"

"Can we go now?" Anji interrupted. "Perhaps, if we're quick enough, we can still save them."

But Sanniah shook her head. "It's not *that* fast, and I have no way of communicating with their carriage. Those that go to the Great One carry only the chosen—they reach the entry point, disgorge their passengers, and immediately return. That way," she said bitterly, "if the sacrifices realize the truth too soon and try to run, the Great One will catch them before they go far. Besides, even if I could speak to them in the carriage, they would never believe me. Not without proof." She crossed to a narrow window and stared out at the city below. "Once the truth is revealed, I expect riots. Perhaps some zealot will kill me."

"You don't *have* to share the full truth," Mia suggested. "Say we kill the monster. Maybe she'll just spontaneously stop choosing new people, and only you and your uncle will be the wiser that she's dead."

"No." She turned back from the glass, jaw set and head high. "The full deception dies with her. I won't allow our murderous priesthood to lie their way out of this again. Perhaps this will shake faith in the gods." She shrugged. "Perhaps it should."

"You share your uncle's unbelief?" Anji asked softly.

"I...have questions for any divine being who stood by and let our people be led astray. Maybe this is a punishment for our own faults—the lives we've sacrificed to the Great One may be a way to balance those that her children have taken in the Beyond. And my parents were not guiltless. Mother knew the truth, and she could have taken action. But she accepted the system as it worked, and she paid for it with her life. I won't make the same mistake." Considering Anji, she asked, "You believe?"

"I believe the High Queen guides my steps, yes."

"You've seen this High Queen of yours?"

"No, nor have I directly heard Her voice. But I believe I've felt Her presence," she replied, "and in any case, she's never demanded blood sacrifices of Her people."

The corner of Sanniah's mouth ticked upward. "An improvement on our current god situation. But if we can kill the Great One, I want it *known*. Every lie, every deception, regardless of the cost."

The queen was ready to burn it all down, I mused, and

frankly, I respected that.

"What's your plan?" asked Anji.

She opened her communicator again. "When I took the throne, I was given the access codes to the emergency broadcast. If I trigger it, ever device across the land will show my message."

"Those things can transmit images," I said, following her train of thought. "So we get to the Great One, you show them what she actually is, and you broadcast her death."

"I'll do a second broadcast of her corpse," Sanniah corrected. "Once we've slain her."

"No offense, lass," said Anji, "but have you received martial training?"

She put the communicator back in her pocket and cupped her hands, and a globe of fire the size of a golf ball blazed to life within them. "Not yet, but I can help."

Anji's eyebrows rose. "Can you throw that?"

"Better." She pulled her hands away, and the tiny fireball hovered in front of her. With a whispered command, it shot at the wall and fizzled out against the stone. "I don't think it's sufficient to *kill* the Great One," Sanniah admitted, "but perhaps I can harry her."

"I don't know about y'all," said Mia, glancing around our group, "but I'm not turning down flaming missiles. So that's Sanniah on fireballs, me with the .454, Anji with the .38, and him with arrows," she continued, nodding to Fanakel.

"I have blades as well," Anji protested.

"Of course, but I'm talking about distance weapons. What if we spread out and distract the Great One? That would give Suze a way to sneak in with the sword."

Sanniah's forehead crinkled around her large eyes as she looked at me. "*You* are the best swordsman in this company?"

"No, that's Anji," I replied, "but I'm the one with the sword designed to kill the Great One's children. Want to see if it works on Mama, too?"

"What does it do?"

"Cuts through them and sets them on fire."

"Ooh," she murmured, and I pulled the blade free to show it off properly. "What gives it such power?"

"Complex forging and spellwork that took many lives," Anji said quietly. "Aen crystals set in the hilt. And an elemental trapped at its heart to hold everything together."

Her head tilted. "Elemental?"

"Incorporeal beings found in our worlds," she explained. "We came here in part to free the one in the sword. He says he's in agony."

"So why not break it?" she demanded.

"Because that would kill him," I said. "The only way we free him is to eliminate the threat for which the sword was built, which is the horde of children you've been exporting. If we kill them and their mother, maybe that'll be enough to release him."

Sanniah's face softened. "Can he hear us?"

"I think so. He's too strained to speak, but I think he knows what's going on. So let's not waste time," I said, sheathing the cursed weapon. "How soon can we leave?"

She glanced out the window at the clear purple sky of afternoon. "Get your things. We go now."

CHAPTER 12

At the top of a particularly tall tower—which, thank God, included an elevator—sat a landing pad and three pale blue, slightly bulbous aircraft. Well, I assumed they were aircraft, given their fixed wings and altitude, but I didn't ask for details as Sanniah strode toward the guard on duty by the door. "Greetings, good sir," she said in a tone that welcomed no argument. "I am taking my honored guests on an aerial tour of the city. We'll return by nightfall."

He stood at attention, though his face turned ever so slightly as he took us in. "Do you not wish a pilot, Your Majesty?"

"No need." She smiled perfunctorily, then ushered us toward the largest of the vehicles. A tap on the side panel caused it to pull away from the body and rise, revealing more of the Unaran-scaled benches I was coming to loathe.

Sanniah lowered the door behind us, then climbed into the cockpit and pulled back her veil. "Well, let's see how this goes," she muttered as the engine rumbled to life.

"Just checking," I said, leaning up between the front chairs, "but are you, uh... *licensed* to fly this thing?"

She turned to me and grinned. "Who's going to tell me no?"

"All technicalities aside…"

"I've been instructed in the basics," she said, which was less reassuring than she'd intended. "Takeoff and landing are the only difficult parts."

"Great," I replied, forcing enthusiasm into my voice,

and traded glances with Mia. She cocked an eyebrow, and I told her, *We're going to die.*

Mia shook her head.

This isn't good. Remember when Uncle Malachi taught me to drive a manual?

She leaned toward me and patted my knee. "Breathe, Suze."

"Is everything all right?" asked Sanniah, glancing over her shoulder.

"Just fine," Mia lied. "Suze gets a little weird with heights. Take us up."

"I see. Nothing to worry about," she said to me, and depressed a button in the console.

The craft rose with sickening speed, and after a quick, "Oop!" from the cockpit, it leveled out and hovered. "Sorry about that," said Sanniah. "I said that taking off was one of the hard parts. Anyway, here we go."

We banked, doing a slow loop around the palace, then headed to the northwest, away from the city center. As we sped toward the waystation, Anji climbed to my bench, then said, "Sanniah, a thought. I didn't see any vehicles like this on our trip from Acanna."

The young queen laughed. "I would think not. They're uncommon."

"And…who has them?"

"Me, obviously. The temple has a few. Our soldiers have a modest fleet, but they're seldom used."

"But not the common folk?"

"Oh, no. Most people take the carriages when they travel—they're inexpensive and efficient. This is something of a rarity, but my mother fancied them, so now I have three."

"Mm." Anji considered that briefly, then asked, "So what will people think when they see you flying over, heading toward the mountains?"

"They may be puzzled," she admitted after a brief hesitation, "but my uncle and his inner cadre travel in this fashion all the time. Besides, what can hurt us from the *ground?*"

That sounded entirely too much like tempting fate for my taste, but Anji took it in stride. "You tell us—this is your terrain. I'm more concerned about what happens when your uncle wakes and finds us all missing."

"He may pursue us," she replied, "but his craft are no faster than mine, and we have the early advantage."

Momentarily satisfied, Anji sat back on the bench, but Sanniah took her turn. "I've been wondering—how did all of you come to speak our language?"

"We don't. Most of us have two-way translators," I explained.

"Huh. And the rest?"

"Just me. It's either a property of the sword or my own quirkiness, but I don't need a translator."

"Fascinating. And these translators, how are they made?"

Anji grinned and cracked her knuckles. "Do you want the short version or a proper lesson, lass?"

As the dwarf lectured her captive audience about the fine art of forging, I looked out the windows at the city below, which was rapidly flattening. Once over the wall, the settlements continued, albeit in clusters surrounded by golden meadows and fields. A river meandered beside them, heading west, and I thought of the dead Falova, the stinking waterway in which little to nothing survived.

Somewhere, deep in the Kopaati desert, my biological father languished, helpless to save himself. I *would* find him, I promised myself...assuming, of course, that I survived my encounter with Unara's false god.

Briefly, I wondered if it were possible for me to manipulate the river from that height, and then I thought better of it. If we made it back alive, Sanniah might face riots and worse. No need to add rogue waves to that list.

I turned to look at Mia, who'd made herself as comfortable as she could in the squished second row and closed her eyes. "Feeling okay?" I asked.

She cracked one eye open and nodded. "Relatively speaking. Why? I'm just napping, nothing to worry about."

"No, I mean...uh..."

I left that dangling while I tried to think of the most polite phrasing for my question, but Mia beat me to it. "I fed again?"

"Uh...well...you haven't done that in a few weeks, and—"

"I feel fine. Less hungry than usual. I'm not going to turn into some slavering, unstoppable force of seduction," she added with a smirk.

"I know, I just—"

"You worry. I get it. I mean, I'm also slightly weirded out that you can carry on a one-way conversation in my head these days, but...eh."

I leaned against the window and groaned. "We used to be *normal*."

"Did we?"

"Closer to it," I allowed. "What do you think would have happened if I'd followed you to New York right after school?"

She laughed to herself. "Aw, man...well, I had the internship, and that was enough for a shitty apartment. We'd probably have been roommates. You'd have found some waitressing job or whatever to tide you over. I'd still have hooked up with Raquel...she'd still have cheated on me...my internship still would have ended, so it'd have been you financing the shitty apartment for a while. But that would never have happened."

"No?"

"Nope. Not with your dad gone and Malachi all alone. You've always been a family sort of girl."

"When you've only got two people in the whole world who claim you, you tend to worry about them," I murmured.

"I'm not criticizing. And besides, even if you had run

off with me, Terj would have tracked you down."

I turned my face toward hers. "You think his range would have extended that far?"

"Don't know. Maybe. But what better option would he have had in town? My mom? Duffy Shoemaker?"

I thought of poor, deluded Duffy, our former classmate who'd barely received more than acne during puberty, yet somehow thought he was God's gift to women—particularly Mia, long the object of his desire.

"How long do you think Duffy would have lasted at the cabin?" Mia asked. "One night? Two? He'd probably have wet himself and run for it the first time he saw an Outsider, and then something with wings would have snacked on him. Nah," she said, closing her eyes again, "Terj knew what he was doing."

"You think?"

"Suze, you've had that fucking sword for what, two months? And look where we are now."

It had, I reflected, been one hell of a long, strange summer.

Deciding to follow Mia's lead, I wedged myself in place and tried to sleep. *Hey, Terj?* I tried. *Can you hear me? We're getting close.*

There was no answer, and I hoped that despite the pain, he was somehow aware that we hadn't abandoned him to his fate.

Our flight path followed the carriage spur that ran toward the mountains. I spotted the occasional signs of habitation below us, first true towns, then clusters of buildings indicative of settlement, and then the occasional farm abutting the tracks. The final waystation was a one-story stone building in the middle of a pasture, but the tracks went on, a thin scar through the grass, as the land turned wilder and the mountains rose ahead.

A few hours into our flight, I looked down and saw the

small carriage that had delivered the two chosen ones to their god that day heading back toward Dalienn. "Guess we're going the right way if even the carriage is running in the opposite direction," I weakly joked.

"It has no will of its own," Sanniah replied. "Magic directs that carriage's journeys."

"No conductor?"

"Too risky," she said bitterly. "We can't chance someone learning the truth, now can we?" Glancing briefly at me over her shoulder, she said, "Mother explained it to me just before she and Father were forced to take that journey. The carriage runs to the end of its line, near the entrance to the Great One's lair—it's a tunnel cut through the mountain with a long set of stairs carved inside. There's a spell on the carriage that tells it to reverse once it's been unburdened. The chosen then have no choice but to go forward, and once they enter the tunnel, a set of heavy doors closes behind them."

"A trap," I muttered.

"Exactly. And the doors won't open again for three days, just in case anyone starts up the staircase and has second thoughts, so we can't enter by the main route. A second barrier door awaits at the top. There's a little platform at the end of the tunnel, apparently, just big enough for the chosen. Once they pass through, that door closes as well, and then they have nowhere to hide."

Mia hissed. "That's brutal."

"Yes. Fortunately, the poor chosen don't live long."

"Question," said Fanakel, leaning over Mia's seat. "If the main route is blocked to us, how do we get in? From the air?"

Sanniah groaned. "That way is *also* blocked, but perhaps less so."

"Meaning?"

"Some of the Great One's children are born with wings," she replied. "Thus, there's a metal grate constructed over the valley where she makes her home to prevent them from escaping. I've not seen it in person, but perhaps the gaps are large enough to let us in."

Fanakel started to speak, but I beat him to it. "We'll cross those bridges one at a time. You just focus on keeping us in flight, yeah?" To Fanakel, I added, *We'll figure this out. No sense in making her panic about a possible non-problem while she's at the controls.*

While he didn't seem fully convinced of my logic, he let it go and sat back on his bench.

Finally, as the sky began its shift toward a vibrant alien sunset behind the jagged black rock, Sanniah said, "There, the end of the tracks. Do you see?"

I peeked over her shoulder and saw the end of the line, at which point a wooden bumper separated the smooth order of the carriage path from the scrub and fallen stone. About twenty yards ahead, carved into the rock, stood a portal about eight feet high. As Sanniah had predicted, a pair of dull metal doors blocked the way into the mountain.

"Why don't you circle the peak," I suggested, "and see if you can't find a relatively flat spot partway up on which you can put us down? We may have to climb."

Sanniah did as I asked, and on the western side of the mountain, she located a shelf barely large enough for our craft. White-knuckling—well, in her case, it was closer to pale orange—the controls more than I'd have liked, she landed with only a slight bump and sighed. "Good job, kid," I said, patting her shoulder, and depressed a release button for the door.

I stepped out on the uneven ground, conscious of the gravel and the rather unfortunate drop just five feet beyond me, and slid aside as the others made their exit. As Sanniah joined us, Mia scrunched up her face. "It's too warm up here," she murmured, "and does anyone else smell rotten eggs?"

"Sulfur," I said, and cut my eyes to the peak rising above us. "Uh, Sanniah, *where* is the Great One's lair?"

"Inside," she replied, pointing up at the summit. "There's a valley at the top of the mountain, or so I was told."

"A valley," I repeated, wondering if something had been lost in translation.

She nodded, then cupped her hands into a bowl. "There's a rim, you see, and then instead of coming to a point, the land dips into a valley big enough to hold her."

I looked at Mia. "A high valley, and now the smell of sulfur. Are you thinking what I'm thinking?"

Mia frowned briefly before the gears clicked. "Oh, *hell*. That's a caldera. It *is* a volcano god."

The young queen's head tilted. "Volcano?" she repeated slowly, hesitating over the unfamiliar syllables.

I realized it hadn't translated, which had to mean that Sanniah had no word in her language for what we were discussing. "A mountain that periodically erupts," I explained. "Spits red-hot liquified rock, gasses, sometimes more...no?"

Difficult as it was for me to gauge Unaran expressions, I thought she seemed taken aback. "Do mountains *do* that in your worlds?"

"Yeah. And I think this one does, too," I said, looking at the rim above us. "Maybe it's been sleeping for an age, but I bet it's not entirely dormant. Do you ever notice smoke rising from the peak? I thought I saw smoke coming from the mountains all the way back in Acanna."

Hesitantly, she nodded. "No one knows why. The priests say it's a sign that the Great One is upset—"

"*Suze*," Mia interrupted, grabbing my shoulders, "can you trigger an eruption?"

"I'm sorry, *what*?"

"Magma's kind of a liquid, right? Can you manipulate it? Make it come bursting out, kill whatever's in the caldera?"

"I..." I paused, thrown by the question, then shrugged. "I can try. Let me see if I can feel it..."

The rest of our party waited while I took a seat in the vehicle's doorway and closed my eyes. As I opened my senses to the presence of water, I felt the moisture heavy in the air, the shining ribbon of the nearby river, and even a small lake within the caldera, but if there was a magma chamber located below, it remained hidden from my view.

"Sorry," I said, opening my eyes again. "I can't even sense it. Magma's rock, anyway, so I think that's beyond my abilities."

"Shit," Mia muttered.

"It was a good thought."

"I'm sorry," said Sanniah, "I...I don't understand..."

"As the one-time volcano geek of Crockett Elementary's fourth-grade class," Mia replied, gesturing to the rocky rim above us, "let me give you the short version. If your world is anything like ours, then the ground you walk on isn't one solid piece—it's smaller, albeit huge, chunks kind of floating on whatever your world's mantle is. The places where those chunks come together can be geologically active. Mountains forms, earthquakes can be triggered...and sometimes, you get volcanos. They're like giant pimples," she explained, "only instead of the usual gunk, you've got this chamber of magma—"

"Molten rock," I offered.

"Right. When the pressure from the magma gets too great, the volcano explodes."

Sanniah's mouth hung slack. "This...you've seen this happen?"

"Not in person, but we've documented it. What you may have here is a caldera," Mia continued. "Sometimes, when a volcano erupts enough to empty out its magma chamber, it collapses in on itself. But even volcanoes with calderas can erupt again if the magma refills. You see smoke on occasion, and we're smelling sulfur now, which is a bad sign. Either water's bringing it up from below, or you've got vents and an eruption on the horizon."

"The magic you use to hold the Great One here,"

Fanakel began, "does it support the mountain in some respect?"

"Shit," I muttered. "What if, by building that prison for the Great One, they inadvertently stopped their local volcano from blowing?"

"It's possible," said Mia, and glanced at Sanniah, who seemed more distressed by the minute. "Long story short, the Great One may actually have done you a favor. But that's something to worry about later," she added, and pointed to a rough trail cut into the rock. "Looks like we're not the first to use this landing site, eh? Let's get up there and take a peek before we lose the light."

As I was standing closest to the trail, I ended up leading the pack, which was something I would quickly come to regret. After a ten-minute scramble with my scabbard bumping against my legs and the ground, I reached the caldera rim, then pulled myself over the top and stared down at a nightmare.

The good news was that Sanniah was right about the metal lid stretching across the caldera. The grate seemed reasonably sturdy and free of rust, and while we could probably squeeze through the holes, I doubted that the larger Outsiders would fit. But that was the only good news.

Below, in the middle of the caldera, squatted a creature out of my nightmares. Its body resembled that of a spider, deep purple in hue, though it had ten legs and came equipped with a hooked scorpion tail. Its head, however, seemed more lupine in shape, though hairless, and a ring of eyes stretched at least halfway around its skull...many of which now appeared to be trained on *me*, the idiot who'd brought Aen chunks to the party. As the creature stood, I tried to gauge its size, but my brain settled only on *cruise ship*.

"Oh, shit," I whispered. "Oh, fuck. Oh, no, *no*, that thing is *big*..."

Clustered around the Great One were thousands of

gray blobs—boulders, I thought, until one opened with a sharp crack, and a winged monstrosity emerged, shook itself, and took to the sky, aiming right at me.

Those were *eggs*, I distantly realized, too stunned to fully process what I was seeing, just before the sound of Mia's gun brought me back to my senses. The newborn Outsider squealed and splatted on the barren ground below, and I saw the horrifying truth: the creatures that had terrorized the four worlds, the things that broke down my door and flew down my chimney and barely fit into my uncle's chest freezer, the monsters I'd been tasked with killing...they were *hatchlings*.

The others had joined me at the rim, and judging by the looks on their faces, they shared my sentiments about our situation.

"Good place to lay," Mia muttered. "The ground must be warm—"

"Forget the ground," I said, and pointed to the lake at the heart of the caldera. It wasn't huge, maybe only a few acres in size, but I could feel it—and I knew damn well that it wasn't purely water. "The volcano's not dormant, and I'm smelling sulfur, so what do you think the pH of *that* is?"

"*Ooh.*"

"Lasses?" Anji interjected. "The Great One appears to have noticed us..."

"Hold your fire. I'm going to try something," I said, and reached for the lake. It responded after a moment's concentration, rising in a nearly spherical blob to reveal thin fissures in the damp bed. "Maybe we can burn that thing—"

"Wait," Sanniah ordered, and scrambled to pull out her communicator. After a few taps, she stared into the screen, took a deep breath, and feigned composure—and she left her face uncovered by her veil. "My people," she said in a practiced voice, "I do not address you lightly. The news I bring to you this evening will be, at best, disturbing, but I ask for peace and order."

She paused to nervously lick her lips.

"You have been deceived," she continued. "By your rulers and by your priests, the very people you should have been able to trust. This deception is ancient, and it has so permeated our culture that I fear what the morning will bring. I do," she said, and weakly chuckled. "But as a wise priest once told me, the ugliest truth is more precious in the sight of the gods than the most beautiful lie."

I kept silent but sneaked glances into the caldera, watching the Great One as she considered us.

"Like you, I was raised in the faith," said Sanniah. "Taught to love and revere the gods, especially the one who has so graced us with her presence. Who shows us her favor and love, and asks only that we send her children into the Beyond. The Great One." She stared into the camera, letting that sink in, then said, "What I have come to learn since then, from my mother and from the high priest himself, is that the Great One is no true god. She's no god at all. See for yourselves."

With that, Sanniah held her communicator over the caldera with one hand, then shot a trio of fireballs into the dimming sky. They plunged through the grid but hovered near it, illuminating the creature below.

"*That,*" said the queen, "is the so-called Great One. You've heard it said that Kuvarand oo'Ilth sha'Volng convinced her to live among us. That's partly true. He sought to draw a god here. Instead, he brought forth a monster, but he was too proud to allow word of his failure to spread. That creature has been locked here in the mountain ever since, laying her eggs and feeding on our people." She turned the camera back to face her and slowly nodded. "Yes, I said 'feeding.' Those who are chosen to join her—your friends, your children, your spouses, your parents, *my* parents—are sent here not to dwell in the presence of the divine but rather to feed her appetite."

With that, Sanniah turned the communicator toward the four of us. "These people have come from the Beyond, where the Great One's children kill their kind. Oh, there was never any command to send the children away," she said sarcastically. "Our forebears simply realized that if we didn't dispose of them, they would kill and eat us. So that's why the tunnel was built, long and strong. It's protected our lives, but at the cost of others'. No more."

Flipping the communicator toward herself once again, Sanniah said, "We will do our best to end this evil *now*. Our force is small but willing, and if the true gods are merciful, the sun will rise on a freer Banilgh."

Leaving the device open, she whispered, and it rose from her hand to hover over her head, twisting and bobbing with the movement of her body. "Very well, Susan. What do we do?"

"Pray that this works," I replied, and hurled the lake at the Great One.

Fun fact: volcanoes can produce some strongly acidic bodies of water when the right gasses bubble up. Maybe these lakes aren't quite strong enough to immediately dissolve holes in the boats of hapless scientists, but they can cause *nasty* burns to exposed tissue. I mean, there's a reason why you don't want to bathe in sulfuric acid.

The monster screamed when the lake splashed over her, soaking her back and head. I pulled the liquid back together as quickly as I could, then doused her twice more, until she sank to the ground and drew her legs beneath her. I made the acidic sphere coalesce once again, hoped this would work quickly, then thrust it down over her head, holding it in place as she thrashed and even for a moment after she slumped and stilled.

With that, I tossed the deadly lake back into its bed and said, "Sanniah, more light. Let's make sure it got her."

She obliged with another volley of fireballs, which hovered around the creature's wounded head. For a moment, I thought the lake might have done the trick—if

I hadn't burned the creature to death, I'd at least drowned it.

Then I noticed a patch of acid-pocked flesh atop the Great One's skull begin to change color and knit back together.

"*Fuck*," I muttered. "She's regenerating."

"Are you kidding me?" Mia groused, while Anji mumbled a prayer to the High Queen and Fanakel readied his bow. "Shit. What's plan B, then?"

I smiled grimly, then patted the scabbard at my side. "This thing was made to kill them."

"*Suze*. No, absolutely not, that thing is enormous—"

"It's our best chance," I insisted, and hoisted myself onto the metal grate. "So I'm going to need you to keep her distracted until I can get down there, okay?"

Mia reached up and gripped my wrist. "Susan Cole, get your ass back here! That's insane!"

"I'm carrying a weapon that was designed to kill Outsiders. Surely it'll put a dent in Mama."

"And if it doesn't?"

I locked eyes with Mia, then rotated my arm so that I could grip her wrist in turn. "If this doesn't work, get the sword and take it back to the four worlds. Don't let Terj suffer any more than he has to."

"Suze—"

"I'm not going home with this sword still attached to me. One way or another, this Watcher gig ends tonight. So promise me that if something happens, you'll get Terj out of here."

Though she looked like she wanted to drag me off the mountain, she released my arm and muttered, "Okay. Be careful."

"Will do. Cover me," I said, then swung my legs through an opening in the grid, held on to the cross-pieces, and lowered myself through.

Had I been a proper action hero, I'd have treated the grid like a giant set of monkey bars, crossed the caldera hand over hand until I reached the Great One, then jumped down on her back to fight her. But since I've never been able to do pullups, I instead dangled over the stone floor for a few seconds, trying to find the softest spot to land, then released the bars and fell about ten feet onto a sad, prickly bush that did barely enough to keep my legs from breaking. Before I could pick myself up, the light show began by my quarry: a rain of small fireballs like a fracturing comet in the twilit gloom, a hail of arrows, and the percussion of Mia's and Anji's pistols firing until they emptied the magazines and hastily reloaded. The .454 slugs that had sufficed to blow holes in the Outsiders didn't do nearly as much damage against their mother, but the wounded monster still curled in upon herself as her body tried to heal.

I might have felt sorry for her had she not been the cause of so much fucking misery.

With the Great One distracted and temporarily immobilized, I took off as quickly as I could run, staying close to the caldera wall and dodging eggs as big as I was. As I prayed that the hatching could wait *just* a bit longer, I drew nearer to the Great One even as common sense bellowed for me to get out of there.

Suddenly, despite the continuing barrage from above, the monster raised her battered head and stared at me.

I stopped in my tracks and pulled the sword free, wrapping my hands around the hilt as I stared the Great One down in turn. "You want this?" I shouted, my voice echoing across the stone. "Come on, big girl! Take it!"

She *roared*, a primeval noise that would have made a sound designer for a dinosaur movie green with envy, then rose and began skittering toward me.

"Come on!" I yelled, tightening my grip and pointing the blade at the ground. "Is that the best you can do?"

The Great One paused when Sanniah landed a particularly effective handful of fireballs on her stinger, which Mia promptly pierced with a pair of bullets. But the lure of the Aen crystals—or maybe fresh meat—proved too strong, and on the monster came, dragging her injured tail behind her.

I held my ground as the floor around me shook with her thunderous footsteps, keeping my eyes on the creature's impossibly wide jaws and sharp fangs. As my heart stampeded in my chest, I sized her up as well as I could, looking for weak points in her defenses. Her body seemed pretty well armored, but her hairless neck, though thickly muscled, presented a possibility.

Distantly from above, I heard Mia scream my name as the Great One bore down on me, mouth wide. I kept the sword lowered and waited until the head rose above me. It seemed to pause at the top of its arc for a bare moment, and I held my breath.

This was for Uncle Malachi. For the Watchers before him.

For Terj.

For *me*.

Like a flash, the head descended to eat me whole.

In that split-second, I ducked, rolled toward the creature's torso, then stood and jabbed the sword upward in time to make contact with its throat.

The flesh above me exploded in flame.

I cried out but kept the sword lodged in the Great One's neck, widening the gash while trying to dodge the fire. My lungs burned from the acrid smoke, and a glut of ichor poured from the wound in a stinking baptism, but I managed to stab the beast three or four times before she started to retreat.

"Oh, no, you don't," I said, wiping the black goop from my eyes, and ran after her.

I hacked at anything I could reach—the back legs, the armored carapace, the limp stinger. Anything the sword touched ignited like dry grass in a wildfire, until finally, with a last screech of pain, the Great One fell. She twitched briefly, and once she went still, I wondered if I'd witnessed her unimpressive death throes.

"Should I put out the fire?" I called toward the grate. "I think she's—"

Like tripped mines, the eggs scattered around the caldera began to explode. For an instant, I freaked out, thinking they were hatching, but the jets of flame that shot from within set my mind at ease.

"It's like killing a vampire!" Mia shouted down to me. "Take out the sire, and his children follow!"

I might have been more talkative had I not been caught between the burning Great One and the eggs all around us, and I stood there as if warming myself by the flambéed corpse until the hissing and crackling ceased. After a few minutes, even the Great One's flames began to sputter and die, and after stepping well out of the splash zone, I pulled up the lake one last time to extinguish anything still smoldering.

It wasn't until I put the lake back that I felt the sword disintegrate in my hand.

I glanced down to see the blade crumbling into sand by the light of Sanniah's hovering fireballs and gasped. The process accelerated as the decay moved toward the hilt, and before I knew what was happening, I was left holding nothing but the three Aen crystals and a palmful of grit. I stared dumbly at what little remained of my weapon for a second before a pained scream echoed across my mind and just as quickly fell silent.

"Terj!" I cried, holding the crystals close to my face as if I might see motion within their depths. "Can you hear me? Are you okay? *Terj!*"

Somehow, in my panic, I felt a faint breeze ruffle the back of my shirt, and I whipped around to find the source.

Though we'd almost lost the light, I could just make out a humanoid-shaped disturbance in the air, a barely visible indication of a presence. The wind strengthened as the disturbance's form solidified—well, as much as air *could* solidify—and I felt more than heard a long sigh of relief.

"Terj?" I whispered.

Susan?

Laughing in my shock, I tossed the crystals aside and threw my arms around him.

It's strange, to say the least, to make contact with an elemental. If they're not concentrating, physical bodies go right through them. But Terj seemed just as eager to touch me as I did him, and I felt the resistance of his form against my body, air made nearly impenetrable, as he embraced me.

Better? I joked.

His giddy amusement flashed against my mind. *Marginally.*

It's nice to finally meet you.

Likewise. His grip tightened briefly before he withdrew. *Sorry, I…I'm not strong…*

Take it easy, Terj. I've got this, I told him, then wandered up to the Great One, *just* to make certain it wasn't coming back. The thing was charred almost beyond recognition, however, and I was contemplating my work until I heard footsteps behind me.

"Susan?" said Anji.

I turned and grinned. The dwarf carried her forged lighter, a small torch to illuminate a path over the uneven ground, and she was beaming widely enough to split her face.

"Think I might be out of a job," I said, and cocked a thumb toward Terj. "My sword's busted, anyway."

"Glad to see you," she told him, then pointed at the Great One. "Do you think we should take a trophy? Just in case someone wants proof?"

"Proof more than…oh, crap, shine that over here," I muttered, and Anji obliged while I recovered the Aen crystals. "We've got these," I said. "Pretty clear proof that the sword's gone, and since Mama's dead, I don't think we're going to be seeing Outsiders again."

"You may be right," she replied, rubbing her chin

scruff, "but a trophy wouldn't hurt. How about a tooth?"

"I didn't exactly bring equipment for dental surgery…"

"Don't let that stop you, lass," she said, and headed for the Great One's mouth. "Here, be useful and hold my light."

"Be *useful*?"

Anji glanced up at me and smiled again. "Teasing. Come on, I want to get out of here."

While I handled the light and Terj hovered nearby, Anji managed to wrench one of the Great One's smaller fangs from her mouth, which she presented to me. The tooth was nearly as long as my arm and dripping ichor at the root end, but it was a souvenir, and I wasn't feeling incredibly picky that evening.

"So, uh," I began, cutting my eyes toward the grate, "how do we get out of here?"

Anji turned to Terj. "Think you can give us a lift?"

Honestly? No. I'm exhausted, and I'd rather not drop you.

"Mm. Fair. Well, then," she said, pointing her light toward the caldera wall, "we climb."

As it turned out, *Anji* could climb. I was stuck in the caldera with Terj and my giant tooth until Sanniah powered up her craft and lowered an emergency rope through the grate. Tying it around my waist and praying my knots didn't come undone, I held the tooth between my knees and let the onboard winch pull me up, then passed the tooth through the bars and hoisted myself the last few inches. Once I had the rope off, I sprawled atop the grate and stared up at the early stars, feeling more drained than I'd ever been but curiously at peace.

After a minute, a distortion I recognized as Terj appeared over my face. *We should probably go. Sanniah wants to get back in case there's anything she can do to stop the riots.*

"Yeah? Okay," I mumbled, and groaned as I sat up. With the tooth in my arms and the empty scabbard hanging at my side, I let Fanakel help me aboard, and I collapsed onto the first bench by my abandoned backpack.

"Want to join me?" I asked Terj, patting the empty portion of the seat. "I'll squish…"

No need. His form dissolved in an instant, but I heard his voice all the same. *I don't actually require much space.*

"Are you sure? I don't mind sharing."

Rest, Susan, he insisted. *Also, seeing as you're covered in ichor, I doubt that anyone will want to share until you've showered.*

"What?" Oh," I mumbled, looking down at myself. "Forgot about that…"

"You're fine," said Sanniah, who by then had put her communicator away. "Assuming I still have a throne in the morning, I'll have the seats cleaned." She turned and smiled wearily at us. "So…want to see how much of my capital is on fire?"

CHAPTER 13

I don't remember much of the flight back to Volng. Physically and mentally exhausted, I passed out almost as soon as we were in the air, waking only once when I began violently shivering and Mia covered me with a towel from her bag. "Shh," she soothed as I whimpered and curled up against the window. "You're okay, Suze. It's over. Hey, Sanniah, could we get some heat going back here?"

"I don't think that's from a chill," said Fanakel, but by then, the voices were fading again.

The next thing I knew, we were circling the city, and I stared blearily down at the streets below, trying to pull sense from the nighttime lights. Anji, I noticed, had moved to the copilot's seat beside Sanniah—she alone among us fit. "That's the temple," Sanniah told her. "See the braziers at the top? Those are lit at sundown."

Anji whistled softly. "Look at the crowd."

In the glow of the temple's lights and the street lamps, I made out motion below and realized it was a surging throng in the streets, surrounding the temple for a couple blocks in all directions. I feared the worst as we headed for the palace, but to my surprise, the area outside its walls was pretty calm—a handful of people being held at bay, but nothing like the chaos elsewhere that night.

Sanniah flew to the landing pad and put us down with a beginner's jolt, and half a dozen guards sprinted up to meet us. "Your Majesty," said the nearest as she opened her door, "are you hurt? Are you…"

He turned his head and averted his eyes, and with a

grunt, Sanniah ripped off her veiled headpiece and tossed it away. "Look at me when you're addressing me, sir."

The guard hesitantly faced her again, but when no reprimand came, he found his courage once more. "How could you *do* that?"

"I did what needed to be done," she protested. "What Mother *should* have done—"

"No, Your Majesty, you misunderstand. How could you do that without telling us? We would have assisted you…"

The rest of the guards, who stood back at a respectful distance, nodded their vehement agreement.

Sanniah smiled. "I don't doubt that, nor do I doubt your loyalty. But we had to move quickly while my dear uncle was indisposed." Rolling the tension out of her shoulders, she asked, "Any word from him? Screaming curses? Promises to destroy me?"

The head guard's expression shifted toward a grimace. "Word from temple security is that he took his own life shortly after your broadcast. They're begging for reinforcements.

"Coward," she muttered, "but at least that's one task off my list. Did you authorize assistance to the temple?"

"Minimal," he replied. "I was waiting to speak with you first, Your Majesty."

"Mm. You know, they've done such a wonderful job to this point. Surely they can manage a few pointed questions from the faithful. Perhaps the Great One will come to their aid," she said. "Recall our forces if you can. The temple is on its own."

While Sanniah left the priests to fend for themselves, her guards trebled their presence around the palace. She had us shown to a quartet of large guest rooms, which necessitated servants scrambling to drag in extra beds for our comfort. I barely noticed the commotion at the time.

My head felt foggy, and I found myself standing dazed by the door of my room, pack on my shoulders and giant tooth in my arms, until Mia came to my aid.

"I've got this," she insisted, and shooed Fanakel and Anji off to bed.

"Where's Terj?" I mumbled as she locked the door behind her.

"Probably stretching his legs...or whatever he has, I don't know. He's been quiet for hours. But *you*, my dear, are getting a bath."

"That can wait until morning—"

"Yeah, no. Come on, put your stuff down," she coaxed, and once I was unburdened, she nudged me into the bathroom.

The tub, like that at Dagerah's home, was grossly oversized for Unarans, comparable to a hot tub, but I paid it little attention as Mia opened the taps and started adjusting the temperature. One wall of the bathroom was fully mirrored, and I stared uncomprehendingly at the figure in the glass, who, though about my size and shape, appeared to have rolled in tar.

"Mia?" I asked.

She looked up, saw the problem, and tutted. "That's why you're not going to bed just yet, and I think you should say goodbye to whatever you're wearing. You've got spare clothes in your bag, yeah?"

"Uh-huh."

"Okay. Well, I'm going to find something for you to sleep in, and you're going to scrub off. Do you need help?"

I shook my head. Once she'd stepped out, I started the slow process of undressing, fumbling with the bungee cord that held the ichor-stained scabbard against me, then peeling off my layers. What wasn't coated with muck was damp with sweat, and I kicked the gross, stinking lot into a pile before sliding into the bath. The warm water was a balm to my aching body—I had, I mused, probably overexerted myself—and once I rinsed off my face, I leaned against the side of the tub and closed my eyes. *This was nice...*

Don't fall asleep in there.

My eyes flew open, and I sank into the water until the oily scum on the surface covered me to my neck. *Where are you?*

On the other side of the door, Terj assured me. *You felt like you were drifting off again, and since it's been a long night, do we really want to explore just how far your abilities can go at this moment?*

Huh?

Last I checked, you can't breathe water.

Right. Though not entirely convinced that I was alone in the bathroom, I made myself reach for the shampoo and start lathering. *Where are you sleeping tonight? I don't think Sanniah knew what to do with you...*

Well, since I don't exactly sleep...

Where do you want to rest, then? Or do you? Must be nice to take to the air again.

He paused before answering me. *I haven't quite done that yet. It's...*

Overwhelming?

Yeah.

Take your time, I told him. *Look, we're just going to sleep this off unless an angry mob shows up with a guillotine. If you want to explore the city, don't let me stop you.*

You won't leave without me?

He sounded nonchalant enough, but I heard the undercurrent of fear in his voice.

I'm not going anywhere without you, Terj, I promised. *We're taking you home. But for now, you're not hurting anymore, are you?*

No, he replied, the thought colored by incredulity. *No, I'm not. I'm weaker than I remember, but—*

You've been through hell. It's okay. Recall the part about how I'm going to crash as soon as I'm clean? I can barely think straight.

You're exhausted.

He fell silent, and I thought he might have left on his

exploratory tour before he asked, *Would it be all right if I stayed with you tonight? I won't bother you, I—*

Of course, I said, and ducked down to wash my hair clean. When I surfaced again, I contemplated the sludge floating atop the bath, then lifted out the top inch of water, poured it into the sink, and let the tap run for a moment to fill and reheat the tub.

I had to freshen my bathwater twice more before I felt clean and de-ichored, and I emerged in a slightly too small towel to find that Mia had left my nightclothes on the hastily reconfigured beds. *Terj?*

I'm looking out the window.

Thank you, I said, and dressed. With a final squeegeeing of my wet hair, I crawled into bed and groaned.

Want the lights off?

Yeah.

I think... The room suddenly went dark, and Terj sighed. *Harder than it should be.*

We're going to get you home. Don't worry.

With that, I knew nothing more until I screamed myself awake a few hours later, convinced that an endless horde of Outsiders was about to overwhelm me. *You're safe*, Terj soothed. *They can't hurt you anymore, Susan. It was just a dream.*

I sat up in bed and cupped my hands over my face, feeling the jagged scar on my left cheek—the thick red line from my eye to my mouth where an Outsider had ripped my flesh open. Maybe it would have healed better had I been able to go to the hospital, but the nearest one was outside the radius of the magical tether that had bound me near the Crossing.

The last two and a half months must have sunk in at that point, there in the darkness, as I took a deep breath and burst into tears. I didn't know what I was crying for—my dad, my uncle, the life I'd known, the girl I'd been—but I bawled until my face was wet and my nose was running, and then I felt Terj beside me, a faint pressure as his arm wrapped around my shoulders. I turned and buried my face against him—and really, as dark as it was in there, it was easy to imagine that I wasn't clinging to almost nothing at all.

Forgive me, he begged as I sobbed in his arms. *I'm sorry, Susan, I'm so sorry…*

I lifted my head and felt for his face, and my fingers brushed against a firmer patch of air that might have been a cheek. *We're free, right? That's what matters. And you know I forgive you.*

Still sniffling, I released him and tried to make myself comfortable again, and the blankets seemed to rise of their own accord to tuck me in. *Terj?*

I'm here, he told me, and with that promise, I allowed myself to sleep.

Morning came too early for my taste, but I felt much closer to normal, if still unusually achy, when I crawled out of bed. I might have slept all day, but one of the servants knocked about an hour after sunrise to check on my needs—a doctor, a launderer, breakfast? I asked her to throw away my ruined clothing, but she insisted that the leather scabbard was far too nice to be discarded and said she would bring it to a specialist in the stables for cleaning. When she offered breakfast a second time, I took stock of my stomach and tried to recall when and what I'd last eaten—maybe a handful or two of granola on the flight out to the mountain the previous afternoon. Hunger beat the need for sleep, and she offered to wait until I was decent to show me to the dining room.

I slipped into the bathroom with mostly clean, if rumpled, clothes and the bare-bones toiletry kit from my pack and assessed the damage. Brushing my teeth was a start, and while my hair crimped and curled in the random fashion of a night spent air drying on my pillow, it was salvageable in a ponytail. My face was puffy, my arms and legs bore a fresh set of cuts and bruises, and there was nothing I could do to hide my scar, but at least I didn't stink of ichor.

So, said Terj, *how's the first day of unemployment going?*

I turned and found him hovering on the threshold of the bathroom, barely visible in the shaded gloom. *I kind of thought there'd be more sleeping in, but food's also nice. How are you feeling?*

A little stronger, I think. The swirling air and dust that comprised his form shifted, and I laughed as I realized he was miming a bicep flex. *Not fully restored yet, but I'll be honest, this is a vast improvement over this time yesterday.*

I thought back to the waystation in Dalienn, where we'd watched the two doomed to feed the Great One obliviously depart to their deaths. That hardly seemed like the previous day. I wondered if the families of that young couple had seen Sanniah's broadcast, and if so, how they were holding up.

There's nothing we could have done, Terj reminded me.

I sighed and looked back in the mirror. *I know. It just sucks that they died for nothing. If we'd come one day sooner...*

We still wouldn't have made it unless Dagerah could have been convinced to leave early.

I hope he's okay. The village priest had come to the city to see his sister—surely he hadn't been caught in the temple mob the night before.

Think of it this way, said Terj. *Because of what you did, no one else will ever take that ride. No one in the four worlds will die from an Outsider. And no one will ever be bound to that goddamned town ever again.*

What, I teased, *you don't like Cole's Crossing?*

I've spent way too long there. He paused, then asked, *Are you thinking of staying in the Crossing?*

I don't know. Hadn't gotten that far. I straightened my ponytail, then gently rubbed my scar as if I could somehow press it back into my flesh.

You're beautiful.

With a snort, I cut my eyes to Terj. *Thanks for trying, but you already told me that you can't judge physical appearance.*

I meant what I said. You're beautiful in the ways that matter.

I stared at him for a moment, then smiled to myself. *You're not so bad yourself.*

His amusement echoed in my mind. *I'm broken in more ways than I can count, but the effort is appreciated.* With that, he moved from the door and asked, *Shall we?*

I stepped into the hall, where the servant was waiting, and sensed Terj hovering invisible at my side. An elevator brought us down from the tower where we'd slept into the main part of the palace, and after a brisk walk through a few corridors, the servant opened the doors to an intimate dining room, where the rest of my companions and Sanniah were already tucking in. Guards posted on the doors nodded as I entered, and the queen rose and gestured toward the buffet. "Good morning, Susan. Eat as much as you like, and if there's nothing here to your taste, I'll have the kitchen make whatever they can."

"It smells great," I assured her, and loaded a plate as my awakened stomach roared for food. Whoever had set up the dining room had used what probably passed for a high-top table for Unarans and replaced most of the chairs with benches, so I was able to snag a seat beside Fanakel without banging my knees into the furniture.

"Where's Terj?" Mia asked, glancing around the room.

Here. He manifested briefly near the tray of juice pitchers, waved, and vanished again.

Sanniah dropped her spoon in her surprise, but Anji came to her aid. "If one is unaccustomed to elementals, it can take time to acclimate."

"I…I'm sorry," she said, looking toward the place where he had been, "I don't mean to be rude…"

Believe me, I'm not in the mood to take offense today. How's your riot situation?

"Is the temple still standing?" I asked between bites of hot, sweet bread.

Sanniah winced. "Standing, yes, but severely fire

damaged. We've received reports of several priests and rioters receiving medical care overnight, and news is still coming in from the provinces." She took a sip of juice, then said, "As you might imagine, some of the families of the 'chosen' didn't take the news well."

I made a face. "*How* not well?"

"We've got mob justice and a few dead priests on our hands." She sighed and shook her head. "It's not right. The local priests were almost as deceived as the laity— they're not the ones who chose and announced the next sacrifices. But emotions are running high right now, and since just about every family has sent at least one son or daughter to the Great One over the generations, you might not be surprised to learn that the provincial authorities are turning a blind eye to much of the violence."

"What's your plan?" Fanakel asked.

"After we eat, I'll be broadcasting again, asking for peace and announcing my uncle's suicide. He was the driving force behind the recent deaths, so perhaps his end will give some of the families the vengeance they seek."

As she tucked in again, I said, "The priest who brought us here, Dagerah, is visiting his sister in town. Is there anything you could do to check on him? He was very hospitable to us, and I'd hate for something to happen to him."

Sanniah nodded. "Certainly. That was Dagerah…"

"oo'Fin sha'Acanna," I finished. "I don't know his sister's name…"

"We'll find her," she said, and popped another piece of bread in her mouth with a satisfied groan. "Sorry, this is really good, and I'm always so concerned with manners when I dine with aristocrats…not to suggest that you aren't," she hastily added, having heard herself, "but—"

Anji chuckled and patted her arm. "You've never seen dwarves feast, have you, lass?"

"Afraid not."

"Well, let's just say that even the highest-born dwarf

gets a little sloppy during the toasting. And it's *fun*," she added with a warning glare for Fanakel. "I'm sorry if Nokan'ti can't appreciate it."

He grunted as he sawed off a piece of roast meat, which my stomach had decided was close enough to beef to pass muster. "I take it, then, that you've never feasted with elves."

"We aren't typically invited to such, no."

The corners of his mouth curled as he took a bite. "There's a wine my aunt favors. It's about twice the strength of ordinary wine."

Anji started to grin. "Yes?"

"And if you knew anything of elven custom, you would know that a proper feast requires the participants to drain their cups by the end of each course." He paused, then met her twinkling eyes. "All seven of them."

"Oh, no," said Mia, laughing.

"Oh, yes. A good feast doesn't end without a fight, some singing, and at least one person asleep on the floor, especially not when my aunt chooses the beverage. All of that is to say we're not appalled by your table manners," he said to Sanniah.

As he reached for his glass, Anji murmured, "A pity we don't get along better. I think I'd enjoy a feast like that."

Sanniah looked back and forth between them. "Your peoples are at odds?"

They nodded. "We had a nasty war about a hundred years ago," Fanakel explained.

The queen frowned. "Concerning what?"

The elf and the dwarf shared a long look, and Anji said, "Religious differences, more or less."

"Things…escalated," Fanakel added. "Unfortunately."

The two sat in silence for a moment, both picking at their plates.

"In retrospect," said Anji, "there were probably mistakes on both sides."

"I'd concur," murmured Fanakel.

Anji glanced up at him, smiled briefly, and returned to her meal.

Sanniah left us shortly thereafter to make her second broadcast, though she encouraged us to eat as much as we wanted and enjoy the palace. "Maybe don't go wandering outside," she added, "but the gardens within the walls are lovely, should you want some fresh air."

Frankly, what I wanted most was to go back to bed, but I stayed with the others while we satiated our appetites. As Fanakel started to rise to hit the buffet again, Anji stopped him with a raised palm. "Son of Nokan'ti, a moment?"

He frowned bemusedly but sank back onto the bench. "Sure."

She scowled at her plate as she collected her thoughts, then raised her face toward his. "I...I just wanted to say that while I am fully aware of the...*tension*...between our kingdoms, I hold no particular animosity toward you. You've been a valuable member of our company, and I..." She hesitated, then smiled at him. "I respect you, son of Nokan'ti. And if we soon part and go our separate ways, I wanted to say that. I'll admit that I didn't see much use for you in the beginning, but I was wrong. So." She shrugged and picked up her glass.

"Fanakel," he said softly.

Anji cocked an eyebrow. "Come again?"

"We do not hide our names from everyone, only from those subordinate to us in some way. That's why, even now, I couldn't tell you the names of my father and my aunt if you put a blade to my throat. But...I don't mind that you know mine. I don't even really mind that you use it."

She started to grin again. "Are you saying..."

"That the respect is mutual, daughter of Blackhorn Mountain. And if anything, you are the superior fighter."

"You know," said Mia, "we did all just attack a giant monster together, so surely some things overcome politics...right?"

"It's a little more than *politics*," Fanakel replied.

"And I dare say that Susan did the real work yesterday," Anji pointed out.

I held up my hands. "Team effort, y'all. I just happened to be the one to whom the damn sword was attached."

"You were pretty badass," said Mia.

"I got lucky."

"Mm. Guys?"

"I agree with Mia," said Anji, and Fanakel nodded.

That's four for Team Badass, Terj added, *so do the graceful thing and agree, Susan.*

I rolled my eyes and lifted my glass. "*Fine.* Thank you."

With that, Fanakel got up for seconds, only to be confronted with Anji's smirk as he returned to the table. "I'm hungry," he protested as he settled in with his loaded plate, "and my stomach's bigger than yours."

"Oh, I'm not criticizing," she quickly told him. "I merely had a thought."

"What's that?"

"Well…" She paused to consider her stubby fingernails. "You know that my father is a signatory to the Peace of Meali, yes?"

His brow furrowed. "Yes…"

"And so are your father and aunt."

"Naturally."

"So…I've seen Father's copy of the treaty. Everyone signed copies so that there would be no question about the terms."

Fanakel nodded. "I've heard that. Where Nokan'ti's copy might be, I can't say, but I'm not surprised that your father has one."

Her little smirk deepened. "Having read the treaty a few times, I remember the names of the signatories."

The elf's eyes widened as he followed her train of thought. "You…"

"Want to know your dad's name?"

He glanced guilty around the room as if afraid of spies,

then leaned toward her across the table and whispered, "*Yeah.*"

"Enoul," she whispered back. "And your aunt is Enarl." She straightened, then raised her juice glass to him in salute. "Deploy that as necessary, my friend."

Fanakel chuckled. "If I did, I'd probably end up begging for shelter at your border."

"Ours is actually a lovely country. Not nearly as many trees as in yours, and things are probably a bit shorter than you'd prefer, but it's not a wasteland."

"Can confirm," said Mia. "One hell of a shiny temple, too."

"So…*if* they threw you out," Anji continued, "and we were your only option…you know, could be worse. You could end up in Ti'cal."

Both dwarf and elf grimaced at that.

"Where's Ti'cal?" I asked.

"That's probably something you should know," Anji replied. "On Kopaat, the tunnel opens in the desert, yes? Major feature of the continent of Echoril. Roughly equidistant from the tunnel are Daril to the northeast and the Meali Republic to the southwest, and Taln'een is then northeast of Daril. Do you follow?"

"I think so…"

"Good. So, rising far south of Daril and flowing north to empty into the sea is the Falova. Ti'cal is the kingdom that grew up around the headwaters and the southern reaches of the river. Major fishing industry. It was once prosperous, but in recent years, with the river having died…"

I sucked my teeth. "Ouch."

"Exactly. I don't follow Ti'cal very closely, but I've heard reports of food shortages. Daril has the sea to feed it, but Ti'cal has only the Falova."

"Speaking of Falova," I said, reaching for the breadbasket on the table, "I intend to go in search of him once we get back. Not quite sure how I'm doing it yet, but that's on the agenda."

"What about that elemental who carried us across the desert?" Fanakel suggested. "Do you think he'd be willing to assist again?"

Almost certainly, said Terj.

"But I hate to keep imposing on him," I said. "He's carried us twice, now. I don't want him to think I'm taking advantage of him…and the only way I know to get in touch with him is to make a freaking thunderstorm, which is no guarantee."

I could carry you.

"*You* need to take it easy and rebuild your strength," I told Terj. "I'm not asking that of you."

No, you're not asking—I'm offering. I _want_ to help, he insisted. *And if I didn't have to carry the whole group—if maybe the two of us could do this—then I wouldn't need to rest so often.*

"You know," said Mia as I started to argue, "that's not something we have to settle today. Why don't we put a pin in all future rescues until we get back to the Crossing, huh?"

"But—"

"No buts, Suze. Here, eat this," she ordered, pushing the breadbasket toward me.

Sometimes in life, you need to shut up and listen to your best friend.

I ended up carrying the half-emptied breadbasket back to my room with me, and I fell asleep again with it on the nightstand, just in case. The last thing I remember before I dozed off with a full stomach was Terj's voice: *Rest easy. I'll be here in case the dreams return.*

Sanniah's word was good. She made a broadcast that morning to plea for peace, stressing that the village priests the people had always known and trusted had also been kept in the dark. "At most," she said, sounding far older than sixteen in the recording I watched later that evening, "they understood that the tunnel was necessary because the Great One's children were dangerous. Her true nature was hidden from all but the highest priests...and since my dear uncle ended his own life last night, he faces the gods' judgment now, which is more terrible than anything I could administer. I understand that his death doesn't bring back your loved ones," she continued, staring into the camera with her face again unveiled. "It doesn't bring back mine, either. He sent my parents to die so that he could have someone more easily ordered about on the throne." She smiled coldly then and said, "I am young, true, but I believe I'm more than he anticipated."

Following her broadcast, she asked an aide to track down Dagerah, who was discovered sheltering in his sister's home near the city wall, hiding in her spare room and quietly falling apart. She sneaked out of the palace to visit him personally, and as his sister and her husband raced to tidy their home, she sat with him in the presentable living room and thanked him for what he had done. "I know this is a shock," she told him. "The truth was a blow to me as well, and I learned it from my mother's lips the night before she and my father were sent on that last journey. Perhaps it was a beautiful lie, but the cost of maintaining it was far too great."

With his sister's blessing and thanks, she posted a guard at their house, explaining that we were concerned for his safety. "Frankly," Sanniah reported over dinner that night, "I suspect that the greater danger to him is himself, not an angry mob, but I hope that now that the false god has been cast down, he'll find peace elsewhere."

Fanakel considered her as she ate. "You still have faith?"

"I believe that the gods' ways are sometimes unfathomable," she replied, "and while the Great One caused much harm, she also served us in various respects. After all," she said, cocking her head, "we were the only nation around with a god dwelling within our borders. Our neighbors helped pay for the tunnel's maintenance, and foreigners made pilgrimages to our temple. We thought ourselves a blessed people." She shrugged. "As I said, a beautiful lie. But now that the rot has been removed from the temple, I have hope that we can come together and start fresh."

She was, I mused, very young, and blessed or cursed with the optimism of youth. But she was bold, and I hoped for the best. The hundreds of bouquets of flowers left on the palace steps during the day certainly suggested that she'd found favor with one segment of the population.

"What will you do with the tunnel?" Mia asked. "Tear it down?"

Sanniah shook her head and took a sip of wine. "No. The tunnel remains."

"Why?"

"As a sign," she replied. "A reminder of the cost of pride and deceit. I won't pay for its maintenance any longer, so over time, it will crumble, as it should. Perhaps people in the provinces will steal brick to reuse in other building projects. Someday, long after I'm gone, all that will remain will be the odd bit of rubble in a vague line across the fields…or so I hope." After another pause to drink, she added, "In the meantime, the tunnel easily marks the weak place between our world and the Beyond. Perhaps someday we may send emissaries."

"Or we could just pop up here on vacation," I joked.

She grinned. "And you would be welcome. Truly, I'm in your debt…all of you," she said, looking around the table. "Should you ever have a need, call upon me."

Morning broke on a city dampened by an overnight rain, and the rooftops below my window seemed to glisten in the dawn light. Feeling better than I had in days, I bathed and packed, grabbed breakfast with the others, and met

Sanniah in her throne room for our sendoff. While she wore a delicate golden crown, the veil was nowhere in sight, and I silently applauded her.

With her chief ministers gathered around, and broadcasting to her people, she thanked us for our service to Banilgh and to Unara at large, and then a servant began to pass out small, wrapped boxes. "Copies of my broadcast of the Great One's defeat," Sanniah explained. "Should your peoples require proof, I hope this suffices."

The servant paused at the end of our line, flummoxed to still be holding a fifth box, and I accepted it on Terj's behalf. "If this doesn't do it, I hope the big tooth will," I told the queen.

"It's being securely wrapped for transport, I assure you. What remains of the creature's skull will be brought here in the days to come, should you need additional pieces."

"Then I think I'm set for souvenirs," I replied, chuckling.

"Not quite yet." She beckoned to another servant, who unwrapped a cloth-covered bundle to reveal my leather scabbard, cleaned and oiled. The bungee cord was gone, replaced by an actual belt, and I received it with thanks. "Try it on," said Sanniah. "Let's make sure it fits."

It did, to my relief—as much as I'd eaten in the last day, I wouldn't have been surprised to have put on a few pounds—but as I started to unbuckle it, she stayed me. "Since you lost your weapon in doing us a favor, it wouldn't be proper for us to send you away with an empty scabbard."

Oh, believe me, Terj interjected, *no one's upset to see the last of* that *thing.*

"Be that as it may, I'd like to try to replace it." Another servant stepped forward, awkwardly carrying a long wooden box, and opened it to reveal a lovely steel blade, albeit one grossly oversized for the Unaran physique. "Two hundred years ago, the king's youngest brother grew into a giant," Sanniah explained. "He was so large that standard weapons seemed like toys in his hands, so this sword was forged for his use. Tragically, he died a young man, and the sword wasn't completed until after his death. It's old but new," she added, grinning. "And it should be used for good."

I carefully removed the sword from its box and wrapped my hands around the leather-covered hilt. The fact that I could hold it with both hands suggested how big its intended owner had to have been. There were no Aen crystals set into it the hilt, of course, but the pommel had been finely etched with a decorative motif of leaves—in all, a beautiful weapon.

"Are you sure?" I asked Sanniah.

She nodded. "Take it with my thanks."

I slid it into the scabbard—an excellent fit, even if the replacement wasn't magically forged like its predecessor.

Soon, Sanniah escorted us to the landing pad on the tower roof, where the largest of her aircraft awaited, loaded for transport. "I'm afraid it'll be a long flight," she said apologetically. "Arrangements have been made for you to overnight in the waystation at Joh, and from there, you'll fly to the weak point of the tunnel tomorrow." She hesitated, then awkwardly hugged us all, excepting Terj, who was conserving his strength and remained invisible. "Safe travels," she bade us as we boarded. "And may the gods see you home."

Our pilot and copilot were polite but quiet—in all fairness, I'm sure we freaked them out—and I soon caught myself dozing as we flew along the carriage line away from Volng. I woke to eat in the early afternoon, embarrassed to find that I'd slept so long, but no one teased me, and Terj told me not to feel bad. *For the last two and a half months, you've been dealing with monsters in the night, angry monarchs, and other delightful stressors. You're more exhausted than you realize.*

You don't have to coddle me.

I'm not. I have learned a thing or two about you of late, and I know what "drained" feels like with you, so stop beating yourself up over a damn nap.

I frowned into space, able to sense Terj's presence but unable to see him. *You're still connected to me? Even without the sword?*

In a way. You feel me, don't you?

I know you're here…

And you're the only one who would know that if I didn't periodically announce my presence. I'm not exactly making myself known right now.

Is that not the elemental bit of me showing through?

Possibly, he allowed. *But with a bond like the one the sword forged…I mean, you and I may always be a little more attuned to each other than circumstances would dictate. Magic can have side effects.*

Huh. I dug through the granola bag, hunting for chocolate. *Well, as I've said, if I have to get stuck with someone, I could do a lot worse than you.*

He chuckled in my mind. *Still contemplating that road trip? You, me, Mia, the mighty Accord?*

Think we could squeeze Anji and Fanakel in there, too?

If I stayed like this. Wait, would Anji need a booster seat?

Do you want to suggest putting Anji in a booster seat?

You know, I think she might find a way to kill me if I tried. But in all seriousness, what do you plan to do? Terj asked me. *Assuming we don't die in the desert while trying to find your father, what then?*

I slowly munched on a handful of increasingly stale granola as I considered the question. *Don't know, really. Go home, pack my stuff, see the world beyond the Crossing?*

Terj was quiet for a moment, then asked, *You wouldn't consider staying somewhere in the four worlds?*

Where would I go? I've gotten by this long on bravado and charity. My mother wants me dead, and my dollars are worthless.

You have three Aen crystals, he pointed out. *That's a small fortune, you know.*

Is it?

Trust me. They're in the bottom of your bag, yes?

I nodded. *You feel them?*

I do. And if you wanted to sell them, I suspect the maladetas could find a buyer. You could set yourself up in one of the human countries…maybe Meali, he suggested. *Or there are certainly human settlements on the other worlds. You're not limited to Kopaat.*

Something to think about, I replied, and fished out another handful. *What about you? Assuming we make it out of the desert, what's on your agenda?*

Terj didn't sigh—physically, he couldn't—but that's how my brain registered his response. *Honestly? I don't know. There's no family waiting for me, but that's true for nearly all of us. I guess I could go exploring, ride some storms, see what's out there.*

I hesitated before asking, *Is that what you want?*

Not particularly, he admitted. *Freedom is a wonderful thing, but I don't yet know what to do with it, and…* Again, he seemed to sigh. *If I tell you something, will you keep it in confidence?*

Of course.

Well…I've constantly been with someone for most of the last five hundred years, and I…I'm just not sure how I feel about going off on my own yet. Someday, he hastily insisted, *but right now—*

Stay with me, I offered. *We can figure ourselves out together.*

He didn't even pretend to disguise his relief. *You mean it?*

Can't you tell?

Thank you. Is the Grand Canyon still a possibility?

Don't see why not, I said, and put the granola away before I could eat it all.

As the sun sank in the violet sky, we landed beside the waystation in Joh, just as the last carriage of the day was pulling in. By the time we'd gathered our things, Vashir had emerged to meet us, and I was thrilled to see that the priestess was alive. *Well* might have been an overstatement—she looked a bit rumpled and haggard, and I doubted that she'd slept much in the last days—but she extended her hands in welcome and led our group into the building and up to her apartment to eat. As I settled in on the floor cushions, I noticed that she'd changed her décor: the three small alcoves in the sitting room where I'd seen altars of flowers and incense set up on our previous visit were down to two, the middle one having been scoured clean.

"So," I murmured to the others as Vashir slipped out to bring up food, "if one wanted to make small talk with a priest after recent events, what might one safely bring up?"

The answer to that, thanks to our pilots, was kajuvel. Despite their small stature, Unarans were born runners, and relay race teams were as closely followed as football back home. Some of the upcoming stars were sons and daughter of Joh, and as one of them turned out to be Vashir's niece, she was only too happy to speak of her team's latest victories.

As before, we slept in a private room that night so as not to worry the other travelers, and we set off with the dawn. Around noon, the copilot said, "Look down to the right—that's Acanna."

From what I could see, their temple was still standing, though the people working in the fields stopped and stared up at us as we passed overhead.

"Not many flights come out this way?" Mia asked.

The pair up front laughed. "Seldom, if ever," said the pilot. "Just a little farther, now…"

Looking up between their seats, I could barely make out the bend in the tunnel where its arms met. The orange brick structure grew larger in our view until our pilot put us down gently in the tall yellow grass. I grabbed my gear and stepped out, grateful to be on solid ground once more, then considered the solid wall ahead of us. "So, uh…did the queen give you any particular instructions about how to get us *inside* of there?" I asked, leaning back into the aircraft.

"She did," said the copilot, who exited with a small

black bag in his hands. "Stand back, if you please."

While we retreated, he waded through the grass to the tunnel, then dug in the bag and extracted a circular red object. This he affixed to the bricks, and after tapping a sequence on its surface, the circle turned blue and began to beep. As the copilot jogged away to join us, the beeping increased in tempo, and then, with a little puff and a gentle spray of masonry chips, a neat hole appeared in the tunnel.

"Those disintegrate anything within their radius," he explained as we stared at the impossibly near detonation, "but sometimes, there's a bit of blowback. It's safe now."

"I need one of those," Anji muttered as we adjusted our packs and headed for the hole.

The pilots watched from the far side as we stepped into the tunnel. As soon as I'd lugged my giant tooth within the structure, I felt it—the potential of Aen-laced air, coming from straight ahead. Hoping for the best, I pressed against the brick on the opposite wall. To my relief, my hand and wrist passed through as if I were pushing against pudding, and I turned back to wave and to catch a last glimpse of the weirdly purple sky. "It works! Please thank the queen for us," I said, then stepped through the wall and emerged in the darkness of the Crossing.

Seconds later, the others joined me, and I felt Terj's excitement to be that much closer to the Aen. I looked back at the wall leading to the Outside, which seemed deceptively solid, and fought down a giggle of relief.

"Well, shit," said Mia. I heard the sound of a zipper, and a moment later, her flashlight clicked on. "Home again. You think Ms. Quince is still waiting for us?"

"We've only been gone...what, six days? She'd better be," I replied, then started to reach for my sword before I remembered that the one I was carrying wouldn't light up like its predecessor. "Shall we go find out?"

CHAPTER 14

We emerged from the cave into the bright sun of late July. Even within the shelter of the woods, the humidity attacked like I was being smothered by a hot, wet blanket. "Thank God the cabin's air conditioned," I grumbled, then ducked through the hole in the fence around the ersatz asbestos mine and headed up the trail—a trail that thousands of Outsiders had worn, and that none would ever walk again.

That was something, at least. Cole's Crossing would never know, but they'd sleep with one fewer danger lurking in the darkness.

As we neared the cabin, I assessed the scene: Uncle Malachi's old truck parked in its usual spot, Mia's Corolla and my Accord parked nearby, and Ms. Quince's white tank of an Altima behind them on the dirt path, pointed toward town. I didn't see any blood, ash, or major damage to the cabin, which was reassuring, though I could make out the barrel of a rifle through a cracked front window and hoped the maladetas hadn't had to use it.

Before I could reach the porch, the front door flew open, and Ms. Quince laughed aloud. "You're alive!" she cried, running down the short flight of stairs, and met me with a brief but crushing hug before she assaulted the others in turn. "What are you carrying? What did you find over there? Did you..." Her eyes flicked to the hilt at my hip, and then she frowned. "Wait...what did you do to Firebrand?"

Destroyed it, said Terj, appearing at my side in a gust of wind and dried leaves. *That one's a gift.*

Ms. Quince gasped and retreated a pace, one hand flying to her mouth. "You...how..."

"Let's just say that Outsiders won't be a problem going forward," I replied, then waved to Ganeel as she peeked out the door. "Is there anything to eat? I think I could do some real damage to a pizza."

"*Ooh*...Little Italy?" Mia suggested.

Anji perked. "I'll join you."

"What is pizza?" Fanakel asked with a suspicious frown.

"It's *quality*, is what it is," said Mia. "My wallet and keys are in the cabin. Want me to make the drive?"

"No, thanks," I said, and smirked at the stunned maladetas. "Sword's gone. *I'll* do it."

Shotgun, Terj called.

"But *what* has happened?" Ganeel demanded as Mia pushed past her into the house. "Firebrand...you..."

"We did what you couldn't," I said, following Mia, "and we'll tell you everything after we take care of priorities. Now, what does everyone want topping-wise?"

I braced myself on my way through town, just in case the leash the sword had placed on me was still intact somehow and I was about to hit a wall of pain, but I put Cole's Crossing in my rearview mirror without anything worse than a vulture sighting on the side of the road. Terj remained invisible beside me, but I could sense his pleasure, particularly once I rolled down his window.

I don't mean to judge, I said as we picked up speed on the two-lane highway, *but tell me you're not riding along with your head sticking out.*

So what if I am?

I smiled to myself. *Feels good?*

Incredible.

Personally, I found the smell of the pizzeria more

exciting than the wind in my hair, and I lingered in an old chair in the lobby, breathing it in and drinking a Pepsi, while I waited for my order. Terj remained in the car—quite contentedly, by the feel of it—though he seemed confused when I returned with my arms full and opened the back door. *Don't you think the boxes would be safer up here?* he asked. *In case you brake hard?*

You're already sitting up there, I replied.

I'm not really sitting, you know, so—

Keep your seat, I insisted, and wedged the pizzas in the floorboards. *Enjoy the ride.*

When I buckled myself in, he quietly said, *Thanks, Susan.*

For what? You called shotgun, didn't you?

Well, yes, but...thank you.

I reached across the center console, and an almost transparent hand appeared to grip mine. *Least I can do.*

Terj said little on the way back to the cabin, but I could tell that he was still having a good time. It was strange, I mused, to be so attuned to another's moods, and I wondered if we'd always be like this. Assuming Terj eventually went on his way, would I still sense him so strongly whenever our paths crossed again?

That the notion of *not* feeling him by my side seemed oddly wrong was, I assumed, a side effect of the weeks we'd spent in each other's company. Nothing to worry about, I told myself, and sped home before the pizzas could cool.

By the time we returned, Mia, Anji, and Fanakel had done a fair job of filling the maladetas in, and the two women were watching open-mouthed as Mia's compact replayed Sanniah's broadcast of the Great One's end. "I come bearing 'za," I announced, dropping the boxes on the counter, but the maladetas ignored me until the recording ended.

Ms. Quince looked up at me as I leaned against the wall, laden plate in hand and garlic on my fingers.

"Merciful gods, child," she murmured. "*That* was the trouble all along?"

"Yup," I said around a massive bite of cheesy dough.

She slowly exhaled. "Malachi would be so damn proud of you. I hope you know that. And Barnaby, naturally, but after everything your uncle endured—"

Everything you put him through, you mean? Terj interrupted, manifesting a few feet away from her chair.

Ms. Quince turned and glared up at him.

I'm not letting this go, Ardielta.

"And what would you have me do?"

Own responsibility for your choices, for one. More than that...I'll think about it. She started to speak, but he cut her off. *Oh, no, Taln'een isn't getting off that easily. You assholes put me through five centuries of hell. You owe me.*

"That...is probably fair," Ganeel admitted. "What do you want in recompense?"

I don't know yet, but I'll find you when I do. Fanakel, chin.

"Huh? Oh," the elf muttered, catching an errant glob of sauce, then grimaced. "Susan, do you have a spare razor, by chance? Mine has dulled."

"Sure," I said between bites. "*Or*, hear me out, you could get a little scruffy."

Fanakel cocked an incredulous eyebrow as he dunked another garlic breadstick in marinara.

"What? You look good with a 'three days in the woods' beard."

Anji hissed. "Ooh. Would we really call that a beard?"

"Close enough," he muttered. "But, uh...thanks. I think."

At that, Ms. Quince rose and folded her arms. "Young man, you have nothing to worry about."

"Besides obvious indications of mixed parentage in Nokan'ti?" he countered. "It's not *great*."

Her lips curled into a faint smile. "Once your father sees this recording, I doubt he'll complain about the beard ever again."

"You're assuming that he'd agree to watch it," Fanakel replied. "The next time I show my face in the Greenwood, he'll probably throw me in a cell for a month before he bothers to ask where I've been."

The maladetas exchanged glances, and Ganeel said, "Tell them, daughter."

"Tell us what?" I asked.

"*Well,*" said Ms. Quince, drawing out the word, "things have been quiet around here in your absence, so we went into the tunnels and sent messages to our sister clans about what you were doing. Word has reached your families," she told Fanakel and Anji. "Your father, I understand, was stunned," she said to Fanakel, "and as for you, Anji, the Great Temple has been sending up daily prayers for your safe return."

The princess smiled at the news.

"Dare I ask about Daril?" I muttered.

Ms. Quince grunted. "We declined to mention your claim to the throne. My sister in Deoni reported that the queen seemed...*pleased*...that you'd gone Outside."

"Shocking," I deadpanned.

"Yes, well, I suppose we'll need to send word again that the greatest heroes in the four worlds have returned triumphant. *Ah,*" she snapped as our faces shifted. "You could use a little good publicity, and remember that legends aren't written about the overly modest."

"We just—"

"You killed every Outsider in existence," said Ms. Quince. "We've already heard reports of the things spontaneously bursting into flame in Ildon. So what I propose to do is record this recording," she said, holding up the Unaran compact, "and pass it around. Perhaps we could tarry here for a day or two," she suggested. "Give the recording time to circulate. I'm sure you could use a little rest before your next journeys—and Mia, I've been by Antoinette's. She told me to tell you that she hopes you're doing well and can't wait to have you back."

"That's great," Mia mumbled, though she didn't sound overly enthused.

"Anyway," Ms. Quince continued, "it will take a bit of concentration to convert the recording into something transmissible." She wiggled the closed compact between finger and thumb. "If I may borrow this, Ganeel and I can go back to my house for the night and do what needs to be done. If any of you wish to come with us, I know the bed situation here is rather dire."

The four of us glanced at each other questioningly—I already knew that Terj wasn't leaving my side—and we shook our heads. "We'll manage, thank you," Fanakel told them. "Assuming there's anything left in the pantry…"

"Oh, don't worry, I restocked," said Ms. Quince, rising. She'd slipped into jeans in our absence, as had Ganeel, who wore them awkwardly and kept tugging at her shirt. "We'll see you in the morning, then. Let you have a chance to unwind."

They quickly grabbed a few items and departed, and I listened until the sound of Ms. Quince's car faded in the woods. "So," I said, surveying the tidier if still decidedly under-furnished cabin, "same arrangement as before?"

Fanakel sighed, but he nodded and began unpacking his bedroll.

On Mia's suggestion, I drove out of town again for dinner, this time to introduce our companions to the wonders of Chinese takeout. Clean and full of fried rice, I sank into bed with a feeling of contentment I'd almost forgotten, then scooted toward the far side to leave room for Mia.

A quiet voice roused me in the night, and it took me a few seconds to recognize it as Terj's. *Susan? Are you awake?*

I am now, I replied in kind, and squinted at the glowing numbers of the old digital clock. Barely past eleven. *What's wrong? Bored?*

Come eavesdrop with me.

I snorted at that. *You're not even going to try to pretend you're not spying?*

I won't lose sleep over it.

You don't sleep, I pointed out, but rolled over and saw that Mia's half of the bed remained empty. *Where's Mia?*

Porch. Come on, be stealthy.

Quietly, trying not to stub my toe in the darkness, I crept out of the bedroom and into the main room of the cabin. Fanakel had made his bed on the far side, near the cold fireplace, and seemed to be deeply asleep, but the recliner Anji had claimed was empty and upright. Suspicion mounting, I made my way to the closest of the front windows and knelt beside the wall, where I could sneak occasional peeks through the dirty glass.

As I'd suspected, the missing were together, sitting on the porch steps and softly conversing while the crickets chirped. Considering the state of the drafty, aged cabin, I didn't have to strain hard to listen in.

"It's stupid," said Mia, and swigged from one of the longnecks I'd picked up with the Chinese dinner.

"It's not," Anji protested.

"Yes, it is. I've got a place here, I've *probably* still got a job, and…" She heaved a long sigh. "I don't want any of it."

"You did tell me you didn't want to work in the restaurant forever—"

"Yeah, but right now, Antoinette's is what's paying my bills. I don't have massive savings, I don't have anywhere to go outside the Crossing…hell, I took at stab at New York, and that was a colossal failure. But…ugh," she muttered and drank again.

Anji sat quietly, waiting her out.

"The thing is," said Mia, "I spent the last, like, ten weeks as a badass trainee gunslinger or something, and I just don't want to back to being Mia Randolph, Waitress Extraordinaire, who's bunking at her best friend's place because getting a rental house would be too expensive.

Don't get me wrong, Suze has been a lifesaver—she only asks for help with utilities and food, you know? But I don't want to be living like this when I'm thirty, Anji. I don't want to die in this town."

The princess grunted noncommittally.

"On the other hand," Mia muttered, lifting her beer, "the money I have won't get me far, so it's here or homelessness. Guess there's not much call for monster slaying, huh?"

Silence descended between them, Mia taking the occasional pull and Anji staring into the trees. I'd almost decided to slink back to bed when Anji said, "Come with me."

"Sorry?"

"Back to Heartfast. Come with me. It's not nearly as provincial as the little towns—we have our share of oversized visitors," she added, gently elbowing Mia in the side—"so people wouldn't stare much."

"And do what?" Mia asked.

"Stay with me." Anji sped up as she warmed to the subject. "I'll tell Father that I've agreed to train you in swordsmanship, and you'll train me with firearms. We can find a room for you in the palace. My siblings have entourages, so Father won't begrudge me a single friend, especially not if we're tutoring each other—"

"Slight problem: your dad saw me before second puberty. He wouldn't let me stick around."

"If I ask him, and once he's seen what we did…"

Mia shook her head. "He's not stupid—he'll figure out that I've got tekori in me. You think he'd really give a parasite free run of the palace?"

"You are *not* a parasite," Anji insisted.

"That's not what you people say. I've heard it from dwarves, from Fanakel…"

Anji gripped Mia's free wrist. "They're wrong. And you don't have to feed like…*that*. Do you?"

"I don't think so. I mean, it feels great when I do, but

I've been able to get by with big portions of real food. Succubus or bottomless pit, those are my two modes," she joked.

"What *is* a succubus, anyway?"

"Mythological sex demon."

"Mm. But I'm serious, Mia, come with me. Father will understand, and we'll make this work, and I…I don't want to say goodbye to you," she blurted, then stiffened, hastily pushed herself to her feet, and started walking down the stairs.

"Anji, wait," said Mia.

"I—"

"*Wait.* Please." With the stairs between them and Mia sitting, they were almost at a height, and Mia gripped Anji's tense shoulder. "What are you saying?"

Anji didn't answer her for a long moment, and her muscles remained tense. Finally, she said, "Please be patient with me."

"I'm right here," Mia replied.

"I…" Anji sagged as she sighed. "Perhaps you think me a coward, and I deserve that. I've heard all my life that what I want is wrong, but…but with every fiber of my soul, this feels *right*," she confessed. "And I…I'm trying, I am, it's just…"

"I'll wait."

She turned to Mia, her cheeks damp above her short beard in the porchlight's glow.

"I will wait for you," Mia said slowly. "You know, it wasn't so long ago here that there happened to be men and women who lived with very *good* friends of the same gender. Never married, died single, just…moved in with a great buddy one day and set up house together. People didn't necessarily talk about it, and it wasn't like they were legally married, but they did what they could. And if all we can be to each other is good friends…I could be okay with that, I think. Not perfect, not what I'd choose, but if that's all I can hope for, then I'll still wait for you."

Anji stared at her, her expression shifting as she processed that. "You mean—"

Whatever she'd intended to say next was cut short when Mia darted forward and kissed her—briefly, fairly chastely, but leaving no question as to her intentions. Anji pulled back in surprise and took a step toward the ground, panting, then mustered her courage, ran back up the stairs, and pulled Mia into her arms.

You knew this was coming? I asked Terj as I sneaked back to bed, giving the two of them some privacy.

It's been building. Rokund probably won't be thrilled by Anji's new sparring partner, so let's hope the maladetas are right about their publicity campaign.

I gently closed the bedroom door and crawled beneath the blankets. *Well, I think we should do the adult thing and play dumb.*

Wisdom is not antagonizing the woman with better sword skills, he concurred. *Sleep well, Susan. I'll fill you in tomorrow if anything develops.*

As much as I wanted to vegetate in front of the TV in the cabin for, say, the next month, there was the *tiny* matter of the home and business I'd neglected since May, and so I got up early the following morning to put in a brief appearance.

Sunday mornings were quiet in Cole's Crossing unless you counted the parking lot at Grace Methodist. It wasn't a flashy church—Reverend Bowers still wore a suit underneath his robe, and the organist hadn't lost her job to a praise band—but since Grace was the only church in town, proximity won out over style for a good chunk of the local churchgoing population. As I drove past the graveyard where my dad and generations of Coles were buried, I thought about what Ms. Quince had told me— about how the occasional maladetan woman would sneak her son through the tunnels and into my hometown for a better life. How many of the people sitting in that church or buried beside it had ties to another world? Did they know? Were there closely guarded family secrets, or was the whole "not entirely human" thing swept under the rug? And if they did know, were these maladetan descendants the force that had covered up the tunnels' existence with warning placards about asbestos?

I wondered if those immigrants had regrets later in life, if they ever dreamed of a world in which the air itself felt alive with potential and woke longing for home. Perhaps they never looked back. Finding themselves in a far more patriarchal society than the one into which they were born, where the women didn't live for centuries and couldn't work magic, had to be liberating for those maladetan sons.

Did their mothers ever return to check in on them? To see their boys bowed by age but surrounded by families of their own? Or did they stay away, knowing that their sons would be unable to explain their presence to anyone in their new lives?

My thoughts darkened as they turned toward Erianthe. At least those maladetas has tried to give their kids better futures, unlike *some* mothers. I imagined her smiling at the news that I'd gone into the perilous Outside, from which no one ever returned—the trash taking itself out. And now that I'd not only come back alive but done so with video and a souvenir, what would she think? Surely the maladeta in Deoni would show her. Would Erianthe express superficial happiness at the end of the Outsider threat? Would she fume behind her smile? Would she lock herself in her room and quietly freak out?

Pulling into my driveway, I raised the garage door and parked in the cluttered gloom.

I wasn't safe in the four worlds, particularly not on Kopaat, as long as I remained Erianthe's dirty little secret. Maybe I could find patronage for a time, but I'd always be looking over my shoulder, waiting for someone to handle the problem for their queen. And yes, I understood that the issue was bigger than my feelings over being abandoned (and, lest I forget, almost being executed). Erianthe's marriage was a contract: the Cirivantan navy would help defend Daril's interests in distant Ga'besh, and in exchange, a child of the Terol line would sit on the Darili throne someday. My existence was proof that Erianthe couldn't uphold Daril's end of the bargain. In a way, I felt for her, a girl who'd been burdened with a crown too soon, found illicit comfort in another's arms, and ended up with a baby she couldn't afford to keep. She'd delivered me alone in the woods, and I couldn't imagine what that must have been like—unassisted, unmedicated, probably terrified, and so very far from home, enduring the pains of labor to bring forth her literal problem child.

Had she looked back when she left me lying there and returned to the tunnels? Had she fought the urge to hold me when I cried? Or had she, surely exhausted and bleeding, hurried away with relief?

I pitied the girl she'd been, but speaking as the newborn left to die beneath an alien sun, that pity was somewhat tempered by anger.

And it wasn't just me whose life she'd tried to ruin—well, in my case, end. She must have felt *something* for Falova if she'd willingly…

Yeah, I still didn't like to think of the mechanics of my own conception.

Regardless, Erianthe had ordered Falova kidnapped, extracted from the river he'd claimed, and carried into the desert, where he could die or live but probably wouldn't trouble her again. The river had died without him, a scourge on Daril that had lasted for most of her reign…and on Ti'cal, I mused, whose fishing industry had evaporated.

I climbed out of the car and walked into the house to check on the place. Aside from a blinking microwave clock, evidence of a summer power outage, and a few dead bugs in the windows, the house seemed to be as I'd left it. The yard looked decent—I had my lawn service on monthly auto-debit—and though I found my mailbox stuffed, nearly everything inside was junk.

With the flyers trashed, I turned to the task of cleaning out the fridge, then ran the taps and flushed the toilets to make sure everything was still working. The air conditioner wanted a new filter, and I installed one from the stash Dad kept in the garage, yet another dwindling sign of his presence in our home.

I was going back into the Kopaati desert to find my father. My *biological* father, to be clear. Did he have any idea that I existed? Had he known of Erianthe's pregnancy before she sent her goons after him? And if he hadn't known, how would he feel to learn that he'd sired a rogue?

I *wanted* to meet him. I'd never seen commonalities between my face and Dad's, and I'd been too preoccupied to notice the features that Erianthe and I shared until later...would I find anything familiar at all in an incorporeal being?

Glancing at the refrigerator, I noticed the last photo that Dad and I had taken, just before I went back to college after the Christmas holiday. We'd been in the Grace Methodist fellowship hall at the town's family-friendly New Year's Eve party, our arms around each other and silly party hats on our heads, clutching plastic flutes of sparkling grape juice and grinning. He'd died ten days later, but not before he'd added that picture to the kitchen photo gallery.

God, I missed him. And now, with Uncle Malachi gone, too...

I must have cried alone in that quiet kitchen for ten minutes, sitting at the island with my face in my hands. Terj was right—I hadn't yet mourned my uncle properly, and being home after the insanity of the last months brought the familiar grief rushing back like a tidal wave.

And then came the knock at the door.

Drying my face on a paper towel, I pulled myself together and went to the front, where I found Ms. Quince on the welcome mat. "Hello, dear," she murmured. "Thought I heard a car over here. Are you all right?"

I shook my head.

"May I come in?"

I stepped aside to admit her and closed the door, and when I turned around, she hugged me tightly. "It's more than you ever should have borne. I know that," she said, rubbing my back. "You did a wonderful thing, but that doesn't make it an *easy* thing to move past…"

"It's not that," I mumbled into her shirt.

"What is it, sweetie?" she said, and for a moment, I imagined her once more as the kindly neighbor I'd always known.

"I miss them *so much*," I whispered, then started to cry again.

She didn't have to ask for clarification. "Oh, Susan," she said, and shepherded me back to the kitchen. "Sit down, I'll make you a cup of tea."

I'd calmed to hiccupping by the time the kettle whistled—Ms. Quince insisted that microwaved water tasted off—and she pushed a chipped mug in front of me. "Talk to me," she said, taking a seat at the island to my right. "Is there something I can do?"

"Not unless you can raise the dead," I muttered into my steaming drink.

"Unfortunately, that's beyond my power." She waited while I took a tentative sip, then said, "I know you're hurting, honey. I know you miss them. But you should know that wherever they are, they are *so* proud of you."

"You can't know that."

"I do," she insisted. "I knew the Cole boys long before you entered the picture, little miss, and I watched you grow up. Barnaby used to say that you were the greatest gift of his life, do you know that? And Malachi—that man adored you. Now look at you," she continued, "the last

Cole in the Crossing and the bravest of them all."

"I'm not really a Cole, though, am I?" I said, cradling the mug.

"You are in all the ways that matter," Ms. Quince replied. "And wherever you go from here, whoever you become...you'll carry your family with you."

I gave her a little smile. "You don't think I'm going to stay in town?"

"Not forever. You can't." When I frowned, she explained, "The rogue elementals I've known of, corporeal and incorporeal alike, have shared two traits. They're always more powerful than their elemental parents, and they never grow old. I've seen them be *killed*, now, but they don't die. So while you can stay here for a time, there will come a day when your face will be too young. Besides," she added as I took that in, "I can't imagine you lingering here as a young woman for the next few centuries. Surely there's something else you'd like to see beyond Cole's Crossing."

"Don't know," I said with a shrug, "but I'm going to go find my father first. Take him back to the river. Seems like the right thing to do."

Ms. Quince sat beside me in silence for a time, letting me drink and stew, then said, "I've noticed in this part of this world that people tend to have a fairly rigid, limited view of what a family can be. Know what I mean?"

"I guess."

"Your dad and your uncle loved you dearly," she murmured. "But Susan, they wouldn't want you to be alone if you could have more family by your side. Now, I'm sure both of them would like a strong word with your mother, but from all we know, Falova is blameless in your abandonment. I don't think they'd be upset if you reached out to him."

"Maybe," I allowed, "it's just that...I mean..."

"You feel like you're being disloyal? That seeking your biological father is somehow an insult to Barnaby?"

I nodded and clutched my cooling tea.

"Little one," she said softly, wrapping an arm around my shoulders, and I leaned against her. "Your dad will always be your dad, and no one can take that away. You hold him close," she continued, reaching over to pat my chest, "and you always will. But I'm telling you as someone who knew him *pretty* well that he would want you to find Falova. Not to replace him, but to expand your family. Love is not measured out to us at birth, to be carefully hoarded and rationed only to a handful of people," she told me. "Love is infinite, a self-replenishing resource. And if I know Barnaby at all, he'd be crushed at the idea that you'd go on the rest of your life without ever loving anyone new."

After a moment, when my throat no longer felt so tight that I could barely breathe, I mumbled, "You're not just saying that?"

"Not at all. And I also meant it when I said you were the bravest of the Coles," she replied, giving me a little squeeze. "Malachi couldn't have done what you did."

"I don't know, if he'd had the chance…"

Ms. Quince sighed. "And I should have given it to him. I…admit that. In all honesty, though, I don't think he'd have made it as far as you went. You are remarkable, my dear, and if Malachi were here right now, he'd tell you so himself. Of that, I have no doubt whatsoever."

She released me and slipped off her stool, then patted my shoulder and headed for the door. "I should be getting back to my place before Ganeel panics. Between you and me, she's not acclimated well to this century. I doubt she'll be sorry to return to Taln'een."

"How much longer will you stay here?" I asked, turning to watch her go.

"If you lot are up to it, I thought we might leave tomorrow. We'll need fresh provisions to make it across the waste, so I'll shop today. Don't suppose there's any need to maintain the funds I'd set aside for my replacement here," she added with a smirk. "We can have the *good* granola."

"Do you want company? Shopping buddy?"

Her expression shifted toward true pleasure. "Well, now, since Ganeel's terrible in public around here, I just might."

We took her car out to the big grocery store in the next town, the one that had rendered the Cole family's general store far less necessary than it had once been. While Ms. Quince drove, I left a message on my store's old answering machine for Annie Plunkett, assuring her that I was alive and well, thanking her for picking up the slack in my absence, and telling her to make whatever purchases she needed until I got back.

When I hung up, Ms. Quince asked, "Are you planning to keep the store?"

"I don't know," I admitted. "Kind of feels like sacrilege to sell it, but if I don't stick around…"

"You could sell it to Annie. She knows that place as well as Barnaby did, and she'd take good care of it. But," she added as I considered that alternative, "this isn't a matter that has to be decided today, right? Today, we buy supplies for our journeys." Turning at an empty four-way stop, she asked, "Any idea as to what the others plan to do? If you and the elemental go off alone—"

"Terj."

"Terj," she said, and I knew I wasn't imagining her discomfort. "Do Fanakel and Anji intend to go home immediately? And Mia, what are her thoughts?"

Scenes from the previous night's spying flashed in my mind's eye, but I pushed them away. "I don't know. I don't think Mia wants to stay here, but as for the others…"

"Mm. Well, if there are no *firm* plans, Ganeel and I spoke last night, and we have an idea. What if all of you returned with us? I mean, the three of them now, and you two when you're ready," she clarified. "The longer Anji and Fanakel wait to go home, the longer the news has to circulate, and the longer we have to ensure that the transitions will be smooth."

"What do you mean?"

"I'm not overly worried about Anji—Rokund is a reasonable fellow, and I think he'll be glad to have her back, no matter how long she's been away. But Fanakel left home under slightly less authorized conditions, shall we say, and we want to be certain that he'll receive an appropriate welcome."

My eyebrows rose. "You think that after everything we've done—"

"I've known my share of elves, Susan. We can build the king's son into a hero, but there's no erasing his mother. Our goal is for Fanakel to be respected—putting him fully on par with his siblings in his father's eyes would be a task for the gods."

"Assholes," I muttered. "Bunch of gorgeous pricks in their fucking treehouse."

She chuckled and swerved around a flattened squirrel. "They can be useful on occasion, but...*yeah*. Anyway, let's run that thought by them. And Mia, assuming she wants to come."

I waited until Ms. Quince had passed a rumbling old pickup truck out for a Sunday drive, then asked, "Is there anything you can do to help Mia find her father?"

"Perhaps," she allowed after a moment's consideration. "And if Mia wishes to search for him someday, I wouldn't be opposed to assisting her. But that's something she'll have to decide she wants to do. I know you've been through a lot this summer, but so has she," Ms. Quince murmured, "and if I were you, I'd let Mia set the pace in that area."

"Oh, I wasn't going to push it. I was just curious."

She smiled beneath her sunglasses. "Then yes, we do

have our ways."

"Speaking of," I said as Ms. Quince pulled up to the grocery store, "before I go running out into the desert, I've got a question."

"Only one?"

"One big one. Whoa, he's not looking—"

"I see him," she soothed as a bright yellow dually backed into our lane. She pulled into his vacated spot and parked but kept the engine running, as the late July morning was unpleasantly warm at best without air conditioning. "Now, what's on your mind?"

"It's occurred to me," I said, drumming my fingers on the armrest in the door, "that if I locate Falova, I don't know how the hell to get him back to the river."

Ms. Quince peered at me over her lenses. "Sorry, I don't follow."

"I mean, he was removed by magic, right? How do I remove him from wherever he is now? Like…how do you transplant an elemental?"

She grunted. "It's not easy, and it would have to be with the elemental's consent. We have records of it being done after massive natural disasters in the distant past. What happened to Falova was almost certainly not consensual, and that's the kind of magic that only a suicidal maladeta or a very well-trained human with *ample* amplification from Aen crystals would be able to accomplish."

"Not an elf?"

"Surprisingly, no. They can use the Aen to affect most living things, but they're not particularly effective against elementals. That was why my people were necessary to complete Firebrand. But back to the matter of Falova—I don't think a maladeta had a hand in his removal."

"The air elemental who told me he was alive to begin with said that Falova believes it was three humans who took him into the desert…"

"That would make sense," she said. "Teamwork would

be necessary for a task that large. But here's the issue: when an elemental becomes sedentary, they fuse part of themself with whatever they join. If they willingly allow themself to be relocated, that part leaves with them. In Falova's case, part of him is still there in the river. Wherever he's been dumped, I doubt he's properly 'joined' it, so to speak. So all you would need to do is convince him to come with you. Well, that, and bring something with you large enough to carry him. They're *very* easily compressed, but he'll need to travel in water."

I thought briefly of the goldfish I'd carried home from the county fair in a plastic baggie, the one that had lived two days before I found it floating upside-down and gave it a sea burial via toilet. "How big a container are we talking about?"

"Size wouldn't be the most important thing. You just want something sturdy enough to survive the trip."

I squinted at her. "Like…a thermos? Would that do it? Hard to break, won't lose water?"

She mulled it over. "You know, strange as that sounds…I think it would. *If* you can convince him to get in there. Considering what he's been through, that might be the biggest hurdle."

I tried to imagine how that meeting might go: *Hi, I'm the daughter you never knew you had. Could you climb in this small, cramped space, please?*

"Rescue by thermos," I muttered. "Hell, not even the weirdest thing I've done this week."

"That's the spirit, dear," said Ms. Quince, and opened her door. "Come on, let's get going before the after-church crowd swarms the place."

CHAPTER 15

"All I'm saying," Mia groused as we hiked through the Kopaat-bound tunnel the next morning, "is that it would be entirely possible to get motorcycles down here."

"Possible, yes," Ms. Quince replied. While she sported her maladetan garb once again for the journey home, she'd strapped on an LED headlamp, an incongruous addition to her long blue dress and hooded gray cloak. "But not *practical.* Assuming you were to safely get a bike down the staircase in the dark—and good luck with that, those things are heavier than you might imagine—how would you possibly carry enough fuel to make your effort worthwhile?"

"How long are the tunnels—like, what, ten miles? Fifteen? Decently flat? You could cut a half-day trip down to half an hour at most, and that's if you slow down in the dark."

Overdriving one's headlights wouldn't be hard down there, I mused, watching the colorful streaks of lightning run through the rock around us. The effect was pretty but didn't improve the poor visibility.

"Granted, and I agree that a motorcycle wouldn't be a bad thing to have *in the tunnels,*" said Ms. Quince, "but what happens once you hit the wasteland outside? Those aren't easy conditions, and you probably wouldn't get more than a couple hundred miles before you ran out of fuel, *if* you had a touring bike."

But Mia wasn't giving up. "Okay, so how far to a road?"

Ms. Quince laughed. "Define 'road.' You've experienced the joys of Darili highways, have you not?"

I cringed. The long road from the hinterlands to Deoni had been nothing more than a rutted dirt track for most of its length.

"So, to recap: limited fuel that can't be replenished, you're off-roading, and once you find a road, it'll be a hazard at best," Ms. Quince continued. "From the tunnel opening to Deoni—and that's as the crow flies, mind you—"

"The what?" asked Fanakel.

A straight line, Terj explained. While I couldn't see him, I could feel his presence in the darkness. *Imagine that you're making the journey by air, without regard for ground impediments.*

Ms. Quince's light bobbed as she nodded. "Precisely. Now, I'm estimating, but I'd be surprised if the trip from the tunnel to Deoni were less than seven hundred miles."

Sensing my shock, Terj seemed to chuckle in my mind. *We've been fortunate thus far. I've yet to see any method of transportation in the four worlds that can surpass elemental speed.*

"Okay, then, forget the bike," Mia mumbled. "How the hell are we getting back to Taln'een?"

Ganeel sighed. "That, child, is the tricky part. We pray for the gods' favor but plan for a walk."

"But do we even have enough water to make it to civilization?"

"We *pray*."

Ms. Quince glanced over her shoulder at Mia. "There *is* a plan beyond prayer. The tunnel lies along the primary corridor between Daril and the Meali Republic, and merchant caravans aren't uncommon. Even travel by chiquiw would be better than travel on foot. We can generally negotiate passage—a maladeta isn't a bad addition to a traveling party—and I'm fairly confident that we can work out a way for all five of us to get a ride...that is, assuming a party passes by. That would be where prayer comes in."

"And what if those Darili guards are still on duty?" Anji asked.

Ganeel snorted. "You know, having seen Daril's finest warriors in action, I'm not overly concerned."

While I appreciated her confidence, I wasn't keen on having another run-in with the guards. Bluster and a magic sword had gotten us past them the first time, and now that I was carrying an ordinary blade, I didn't care for our worsened odds. As I made my way through the darkness behind the maladetas, overly burdened with my trophy tooth lashed to my backpack, I prayed to any convenient deity for a little luck.

Unfortunately, that luck turned out to be a mixed bag. The end of the tunnel had barely widened beyond a bright pinprick in the distance when we began to hear raised voices, and the argument came and went as we neared. By the time we emerged, the parties were locked in a tense standoff: the damn Darili guards on the one side, and a large dwarven carriage on the other. Unlike the carriages I'd seen back on Ildon, this one was the size of an RV, and the translucent window panels of quartz revealed that the back half of the rig was loaded with boxes. Three dwarves stood by their carriage in belted tunics, leather vests, and dark trousers, overdressed for the summer and already sweating in the morning sun.

"What's the meaning of this?" asked Ganeel as she stepped from the tunnel's shadow.

The four guards and the dwarven trio turned as one, and the guards' hands went to their swords. "You returned," said the blond guard with the ponytail, stunned.

Ganeel shrugged. "My travels take me where I must go. Again, what's your quarrel with these...merchants?"

The dwarves nodded, and their apparent leader, a redhead who wore his beard in four red braids, bowed to her. "Greetings, and the High Queen's blessing upon you. Could you translate, please? Our translators are poor things, and we cannot make these humans understand us."

"Of course," she replied as the rest of us exited the tunnel. "Why have you stopped—"

"*You!*" the blond guard yelped, pointing his sword at me. "Get back! Return to your post, damn you!"

"*Excuse* me?" I snapped, drawing my sword in turn. "I don't have a *post*, asshole, and I don't take orders from you."

His smarter companion, the guard with the brown crewcut, started to intervene. "The Watcher—"

"Is now unemployed," I interrupted, and showed them my new blade. "Looks a little different, doesn't it?"

The four guards gaped, and the third, whose short, pale hair had done his pink scalp no favors, managed to recover first. "What...what have you done to Shadowbane?"

"Destroyed it," said Ms. Quince. "*And* all the Outsiders. There are none left to trouble us," she said with a cold smile, "so the sword has served its purpose. Now, why are you harassing these dwarves?"

The guards exchanged glances, and the smartest of the bunch cleared his throat. "These appear to be merchants—"

"We *are* merchants!" the leader of the dwarves interjected. "We've been trying to tell them for hours! We're bound for the market in Genutil with hunting and fishing supplies," he said, thumbing one hand toward their carriage.

Ganeel grunted. "Not Deoni?"

"These are not wares for city folk, nor are they scaled for human hands," he replied. "The great summer market will be held in eight days' time for the far northern settlements. We've secured permission to trade," he added, and pulled a folded sheaf of papers from within his vest. "See?"

She took the papers from him, briefly scanned them, and handed them back. "All seems to be in order, if my Lower Dwarfish is still decent. You come from Meali?"

"No, Silverhold...Great Mother?" said another dwarf,

cocking her head. "You are of Taln'een, are you not?"

Ganeel nodded in acknowledgement. "Yours has been a long journey."

"Silverhold is in Duvila," Ms. Quince whispered to me. "It's the continent between Echoril in the north and Antinil in the south."

"Yes," said the lead merchant, "and we've been arguing with these fools since before dawn. We'd like to proceed before we broil alive."

She nodded, then turned her attention back to the guards, who looked shiftier by the minute. "These are merchants bound for Genutil. Let them pass."

"They said there's a toll, Great Mother," the female dwarf offered.

Ganeel's expression hardened as she stared the men down. "*Is* there, now? And on whose authority is such a toll levied?"

The guards' apparent spokesman rubbed his neck. "Well, you see, the queen—"

"For the last time, this is not Darili territory," she snapped. "The tunnel was purposefully built in no-man's-land so that none could control its use. You have no claim here. Stand down."

"Actually," said the fourth guard, who wore his dark hair in a long braid, "I think we have an *excellent* claim. We're the ones who've guarded these lands against Outsiders, and it's only fair that Daril receive its due compensation."

"We have laws," Ganeel protested. "Treaties. Your actions are pure thievery, and were we to ask your queen, I sincerely doubt that she would have any knowledge of a toll scheme."

"But Her Majesty isn't here to be asked, is she?" he retorted. "So in her absence, you'll just have to trust us."

How do we want to play this? I silently asked my companions.

Beside me, Mia sighed. "Let me. Ears."

Fanakel immediately slapped his hands into position, and as the dwarves watched bemusedly, Anji told them, "Do as the elf does. Explanations later."

Though still perplexed, they were willing to listen to a fellow dwarf, even one with a questionably short beard. As soon as they'd blocked their ears, Mia turned on the charm. "Boys," she purred, sashaying past Ganeel, "*boys*, come on. I know you've been out here for a long time, but surely we can reach an agreement...can't we?"

Within minutes, she had them and their two awakened companions packed, mounted, and on their way back to Deoni, riding as hard as their chiquiws could run. We watched until the cloud of dust behind them faded to haze, and then Mia rolled her eyes and mimed uncovering her ears.

The dwarves backed away from her. "You...are you..." the female merchant began.

Mia nodded. "Half tekori...probably. Sorry for the shock, but it was either do that or shoot the bastards, and frankly, I've had enough killing this week."

"These are my companions in arms," said Anji, stepping between them before the merchants could protest further. "That one," she continued, pointing to me, "was the Watcher until a few days ago."

The dwarves' eyes widened. "We'd heard rumor that the Watcher had gone Outside," began the third, the only one of the trio with a short sword at his waist.

Anji nodded. "She did. We accompanied her. The Great Mother speaks the truth: Outsiders will trouble us no more." Pulling herself to her full height, she said, "I am Anjikora of Blackhorn Mountain, daughter of Rokund Elf-Bane. The High King's and High Queen's blessings on you all."

The other dwarves stiffened, then quickly bowed. "Princess," said their leader, "this is...well, this is wonderful news, but one would hardly expect to find a lady like yourself in such, uh...company."

"It's a long story, and one I wouldn't mind telling," she replied. "The five of us are bound for Taln'een. I hate to impose, but is there any way that you might be persuaded to give us passage? We'll gladly share our supplies."

They hesitated, and their leader absently tugged at his beard. "We'd certainly welcome you, Your Highness, and the maladetas, naturally, but, uh..." He eyed Mia and Fanakel, who stood by silently, waiting.

"Perhaps," said Ms. Quince, pulling out her compact-like device, "we could change your mind."

She sat on the carriage's step, the better to show the dwarves the recording. I watched their faces, trying to gauge how far along the clip was by the screams and shrieks of the Great One. By the time Ms. Quince closed her communicator, the dwarves' faces had paled, and they looked at us with a mixture of horror and awe.

"I helped train them," Anji said quietly. "And I trust them. Should they do anything to harm you or your cargo, let the blame fall on me."

The two male dwarves traded glances, but their female companion pushed them aside and opened the door. "Welcome aboard," she said. "Taln'een, was it?"

Anji thanked her, and the others headed for the carriage, taking the giant tooth to ease my load. I hung back with Terj, and Mia hugged me tightly. "You two be safe out there, okay?" she murmured. "I don't like this one bit."

"We'll be fine," I assured her.

We'll find you in Taln'een, said Terj. *Safe travels.*

"You, too." With a last squeeze, she released me, flashed an uncertain smile, and headed into the carriage.

The female merchant stuck her head out the door once Mia boarded. "Coming, lass? There's room."

"I've got another stop first, thank you," I replied, and though she seemed poised to argue about the wisdom of leaving me alone in the wilderness, she closed the door, and the carriage flew away.

I shifted my pack on my shoulders and squinted up at the sun. *You and me, huh?*

Hold on.

Before I could ask questions, a gust of wind swept me off my feet and into the air, and I laughed nervously as I came to rest on an invisible cushion. *Little warning next time?*

Terj appeared beside me, translucent but defined against the bright sky. *Sorry. Let me have my fun.*

Yeah, yeah. I shrugged off my bag, and my aching muscles seemed to sigh with relief. *Are you okay to do this? Strong enough?*

I'm feeling better already, he insisted. *Just being within the Aen...don't you feel the difference?*

Oh, I can feel it, but I don't want you to overexert yourself.

Let me worry about that. Which way are we going?

My eyebrows rose. *I have no idea. I don't even know how big this damn desert is.*

Mm. He thought for a minute, then said, *Try this for me. You can sense water in the distance, yes?*

To an extent...

Try that. See what's out there.

Obliging him, I closed my eyes and tapped into my newly awakened senses. Even in the dry wasteland, I could feel the hints of water in the air...

....far to the north, the narrow sea between Echoril and Genutil...

...the ribbon of dead water that marked the Falova's course...

...and then, due south, I picked up on concentrated water somewhere over the horizon.

There's a lake or something south of here, I told Terj. *Not sure how far away, or how big it is, but if there's an oasis, maybe there'll be an elemental around who can point us in the right direction.*

It's a beginning, he replied, and started to push us along.

A moment later, after profusely apologizing for almost sending me and my gear blowing backward to our deaths, Terj put together a windshield and tried it again. *Much better*, I said, working to slow my hammering heart.

I could feel his fear and embarrassment. *I didn't even think about—*

You've never carried a passenger, have you? You're learning.

I could have killed you.

But you didn't. Calm down.

Terj said nothing for a few minutes, then quietly asked, *Why do you keep putting up with me, Susan?*

I mean, I like to think we're friends by now.

He didn't answer that, but I sensed his flash of surprise and pleasure.

Despite Terj's optimism about his condition, after a few hours in the air, he was desperately flagging. *I'm sorry*, he said, disgust coloring the thought as he set us down atop a treeless hillock. *It's harder than I imagined…*

You're doing well, I insisted. *Better than I could have.* We had to have covered at least a hundred miles that morning, probably more, though I could tell that Terj wasn't as fast as the other air elemental had been.

I'm weak, he grumbled.

Terj, give yourself a break. This is more than I should ask—

I've got to keep you safe out here. If I can't even carry you…

"Terj," I murmured, and his suggestion of a face turned toward mine. *If I have to walk, I will. Okay? Thank you for coming out here with me.* I wiped my brow—the dry summer air was far less pleasant without the breeze of flight—and unzipped my tent's carrying case. *I'm going to put up some shelter and eat lunch. Why don't you rest?*

I can help—

Please rest.

Reluctantly, he let his form dissipate, and I pitched the pop-up tent and opened a bag of dried fruit. I allowed myself a cup of water, no more, then stretched out in the warm shade and folded my arms behind my head. *Terj?*

I'm here.

You're welcome to come in.

The fabric around the door fluttered ever so slightly with his passing, and I sensed him against the far side of the tent. *I'm going to close my eyes for a few minutes,* I told him. *Long walk this morning, and I shouldn't be this tired, but my brain thinks it's midafternoon, and I could do with a nap. Is that all right?*

I felt his wariness—he suspected, and rightly so, that I'd proposed a break for his benefit—but exhaustion won out over his pride. *Sounds wise,* he replied, and soon stilled, the closest he ever came to sleep.

When I awoke, the sun was beginning its decline, and though the air was still miserably hot, Terj seemed refreshed. I packed and braced myself for the upward surge, and we were off once more.

As twilight fell and the clouds burst into oranges and pinks in the west, I finally spotted the source of water in the distance: an oasis perhaps four or five acres in size. The grass around it was lush and green, and even a few trees grew near the bank. A short distance away, though farther than I'd have anticipated, I spotted five chiquiw-drawn wagons pulling into a rough circle.

We should land before we're upon them, said Terj. *Unless you want all sorts of questions about how you happened to fall out of the sky.*

He had a point, and he put me down far enough away that I was decently red, sweaty, and gritty by the time I walked up to the campsite.

A bald man—human, I assumed on first glance—who'd been attaching feed bags to his chiquiws' harnesses stopped and stared at me. "Where did *you* come from, girl?"

"Hiking," I replied, and made a show of wiping my face on my T-shirt. "Long day. Is something wrong with the oasis?"

He chuckled mirthlessly. "First time passing through the waste, eh? You'll give that spring a wide berth if you're wise. The elemental's a menace."

I thanked him, and when he turned back to his animals, I slipped away, heading for the water.

The tall grass brushed over the tops of my boots as I approached the shore, and I paused a few yards from the bank, watching the barely ruffled surface of the spring-fed lake. *Good evening*, I thought. *I'm Susan. Is there a name by which I may address you?*

The lake began to churn, and a figure rose from the depths, its head, arms, and torso composed entirely of water. He towered over me at first, about eight feet tall and proportionally broad, then considered me. I could feel his confusion.

I am myself, he replied after a moment's reflection. *What are you?*

A rogue, people say. My father was one of your brothers. Nodding toward my silent companion, who remained unseen to my left, I said, *This is Terj. He's helping me search for my father out here.*

The water elemental shrank a couple feet, no longer readying for battle but still perplexed. *Your father, you say?*

I nodded. *He was taken from the Falova River and carried somewhere out here. I don't know where he was dumped, but I'm trying to bring him home.*

His thoughts seemed to soften. *I have heard stories of him. Deeper in the waste...that way*, he added, pointing to the south. *I cannot tell you where he lies, but yes, I have heard him spoken of.* His head cocked as he studied me. *A rogue. Fascinating. It has been years since I last saw a rogue...*

I hesitated, hoping I wasn't pressing my luck, then asked, *Would you mind if I made camp here? I don't know those people*, I said, nodding toward the wagons, *and since we're rather outnumbered—*

Make your bed, he replied. *I will allow it.*

Thank you, I said, and smiled. *I'll try not to disturb you.*

As the water elemental conversed with Terj, I set up my tent again and arranged my sleeping bag. That accomplished, I rummaged through my pack until I found my chemical heater kit. I started the heater and pulled together the few ingredients I'd need for pasta, then began to open one of my water bottles to fill the pot.

What are you doing?

I glanced up to find the elemental watching me from the edge of the spring. *Cooking dinner. Is that all right?*

You require food, yes? Water?

I shrugged. *Corporeality has its drawbacks. Body needs feeding, and poor Terj knows how heavy my water supply is.*

You are carrying water?

Enough for a few days. I don't know how long we'll be out here, so I'm trying to ration it.

He withdrew from the bank and motioned me closer. *Take what you need, little sister.*

I frowned. *Are you sure?*

Certainly. Come, drink.

Sensing no warning from Terj, I filled my pot and thanked my host, then set it to boiling and whipped up my mediocre spaghetti. Dinner was nothing special, but it was filling, and I risked asking the elemental if I might wash my dishes. He allowed it, and as I rinsed my silverware by flashlight, he asked, *Are you dirty as well?*

A little grimy, I allowed. *It's hot, and it's been a long day.*

Bathe. The spring is safe.

It was also cold, but I wasn't complaining. Kicking off my shoes on the bank, I waded in with my clothes still on, then submerged myself to ease the shock of the temperature change. When I surfaced, I felt Terj hovering nearby, watching. *I'm okay*, I told him. *I can swim, you know.*

Sorry.

The water elemental's amusement rushed into my mind. *He worries about you. Unnecessarily, it would seem.*

It's appreciated, I replied before Terj could be embarrassed.

I sank again, rinsing my hair and washing the grit from my skin. A few minutes later, much cooler and a bit less gross, I walked out of the spring and concentrated until the water I'd accumulated pulled away from me in an amorphous blob. I dropped that back into the spring and nodded to the elemental in thanks, then slipped into my tent for the night.

Are you coming, I asked Terj, *or do you have more exciting plans?*

He laughed softly. *I'll be up for a while, but I'll be around. Sleep well, Susan.*

Exhausted as I was, I did just that.

It wasn't daylight that awakened me, but rather the sound of my tent's zipper being slid open.

"Terj?" I mumbled, blinking blearily in the darkness. "That you?"

When the door flap dropped, I saw a large, decidedly solid form on the other side and knew the answer to *that* question. Before I could do more than yelp, the man outside my tent grabbed my feet and dragged me out, still cocooned within my sleeping bag.

"Hey!" I shouted, reaching for my sword, but he was too fast. Kicking and clawing instead, I made contact with his skin and thought I might squirm my way to freedom, only for a second man to sit atop my chest.

"Don't you know it's not wise to travel alone, little girl?" he murmured, his breath foul in my face. "You'd better come with us. We'll take care of you, don't—"

His lies ended in a scream as he was yanked into the air. While his buddy stared upward in horror, I scrambled to freedom and ran toward the shore. A scream and a loud thud told me that Terj had dropped the man, but I didn't dare to look back.

Before I reached the water, the first man grabbed my shoulder and spun me around. "You're not going anywhere," he said, and the knife in his free hand gleamed in the moonlight. "Let's be smart, now…"

I didn't bother asking permission before I summoned a

ball of water from the spring. Terrified and infuriated, I threw it at my assailant, but I didn't release my grip, instead holding the water around his head like a fishbowl.

Dark as it was, I couldn't see the details of his expression, but he dropped his knife and released me as he swatted ineffectively at the water, trying to clear an airway. He gurgled and sank to his knees, then fell and went still.

As I stood over him, shaking, I heard the elemental's voice behind me: *Let me help you, little sister.*

I nodded and stepped aside, and a pair of unnaturally long arms made of night-black water rose from the surface and pulled him under. I didn't know if my attacker was dead by then or only unconscious, but something told me he wouldn't escape the spring.

Susan? Terj called, hurrying to my side. *Are you hurt?*

I'm okay, I said, which wasn't entirely untrue, but I didn't resist when Terj solidified enough to hug me. *I'm okay.*

You're trembling.

I just killed a man...

So did I. Teamwork.

I stiffened when I saw torches approaching and heard angry shouts. *Terj...*

Guess they found their friend, he replied, and his grip on me tightened. *Let's go—*

Peace, the water elemental interrupted. *Allow me.*

When he rose from the spring that time, he was at least twenty feet tall, and the approaching mob stopped in their tracks. *If you want to live, take your wagons and leave*, he thundered.

Loyalty only went so far, as the mob turned and retreated to their camp. I stayed in Terj's arms until the wagons set off into the night, their drivers shouting at the sleepy chiquiws, and only then did he relax his hold.

If you could bring the body closer, I will dispose of it, the water elemental said.

Terj took him up on his offer, plucking the mangled

corpse off the ground and dropping it into the spring. As he returned to me, the other elemental urged, *Take your rest, little sister. They will not return tonight.*

I found my sleeping bag and carried it back inside the tent, then remade my bed and pulled my sword closer. Before I could zip the door, Terj entered, once again insubstantial but unhidden to my senses. *Do you want to be alone?* he asked.

No.

Then I'm here to keep the watch.

You need your rest—

Let me worry about that.

But though I knew I was guarded, sleep refused to return that night. Instead, as I lay awake and listened to the stillness, I grew vaguely conscious of a strange sensation, almost like a tug on my innermost being. I couldn't name the source—hell, I could barely describe it—but the longer I analyzed it, the surer I grew that it came from the south.

At dawn, I made a quick breakfast of granola, apologized to the water elemental for the night's disturbance, and thanked him for his hospitality and assistance.

It was no trouble, he assured me. *I did little.*

I wouldn't call sending the rest of those merchants screaming into the night "little."

He chuckled. *I've done far worse.*

As I packed my gear, he said, *Little sister?*

Turning, I found him still raised a few feet above the surface, watching me. *Yes?*

Yours is a remarkable talent, you realize. I've not seen its like.

I shoved my rolled-up tent into its case and zipped it closed. *What can I say? Rogue.*

He watched me for a moment more, then said, *I have always thought that a poor name. The thoughts attached to the term—unpredictable, ungovernable, dangerous. And perhaps you are all those things,* he allowed. *But you are the most interesting of our kind. The most gifted. Perhaps you should be feared, yes, but also celebrated.*

Thanks, I replied, shouldering my bag, *but I think you might be in the minority on that one.*

You think so, but then you're approaching this from a human perspective. It was not we who named you rogues. With that, he lifted a hand in farewell. *A safe journey to you both. Should you pass this way again—*

Keep going? Terj joked.

The other elemental paused, processing that, then laughed. *You are a strange one, brother. But no, should you need a resting place, be welcome here.*

We thanked him again and took our leave, flying quietly through the warm morning air. I made myself as comfortable as I could, leaning on my bag as a lumpy backrest, and concentrated, trying to feel water to the south. A few spots seemed promising, but none were large, certainly not compared to the oasis we'd left.

I guess that was the biggest lake for miles, I thought. *There's very little of substance around us.*

He's fortunate, Terj replied. *That lake is constantly replenished by the spring beneath it, so he doesn't fear the dry season. Anyone else out here...*

Sounds unpleasant.

For one born to water, absolutely. He hesitated, then asked, *Are you all right? You're not dehydrated, are you?*

I'm fine, I assured him. *Our host was very generous.* Giving up on my bag, I stretched out atop the cushion of air and linked my hands behind my head. *Wonder why he's so aggressive to other travelers.*

Because they don't respect him. He doesn't mind if their animals drink—they're dumb beasts, and they can't help where they're driven. But he's dealt with more than his share of obnoxious merchants and soldiers and the like, and so he's made a reputation for himself.

I closed my eyes and smiled. *Sounds like you two got acquainted last night.*

He's talkative, and I...

You were silenced for a long time, I said when Terj's voice faded in my mind. *If you want to sit up all night chatting, I'm not going to fault you for it.*

He seemed to sigh. *The problem is that I'm trying to remember the etiquette. I was very young when I was captured—I mean, a water elemental of my age at the time would still be unattached*, he said. *Compound youth with several centuries stuck in that damn sword, with only humans to observe, and…I fumble.*

Surely he didn't hold it against you…

Oh, no, he was gracious once I explained the situation. I just feel…

Detached? I offered.

Yeah, he said after a brief pause. *Like…so, long before your dad and Malachi, the town fathers used to host dances for entertainment. Jacob Cole was a skilled dancer, and Joseph after him. A man would serve as the caller, and seemingly every adult there knew the steps—complicated steps, not that hug-and-sway thing people seem to do these days.*

When did you ever go to a modern dance?

Never, but Malachi had an eclectic taste in movies. Anyway, I used to wonder when they were all taught how to dance, how to move in such a stylized fashion. Now, here, trying to interact with my own kind…honestly, it feels a little like jumping into the middle of one of those dances without the first clue as to what I'm meant to be doing.

I rolled over and raised up to look behind me, but Terj remained invisible. *If you ever want to learn to bust a move, I can do a mean Electric Slide.*

His amusement rippled across my mind. *Maybe I'll take you up on that someday.*

Steeling myself, I looked down through the air on which I was riding and watched the ground rushing by below until my stomach protested that this was a poor life choice. *Question*, I said to Terj, rolling over again to calm the part of my brain that was screaming about imminent death.

Shoot.

Some of the other elementals I've met call me "little sister."

Kingkiller didn't, but the guy who carried us across the desert twice, and the one last night…

It's common, he said. *Remember that most of us are parentless—we spontaneously generate at the edge of the Aen. Most of us also lack names, so we refer to each other as "brother" or "sister." "Little" gets tacked on for those who are obviously young—I had my share of it before my capture. It's not meant as an insult,* he added. *As a people, we're not great at timekeeping, but as it's not unusual to find elementals who are thousands of years old, they're very much aware that you're young by comparison.*

Ah. I stared up at the wispy clouds hanging high overhead. *You never use it.*

I called the one we just left "brother…"

With me, I mean.

Terj paused. *Well…you have a name, and you've always been Susan to me. Does that bother you?*

No, I replied, *I was just curious.* I thought for a moment, then pressed, *You <u>really</u> have no parents? No actual family?*

None. But on the bright side, there was no one to miss me while I was stuck on Earth.

That's not a good thing, Terj.

I tried to relax, but the thought gnawing at the back of my mind finally broke free. *Do you think my father will like me? I know it'd be a shock to find out you've got a grown kid, but…*

Terj's voice was gentle when he answered me. *I know that very few of us ever actually procreate. It's rare for us to have children at all, let alone produce a rogue. He may be surprised, but if he rejects you, I'll be stunned.*

You're not just saying that?

I don't lie to you. And should he turn out to be an ass…

Yes? I prompted.

I'll look the other way if you dump him in a sewage pond.

"Eww," I muttered.

Susan, the dwarves may have figured out flush toilets, but you and I both know they haven't shared that technology with Daril. Waste has to go somewhere…

Great. Watch me be the first rogue to die of cholera.

Eh, your power has awakened. I doubt you ever really get sick again, he replied. *But if you do, I think I'm strong enough now to hold your hair back.*

What a prince.

Says the princess.

I groaned. *Don't remind me of that right now, okay?* I said, then closed my eyes and focused on the distant water, which sparkled in my senses like diamonds in a coal mine.

CHAPTER 16

All day, we scoured the wasteland for any sign of elemental life, all for naught. The four little ponds we spotted and searched were uninhabited—they were hardly bigger than dinner plates, pitifully shrunken in the unrelenting summer heat—and we didn't encounter another air elemental all day. I couldn't blame them. Had I been able to fly anywhere on Kopaat, I sure as hell wouldn't have stuck around the miserable desert, though a clue as to my father's whereabouts would have been most welcome.

The only help I could offer Terj beyond finding puddles was my pull to the south, which had grown stronger all day. As we made camp that night beneath the brilliant stars, alone in the wilderness, Terj urged me to sleep, but the surety that what I wanted lay just over the horizon tugged on me like a magnet. Restless, I tried eating my feelings, but granola wasn't cutting it. I drank a few mouthfuls of water, careful to preserve what I could, then forced myself to bed down and try to relax.

Sleep came only in brief spurts, however, bursts of formless dreams interrupted by my unquiet mind, and I gave up long before dawn. By the time the sky began to lighten, I'd eaten, packed, and pulled my increasingly unruly hair back in a ponytail, and Terj lifted us off the ground. *Where to?* he asked.

I pointed due south, and on we sped.

About half an hour later, as dawn broke to our left, the mental tug grew strong enough that I knew we had to be close to the source. *Down, down*, I urged, and Terj carefully dropped me atop a barren little hill. I looked around, seeing nothing but dirt and sand and scrawny scrub vegetation, but there was *something*...

Screwing my eyes closed, I focused...and there it was, about ten yards beyond the foot of the hill at the bottom of a depression. Barely visible even to me, more of a moist spot than a body of water, but something deep within me insisted that I approach. Dropping my bag, I ran down the hill and across the hard ground, then came to the edge of what might once have been a little pond, a bowl no more than a few inches deep. Whatever had filled it had long since evaporated, leaving a damp patch at the deepest point of the indentation.

Hello? I called. *Is anyone there?*

But the part of myself that had propelled me toward this place knew the answer even as I asked the question, and it swelled with the strangest sense of joy as a wary voice answered me: *Who is there? I cannot see.*

I hurried down the slope and stepped carefully across the cracking dirt, then leaned over the dregs of the pond. *I'm Susan. Are you Falova?*

His initial fear melted in an instant, replaced by an overwhelming burst of comingled surprise and awe. *You...*

Hi, I said, and waved down at the moist earth. *I could be wrong, but I think I'm—*

Soul of my soul.

Yes. That was it. *That* was what I'd been feeling, the growing proximity to this being with whom I shared such a primal connection.

I adored my dad, and I'd have given anything for five more minutes with him...but as I knelt beside the place where Falova hid, the part of myself that had awakened within the last months cried out in recognition.

I heard a rumor, he continued in a rush, *but I could not believe it, I thought surely it was impossible, but...you exist. Soul of my soul,* he repeated, the thought colored by wonder. *How did you come to this cursed place?*

I glanced up as I sensed Terj drawing closer, then pointed to him. *My friend gave me a lift. I wanted to find you.*

And you did. Now I can die content, he replied, his mood shifting toward wistfulness. *To see you at the end…my child,* he said softly. *My beautiful child. Thank you—*

What do you mean, the end? I interrupted.

I will die today, he said—frankly, far too calmly. *This pond always shrinks in the dry season, but this year has been particularly bad. The sky is clear, the air is warm, and the last will evaporate by midday. But your presence is such an unexpected pleasure, and if I could trouble you to stay a little longer…*

Wait right there, I told him—stupid, in retrospect—and took off running for my bag. I puffed back to him shortly thereafter, unscrewing my new thermos. *You're not dying today. We've come to take you home.*

Home? he repeated, and a shadow of fear crept into the thought. *How?*

Do you see this? I asked, holding the open thermos above the damp spot. *If you're willing to ride inside, it'll protect whatever's in there from evaporation, and we can get you back to the river.*

But Falova's fear deepened as I spoke. *I…* he started, then fell silent for a moment before trying again. *I do not…I do not know if that would be wise…*

At that, Terj manifested and hovered over him until the two were face to face—or so I assumed, as there wasn't enough water left for my father to create any sort of form. *You're frightened,* he said. It wasn't a question. *I understand. It must have hurt terribly when you were ripped from the river.*

You cannot imagine.

Oh, yes, I can. Did you ever hear about our brother who was killed by maladetas to forge a sword?

I did. Years ago, but yes…

They only thought they killed me, Terj replied, his voice carrying a bitter edge. *Susan freed me from centuries of pain. She's here to help you. Work with her.*

I get it, I added. *Nothing like a stranger asking you to put your life in her hands, huh? But if you could try to trust me—*

Soul of my soul, I trust you, he replied, *but…*

You're afraid. I would be, too. Taking a seat beside him, I sighed and put the thermos down. *And I know I'm asking a lot. But you're right, there's not much water left. You can die here, or you can take a chance with me.* I paused, collecting my thoughts, then said, *My name's Susan. I'm twenty-three. I spent about two months as the freaking Watcher, and that was miserable, but I met Terj here, so not a complete loss. And we killed this giant spider…monster…thing out beyond the Aen a few days ago, so I'm not exactly the Watcher anymore. Uh…I grew up in this little town at the Crossing, on the Earth side…I've got a grocery store there, but it's nothing special. I'm nothing particularly special, or I wasn't before getting stuck with the magic sword I just destroyed, but—*

Susan.

I sniffed and realized my eyes had begun watering. *I'm sorry, I'm babbling, but I'd really like to try to save your life, and—*

What do I need to do?

He sounded resolved, despite his lingering fear, and I hastily got back on my knees and retrieved the open thermos. *I'm going to pull whatever water is left together and out of the dirt. Can you hold on to it?*

I…I will try…

Let me know if this hurts, I said, then took a few deep breaths to calm my pounding heart, cleared my mind, and focused on the water before me. Carefully, doing my best not to leave a single drop behind, I brought the traces of moisture together into a small sphere, half in and half out of the soil. *Still with me?*

Yes…

All right. Here's the fun part, I said, and held the thermos close. A nudge of power was all it took to send the entirety of the remaining pond into the bottle, and I peered down at the little liquid sloshing within. All told, there couldn't have been more than a few tablespoons. *Falova? Are you in there?*

I…yes, he replied, shocked. *Yes, I am.*

My shoulders sagged with relief as I gently set the thermos on the ground and pulled a bottle of water from my bag. *Here, this might make it more comfortable*, I said, and filled the thermos three-quarters of the way.

Falova's tension eased a degree as the water rose. *Thank you.*

Sure. Now, I'm going to screw the top on, I explained, holding it above the bottle so he could see. *I'm sorry, it'll be dark in there, but you'll be safe until we reach the river. Ready?*

I trust you, he thought, and voiced no complaint as I sealed him inside.

With that accomplished, I stowed the thermos in my bag, tucking it carefully among my rolled clothes, then stood and shouldered my gear. "Shit," I whispered.

That's a good "shit," right? asked Terj.

Yeah. Yeah, that's pretty good. As he dematerialized, I smiled and gripped the straps of my bag. *Want to go find that damn river?*

Strangely, I don't have any better plans today, he replied, then scooped me into the air and set off.

I wasn't surprised that Falova said nothing to me for the first hour of our return journey. He'd had a day already, and it was barely morning. I, too, was mired in my own thoughts for a time, but as the silence stretched, I looked back toward Terj and asked, *Is he okay?*

I haven't heard a peep from him, Terj replied. *Have you?*

I shook my head. *Maybe he doesn't like heights, either, huh?*

More likely he'd made his peace with the idea of dying, and now you've thrown a massive wrench in the plan. That's not a bad thing, he hastily added, *but think of it like this: he arrived in the desert under traumatic circumstances, he's been isolated for years, he'd probably given up hope, and now you swoop in.* Terj seemed to chuckle. *You took off sprinting, Susan. How did you find him?*

I felt him, I replied. *It's the weirdest thing, but I've been sensing him for more than a day. Like some long-range version of Marco*

Polo, I joked. *And then I got close enough, and…I __knew__ we'd found him.*

That's not altogether surprising…

No, like… I struggled briefly as I combed through my scattered thoughts, then said, *When I met Erianthe, I had no idea who she was. She practically told me she was my mother, but I was clueless until Fanakel and Anji spelled it out for me. But as soon as I reached Falova, something in me recognized him.*

Ah. You heard what he called you, yes?

"Soul of my soul." Guess this isn't a "little sister" situation, eh?

Hardly. Look, I can't speak from experience, but my understanding of how we procreate is that the child is the result of a blending of the parents' essences. Falova wasn't being poetic. Whatever it is in you that recognized him was probably recognizing its source.

Strange, I allowed after a moment's consideration, *but useful, I guess.*

How so?

I mean, I have no idea how I'd do a paternity test on us.

Terj laughed in earnest. *I would say that's unnecessary.*

We fell quiet, and I watched the world brighten with one arm around a bag strap, just in case of turbulence. Eventually, however, my anxiety got the best of me, and I quietly asked, *Falova? Are you all right in there?*

He sounded a little dazed but not upset when he answered me. *Relatively comfortable, thank you. Could you tell me where we are?*

Somewhere in the wilderness. Sorry, I've yet to really learn Kopaati geography…

I thought the attempted conversation had fizzled out, but then Falova said, *You mentioned that your home is at the Crossing.*

That's right. The tunnels are anchored on Earth, and my hometown is just above their nexus.

But…you are Erianthe's daughter, are you not?

I am, I admitted.

Fear surged back into his voice. *What has become of your*

mother? I've worried all these years that something terrible must have befallen her…

What do you mean? I asked, my stomach clenching.

The men who attacked me, did they come for her as well? Was she driven from Daril? Does she live? When I didn't immediately respond, he pressed, *Please tell me. The love I hold for your mother has not changed, and if she is in distress, if there is anything I can do…*

My heart broke at his plea, as I heard the desperation within it. I turned to Terj, whose only commentary was a muttered, *Yikes.*

That's very helpful, thank you, I shot back, then returned my attention to my father. *Erianthe is alive and well. She's still in Daril. Married a guy from Cirivant…they have at least one child*, I said, recalling Anji's unfavorable assessment of the crown prince.

His fear shifted toward relief, then was just as quickly overshadowed by deep confusion. *But…you do not claim Daril as home? Why?*

I hesitated, trying to come up with a delicate answer.

I apologize, said Falova, *I have upset you. If you and your mother have quarreled, I do not mean to—*

No, no, I interrupted. *It's fine. Uh…I didn't actually meet her until a few weeks ago. I wasn't raised in Daril.*

He made no effort to mask his surprise. *She sent you away?*

She…well, I'm piecing this together from what I've been told, but…look, we don't have to talk about this today. You've had a shock already, and I don't want to make things worse—

Soul of my soul, he said gently, *I feel your sorrow. Tell me the truth.*

My eyes pricked as my throat tightened. *Erianthe was engaged to this prince named Narod when she was young.*

I recall. She told me she had no desire to be with him, said Falova. *She wept often when she spoke of her engagement. I suggested to her that she break it, that her life was too short to waste it in an unhappy union.*

And you two...um... My mind refused to complete that thought.

Fortunately, he seemed to understand my unease. *I fell in love with Erianthe, and I told her as much. She loved me as well, and after her father's death, she would sneak away from her own mother's watch at night to visit me in the courtyard garden...*

There was a tenderness to his voice when he spoke of her that I found difficult to reconcile with my own impression of Erianthe.

She told me that she did not love the Cirivanti boy, Falova continued. *She loved me, and while neither of us knew what form that love could take, she craved our time together.*

What happened? I asked.

His thoughts darkened. *The men came one night, three humans with talent and Aen crystals to strengthen them, and they tore me from the river just beyond the castle walls. I recall little but pain during the journey out to this wasteland, but I do remember them debating whether they should kill me. Whoever had paid them for their work wanted me dead. They finally resolved to abandon me in the desert instead, and one of them took pity and found that pond. Then they fled for Ti'cal.*

Why Ti'cal?

I do not know, but I remember that they feared returning to Daril. They did not trust the one who engaged their services. All this time, I thought that someone might have attacked Erianthe...

I didn't want to hurt him. I'd just met the guy, and I didn't want to deliver a crushing truth in the first hours of our acquaintance, but I couldn't see a way to avoid the blow.

She wasn't attacked, I told Falova. *When she realized she was pregnant, she hid in her room and faked a long illness, then left Kopaat, went to the Crossing, and came out on Earth. It's wooded there, pretty remote. She had me there in secret, then left me to die and went home.*

His response was horror unformed into words.

My uncle found me, I continued. *Or the man who I called my uncle, I mean. He was the Watcher, and he lived out in those woods alone. He couldn't keep me safe, so his brother raised me. My dad,* I added, and braced myself for Falova's reaction.

His response was slow in coming as he digested what I'd revealed, and to my relief, I heard no anger. *Were they good to you?*

The best. They treated me like I was their blood. I always knew I was adopted—it's not every day someone in my town finds a newborn in the woods—but they never made me feel like I was less than family.

I would like to meet them, if that is possible. Thank them.

Unfortunately, they're gone. Dad died about a year and a half ago, and Uncle Malachi died a couple months back, and... I laughed to myself to keep from crying. *It's been one hell of a summer, you know? You're orphaned, then you find out your biological parents are still around, only your father doesn't know you exist, and your mother tries to execute you—*

What? he demanded, the thought as sharp as a cracking whip.

Yeah. Exile back to the Crossing to fight monsters for the rest of my days or execution, those were the options.

But...but why? he sputtered.

Because I'm an inconvenient truth. She married that Cirivanti, and part of the deal was that his kid would be king or queen someday. Well, apparently, the law in Daril is that the ruler's eldest child inherits, and that would be me...

I didn't belabor the point. Dwelling too long on the fact that my mother had dumped me in the woods to save a marriage treaty just left me depressed.

Anyway, I said, *I'm here now to get you home, and...and that's me, I guess.*

I'd just opened a bottle of water for a quick swig when Falova found his voice again. *I cannot believe this. Erianthe...she would never do that. Not her.*

You think I'm lying? I replied. *Terj can back me up—*

No, I believe you, he quickly amended. *I misspoke. I...do not want to believe that Erianthe could do what you tell me she did, but...*

I saw everything, Terj murmured. *And I'm sorry. A betrayal like that—*

She tried to kill our daughter. Sadness and anger swirled around the thought. *I love her, and she told me she loved me, and…and she…*

She probably orchestrated your attack, said Terj. *Perhaps her mother, I don't know. But with you gone, and Susan gone, no one remained to tell the Cirivanti prince that his intended had been unfaithful and could never fulfill the terms of their treaty.* He paused, then suggested, *You could make the truth known. Bring her to justice.*

Sensing Falova's uncertainty, I said, *This doesn't have to be decided right now. Let's just focus on getting you back where you belong, all right?*

Thank you, he said softly, and fell into a deep silence for the rest of the morning.

Terj had certainly strengthened, but the constant travel drained his resources, and I didn't complain when he put us down for the night still south of the oasis. Though the elemental there had proven friendly, I didn't feel up to risking another encounter with a merchant caravan, especially not with the cargo I carried.

While I pitched my tent and started dinner prep in the waning light, I could sense Terj and my father conversing on the edge of my hearing, carrying on a semi-private conversation that I didn't interrupt. Falova had spoken little all day, asking the occasional question about the land we crossed or prying for bits of my history that I'd neglected to mention. I told him about my fairly mundane childhood, my average college career, and my brief stint as the Watcher, and with those highlights covered, I found little else to say. Honestly, I didn't want to press him, especially considering the bad news I'd dropped on him like an anvil, and so I was content to leave him alone until he wanted to talk. I'd even managed to snag an afternoon nap with Terj's coaxing.

Being the only member of our party who needed sleep and feeding made me feel a little awkward, but no one gave me grief as I made the best of an overpriced MRE and stretched out in my sleeping bag. A touch on the paranoid side after our night at the oasis, Terj remained on guard outside the tent, but I kept my backpack with me, just beyond my flashlight and sword. I was tossing a bit, trying to get comfortable, when Falova said, *Susan?*

Yes?

I am sorry that I could not be what you needed.

I rolled over to face my bag in the darkness. *It's not your fault. You're the one who was abducted…*

But even if I had been unharmed, if Erianthe had simply left you on the bank and walked away, I could not have raised you alone. You would have needed food, clothing, a safe place to sleep…not to mention someone to teach you to speak and move as humans do. And…I am truly grateful that you had a family, he said slowly. *That you have lost them is tragic, and I fear I would make a poor substitute.*

I lay there for a moment, trying to glean his unstated meaning. *So…what I'm hearing is that after you're safe, we should go our separate ways?*

No, of course not! he replied, sounding shocked at the suggestion. *Unless that is what you wish—*

No, sorry, I thought you—

Soul of my soul, I can give you little, but anything I have is yours, Falova insisted. *I want to know you. All I meant is that compared to what you once had, I am a poor second option.* He hesitated, then asked, *Did you think I would not want you?*

I was glad he couldn't see my eyes watering. *Erianthe tried to kill me, so I kept my hopes low.*

What your mother has done is abhorrent. I could not have kept you alive, but that does not mean I do not want you. He seemed to sigh. *I said I am grateful for your family, and I am, but I mourn the fact that someone else watched you grow up. Tell me the truth,* he said in a rush, *was your father good to you? Did he love you?*

Yes, I managed as my face scrunched against my tears. *Dad was great. Don't worry about that.*

You miss him.

A tiny sob escaped in spite of my best efforts. *Yeah. Him and Uncle Malachi both.*

I am sorry for your pain, he murmured. *They should be proud of you.*

I like to think they're not totally disappointed, wherever they are.

You jest, but you need not hide your feelings, Susan.

I flopped onto my back and stared up at the dome of the tent. *I don't even know what I feel anymore. I barely recognize the person I was two months ago, and...I mean, I'm in a tent in the middle of nowhere, on a world I've barely explored, within arm's reach of a fucking sword, having a telepathic conversation with my father, who's hanging out in a thermos. This is...not what I thought twenty-three would be like. At all. I don't know what to do with myself, I can't really go home again, I've got powers I'm still learning to use, my mother has me on her hitlist, and frankly, I'm scared.*

But you are not alone, he pointed out.

I appreciate the support.

More than me—the one outside, the one you call Terj, he is very protective of you.

I snorted. *He still feels bad about drafting me to be the Watcher.*

Perhaps, but he is genuinely fond of you. And...

And? I pressed.

And he cautioned me in the strongest of terms against wounding your feelings, said Falova. *Unnecessary, but he did.*

Surprised, I rolled over toward the bag again. *Did he <u>threaten</u> you?*

In exquisite detail.

What did he say?

That does not matter now. But I did learn something from it.

I'm afraid to ask, I replied.

Have no fear. What I learned is that while your family loved you, they are not the only ones.

I scowled in the dark. *Are you—*

I have said enough, he insisted, though I could hear the smile in his voice. *Sleep, Susan.*

Groaning, I flipped over, wishing the ground were softer. *Terj is already bossy about my sleep schedule. Don't you start, too.*

He is only concerned, said Falova in a tone of placation. *And he probably knows as well as I do what exhaustion can do to a corporeal being. You need rest.*

I'm not an invalid. You don't have to be concerned.

Would you mind terribly if I were a little concerned? he asked.

Though my face was still damp, I smiled against my pillow. *Not terribly.*

Glad to hear it. Good night, Susan.

Good night...Father, I said, tentatively trying it out.

Falova said nothing more, but I could feel his happiness from across the tent.

Bless him, Terj pushed us with everything he had. I woke before dawn the next morning and quickly packed, and as he lifted us up and I began to rummage in my bag for granola, he asked me for a direction. *Can you feel the river?*

I can, Falova replied. *Though I fear that in my present condition, I will have trouble guiding you...*

"Hang on," I muttered, then closed my eyes and attuned myself to the water around us. Due north was the oasis, and far to the north was the sea...but there, running in an ever-widening channel to the east of our position, was the dead river. If I concentrated, I could trace its path from its rise in the distant south, beyond where I assumed Ti'cal lay, to its delta in northern Daril.

I wasn't altogether surprised to note that the river seemed just a bit brighter to my new senses than other sources of water did. After all, in some way, I *had* come from it.

East, I told Terj. *Or east-northeast, more precisely. We can't miss it, but it'd probably be better to pick a stretch that's not in*

Darili territory.

The others concurred, and Terj set off at a grueling pace, stopping only when my body demanded bathroom breaks. The sun rose high overhead, then began its descent behind us, and still, he refused to stop for the night.

Finally, I caught a glimpse of the watery ribbon through the wasteland, the dead river glinting in the setting sun. *It smells weird,* I cautioned Falova, *and nothing really lives in there anymore, or so I'm told.*

But that close to home, he was too excited to care about minutiae like the condition of the water. I could feel his anticipation bubbling up, a geyser ready to blow, and by the time Terj deposited us along an uninhabited stretch of the river's bank, I wouldn't have been shocked had the thermos shot from my bag like a rocket. It remained stowed where I'd hidden it, however, and I pulled it free and started for the water's edge.

There was no instruction manual for returning my father to his river, but something told me that pouring the contents of the thermos in the shallows wouldn't be the best alternative. Instead, windblown and dirty as I was, I waded straight into the cold, foul-smelling water until I was waist-deep, then unscrewed the thermos's cap and glanced inside. *Ready?*

His joy didn't require words.

Carefully, I crouched until the thermos was submerged and its contents freed to the water. In an instant, a pulse like lightning shot up and down the river's length, painless but bright as a flashbulb. The smell began to fade a few seconds later, but I barely noticed it at the time, as a figure was rising from the water in front of me. As I straightened and watched, my shirt dripping, the figure took on definition: arms, a head, and finally, the impressions of facial features.

I grinned. *Hi, there.*

My father moved closer, then cautiously stretched out one hand and cupped the scarred side of my face. *Soul of my soul…*

Though his form was comprised of nothing but water, it was firm enough to withstand the assault when I hugged him. His arms wrapped around me in turn, cold against my skin, and his gratitude flooded my mind.

It took me a moment to realize that there was love mixed in as well. Maybe he hadn't known me long, but his sentiments seemed genuine.

I might have stood there until the sun went down had Falova not said, *You are shivering, Susan.*

Yeah, I know.

Perhaps you would be more comfortable on the bank.

He escorted me to the shallows, and when I reached land, I willed the water off of me and back into the river. *Remarkable*, said Falova as the blob plopped in.

I have a party trick, I replied with a shrug, and smiled as Terj approached to join us. *So, what happens now? Will the river live again?*

Falova nodded. *It will take time, but the river can be restored. And you're…all right?*

Better than I have been in many years, he replied. *Thank you both. I cannot repay you…*

There's no debt, said Terj. *Happy to assist. Though you*, he continued, nudging my arm, *might consider getting back in the water. You're fragrant.*

I can't help it, I protested. *I haven't had a real bath in days.*

Believe me, I'm well aware.

"Jerk," I muttered, but smiled at his quiet laughter in my head.

You are welcome to the river, Falova offered. *Anything I have is yours, Susan. Take what you will. Or stay here*, he suggested.

I knew he meant well, but remaining in the wasteland wasn't feasible in the long run. *Thanks, but I think I need to push on. We've got friends waiting for us in Taln'een*, I explained, turning to Terj. *Though if you've had enough of me and want to go exploring, I'm sure they'll understand.*

I think I could stay longer…if you're not sick of me yet, of course.

Reaching out, I found his hand and laced my fingers through his strangely substantial form. *Be happy to have you.*

And once you reach Taln'een? Falova asked. *What then?*

I exhaled slowly and watched the sunset ripple in the river. *Not sure yet. What I do know is that I can't safely stay in this world until Erianthe stops coming for my head. Do you want to confront her?* I asked him. *If she didn't have you kidnapped, she's bound to know who did.*

I imagine that she does, but…

But? I prompted.

He was slow to respond. *I do not expect you to understand, but in some respects, I still love your mother. Confront her as you will, but perhaps you could refrain from revealing my fate.*

Frowning, I said, *You don't want justice?*

I have been returned, and I have met you. For now, that is all I need. Your relationship with Erianthe is a matter for you to decide, but I do not wish to harm her.

Falova was right—I didn't understand why he wasn't ready to burn Deoni to the ground—but it was his choice. *Should I see her, I won't mention you,* I promised him. *And now, I do have a favor to ask.*

Name it.

I stretched out my free hand, and a vaguely boat-shaped structure emerged from the river, comprised of water but solid enough. *Terj has been working hard for days, and it's only fair that I take a turn. Do you mind if we ride along?*

I would be pleased. He stayed close while I grabbed my bag and boarded, and Terj sank onto the single bench beside me. *You can propel yourself?*

Quite well, said Terj. *Steering is another matter…*

No one warned me about that waterfall!

He laughed and patted my shoulder. *We'll know when to abandon the boat this time, yes?*

Practice is seldom a bad idea, Falova interjected, *but perhaps, given the circumstances, I could be of assistance. With sufficient speed, you could cover much of the wilderness by dawn, and I know a place where you might wait out the day, should you wish to avoid detection in Daril.*

You don't mind? I asked.

My dear, he replied, sinking into the river just as the boat pushed off from shore, *for you, it would be my pleasure.*

EPILOGUE

Barely more than a week after Falova's return, the river had already begun its recovery. As we walked the pathway along its bank, I noticed shoots of green comingled with the dead vegetation by the water's edge. The weird stench had entirely dissipated, and when I squinted at the river, I saw a fish slip by. Sure, one fish wasn't anything to write home about, but it had been the talk of the tavern the night before—that, and the crown prince's engagement.

Ganeel had secured lodging for us that evening, a place on the outskirts of Deoni, explaining that she didn't want to be rushed the next day. Travel had been no problem—Terj, stronger than ever, had done the honors and saved us the long trek—but he'd put us down in a secluded place outside the capital so that we could approach on foot and avoid unnecessary questions. People stared enough as it was. Two maladetas on the road would be a curiosity to many, but six figures in hooded gray cloaks, even if one was closer to child-sized, was enough to make even the most intrigued give us our space.

Still, we'd passed an uneventful night in the tavern's main room, eating wild-caught fowl with a tangy berry sauce and bread made from locally grown kirta. Eating while hooded had been an awkward but necessary precaution. Mia would have been strikingly beautiful had she rolled in mud, Fanakel looked every inch the elven prince with a little tailoring assistance from the maladetas and a good wash, haircut, and shave, and while Anji's beard was still short by dwarven standards, it would have drawn notice all the same. As for me, I didn't know whether my description had made it onto a "wanted" poster yet, but my scar was too memorable for me to show my face. Even with the maladetas' ministrations, it had yet to fade, nor had the sword's magical brand disappeared from my palm. The brand had lost its power once the sword had fallen to pieces, Terj verified, and the fact that I didn't need a translator without it only proved my elemental extraction.

As we ate and eavesdropped, the other travelers spoke of three topics. First in the minds of the majority who'd come up from the south was the summer drought, which had been particularly harsh that year. With the end of the dry season perhaps another two months away, the weather loomed large in many minds.

Second was the inexplicable rejuvenation of the river, which had been dead for two decades. People spoke in excited whispers of catching glimpses of fish and missing the stink; one man swore he'd seen the elemental outside of Daril.

But the third topic was of most interest to me. The queen and prince consort had announced the engagement of the crown prince to a princess of Eraneg, a wealthy kingdom on the southern continent of Antinil. Having come to prominence through their silver and gold mines, Eraneg was the undisputed ruler of a good swath of the eastern coast, and their merchant ships were peerless on Kopaat. Some of the travelers in the inn spoke of the princess, second in line to the Eranegi throne, who was supposedly a great beauty. Others, less concerned with her as a person, talked up the benefits of a marital alliance between the two kingdoms, comparing it to Erianthe's advantageous marriage to a Cirivanti prince and Cirivant's subsequent assistance to Darili interests in Ga'besh.

I wasn't in love with Ganeel's timing. True, Anji said that Edes Fulquir was a jackass, but he was still my half brother, and I didn't want to spoil his engagement party.

But Ganeel had insisted: the cream of the Darili aristocracy would be present, she pointed out, and so Erianthe wouldn't be able to conveniently "disappear" me if things went south.

I hoped.

Though the tavern bed was decent, a little lumpy but not painfully so, I hadn't slept well in anticipation of the morning. Dawn found me in the dining room with a cup of a bitter tisane, and Terj, who had stayed out exploring half the night, sat invisibly at my side and kept me company while I tried to pretend that my stomach wasn't in knots.

We stored our gear at the tavern that day, all but a few necessary weapons and the securely wrapped trophy tooth, and followed the river on foot deeper into the capital. As we walked along, I noticed a ripple out of the corner of my eye and turned to spot Falova peeking up at me from the shallows. *Morning,* I said as my sword's comforting weight bumped against my leg.

You are anxious, soul of my soul.

Very.

I wish I could go with you. Erianthe seems to have walled up the river's entrance to the castle, he replied, the thought colored by frustration.

I'll be all right, I said, trying to reassure him as much as myself. *And nobody wants to annoy a maladeta, so maybe I won't be thrown in a cell this time around.*

He didn't seem entirely convinced. *Be careful. If you call for me, I should be able to hear you, even within the walls. Should you come to harm—*

I won't let her out of my sight, Terj interjected. *Susan won't be alone.*

Still, I will be waiting for news, my father said, and the water stilled as he disappeared beneath the surface.

As noon approached and our cloaks began to grow unbearably warm, we crossed the bridge over the dry channel where the river had once flowed into the castle grounds, then approached a guarded entry point. The men on duty, wearing breastplates painted with the blue and green Darili flag, stepped forward to intercept us, and the older of the two extended a hand to halt our progress. "Invitation?" he demanded.

Ganeel lowered her hood and fixed him with her well-practiced stare. "The Great Mother of the Taln'een has come with the bravest warriors of our worlds, and you ask me for an *invitation*?"

He traded uncertain glances with his partner. "Uh…Great Mother, we're only following orders…"

"If Her Majesty refuses to see me, let her say so to my face. We are going in now."

Someday, I mused, when I became a real grownup, I hoped to master Ganeel's mixture of confidence and disdain. It did the trick, and the guards not only backed down but called for a servant to lead us into the castle and up to the ceremonial hall.

Standing at the edge of the lilac runner as a herald announced Ganeel's arrival to the assembled, I quickly took in the setup: a high ceiling supported by stone arches, dozens of long tables groaning beneath the weight of the midday feast, hundreds of men and women in their finery, and alternating sets of banners, the colors of Daril and those of Eraneg, I assumed. At the far end, atop a dais, the diners looked up from their meal in surprise. I recognized Erianthe in one of the central pair of wooden chairs, her brunette ringlets impeccably arranged around a golden tiara set with Aen crystals. To her right sat a thin man with dark hair that hung to his shoulders, who hunched slightly over his plate. While I couldn't make out the details from that distance, I surmised that this was the prince consort, Narod. To Erianthe's left sat another couple, probably the parents of the bride-elect, while beside Narod sat a pair who had to be the guests of honor. Other dignitaries filled in the remaining spots at the table—siblings, perhaps, though I couldn't say.

When the herald's voice died away, he stepped aside, and Ganeel strode up the central aisle toward the royals. "Your Majesties," she said as the assembled nobles stopped eating and turned to stare, "greetings. This is an auspicious occasion."

Nearing, I could see that Narod was squinting down at us, but smiled as Ganeel spoke. "Ah, Great Mother! Your coming was unexpected, but we will find a place for you and your companions…"

"Perhaps we could speak with her *later*," said Erianthe, whose deep, low-cut purple dress, redefining "fitted," seemed poised to release her chest upon an unsuspecting world if she coughed too heavily.

Narod sat up a little straighter, frowning bemusedly. "Certainly, my dear, but I'm sure we can procure a few more chairs in the interim."

Before the two could argue, Ganeel said, "Your hospitality is appreciated, but I did not come to gorge myself. Rather, I have brought some of our worlds' greatest warriors here today." With a nod to the Eranegi royals, she asked, "Have you yet seen the wonders accomplished Outside? I instructed my daughter here to show you, Your Majesty," she said to Erianthe, "but it was my understanding that our other clans would share the tidings, too."

The bride's father, a golden-skinned man with a fringe of white hair, beamed. "Oh, yes, of course! We didn't know what was more astounding, the magic used to replay the battle or the battle itself," he added with a little chuckle. His dark-haired wife, obviously much younger, patted his hand indulgently.

"Well, then," said Ganeel with a smile, "you should be pleased that not only have I brought a copy of the recording to share with all present, but I have brought with me the warriors who slew the mother of monsters in the lands beyond the Aen."

The other diners rumbled and whispered in

anticipation, and with a nod from Ms. Quince, the four of us lowered our hoods. The Eranegi king looked like a kid on Christmas morning, his wife's eyes widened, Narod smiled in delight, and even the fêted couple and the teenage boy and girl beside them looked on with interest. Erianthe, however, stared down from her chair with a frozen expression and quickly paled.

"I realize your guests are eating, and perhaps my timing could have been better," Ganeel continued, softly chuckling, "but if Your Majesties would like, I would be honored to show them why they need never again fear the night-stalking horrors that plagued our worlds for so long and recently returned."

"Please," said Narod, waving her on before Erianthe could protest. The Eranegis concurred, and so Ganeel pulled her compact-like device from her dress pocket, gestured and whispered over its surface, and then turned it to face a stone wall. A frozen image, the beginning of Sanniah's broadcast, appeared to the *ooh*s and *aah*s of the nobles, the picture blown up to many times larger than life yet still rather sharp.

"That is Sanniah oo'Kral sha'Volng," said Ganeel with practiced pronunciation, "queen of a realm Outside called Banilgh. Unless there are a great many translators in this room, I trust that much of what she says will be gibberish"—she paused as the guests laughed—"but in brief, she was explaining to her people what was transpiring. And now, I suggest you brace yourselves."

The recording began to play—where the surround sound was coming from, I had no clue—and I marveled at the low-light capabilities of Sanniah's camera. It had picked up the faces and forms of the four who'd stayed above to shoot at the massive monster, but it had also captured every one of my awkward movements and desperate thrusts. More than that, it showed with great clarity how I'd tossed around the volcanic lake, how the creature had died in flame, and how the giant eggs scattered across the caldera had died with her.

When the recording ended, silence fell over the hall for only a few seconds before the Darili highborn broke out in thunderous applause. Narod stood and clapped with them, and even Erianthe managed a polite smile. The sound rose to a new fervor when Ganeel unwrapped the monster's tooth, and she waited for a minute until the noise began to fade before raising her voice and gesturing toward us. "May I present our heroes?"

"Absolutely," said the Eranegi king.

She turned and nodded to Fanakel. "A son of Nokan'ti, son and nephew to the Twins." He briefly bowed his head as the applause recommenced.

Ganeel continued down the line. "Princess Anjikora of Blackhorn Mountain."

With the cheering that time came a susurrus, which Anji and Fanakel had to have expected. That the two of them were standing in the same room, let alone beside each other, had to be shocking to anyone who knew the first thing about the War of the True Children.

Once the room sufficiently quieted, Ganeel said, "This is Mia, may her ammunition never be depleted."

We knew she wouldn't elaborate. There was no need to put people on edge by announcing a stranger of tekorish extraction.

"And this," Ganeel concluded once Mia had been thanked by the crowd, "is Susan—"

The applause returned with a roar, and I flushed as I waited for it to subside. Apparently, jumping into a volcano with a sword and a prayer made one a crowd favorite.

"Susan," said Ganeel, turning to the high table, "was, until quite recently, the Watcher. The great sword that our peoples forged together has been broken, its purpose fulfilled, and she was the last and greatest of its bearers." She held up a hand to stop the fresh clapping before it could crescendo. "And I bring her before you now because it is only right and proper that a daughter of Daril be recognized by her own people."

Erianthe opened her mouth, but Narod beat her to it. "Of Daril?" he echoed with a smile. "I had no idea that the Watcher had been chosen from our lands. Where do you come from, Watcher?"

He had a kind smile, and part of me hated what I would say next.

"I was conceived in Deoni, Your Highness," I replied. "But my mother delivered me outside the Aen, at the Crossing, and abandoned me in the woods there."

The guests' murmurings resumed once more, and Narod's smile faltered. "I...I'm terribly sorry to hear that, young lady. Do you know why...?"

His voice faded, but he didn't need to finish his thought. "A couple reasons come to mind," I told him. "First, I'm a rogue elemental. I mean, you saw what I can do with a lake."

The young couple beside him—my half brother and his fiancée, I reminded myself—gasped and sat back in their chairs as I beckoned their wine from their glasses and set it swirling around them before dropping it into place.

"I suppose that could be a difficult thing to deal with, having a child with that sort of power," I continued. "Because I was raised outside the Aen, I only discovered it a few weeks ago, so this is all still kind of fresh to me, but the Great Mother here will vouch that I have it under control."

"She has *markedly* improved," said Ganeel.

"But the second issue, I think, is the real reason why my mother left me to die," I said, focusing on Narod's sympathetic expression. "She was engaged to another man when she and my father conceived me, and so I am...problematic."

"That is indeed difficult, but a daughter as accomplished as you should be celebrated by her family, not shunned," said the prince consort. Do your parents know of your deeds beyond this world?"

"Oh, yes, Your Highness. My father is Falova, and he and I had plenty of time to talk after I found him in the desert. You may have noticed that the river is beginning to recover since I brought him home last week."

His jaw dropped, and he put a hand to his chest. "Truly, Susan, you are to be counted among Daril's finest sons and daughters. How did you manage to find the elemental? I thought he was *dead!*"

I felt a soft brush of wind against my hand. Terj had decided to keep a low profile that day, but he stayed close to me, offering silent support.

"Luck and help from my friends," I told Narod. "He's very glad to be back."

"And I'm sure I speak for us all when I say we're grateful for his safe return. But what about your mother?" he pressed. "Does she know what you've done for us?"

"Well, I think she's heard a fair bit of it, but I'm not certain exactly what," I said, then steeled myself and looked at Erianthe, who stared down at me through her frozen mask with wide, frightened eyes. "Hello, Mother," I said, and barely smiled. "I think we should talk."

ACKNOWLEDGEMENTS

Thank you for coming along for the second part of Susan's journey! It's not over just yet, but I think you'll like where she's going...

As usual, my thanks go to the Novel Chicks for putting up with me.

And yes, here's to you, Mom and Dad.

ABOUT THE AUTHOR

When not writing fiction, Ash Fitzsimmons is an appellate attorney and an unrepentant car singer.

Find her online:
www.ashfitzsimmons.com

www.ingramcontent.com/pod-product-compliance
Lightning Source LLC
Chambersburg PA
CBHW031544240626
47153CB00002B/372